A typical *STH* reader

SEX

True Homosexual Experiences
from S.T.H. Writers

Volume 3

Edited by Boyd McDonald

Gay Sunshine Press
San Francisco

3rd Printing 1997

SEX is copyright © 1982, 1997 by Gay Sunshine Press. All rights reserved. Except for brief passages quoted in a newspaper, magazine, radio, or television review, no part of this book may be reproduced in any form or by any means, electronic or mechanical, including photocopying and recording, or by any information storage and retrieval system, without permission in writing from the publisher.

Cover photo copyright © 1997 by Kristen Bjorn.
Cover design by Rupert Kinnard.

All interior photos in this book are to be credited to Athletic Model Guild (except where indicated otherwise) and are published with permission.

All photos in this book are posed by professional models. The fact that AMG models are shown in this book does not mean that they are necessarily homosexual, nor that they endorse any product or particular code of behavior. The stories presented here are true sexual case histories. The fact that they appear in this book does not mean that the editors or publisher necessarily approve of those acts which may be illegal in some states. It is against the law to have intercourse with boys under 18, but we do print memoirs of men talking about their own boyhoood experiences—true case histories.

Library of Congress Cataloging in Publication Data:

 Main entry under title:

 Sex: true homosexual experiences from S.T.H. writers, volume 3

 1. Homosexuals, Male—Sexual behavior. I. McDonald, Boyd. II. Straight to hell. III. Title: Sex.
HQ76.S2 1982 306.7'66 82-15393
ISBN 0-917342-98-4 (pbk.)

The Boyd McDonald interview by Vince Aletti first appeared in General Idea's *File Magazine*, Vol. 5, #3, summer 1980.

Gay Sunshine Press
P.O. Box 410690
San Francisco, CA 94141
Send $1 for complete catalogue of books available.

America's True Perverts

Straight To Hell does not advocate the overthrow of the American Government; Johnson and Nixon and Reagan have already taken care of that.

"Straight" males can be used for fun in bed but they are not worth talking to, their writing is not worth reading, their films not worth seeing, their attempts to give leadership in religion or psychiatry or any field are not to be followed, and they should not be allowed power in business or government because they have proved they cannot handle it. In their craving to express virility — in war, greed, violence, hate, corruption — they have ruined the most promising nation and made America a nation you can't trust. Inadequate use of their pricks has turned America into a nation of pricks.

Some are fun in bed, but only because their membership in the powerful sexual majority gives them a certain ease which is called "masculinity." But under their surface show of virility they are ipso facto, by being "straight," too timid to be of any real interest or value. Only men with balls dare to be different — to be homosexual, for example, or refuse to kill innocent Asians. The frightened ones do what Nixon or the church or somebody tells them to do. Historically, this has been, "Make war and money but don't make love."

Thus they are America's true perverts. Killing is the ultimate perversion and America has become history's greatest killer.

To value people by the value of their bank accounts is another perversion.

To use sex to express hate rather than love is another.

"Fag-baiting" is a sex substitute and sex additive, like sports, war, and displaying money. These are public displays of virility and conformity by men who need all the support from society they can get.

Straight To Hell will not take time to reason with fag-baiters. As an economy measure it will simply retaliate in kind.

We support only the minority of decent American men — a few like Daniel Ellsberg, Anthony Russo, Ralph Nader, and Ramsey Clark Jr.

Most American women are decent. We wish them power.

But it is a man's country — America is "he," not "she" — and the men have ruined it. The majority of American men, as the war and the elections show, are mad in both senses: they are insane and they are enraged. You can't beat them right now, it's true; there are too many. But that doesn't mean you have to join them. If you can't beat them hassle them. We will by pointing out their perversions, insanity, pretence, and lies. We speak for the sane minorities.

The growing importance of women, and corresponding growing impotence of men, offers some hope for the future. Someone — women, blacks, homosexuals — someone who's out of the competitive virility rat race — should take over. The men have bombed.

— *Boyd McDonald*

The Love That Dare Not Speak Its Name: Armpit-sniffing

CONNECTICUT — When I was going to Rutgers back in the early '70s my courses required me to use the Alexander Library a lot. Naturally around the school there were always many attractive young men but for the first few weeks nothing exciting happened.

One evening while I was working in the Reference Room I felt someone staring at me and I looked up from my work and there was a fantastic looking man looking at me. Tight jeans and a baseball cap. We both stared and stared at one another. He started to walk away and I followed him because he looked back several times to be sure he was being followed. I followed him into a very large men's room. He had disappeared when I got into the room and I didn't know what to do because this was the first time I'd ever attempted a liaison in a men's room. The only thing I could think of was to go into a stall, which I did. Soon, there he was standing in front of the door to the stall I was in, rubbing his obviously hard cock through his jeans.

I opened the door and he stepped in quickly and shut it behind himself. He whispered, "Did you save any come for me." I said, "I sure have." He took his jacket and shirt off and hung them on the hook. He urged me to do the same so I did. I was very afraid but extremely excited by him and by the situation. He was about 27 and handsome. He was well built with especially nice shoulders. I embraced him and was immediately aware that he didn't use deodorant and at the end of the day needed a shower, which was a fantastic turn on. We were kissing like mad and I was sniffing and licking those sweaty armpits. He unbuckled my belt and pulled my pants and Jockey shorts down and began to suck my hard dick. I undid his jeans and exposed a pair of pure white Jockey shorts, another real turn on. Down they went and there was a beautiful cut seven inches. I went down on him and sucked him and stuck my finger in his asshole. His ass was firm and round. I also rubbed my fingers in his armpits and sniffed them and made him smell my fingers, saying to him, "Smell your funky armpits." This turned him on very much and he shot his load in my mouth. He then went down on me and I came right away. He left the stall after saying, "See you later, buddy." A week or so later I saw him and he told me he had to go home to wash his "pits" because they stink. I told him not to waste it and we went into the stacks and I told him to unbutton his shirt, which he did. He was wearing an undershirt so I told him to go into the men's room and take it off and he might as well take his Jockey shorts off and to my great surprise he complied with my request. He came back shortly and handed them to me. I sniffed them. The warm, sweaty man smell was very strong. He said he hadn't had a shower in two days. He went back to the men's room and had a repeat performance. I soon found out that he also liked to get fucked. We were in the men's room another time and a stocky young guy came in and went into a booth. My friend told me that the guy had a huge dick and that he liked to sit on it. He went over to the stall, telling me to come and watch after he went in. There on the toilet sat an ordinary looking stocky guy with his shirt off and pants around his ankles, no shorts, with an enormous cock. He had very little hair on his body except around that incredible dick. Rick, my friend, was taking off his shirt and undershirt and one boot and one leg of his jeans and

Jockey shorts. The other guy was sucking Rick's cock and playing with his asshole. Then Rick sat on the other guy and that big dick went right up Rick's asshole. Rick was really riding that cock. He opened the door of the stall and motioned me in. I unzipped my jeans and Rick started to suck my cock. I started to play with his nipples and sniffed his armpits, then went down on him. All the while he was riding up and down on that huge tool. Rick shot his wad, then his friend was getting off in Rick's ass. The other guy gave me a hand job and I came all over his hand and he licked it off.

* * * *

Another time I was sitting in a stall and a beautiful man was looking through the crack in the door. He had dark hair and was very well built, slim, about 6'3", and dressed in elegant clothes — usually not my type. He asked if he could come in. Of course he could because he looked so nice. I opened the door and he came in and I unbuttoned his shirt and undid his belt and pulled his pants down. Bob is his name and he has a well-defined hairless chest. I started to suck his nice-sized cut cock. He didn't want to come, just enjoy himself awhile. He went down on me and then he kissed me. Bob was a great kisser, in fact I think that was what he liked to do best. After that he got dressed and left. Later as the weather got warmer Bob would come in to the library men's room with T-shirt, running shorts and sneakers with no sox. He'd come into a stall and take everything off — no Jockey shorts on — even his sneakers, so that he was absolutely naked. Most of the time he didn't want to come, but sometimes he did. His ass was beautiful and he liked to have it played with.

* * * *

One of the stalls has a glory hole and most of the time it was occupied, but occasionally I would find it vacant. That happened late one afternoon and I saw a guy playing with a small, cut prick in a patch of pubic hair that looked as if it had been trimmed and shaved. I found out later that it hadn't. I looked through the hole and saw a young guy, small, with dark hair, blue eyes and fair skin. He opened his shirt and was playing with his nipples and rubbing his hairless chest and stomach. He had very frayed Jockey shorts and painters' pants. He knew he was being watched and it didn't take me long to realize that Kevin (his name) liked to be watched while he put on a show. His prick was small and very pretty, and hard. He kept playing with himself and then shot all over his stomach and then licked his come off with his fingers. Sometimes I used to try to get him to let me suck his dick. I finally did one afternoon and when I stuck my finger up his tight little hairless asshole, he shot a nice small load. He liked to twist my balls and jerk me off while I sucked his dick. There were many others. If you can use this let me know and I'll send you some more details.
P.S. All true!

Medics Find Some Sailor Cock Too Cheesey

CALIFORNIA — Tid bits from boot camp in San Diego. After reporting to San Diego, all recruits are herded into a big physical examining room. Standing in bare skin were about 40 recruits. All sizes and shapes of cocks. Cut and uncut, long and short, some very large monsters. Standing next to me was a body builder with a great body and a nice long thick cock, but uncut. When the doc got to him he asked to peel it back and watching him straining to get that skin back was more than I could endure and the doctore knew it wasn't going to get skinned, so he was scheduled to return for possible circumcision. I don't remember if he did or not. Can you imagine an 18-year-old kid not playing with himself and skinning his dick when he was much younger?

There were about 200 recruits in my company and they were fat, skinny, great physiques and some that looked like bean poles. Naturally all types and sizes and shapes of cocks too. There was one who had a pair of balls that would make a stud horse envious. There were hanging and swinging as well as uptight balls. Some cocks were smooth as silk and some were dark and others veiny. Some had super large mushroom heads. There were never two cocks alike. One time when all the recruits were stuck in barracks for the weekend, they had a jack-off contest to see who could shoot the furthest. One kid shot 12 feet. I don't recall seeing or hearing of a largest cock contest. We had some kids who had stud horse size cocks and they knew it too.

Before qualifying as a swimmer you had to shower and then come out and get inspected before you jumped into the pool. Well, there was this kid from the hills who was freckle face and kind of slim; he came out from the shower and he had a sizeable cock but it was uncut, so the pool director asked him to skin his cock back, and brother, you should have seen the cock cheese. Actually I think I saw some of the stuff fall to the floor. Whereupon the director yelled at the poor kid and told him, "Don't you ever wash your cock? Look at that cock cheese. You have a cheese factory and don't know it." Exit the kid with a red face and needless to say he was called Cock Cheese from then on.

All recruits are issued boxer shorts. Why I don't really know. But this really made your cock and balls relax and hang all out cause there was no support. Later the guys buy either jock straps or briefs to help relieve the drag, cause we were running all the time and involved in exercise. Remember one hillbilly kid tell us about fucking a cow and a horse because where he come from you were not considered a man till you did that. One kid told about how he and his buddy took a gelding back in the hills and jacked him off, but nothing came out cause the horse didn't have any nuts.

When I was growing up we visited my grandmother, who lived in a desolate countryside. There was a desolate stretch of road, and there is where the lovers went. During daylight when not many used those quiet places, my brother and I used to play around that area — skates, bikes and what have you — and then we noticed condom cans, boxes, papers, wrappers all over, and upon reading the printing, we learned a lot. Then on searching further, we found Jockey shorts, boxer shorts, handkerchiefs, panties, brassieres, etc. It

seemed that when the guys were done fucking they had to wipe with something. The best part was when we found some rubbers that were not used and we tried to roll them onto our little peckers and were simply amazed that anyone could have a cock large enough for the rubber to fit. We also found many rubbers that were full of come. Some were really filled with come.

Psychiatry: Diagnosis

NEW YORK CITY — All this shit about whether men are "straight," bisexual, homosexual, or what, can be cleared up if people would just realize that in public men are "straight" but in private, queer as hell.

Country Club Cock Lover

SANTA BARBARA — Ma got me out of the house by getting the old man to take me to his country club when he played golf. That very first time we went into the locker room, I saw my first male in the nude. He stepped out of a shower stall, a tall, dark-haired, good-looking son of a bitch. Black curly cock hair with a prick that seemed to swing between his legs. When he dried himself that cock of his really flopped around.

I got to see my dad in the raw in this way too. He had a good-size prick hanging from a mass of black hair, but it was not a giant like the shower stud had swinging between his legs. I would sit on the bench nearest the shower stalls and watch the cocks go by.

Most of the time dad would go out on the golf course and I would stay in the locker room. One day a friend of my dad's was taking a shower and he saw I was greatly interested in his cock. In no time this gave him a hard on. He had a very fat cock thrusting out from brown cock hair. He gave me a wink. He was a lawyer.

One time he told me to wait, he would be right back. When he returned he had a buddy to show me, very tall and quite thin. He had a very long slim cock, black cock hair.

It was an American Indian, a caddy, who gave me my first ass fuck. The greens keeper had a shed on the course and it was there that he took me. He dropped his pants and shorts and had me play with this dick. It was the color of cinnamon. Blue-black cock hair. He had 7-8" of cock and had me get down on all fours, my pants and shorts down over my ass. He got down on his knees behind my ass, pulled my buns apart, got his cock lined up to my hole, and went on into me with ease. He worked that big cock in and out of me fast and furious. His hands were on my hips, holding me fast.

He filled my ass with his juice and when he broke free of my hole and saw he had broken through the rubber he used, he laughed and laughed. To him it was a big funny.

I got fucked regularly by this hot-blooded Indian after that.

Secrets of a "Straight"

[EDITOR'S NOTE: The subject of the following article is still handsome in his 40s: pale blue eyes, ruddy shining complexion, trim body, and smooth, hard, hairless hind end. He is attractive in a baseball cap and irresistible in flannel pajamas. But it is his personality that is most alluring. He's a tough blue collar class man from Brooklyn whose recent operation for throat cancer left him with a hoarse voice which makes him sound even tougher. A conservative Irish Catholic, he became drunk and left his wife and children; he lost me when he supported Reagan. But I have gotten over that and have recently spent some time drawing out the secrets which lurk beneath his apparent heterosexuality. He stopped drinking three years ago, and is in fine shape, providing his cancer has been arrested. He dictated the first part of this article as I typed it; the second part is his written answers to a questionaire I gave him.]

I. The Bowery Blow Jobs, Circa. 1976

It was in the late afternoon and it was a very hot and humid day and I was panhandling on Houston Street to try to get some money for wine. I already made the price of two jugs but drank them and I was trying to make enough change for another jug. From the high temperature I began to tire and felt sleepy so I started walking towards the flophouse where I was staying. Without realizing it I walked one block past the flop so I sat down on the sidewalk against this building and began to doze off when this middle-aged man came by and began to look at me. He came over and asked me what was the matter. I told him I feel sick and I need a taste. He asked me if I had a big cock and I told him it's about medium size so he asked me if he could have a look at it. I said I'm not going to take it out on the street — do you have a place to go? He said yes, you can come to my room, it's only around the corner, and I said to him, I just told you I need something to drink. He said, "If I like what it looks like, I have some wine in my room that you can have." I got up as quick as I could because I needed a taste desperately. I began to shake and became very anxious to get to his room. I didn't care what he did to me as long as he gave me some wine. I would have let him do anything. I've never been fucked in the ass but at that moment I would have let him do anything he wanted to do to me. I followed him around the corner and he says this is where I live. There was a woman sweeping the stoop and she greeted him and said hello. He said hello to her and said this is a friend of mine who wants to look at my birds. She said, well, that's nice, he has lovely birds. We went one flight up. He had a small room and against one side of the room was all these fucking bird cages with all these birds making a lot of noise. On the other side of the room was a small sofa bed. He told me to sit down and to pull my pants down. I said, where's the wine. He went to a drawer and pulled out a pint of Thunderbird. It was about threequarters full. He gave it to me and I started gulping it down. While I was drinking he started to jack me off. I told him not to pull my skin back too far because I'm not circumcised. He told me he would go easy. He told me to take my pants all the way off. I didn't have any underwear on so I was naked. He told me to lay back and put my legs up. He started putting his finger in my anus. He

had a long and thick finger and it hurt because I'm tight. When he fingered my anus he started to lick the head of my cock. I started to moan and my cock began to swell. He put his tongue — you know where you piss, where the opening is slit — and I forgot all about the wine because I began enjoying his fingering my anus and sucking on my cock at the same time. He said that he sucked longer and thicker cocks but he liked mine because it was very hard, like a rock. He told me to shove it in and out of his mouth. My whole cock was in his mouth. I started sweating and so did he. I never had anyone suck on my cock like this guy did. I could hear him sucking. He had a lot of saliva and he was drooling. He had a powerful suction. I could have let him do it for hours but then I exploded into his mouth. He took all the come as fast as I came and he swallowed it all. I had to tell him to stop. I told him we'd have to wait a half hour if he wants to blow me again. I told him I liked the way he did it and that it was one of the best blow jobs I ever had. He had a look of satisfaction on his face so he must have liked my cock, but told me that he had to go to work, that I couldn't stay in his room while he was working because he didn't know me well enough, that if I would meet him at midnight I could stay with him until the next morning. I said OK but I'm going to need more wine. He said drink what's left in the bottle and then gave me $2 and said that should hold you until I see you tonight and when I see you I'll pick up a quart of wine.

 We left the room and he went on his way to work and I went to the liquor store and got two pints of Thunderbird and brought them up to the flop that I was staying in and drank them. I passed out on my cot after drinking the wine and did not wake up until the next morning. I didn't bother to see him the next day. I needed a taste so bad I went out and panhandled and made enough money to buy some more wine and forgot all about him. I did not feel like having anyone suck my cock. I just wanted to drink wine. I don't know whether this is after or before. I think it's after. I was working the cars. All morning and afternoon I was wiping windshields for change. I had a couple of partners also working with me. It began getting late and dark towards the evening. We were all wined up and I split and went back to my flop. We had made a lot of change that day to buy enough wine for the three of us. When I got up to my flop almost three-fourths of the cots in the dormitory were already filled with guys sleeping and some were picking lice off their bodies. If there's one thing I could not stomach it was seeing someone that had body lice.

 I drank every day, but always early in the morning. I would take a shower at the Holy Name so I was fortunate enough never to get lice. I tried to keep my body as clean as I possibly could. I would always wash my cock with plenty of soap, pull my skin back and wash the head. Sometimes when I did this I would start jerking off. I got caught a couple of times by the guy who takes care of the showers and he told me to take a shower if I wanted to do anything else I should do it someplace else. I told him to go fuck himself. He told me if he catches me again that he won't let me take any more showers. I said OK I would not do it no more. But I still did it, I just never got caught again. I used to like to jack off in the hot shower with the hot water running over my cock. I would put plenty of soap on while I was jacking off. It felt so good.

 OK, we'll go back to the flop now; we started off with the lice, right? I was sitting on my cot with some of those guys sleeping around me and this guy in the next cot picking these fucking lice off him. I told him to keep them motherfucking lice away from me and my cot. While I said this, this guy was passing my cot and heard what I said. He came over to me and said, don't you

like lice? I said no, I like to keep my body clean so that I don't get lice. He said, how about your cock? I said I keep that clean too. He then asked me if I wanted a blow job. I said maybe. He then said I'll give you a pint of wine if you let me suck you off. I said where can we do it? He took me in this one section of the dormitory where there were two or three empty cots. There were lockers that blocked the view that no one could see us, although everyone knew that this guy gave blow jobs because he probably blew 75% of the Bowery residents anyway. I pulled my pants down and I was standing up. He went down on his knees and put my cock in his mouth before it got hard. I told him not to pull the skin back too far because it hurts. Being not circumcised it would hurt if the skin was pulled back too far. My cock began to swell. He took it out of his mouth and started jacking it off, licking my balls. He told me to sit down on the cot, that he wanted to suck my asshole. I lay down on my back and spread my legs and he spread my cheeks with his hands. This was the first time I ever had anyone suck my ass. He split my crack with his fingers and stuck his tongue in and out of it and it felt funny. I told him to suck me off so he began to suck me off and play with my balls. My cock was very hard by this time. I was enjoying it and I did not want to come. I said you can suck my ass again if you like so he started sucking my ass and I felt like I was going to come. I told him I was going to come so he put my cock in his mouth again. I thought he was going to swallow it. He had a very huge mouth. I think he could have put my balls inside his mouth. I exploded and he started making loud moans while I was coming. So did I. Somebody yelled, shut the fuck up. We pretended not to hear it. He then said that I was very nice, that he would bring over a pine of wine like he promised. When he said this, this other guy came over and went like this to the guy — he didn't say anything, he put his finger on his groin and then in his mouth. The guy looked at me but I don't like to give blow jobs, I liked to be blowed, at that time. I went back to my cot and sat there waiting for him to bring my wine. I had to wait till he gave this other guy a blow job. He came over 15 minutes later and said, here. He gave me the wine. I said thank you. He said, it's me that should thank you.

There was this guy that would walk around the dormitory in only a bathing suit. It was a nylon form-fitting type. You could see that he had a big tool. I thought to myself that it must be at least 10 inches when it swelled up. I did not care for cock at this time. If I saw him today I would love to suck on his big tool. He was a man about 35 to 40. He was very muscular and good looking for someone to be living in a flop house. I never saw him drinking. He would just parade around the dormitory in his tight-fitting nylon bathing suit. His cot was about 6 cots away from where mine was. One morning when I woke up it was about 5 o'clock in the morning. I sat up on my cot and saw this guy that gave me a blow job, I think it was the same guy. I could see the bathing suit guy had a huge cock when he had the cock out of this guy's mouth and was jacking it off. From where I was sitting it looked like it was about 10 inches. It was very thick and circumcised. While he was sucking him off this guy was making all kinds of noises. I'm surprised he didn't wake up the other guys. If anyone else was awake besides myself then they must have been pretending they were sleeping because this was being done in an open dormitory. At least 75 guys. They didn't make fun of the man who paraded around us in his bathing suit; they were afraid to. They weren't in good shape and he was a big muscular guy. After he came, the guy that was blowing said, it's still early, we can do it again. Fifteen minutes later, I was laying down and I could hear them doing it again. I

fell asleep and woke up at 7 when the guy came around to wake us up. He had to be out by 8.

II. "I Want to Gag on It"

You mentioned that you met a youth in a woods. I should say "he met me." I was sitting on a rock near the water when I saw him coming. He was riding his bike. I pretended not to see him standing behind me and I started jacking off. He came over and asked what I was doing. I said, "What does it look like?" He watched me jack off while I looked at the swelling between his legs. He then sat next to me and put one hand on my cock. I said, "Is your cock bigger that mine?" He said it was and asked me if I would like to suck him off. I said OK and he said, "Follow me." I followed him. He had a bike so he got to this other place before I did. That was about 100 yds. from where I was jacking off. It was between these large rocks that nobody could see what you was doing. When I got there he was already jacking off. He had a small and thin body. He was in his teens at this time but had a cock like a man. It was over 7 inches long and thick. I had a little trouble putting it in my mouth. I choked a few times. It took about a half hour before he cum. I took it all until it filled my mouth. He said he liked the way I did it and wanted to see me again. He didn't ask for money but wanted a motor bike. The four years that I saw him I must have sucked him hundreds of times. He never sucked me. One time he asked me to buy him a six pack. He drank 3 cans of beer and started taking his clothes off. He asked me to fuck him in the ass. I did not feel like doing it. He wanted me to fuck him so bad. All the blow jobs that I gave him was in this woods that I first met him.

Then he started smoking pot. It took him longer to cum. Some time I suck him about an hour before he come. I could see him during the warm months but not the winter. I was afraid to take him to my hotel room. The following year the weather got warmer. I saw him in the woods. He had his bike as always. He looked like he was high on something. He got aggressive and I had to push and grab him. I did not hit him. But I was afraid he might hit me. He was about my size now and getting muscular. I told him no rough stuff or no more blow jobs. He said he was sorry. He said, "Please suck me before I come in my pants." A year after this I stopped seeing him. I drank a lot even before I met this boy. I wanted to drink more than I wanted that beautiful *COCK*. I sucked a few cocks after I stopped seeing this boy, but they were men and none of them could turn me on like this boy did. I would cum in my pants or bathing suit while I was sucking this boy's cock. Nobody has ever filled my mouth with cum like this boy could. He be about 26 years old now. I know he never will forget me. I will never forget him. The 4 years that I sucked his cock he would take his shirt off but never take his pants off. He would just pull them down to his knees or sometimes his ankles, but never take them off completely. I did not like this because he could not spread his legs so that I could go all the way between them. I sucked his asshole but I did not like the smell too much. Oh, how I miss him. I would love to suck his hole now, smell or not. I would suck all the shit out of it and swallow it. I don't care how bad it would taste. But the 4 yrs. I had him I guess I didn't appreciate a good thing when I had it. He really liked me to put my tongue in his hole. He told me to clean it out but like I said I

did not like the smell or taste at that time. Boy, do I regret that. Most of the time he would lay on his back when I sucked his cock and licked his balls. When I sucked his asshole he would turn on his stomach. I would bring a beach towel for him to lay on.

How many cocks have you sucked? This boy and 3 or 4 men, maybe more. I used to be drunk a lot. I can't remember. I used to have to be drunk to suck cock. I don't drink anymore and I would love to suck cock, especially big ones that make me choked and fill my mouth with cum. I will suck any cock that's at least 7 inches and thick and will fill my mouth with cum. I don't care if it's a boy, queer or straight. I want to have a man stick a big cock in my mouth. I like to have him hold my head down on it. I want to gag on it. I want to get fucked in the mouth.
What were you wearing when you first met the boy? A bathing suit.
How old were you then? Late 30s.
Please describe how you jacked off when you first met the boy. I started jacking off when I saw the boy coming. I sat on this rock. My bathing suit was pulled down to my knees. I was excited when I knew he was standing behind me, watching. When I saw him coming through the woods riding his bike, I pulled my bathing suit down to my knees. He got off his bike and stood behind me for about ½ minute watching. Then he came and asked if I wanted to blow him. He seduced me. It was fast.
Please describe the boy. He had a little pubic hair around his asshole. He was very thin, about 5 ft. 7 in. Flat tummy, weight 110 or 115 lbs. Narrow boy's ass. He was small except for his *COCK*. It was oversized for his body. He had a face like an angel, innocent looking except for his eyes. His cock was very thick. I had to open my mouth very wide. I would choke some times. He would get a hard on right away and it would stay hard for an hour sometimes. It never got soft until it exploded and his cum flooded my mouth & throat. Sometimes he had so much cum that I had to swallow it and there was some left to fill my mouth. Some would drip out. He asked me if it tasted good. He unloaded large wads. He told me that he did not jack off anymore since he met me, that he saved his cum for me. Sometimes I would not see him for a week. When we would see each other he had a week's load of cum for me. I swear his cock would swell up so big that I had trouble putting it in my mouth and when he cum I couldn't keep it all in my mouth. It was like an explosion. I would lose some of it. I would suck his cock 3 or 4 times and each time he would shoot a full *LOAD*.
How did his cum taste? Creamey. I loved to taste it in my mouth a few minutes before I swallowed it.
How did his balls taste? They tasted sweaty and *salty*. He had big balls. He said to spit on them to make them wet. I would make his cock wet too.
How did his ass taste? I liked his shit-hole but at this time I did not appreciate it. I did not like the taste or smell at this time. I would love it now, especially a boy's hole. I would put my tongue inside it.
Did you give him any flattery or compliments? I would tell him how much I enjoyed sucking his cock and how big it was. He said he saw bigger cocks. I told him his was big enough for my mouth, that if it was bigger it would not fit in my mouth.

Was he really a prize lay, or did you go with him just because he was available? He had a wonderful cock. His cock was the best I ever sucked. His balls were always full of cum, loads of it. He never liked me to kiss him on the lips & face but liked me to kiss him all over the rest of his body. I had to wash my bathing suit every time I would see him. It was full of my cum. While I sucked on his cock I would come in my bathing suit. I never took it off when I was with him. He liked me a little because I was a good cocksucker; we was sex partners. We might have become friends if it wasn't for the drugs. I drank a lot and he smoked pot and took pills. Sometimes after I sucked him I would let him piss in my mouth. I would swallow it too. I never had to jack off. I would cum in my bathing suit or if I was wearing pants my underpants would be soaked with my cum after sucking on his cock.
Did you ever get tired of sucking him, since it took him so long to come? Never. I could not get enough of it. I would have liked to suck him for hours. But my neck got tired.
Was he ever nasty? Did he treat you with respect or contempt? He treated me with respect and I think he was a little afraid of me after I grabbed him that one time. I had to show him who was boss.
Did he ever tell you to do anything? When I was sucking on him he would tell me to spit on his cock & balls so that they would be wet. He would tell me to lick his ass & put my tongue into his hole sometimes. I loved to kiss his cock & belly & chest & his asshole.
What did he say or do while he was coming? He would moan and push my head down hard on his cock. This made me cum in my bathing suit or underpants. I could hardly breathe when he did this. I would some times choke.
What did he do after he came? We would wait a half hour or so and he would let me do it again, or he would go off on his bike & come back in an hour or so. I did not tell him where I lived. He not tell me where he did. He called me Joe and I called him Joe. Some times he told me he would like me to get him a girl. I asked him what for, he said he would like to fuck her & I could watch. I never got him a girl, I wouldn't share his cock with anyone. He was friendly with me.
Were you in danger of being caught and arrested? No, we had 3 different hiding places. No one could see us in the high grass during the warm months. We had some rock cover also. We felt safe & comfortable.
Did you see any other men and boys having sex in the neighborhood? I've seen some other chicken hawks. I never saw them in action though. They would talk to a boy or boys and then go somewhere. Sometimes when I first knew Joe, a chicken hawk would approach him, but Joe would take off from him on his bike. Joe would tell me about this afterward. I asked Joe why he did not go with this guy, Joe would say, because I was waiting for you. That made me feel so *good* that when I sucked his cock I felt I could take his whole cock in my mouth, balls & all. There were lots of boys to look at, some in bathing suits, all ages. A lot of places to go and not be seen. I did not bother with the other boys. I would be waiting for Joe. I guess after awhile the other boys knew I was waiting for Joe. Some times a boy would come over and ask me the time. I was wearing a bathing suit & had a hard on thinking about Joe. He sat across from me looking at the swelling between my legs. He asked me if he could suck me off. Before I could answer I saw Joe coming on his bike. When Joe saw me and the kid and he could see I had a hard on he told the kid to take off. The kid was scared & ran.

South Dakota Sailor Fucks Boston Boy in Mouth

MAINE — Way back during my yute (as Mayor Daly would put it), I was walking up Boylston Street, Boston, on a winter's dark night, in a light snowfall, when a sailor walked past me. I got a whiff of Skin Bracer aftershave lotion, and I hopped up to get in front of him, stopping to gaze in the windows of Shreve Crump. He too stopped, his "p" jacket open, and there was revealed a full, relaxed but most impressive cock. He ignored my stare but I kept walking fast and looking back at his groin. Long before we reached Copley Square it was extending down his left leg. Obviously my glances were received with similar interest. He went ahead of me onto the porch of St. Paul's, which was dark and quiet. When I came up he said, "Cripes! I can hardly walk, it's so stiff." I was rather shy back then and so I restrained myself to a compliment — I was really only a kid and he was a man. "It's sure beautiful," I said. He looked around. The square was deserted and quiet. He took my hand and put it on his cock. I remember clearly the surprise I felt at its heat under the wool of his tight trousers. I felt his cock and, with the other hand, stroked and squeezed his round, firm butt.

He started to undulate his hips and to breathe hard. We strolled to a nearby hotel, also almost deserted, wandered around and ultimately peeked into a pitch dark ballroom, which we entered. Wanting to be near an exit door, we went up to the stage and he leaned against a grand piano while I knelt and started to suck that perfect torpedo. It was an unforgettable cock — smooth, hard and clean. He didn't want to come, so he buttoned up and we left the hotel, still looking for another spot. We finally found a narrow, protected alley on Beacon Street. No windows around and a fire escape at the end, dark and covered with a roof. He stood up a couple of steps so that his cock was at my face level, and I kissed and nibbled his rod through his pants. The taste of the wool and the heat is vivid yet. This time he dropped his trousers, held my head and fucked my mouth. Inexperienced, I got scared I would choke — and did so several times, but he paused once and, still holding my head, planted a long hot kiss on me. When his tongue entered my mouth, I nearly fainted from the excitement. It was a first for me. He came and I swallowed it all proudly, after which he hugged me. As we emerged from the alley we were arrested by cops with drawn guns — there had been a lot of robberies in that area. At the station each of us identified ourselves and stuck by the story that we had gone in there because he was ill and thought he was going to throw up. Upon release (3 A.M.) we shook hands and laughed, but I failed to get his name and address, so worried was I about how I was going to get home and explain to my parents. I had to spend $25 for a cab home — 20 miles — and that was like $75-$100 at today's rate. No problem at home — all in bed. But I jacked off and have many times since over a romantic and perfect experience. He was muscular, chunky and black haired, from South Dakota German stock. His mouth was so clean there was no bad breath — it seemed almost mildly sweet, but that could have been because I was half in ecstasy.

Mississippi Man, 26, Asks Doctor to Beat Him

CONNECTICUT — What a night. It was rainy in the seedy side of Boston's "Combat Zone." I had gone into a peep show about 10 P.M. looking for a hot glory hole and I certainly found one. The hot cock on the other side pulled back and came into my booth, where I stood waiting. He said almost nothing and the fondling continued. He had a room in a motel next door to where I was a house guest and so we drove over there. As we entered the darkened room, lit only by flashing neon signs outside, all I could think of was this sure looked like a Class B movie set. Anyway he turned and said, "I've got to tell you something." "Go on, it can't be any worse than some things I've heard." "I've never done anything like this before." I was dumbstruck. All I could think of was, another fucking virgin. They are such terrible sex. "You'll have to teach me everything." "How come tonight? Is this some bet?" "I just had to. I've spent the whole day in the combat zone and I just never feel fulfilled by girls. I just have to have a chance." You've got the right guy, I said to myself.

We started off with his asking to be slapped around with a doubled belt. Wack, wack, wack, wack, until I realized that you could hear this everywhere. On came the radio to mask the noise. He never opened his mouth except to say, "Beat me harder." I'm exhausted, having been up since 5 A.M. and in classes all day at Harvard Medical School (I was taking a post-graduate course). All this slapping was getting on my nerves so I stuffed my raging hard on down his throat. Of course I got a lot of teeth in the way. A little instruction on swallowing cock was given ("and if you don't behave I'll have to give you ten more hard ones"). I shot over his face; might as well get him right into it. Then he rolled over at the side of the bed and spread his cheeks and said, "Now fuck me." I proceeded slowly, as a virgin asshole really isn't one to fool with. A little patience on my part would make for a better scene ahead. The expected complaints of pain followed but I ignored them all. In fact I hated the whole God-damned position. I lifted him up onto the bed and turned him over so his legs were in the air; my favorite fucking position. Now he would know what was going on. He winced at every plunge but never opened his mouth, as I had the belt as a mouth gag. I shot again up his ass. By now it was about 1 A.M. and I was approaching exhaustion. Well, I thought, I might as well die here as anywhere. So I turned over and made him lick my cock clean of his shit. That was kind of a twist; I thought; I'd never do that myself. (I'm not into scat at all.)

Finally I decided to rest. No way. Now he pleaded for some more beatings; a few more wacks wouldn't be too much to ask. By now he had red welts all over his ass, his back and his legs. I wondered at myself when looking at this (virgin?) man. All the way from Mississippi to Boston for this? I finally said that enough was enough and stood up, pissed into his mouth and got dressed. It was unreal. I'm all dressed; the guy, about 26, is crumpled at the foot of his bed covered in piss and cum; welts all over; here I am all ready to leave and he turns and says, "Please give me five more hard ones." I gave him six and said I hoped he wouldn't forget his trip to Boston. And that's the truth.

* * *

As a physician, can you give any technical advice on how to swallow a huge cock? Most success is due to the ability to actively suppress the gag reflex. About 10% of people have no gag reflex and are in free. The rest have to learn. I tell them that when the cock gets to the back of the throat and they think that they are going to vomit or gag, they should hold their breath and try to keep swallowing. This opens up the throat. Once the cock is down it is best to keep it there as long as possible in order to get the feel of a hard cock so far down.
Can you cite a few examples of flesh you've examined which was a pleasure to touch? Most flesh is sort of boring. The nicest flesh and most seductive meat belongs to the late pubescent male. The new growth of body hair is soft and sensuous. They have nice new thick cocks, most of which have not been tried out. During physicals, many of them swell to full erections. I like to have the male patient leave his underclothing on — it is more private for him and more erotic for me.
Is there any particular group of men you'd like to serve as a physician? The U.S. Marines. Unreal bodies. I took care of them for a long time. They are very homosexually-oriented without having sexual encounters. It is in their training. They relish good head and afterwards are scared to death someone will find out. So they keep their mouths shut. A lot of Marines like to get fucked, especially by sailors.
Have you had patients so alluring and ready you'd like to have sex with them on the spot? And how. I do not make sexual advances on patients but I have had sex with patients who invited it. Each time it happens I wish that I had been stronger and resisted. It is usually only a blow job. But I have also fucked a patient or two who insisted. I just sucked a gorgeous cock on a 22 yr. old blond gas pump number who loved it. He comes to the office a lot. Nice thick one. The sort of cock you dream of when you are on your knees at the suck-hole. I plan on rimming him next. That's the *piece de resistance* that keeps "straights" in line because their girls won't tongue that tight hole at any time. When the anus begins to quiver you have them in your pocket forever. A 45 yr. old "straight" patient came in to tell me that for a *whole year* he has fantasized me fucking him. He likes to suck a cock now and then and is a virgin. Can I face another screaming man? On the schedule for tomorrow night. Did you ever get the photo of that beautiful fireman I sent you? He is a stud!
Where do you look for sex? I like the back of suck movies or dirty bars. I love to suck any size cock.
Please describe the best cocksucker you've had. The best cocksucker I ever actually sampled was a glory hole resident in Chicago. It was an incredible time for both of us. I like a tight drawing and an active tongue, not these wet holes you sort of stick your cock into and it goes back and forth. Not many guys give good head. You can tell who likes to suck and who performs it as a duty.
What's the best cock you ever sucked? The best cock I have ever sucked belonged to a handsome young blond doctor who brought me out. It was a nice sized cock, and as a virgin I didn't gag on it, and life was fine. Since then I see a regular stud with a 9½" cock that is wild. He thrusts his desires down my throat. It is ecstasy.
Please list the place where you've had sex. Toilets, cars, theatres, bars, baths, parks, submarines, ships, airplanes.
Was there any sex on the submarines you served on? Very little homosexual activity *per se*. I used to jack off in the bunk, collect it in the other hand and

then lick it clean. You really had a long haul in the submarines: we would be submerged for over 3 months at a time. Even the Captain began to look good to me.
When you were a medical student, did the other students talk much about jacking off? Yes. All the single ones did. Some were jerking off so much that we wondered if they were getting a conditioned reflex. Med students in general are so horny that they could fuck an animal. All except me. I was apparently out of it. I was asexual then. I have very little sex drive. I was too busy studying and frightened of flunking out. It was sort of a four year depression. I didn't come out of it until I was a Navy Intern. When I interned in the Navy there were 4 gay doctors. Three were out. And then there was me, who soon came out.
Have you ever seen, or heard of, a patient in hospital beating his meat? Of course. I encourage it.
What would be your ideal sex life? If I could have my choice I would have a permanent residence at a glory hole servicing straight workmen. I think sucking off a "straight" man is wild. He goes half crazy and it is a lot of fun for me.
What's the most interesting proposition you ever got: A nearly illiterate young man who worked in a lumber mill came in covered with sawdust, sat on the examining table and handed me a tight wad of a note that said, "How about some fun?" He stood up and took out his cock and that was one of my office sexual transgressions. How could you not?
How do "straight" doctors treat homosexuals? For a long time not one of 300 doctors at our hospital would speak to me at length; I'd sit down at meetings and chairs would be empty either side of me. In 15 years not one straight doctor has invited me to his home. They think of me as weird. Fuck them all. I take care of gays for miles around. There are a lot of us. It takes them out of straight doctors' offices. Straight doctors really have very little idea of gay medicine and the problems we face.
Do you like being an exhibitionist or voyeur? I am fearful of being arrested if I tried any public displays. It is exciting but too dangerous really. Being a voyeur is always a pleasure. Most of my life, as a doctor, is spent as such.
Have you ever, in a locker room, seen a man or boy display his meat and body in such a way that you suspect he's an exhibitionist? Yes. They always do the same thing: they carefully straighten their cocks by pulling down on them to elongate them and then fluff their balls up.
What's the best sex you've had? One time a black dude blew me in a movie theatre in the wings. He never uttered a word but kept looking up to make sure I was enjoying it. I was. He moved his mouth parallel my arousal. It was a perfect blow job. After it was over, he just slipped away into the shadows.
Have you ever had, or given, worshipful sex? I've had a lot of trips around the world but no total body worship. I would like it a lot, however, I give a lot of worship sex and it so turns on my partners they are carried into a state of hypnosis with it at the time.
As a physician, what counsel can you give to asslickers? The two books, *Meat* and *Flesh*, have transformed my whole sexual life to a state of endless, restless excitement. The books keep me so horny that I think the editor needs a good face-fucking. But I tell men not to lick ass unless it is a steady. Clean assholes are still full of bacteria and the danger of hepatitis is immense. Soon there will be a vaccine. What I tell them, when asked, it to get gamma globulin injections

every 6 months, do as they want and if they get sick, for heaven's sake come in right off for diagnostic lab work and care.
Is there anything that can be done to avoid venereal disease? If everyone would wash with soap and water after any kind of sex the VD rate would drop. This would cut down GC right off and maybe syphilis. Gargling does not help unless you use 1/2 hydrogen peroxide and 1/2 water. That kills most of the germs. I'm off to Europe tomorrow. I'm almost too hot to cool down by now.

Hunky Black, 8½" Meats Youth, 11"

PHILADELPHIA — I think your magazine is the greatest fucking thing going. Every time I get an issue I can't wait till my lover goes out so I can settle down in bed, put my cock ring on, grease up my dick with a little Crisco (just a little; I like to feel my dick slide in my hand, not too slick) and settle down for a long session of jerking off. Now that I've got a little collection of your books, I can spend 2 or 3 hours just jacking my dick off. I really enjoyed the interviews with the Marines in Issue 42. I'm Black, just turned 31, 170 lbs., husky (bodybuilding 3 yrs.), big hands, big feet and a big, hot juicy dick. 8½" and about 5" around. I love to have my balls handled lightly while a good-looking cocksucker licks around them and up the root of my dick to my asshole. I also like having my asshole eaten out by an experienced ass licker. Every now and then I run into someone who is really into it and who can take my cock all the way down to the hairs. Boy does that feel good to feel some cocksucker's throat tighten up on the knob of my dick. All of this just leads to the best part — FUCKING. Since I've been 13, 14 years old I've had a thing for white boys, now white men. I love to fuck them and be fucked by them. I've taken some chances in order to get a piece of ass and to give someone a piece. I've fucked on roof tops in New York and deserted houses in Phila. One place where I am always certain to find a big dick for jerk offs, fucking and sucking is in the sauna of the main branch Y in Phila. Three times a week I head down, do my work out (run a mile, lift for an hour) and then head for the sauna and showers. Usually I can find at least 2 or 3 guys who are as hot as I am and seeking some relief. Usually all it takes is a look or a stroke on your cock to get things going. There is nothing better than to have a guy tongue out your sweaty asshole and then changing and sliding your tongue up his shit-hole and feeling it tighten up on your tongue. I usually wind up doing the fucking, sliding my dick up some tight-assed white boy's shit-hole. One of my fantasies is to be a towel boy in the locker rooms of one of the big teams, and to be sexually on call for the players. Baseball, football, big shoulders, narrow waists and long, fat cocks. I'd make sure they were all clean after the big game.

I got a fantastic, juicy, sloppy blow job in a deserted suburban train station in Philly. I just missed my train so I decided to smoke a joint. Light the joint up and just as I did I noticed a boy: straggly Blond hair, thin but with a *nice ass*, looking at me from the other end of the platform. He walked in my direction and asked me for the time. After this he walked down the steps to the street level and around to the back of the station (which was boarded up and off limits). I didn't think anymore about it until about 10 minutes later I heard someone say something to me, and I was all alone on the platform. It was the kid, talking to

me through a boarded up window. "Can I suck on some of that dick," he said. I went downstairs, found where he had removed a board on the doorway to the station and slipped in. The place was a wreck inside; evidently the station was a hangout for kids in the area's beer parties, gang bangs and what have you, since there were a lot of beer cans and scum bags scattered throughout. Went upstairs to what used to be the waiting room and there was the kid. He had opened up his shirt and taken his pants off while keeping his boots on. He looked like an ordinary street thug, young, skinny, a kind of cute face which he'd probably lose in a few years from too many drugs. His best features were his mouth (as you shall soon here) and his ass. Naked it was a sight to behold, arched high and round but not fat, just full and firm, great to feel in the palms of my hands. He sat on a bench. I walked up to him. He unbuckled my belt, unzipped my pants and pulled my jock aside. I was wearing my cock ring so by the time he worked my dick up and out of my pants the whole 8+ inches was up. This kid was a natural and just knew how to suck and nibble around my cock head. He had a lot of spit in his mouth and would make it juice over his lips. He started jacking his cock off. Although the kid was a very fair blond, with fair skin, his dick was almost as dark as mine with a huge knob and thick shaft. It must have been at least 11 inches long and about 6 inches around. I reached for it but he just pulled away saying he wanted to do it himself, and went back to jacking his dick and sucking on mine. He pushed his tongue into my cock slit and swirled it around. This boy knew what he was doing. I was nowhere near coming, as I was holding back, trying to make it last. He had the best mouth, throat and lips it has ever been my pleasure to stick my dick into. I lifted my leg up onto the bench so that he could have better access, and sure enough just like a pro he clamped onto my asshole like a leach. Boy did he suck my sweaty shit-hole out. I asked him if I could fuck him. He said I could try if I could give him train fare into the city (1.85). I said sure, now bend over. He spat a great big glob on his hand and lubricated his asshole. He bent over the bench and parted those tasty looking cheeks and I shoved my cock right up his asshole to the limit. All he did was grunt. It must have hurt like hell but he just grunted. Then he started moaning and asking for more. I was working it in and out and around real slow the way I like it. But he moaned and said, "Come on, bust my ass open with that big black cock." After awhile all I had to do was brace myself against the bench and he did all the rest. He rode my dick like a champion cowboy, wiggling and smashing his asshole down on my dick until it hit bottom. Just as I could feel my body and dick start to tense up getting ready to shoot a load, he pulled himself off my dick, which made a plopping sound, turned around and started sucking me off again, shit smears and all. He really went at it. I must have shot 6 or 7 ropey wads of thick come down his throat. All the while he was pulling on that cannon he had hanging between his legs. When he came he just sort of slumped forward, grabbed me around my thighs, buried his face in my groin and whimpered. He came so heavy that it looked like he had peed on the floor. Now whenever I go to Germantown on business I call him before and set something up. I have since been able to eat his shithole before and after fucking it. Boy is it tasty. Kind of sweet, always clean, pink and tight. He can just about take your tongue off when he clamps his asshole around it. Hmmm. He says he's never fucked anyone so I want to be his first. With an 11 inch cock I figure this kid's ready for the big time. He says he didn't want to ask for the money because he's not a hustler but he really needed the train fare that day.

A Catholic Boyhood
In Long Island Piss-Houses

NEW JERSEY — I implore you to grace your coming issues with more and better shit-hole shots. Speaking of which, my next adventure. One of the sweetest, horniest and riskiest of my adolescent experiences lay in disgraceful, appalling and coarse activities with a Slavic slut of beauty and endowment. I'd enticed him at the notoriously hot and juicy, slimy and unspeakably aromatic underground tearoom of the Hempstead Bus Terminal (Long Island) when I was a mere teenaged slut of 16 or so. I had begun driving, had an old car I loved, and was thereby able to frequent this repugnant sewer of sex more often than as a pre-teen tartlet of 12, bussing in from the boondocks every chance I got. He was truly sucky in every way and we managed all manner of unseemly carryings-on while occupying adjacent, then finally the very same 10¢ shitbowl booth. All this heat was generated between arrivals and departures of unidentified pairs of feet. Some, curious queers, lingered, perchance to peek and share; others, neither, came and went. Quiet moaning and slurping in this stuffy, hot, stench-ridden piss-hole was punctuated by dimes sliding into slits, doors opening and slamming. As his name escapes me, I'll call him Slav d'Amour, in loving deference to his luscious origins. (Poles and Slavs have always caught my eye.) Well, Slav and I would sizzle away many afternoon hours full tilt and soaking our clothes under the bus terminal until quite spent. Then we'd plan to meet at night for more, elsewhere. We'd meet in Hempstead's notoriously busy (harlot) carlot, leaving my car and going off in his usually. Around midnight or later we'd head ironically to his home. He'd pull into the family driveway, next to their big old house in Hempstead, ever so quietly and, incredibly, we'd fuck and suck for hours. It became the safest place for us and we'd carry on stark naked, fogging up the windows in no time. Our noises were miraculously muffled or unheard, for all our animal ecstasies. As his family slept soundly, we never felt very threatened. Much. The danger aspect only added to our hours of the cheapest of cheap thrills. One of this slut's most endearing qualities was his ability to shed clothing in a flash. The instant we coasted silently into the blackness of the drive and stopped, it seemed his clothes would vanish. I drooled at the sight of all that smooth, glorious male skin. Fully dressed, I pounced on him, sliding my tongue down his throat and my hands around his creamy ass as he moaned and hugged and squeezed me all over. I'd kiss, suck and chew this luscious, creamy man-child of 20-plus until he'd tear at my clothes. Slav undressed me, fumbling, moaning, leering at me; in some way his mouth was on me as he tossed away even our socks. He ate me everywhere, hungrily, savagely. He became so thrilled that he would weep and I'd lick his tears as I wet my finger and shoved it in his ass. I swallowed his delicious cock and hairless balls. Hands and lips seemed everywhere. Slav moaned as I licked and fingered his sweaty, tasty privates, his sweaty hands all over me. Our joy became complete as I would tenderly throw this slut of love onto his belly and finger his rosebud of a fuckhole. Suddenly my hard on was sliding home toward his moist rosebud, he gyrating his butt to help us merge. I fucked his tight ass slowly at first, biting his delicious neck and shoulders, then faster, harder, deeper. After a long time (we loved to prolong it as best we could), I shot his insides with hot, fresh boycum. On occasion he'd rub himself

to orgasm on the hot, smelly leather seats as I fucked him. The vision of his smooth, sweaty ass, back and balls glistening in the blackest dark, or first rays of dawn, is with me still, twenty-plus years later. The more we tasted each other, the hungrier we became, until dawn would send us crawling to our separate beds. We would hold each other to the last possible moment, smoke, talk and laugh, until dawn broke, or almost. Filled with bliss and each other, we would dress, roll the car back into the street, he'd start the engine and we'd drive back to the parking lot and my car. How we quietly managed to pull this, our clothes and each other off on several occasions astounds me always. But we managed to overcome our home situations (he, Slavic-Catholic; moi, Italian-Catholic).

One positive aspect of beginning Catholic high school an hour or more from home, in Mineola, Long Island, was the thrill of discovering a notoriously active, exotically "foreign" tearoom there, in the Long Island Rail Road station. Complete anonymity (unlike my Hempstead situation at times) was virtually assured here, and after a long, arduous, holy school day filled with boys, priests, gym, jock straps, showers, smelly lockers and sweat clothes, I was ecstatically wet, horny and nervous thinking of a pit stop at the tearoom. Horny men of every age and type walked, drove or trained into this pit of desire to check out the meat of the moment. The tearoom was tiny. One stall, one urinal, one sink and almost no standing room but near the door. The glory hole between the booth and the urinal could accommodate the various mouths, meats and asses of any magnitude and velocity. I'd spend hours playing and being played with and on. Things got so hot that I'd go there even on weekends with my car, which lent me more options than my bus trips during the week. I'd become so brazen after two years of this scene that when the attendant came in to "clean" I'd just stand there, impervious to his hostile, disgusted glances at all of us homos. If traffic was too heavy in the toilet I'd leave with one slut or another, in my car or his, and drive off into the wilds of nearby Garden City, which had many dark, deserted parking areas. We could park, undress partially, suck, fuck and finger each other. If we were bothered again, we'd simply pull up our pants and drive off to another spot. Back in the toilet, I'd get wringing wet in the hot, airless room while being quickly sucked by the hot, wet mouth behind the glory hole, working feverishly before interruption, with a powerful suction. At times I'd be inside the stall with another brave soul or two and could get my shit-hold licked.

Priests Expect Students to Put Out

I was in a monastery for awhile. Except for jacking off I almost became a virgin. We never even saw another guy naked in the showers. Each shower had a dressing stall in front of the shower. You would go into a dressing stall and undress then enter your private shower stall. Once another guy I met sometime later who had been in a seminary and I were talking about why we left. He stated that the younger guys were expected to let the older priests give them blow jobs. I would have loved it there. He was turned off and wouldn't share any detail. All I remember is that this seminary was in Indiana.

NEW WORKS FROM DENNIS KELLY

[EDITOR'S NOTE: Dennis Kelly is probably the spermiest of contemporary poets. Two of his collections, Chicken *and* Size Queen, *have been published by Gay Sunshine Press. He wrote the following poems for this anthology. "In these poems," he writes, "I've attempted to bring the realism of your prose into poetry. The poems are based on true experiences that I've had recently, as all my poems are. In many ways the prose pieces of* Meat *and* Flesh, *which inspired me to write these poems, are prose-poems, beautiful and startling in all their male nakedness."]*

SPUNK—FEVER

I'm one thankful cocksucker.
I had a delightfully succulent yng turkey for Thanksgiving.
He let me moan & groan over his nice big drumstick.
It was one nice piece of juicey spunkmeat.
It was just the way I like it — uncut & full of creamy jizzcream
I almost choked on it I got so excited.
He was the teenage son of one of my guests.
I was a guest too.
The minute he strut into the room I knew I had to have it.
Adonis-prick'd, sweet-sixteen & never been sucked before.
All puffed-up with goose-down ski-jacket.
Urgent erection stiffly sending out urgent SOS's.
Upturn'd spunk-lips curled nervously.
A pair of corduroys so tight you couldn't help but look at it.
Something inside me quivering to taste it.
His long hair falling out of ski-cap, as he takes it off.
Falling backward into big beanbag, arms behind neck.
Grinningly spreading musk-smelling legs for me.
Wldn't smoke joint or drink because his mother was downstairs.
Helping fix Thanksgiving dinner for later on.
While us guys watch TV Seacock football upstairs getting high.
Refrigerator full of beer in bathroom.
It was all almost more than a girl could take.
And the way he stroked it as he took a piss!
With me there beside him, wanting to fucking touch it.
Wanting to get in touch with it, wanting to feel what he felt.
Foreskin peeled back, glans grinning at me.
Such an innocent face.
But such a low fucking voice & such a mean-looking prick-hose.
He was blond but his pubes were black.
He had pale skin, but his dick was darkest darkmeat.
And with a jizzhose like that, ejaculations do fly...
One needs goggles when confronted with such cumly action.
It was long enough to turn me into a Katherine the Great.
Foreskinn'd spunkmeat, what a fucking treat!

Delicate souffle of dickcheese fondue!
I played a tune never before heard on his rude fleshflute.
There are no words to describe such a humjob.
Just a few strokes & then a nice thick virgin lode.
Cldn't count the squirts I was so delirious.
All I know is, it wasn't enough.
But then when is it ever enough for a nympho?
(He being the nymph of course, not me.)
He's the one that milked out the last drop.
He'd fucked me in the mouth, about a hundred strokes.
But when he milked it, it was with such animal familiarity.
That I shuddered...
Just an everyday crank-it-up experience for him.
That's how he milked out that last drop of opal onto my forehead.
He smeared it over my face, just like J.H. does in the movies.
How many times does he squirt his brains out each day, I wonder.
Spunkcream in the showerroom!
Spunkjuice down the drain!
Jizzlove into bedroom sheets!
Dribbles of it in his fucking shorts!
Wads of it onto his stomach!
Just an everyday occurrence, yet so private it drives me mad!
As I swallowed his load, his mom knocked on the door.
Later, on my pie, she gave me an extra plop of whipp'd cream.
I gobbled it up, like the gobbler that I am.
What a nicely erotic Thanksgiving Day it turned out to be.
I was one *thankful* cocksucker!

PEACHFUZZ AND FORESKIN

I love peachfuzz.
If there's one thing I like better it's cheese and foreskin.
When I find a guy with both I'm in heaven.
One day recently on a morning walk I came across 2 chicken fishing.
Off a dock in the park.
One was older than the other and very handsome.
As I came up to them, the oldest one took out his semi-hard prick.
He began pissing a stream of golden piss into the lake.
With a big worm like that in his hand I wished I were a trout.
So I could nibble it.
I couldn't help but stare.
He let me look.
Even when 2 joggers came by, the kid kept pissing.
Turned his ass slightly so they couldn't see.
But I could.
There was a star stitched onto his bluejeans.
Right there on his fine little ass.
He was delectable to look at and I knew then I had to have him.
After some chit-chat about fishing, he took out a big stick.
He said they used it to knock out the big ones, when they caught them.

I looked him up and down, sizing him up.
Was he a big one?
I told him it was a big stick, but that I bet he had an even bigger one.
In his pants....
He blushed and asked how did I know.
His friend laughed.
Up in the bushes I slipped his bluejeans down to his knees.
His shorts were stiff and smelly.
With dried-up jizz-juice.
He told me he had a hardon almost all the time.
Had to come 3 times a day.
I buried my face in it.
He really got hard.
His shorts were so tight I could barely peel them back.
What I saw made me weak in the knees.
Peachfuzz and foreskin!
What a lucky cocksucker I was!
And his nutsac was tight and bulging with jizz-love.
He told me he had to have it right away.
I grabbed his tight little ass and felt the goosebumps.
I slipped my tongue under the long foreskin and around the head.
I tasted it.
It tasted sweet and sour.
Like sweet and sour sauce.
It was just the appetizer tho.
Soon transparent drools of seminal lube-juice began oozing.
Out of his jizz-slit.
I watched it drip down to the ground but caught most of it.
I sucked his nuts.
They were big for a teenager.
I nearly fainted when I smelled his asshole!
He sat on my face.
I stuck my tongue madly up his asshole.
Then peeled back the foreskin to reveal a slimy head.
Purple with adolescent excitement.
"Is it big enough for you?" he asked.
It was normal for a chicken, 8 inches long, pale and creamy.
He squeezed it, his cock-muscle, engorging the head.
Out of his prick-slit (about an inch long) came a huge glob.
Of lube-juice clear as crystal.
It formed into a big pearl that hung down suspended.
From the kid's prick.
I caught most of it in my mouth.
It tasted fucking good with his tangy dick-cheese.
I was trembling more than he was.
He knew what I liked.
"Suck me off, man," he said.
I impaled myself on his chicken-meat.
He began pumping fast.
Before long I felt the first squirt.
His cockhead grew twice its size as cum came out.

Right away I cupped my tongue around his squirting dickhead.
I stuck my tongue into the prick-slit.
I felt it gush out.
It tasted awful but good at the same time.
With each squirt I squeezed his testicles some more.
I wanted every drop, you know what I mean?
After 4 or 5 shots came the motherlode.
A nice wad, big as an oyster.
It was one long 6" quivering squirt.
I felt every inch of it.
He got weak in the knees, bending slightly.
As he squeezed his whole body thru his dickhead.
I milked it good.
All the veins and arteries surging with each shot.
Each shot of his jizz-hose.
His face afterwards was the face of a chicken.
Who'd crossed the road.
(I knew then why the chicken crossed the road.
It was to get to the cocksucker on the other side!)
I walked home with the kid's spunk in my mouth.
I was one happy cocksucker!

"Straight" Youth Wants Asshole Licked, But Writer Finds It Too Dirty (At First)

CONNECTICUT — Joe, who is 22, wanted to visit yesterday, but I wouldn't admit him until my poison ivy cleared away. He is Irish, French, Italian, has hairless chest, 6', 150 lbs., and well endowed. I met him when moving, as he aided the landlord. He lives a few blocks away. He's introduced me to 18 yr. old Steve, whom he brought to my apt. once when he came over to retrieve his clothes after saying here a few days, and said he'll ask Steve if he wants sex with me. _____ visited last week for about four days on returning from Baltimore. He's a photographer of youth and showed his albums. Joe most emphatically likes to be sucked off, and he erupted most profusely. His thighs and ass are most beautiful. His asshole is quite small and tight, and I did not enter him deeply as he said it was irritating and hurt, so I withdrew. I did not rim too extensively upon our first encounter, as it appeared he had neglected to make use of toilet tissue for some time.

Upon our second encounter I found the taste of his asshole exceptional, as he was clean there and has been so, since. It has a vanilla flavor, and it's most agonizing that he's so tight in that area and not easily accessible, though two of my fingers did enter his hole. Usually his shirt and denim trousers are oil stained from working on cars and motorcycles. His balls, cock and armpits are clean and taste marvelous. Being so young, he tends to be nervous and sweats a lot, which I relieve him of with a tongue bath, which he loves. He wears beautiful white Jockies, and they taste beautifully of his sweaty body after his work as a mechanic. He asks for a tongue bath, especially on his asshole. He often asks me to lick his asshole. I used to pass him on the street when he was a youngster, on his way to school or engaged with his friends sportswise. He used to smile at me so one day I went up to him and talked to him and told him where I lived and that he was most welcome to visit. He noticed my *Advocate* and I asked if he had a girlfriend, and he said he is divorced and has a daughter, and is paying alimony to his former wife, and that his present girlfriend is pregnant by him. I asked him if he was gay and he said he wasn't, and then he asked me if I'd blow him, and I agreed to, so he undressed, and we performed the act on the living room couch, as he had a hard on. He lies on the couch as I perform, but I've not yet drunk of his urine. He lies on his back and on his stomach for ass-licking.

Joe and Jack visited just now. I was with Jack having sex when the bell rang and I admitted Joe, who said he just finished tiling a roof, and will be working at same on Memorial Day at triple time pay. He was sweaty but not dirty. He left this morning as I went to purchase the Sunday newspapers, but he'll probably return again today. He is primarily straight and wishes to be considered such but he is most agreeable to sex with me, but not so much so with Jack, but lately he is more willing to have sex with Jack also. Joe says he plans on marrying his pregnant girlfriend. Joe smells beautiful, always, and tastes likewise, due to his youthfulness. Yesterday Joe wore no underpants. After sexing on the couch, Jack and I both massaged Joe as he was talking on the phone to his girlfriend.

The Making Of A Hustler

NEW JERSEY — I've had a couple of pickups lately. One a little over a week ago was 18. I picked him up hitching home from school. I showed him a porno brochure and asked, "Have you ever had your cock sucked?" He replied, "No, and I don't want it either." I said. "That's too bad, because I'm really good at it." After we made small talk awhile he asked, "What would I have to do?" I knew what he meant but asked, "What do you mean?" "You know," he said, "to get you to suck it."

I pulled the camper off the road and groped him. His cock was hard, cut, average-sized. It took about five minutes until he began to gasp and moan. Then he shot a nice, heavy, sweet load of nectar.

Friday I picked up one hitching to Pa. He's 19, not great looking. He said he was going to a party in New Hope, "Gay party?" I asked. He said. "Are you gay?" I said I am and asked if he is. He said, "No, I don't do it but I let guys do me under the right circumstances." "Are the circumstances right now?" "Yes." I groped his big, thick, rubbery-hard cock. Cut, but nice. Silky smooth. No underpants. He came quickly after jerking off a bit. "Go down on it now," he said. He shot a small wad of very sweet cum. He disclaims being gay but had an instant hard on at the suggestion that I blow him and he knows the language. He was actually a vigorous mouth-fucker and gagged me at times with his ample tool. His body is smooth and hairless. Even his nuts were smooth.

LATER

I got him yesterday again. He's hitching every day. He says he may not be into being sucked every day. He has three girl friends and needed quick fixes because he hadn't seen them recently. His name is Joel.

He likes to thrust a lot. He shot more this time than last and it was just as sweet but he still didn't shoot what I consider an average wad.

His car is broken. He said he didn't think he was into getting blown every day; he was just doing it because he had no wheels and couldn't get out to see his ladies. I told him a ride was available anytime I saw him and he could tell me if he wanted some head.

I saw him again. I asked whether he'd been blown by many and he said three or four. We were nearly to his house when he said, "Would you like to do me?" Afterwards he said one guy had told him he had the perfect cock for chicks because of its size, angle, hardness, and so forth.

Then he said, "Have you ever thought of—er—paying?" I said, "Paying a guy to blow him?" He said yes. I said, "Joel, I feel that the guy should enjoy it at least as much as I. At that we're even. Besides I've never lacked for cock to suck; it's available to those who know where to look."

I wonder whether he'll ask me to suck it again.

I think it is a real shame that people who give these kids like Joel their first blow jobs don't teach them the proper way to take a blow job. They should show enjoyment and give some responses but shouldn't jam those luscious tools down your throat.

"I Ran My Tongue Around My Lips..."

BOSTON — I had flown into the city and stayed at Boston's finest hotel. All night and next morning, an historic blizzard raged. By the time I took luncheon in the main dining room, the city was paralyzed and the dining room almost empty. The head waiter explained how he had to walk in from a suburb as the bus line was shut down. Enjoying a leisurely luncheon in several courses, I was startled to have a young couple seated across from me, one table down, to my right. They were wet and breathless, having run in the snow: a perfectly magnificent boy and girl who looked so much alike, they had to be brother and sister. In keeping with the nature of the hotel, they were richly dressed: expensive and perfectly tailored clothing. I couldn't keep my eyes off the boy: ruddy cheeks, blond hair, athletic build. He wore the traditional blue blazer, white buttoned-down shirt, Wellington rep tie and snug-fitting grey flannels. I recall the rich look of his heavy leather shoes, which buckled on the side. What was even more interesting was the bulge of his groin, which, considering the thickness of flannels, had to be sound in order to reveal itself so handsomely. I returned to my reading; after all it was a formal dining room and he was in company. Then a devilish idea struck me. Maybe by eye contact alone I could shock him. I began a steady gaze over the top of my book at his groin, which I could see perfectly. He seemed not to notice — but finally he had to. At one of his glances I rolled my eyes upwards and nodded. At another glance I silently mounted "WOW!" At that the corners of his mouth just barely curled into the hint of a smile. The next moment will never pass from my memory, so electrifying was it in its significance. He slid downwards in his chair and squeezed his cock, stretching it downwards, so that when he took his hand away it was upstanding all along his thigh, dramatically and perfectly revealed — but safely under the table. When he glanced over again, all the while talking to the girl, I ran my tongue around my lips and motioned with my eyes out toward the foyer and rest rooms. A few moments later he told the girl he was going to "wash my hands" and left. I quietly put down my book and departed from the rear, never passing his sister. In the lavatory, he was standing at a urinal with one of the prettiest, thickest and largest cocks I've ever seen standing straight out. Without a word I went to my knees and blew him. I can remember the feel of his beautiful ass under the flannels. His breath caught and he half gasped, half whimpered as his sweet cream filled my mouth. Without a word spoken, he pulled out a perfect handkerchief and wiped his cock off and zipped up. At the wash basins he said, "Thanks a LOT! That was super." I smiled and thanked *him* and told him he was the most handsome fellow I had ever done. He asked if I had done it a lot and I told him I had. We exchanged names and addresses and I was able to visit the campus of his private school repeatedly thereafter. He had rich parents who had split up and didn't bother with him, and a sister, who was in another private school in another state. We became great friends and had glorious sex all through his prep school and Harvard years. He is now a physician, married and reproduced repeatedly, living out west. He is more than a memory. He enriched my life. If I never had sex again I'd be contented, I think, with that range of experiences with him. I certainly never expect to have better sex.

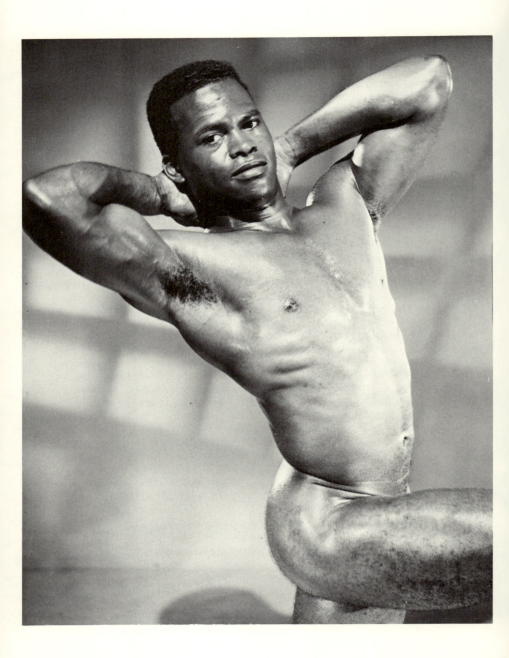

Subscriber Lays "Straight" Student for 6 Months

NEW YORK — Here's one I've been toying with, suitable for embarrassing questionnaire:
Junior in College. Friend and I have a contest to seduce Joe, medium build straight boy, roommate of a friend. I win the race, and we both have sex with him for 6 months, then he moves. He loved to sit on it like nobody's business. Now he lives in Chicago and I believe him when he says he doesn't make it with guys anymore.

- - - -

What makes you think Joe was "straight"? He said so; occasionally would call it "bisexual" but didn't like the word (don't blame him).
Did he talk about girls a lot? Was he a virgin? Not very much pussy talk. He liked girls but was no great success with them. Not a virgin by any means.
Was he attractive? In what way? Yes, he was attractive; lean, average height, wiry, big head of blond curls. Sloppy dresser, more interesting face than the usual "cute college kid." Bright boy, sensitive. No stranger to fags. He was really very sweet, but with a perverse streak.
Did Joe know you're "gay" before you tried to get into his pants? We were college boys; we always talked about sex. *Fetish Times* was popular reading material. He was not a *naif*. I was 20 by this time and almost evryone knew I was gay. I knew him through one of his four roommates, the gay one, so he always knew I was gay.
Did you make any unsuccessful passes at Joe before he finally put out? I had groped him a few times at parties and whatnot before I finally had sex with him. Always playful.
Please give a 1-2-3 description of the first time you "had" Joe: did you undress him or did he strip? What kind of underpants were each of you wearing? Did each of you have hard ons immediately? How did he taste and smell? What did each of you say and do during sex that indicated pleasure? Did he feel guilty after the first time, or try to reclaim his lost heterosexuality? We were sitting in his living room. One of his roommates was upstairs fucking his girlfriend. We were smoking a joint on the sofa and watching a movie. I think we'd been looking at *Penthouse*. Eventually, I just reached over and rubbed his groin. He started to protest, then leaned back. I unzipped his fly and pulled out his cock. Played with it for awhile, then started sucking. Went upstairs to his room to continue in bed. We undressed ourselves. He stripped slowly. He was wearing Jockey shorts, as was I. We both had hard ons before we got in the bedroom. I sucked him for a good while longer and then he fucked me. He was reasonably clean, smelled and tasted of boy flesh with sweat. We had a great time. I don't think he felt particularly guilty; we went back downstairs and watched the end of the movie. He was a horny 20-year-old who'd just gotten his rocks off. I don't think "lost heterosexuality" crossed his mind.
How did your friend, the one who also wanted Joe, get into the act? Joe and I were over at Chip's house, as usual. We all hung out there. Joe had talked to me beforehand about wanting to have sex with Chip. Both of them had expressed interest, so I acted as a sort of go-between, and eventually they were

off in the bedroom. Basically, Joe fucked Chip's face while I watched. We never had sex as a threesome, really; Joe did it separately with both of us after that.
You mention that Joe "loved to sit on it." How did this transpire? It was my idea that he'd like to get fucked, as he liked having his asshole played with so much. He sat on both our dicks, though not at the same time. Joe was about 7", thick shaft, small head; Chip is about 6-7", great balls; I have about 7", thinner than Joe's, but nicely formed, or so I'm told.
When Joe sat on your dick, was he facing you? If so, what expression did he have on his face? He sat on it in all positions. Facing to me, away, sitting on top, lying underneath, face up, face down, sideways. His expressions were priceless, the sincere lust of an earnest young man.
What else did you do? Frequently he would fuck me; usually we fucked each other. Or I would suck his cock. Jacking off, too, when I got tired of sucking — he could go forever without coming. I would frequently suck for nearly an hour to no avail. Not that either of us minded much.
Was there much cocksucking in your relationship? Yes, but usually me sucking him. He tried sucking me a few times but wasn't really into it. Just being nice.
Was Joe always freshly showered and prepared for sex? He was a clean boy. Being a painter, he often smelled of turpentine. I used to meet him at work — he worked in a sub shop — and he would fix me a burger and then we'd walk to his house. He always showered after work, because the place stunk of fried onions, so on those nights he was freshly scrubbed. Having sex was a bit of a problem, as he had straight roommates and I lived at home, but we managed. A friend worked at a motel and would let us into dirty rooms during the afternoon "to watch TV."
During your 6 months between Joe's thighs, did he ever insist he's "straight"? He never really insisted that he was straight, just said occasionally that he thought he probably was.
Was his shit-hole greased for taking your cock? If so, by whom? Did he have an easy shit-hole or a tight one? His asshole was greased, usually by me. He liked it when I took the Jergen's lotion bottle and stuck it up his asshole and squeezed, so it was nice and slippery, which made it easier going in his tight but ready hole.
What condition was his shit-hole in with respect to cleanliness? As clean as anyone's.
How did his shit-hole feel to your dick? How did you achieve friction: did he move his butt up and down, or clutch your dick with his asshole muscles, or did you do all the work? His asshole felt sublime. He had an amazing ass. I was really turned on when he'd have me lay on my back while he straddled me, supporting himself in a spider-like position on all fours and lowered himself onto my cock. Then he would clench and unclench his sphincter and move himself faster and faster up and down my shaft. Other times I'd fuck him doggy style, or in more conventional positions. A typical fuck lasted 20 to 45 minutes; usually he would fuck me longer than I would fuck him because he took forever to come, if indeed he ever did, and his asshole was too new to having a cock up it that sometimes he'd make me stop before I came, but not usually. He liked feeling the hot cum inside his asshole — and like to talk about it. He never ate cum, though, to my knowledge.
Did he come from getting fucked in the ass? Like I say, he didn't come much

at all. I came a couple of times from the hard thrusts of his fat cock in my ass. He only came twice with me — once in my ass, once in my mouth. We had sex maybe 15 or 20 times.

Was there affection and kissing, or was it strictly a cock-and-hole romance? We were friends, or acquaintances at least, before we had sex, so we were on good terms. He wouldn't have yielded to a stranger, I'm sure. Some kissing. Now that you mention it, yes, he was a pretty good kisser, though after awhile he wanted to get down to business. We were fuck buddies; romance was never an issue.

Did he have sex with other men? He had fooled around with his gay roommate, who introduced us, but nothing had come of it and it didn't happen again. I think I was the first guy he came with. Chip followed within a few weeks. The last time I saw him he said he'd had sex with one other man, once, after he moved, but wasn't comfortable doing that kind of thing, as he put it.

Please describe his butt with respect to hair and shape. His butt was small and round, smooth, white, hairless except for in the crack and around his hole. His chest was hairless. Clean shaven, shoulder length dirty blond hair.

Was he always cool or were there moments of embarrassment? Very cool generally, a little uptight about sex, perhaps, but he enjoyed perverted ideas. He was just as hot for sex as I was, and less demanding about what kind than I. He displayed his nudity quite shamelessly and loved to be photographed. He would occasionally tease me about how much I wanted his meat, which he never withheld, however.

Was he tough, to conceal his sexual secrets, or just ordinary, not trying to compensate for homosexuality with a "butch" manner? "Butchness" was not considered a desirable quality. Not that he was effeminate in any way; he was just a guy, not some swaggering beer commercial caricature. None of us were athletes, nor did we know any. They were completely out of fashion in those years.

What evidence did you see that he genuinely liked snatch, apart from the respectability that accrues to anyone in our culture who expresses an interest in it? He would talk about girls he was hot for, almost invariably lean, long-legged beauties; he tended to aim over his head and hence was not too successful. He really wasn't enough of a schemer to play singles games.

Were either of you hurt by the affair or its end? No. It ended as we all left school. I jacked off thinking of Joe for several years after. Chip is my roommate now.

Why do you believe Joe when he says he no longer makes it with guys — had it seemed that he wasn't quite queer and didn't go all out? I believe him because he told me so. He's a very honest guy, with no reason to lie to me. He went all out when he had sex but it was sex, not sex with men, that turned him on. Even when we were fooling around he chased girls, though without much success.

Were all three of you sophisticated about sex? Considering our isolation in the provinces, we were all quite sophisticated and casual about it. I never met any other boys who were so easy going in that way.

Did he ever take both your and Chip's dicks in his ass the same day? No.

Was he ever sore-assed from fucking? Yes.

Apart from his gift for taking it in the ass, was he good at fucking you? Yes. Excellent. I especially remember one night when he fucked me dog style on

the living room floor with his roommates upstairs asleep. We had to stop when one of them drove up outside. But he had crouched on his heels and pumped me rhythmically for a little over an hour, his fat cock sliding in and out nearly its full length with each thrust. Joe definitely knew how to fuck, and like I say, since he almost never came, he could go on till you made him stop.

Did he tell you about beating his meat? He jacked off all the time.

Was he sufficiently interesting so that you jacked off thinking of him? Yes. For years afterwards.

Did he try to conceal his affair with you from his college roommates? Yes. We were fairly discreet. The roommates were all straight, except for our mutual gay friend, and had girlfriends they brought home to fuck, but he didn't want to be thought of as gay or to have me thought of as his "girlfriend," so we kept it quiet.

How many men do you suppose Joe has had sex with? I think three: me, Chip and some man he met in a bar once. Women, I don't know; when I met him, maybe eight or nine.

Was his underwear ever soiled or, worse, didn't he wear any? He wore it, but it was fresh daily, though probably not bleached.

How soon after you began sexual preliminaries did he get a hard on? He had a hard on before I could get it out of his pants each and every time.

Did you pay each other sexual compliments? Yes, he was complimentary, and would say so when he enjoyed something. I flattered him and praised his lithe young body and firm, fat rod.

How did he feel about taking it in the ass? He always displayed enthusiasm and enjoyment. "Fuck that ass," etc. He loved to fuck and he loved to get fucked. He would hump up and down on my cock and you could just tell that he had one of those asses that's born to have cocks inside it. He would really tune in to sex but otherwise I think he was a little uptight about getting fucked; his father was in the military and a real "man's man." But put a dick up Joe's butt and he went wild.

Did you consider Joe Eating Stuff? By all means.

Did you consider his ass Eating Stuff? Certainly prime eating stuff, but meant to be a fuck-hole.

Did you kiss and embrace much? Yes. On the lips and elsewhere. He kissed back. We hugged during sex and would lie entwined around each other afterwards, or spoon-fashion during the night.

Was he an extravert, or quiet? Introverted generally, but outspoken among friends. A nice, shy boy with a wicked tongue. He wouldn't admit in public, of course, to having sex with men.

Was he just an ordinary guy, or extraordinary? If so, in what way(s)? He was extraordinary. He was quite handsome, though no cover boy, but in a very straight sort of way. His features were fine and sharp-edged and his tongue acerbic. He seemed very alive.

Did your dick get shitty when you fucked him? If so, did he care? Yes, we both got our cocks shitty. We didn't make a big deal out of it — just one of the things you have to live with. He did mention it as an advantage of pussy.

Before you had sex with him, was he sufficiently seductive or alluring to give you confidence he would respond to your sexual overture, or even your complete sexual opera? He was a sexy boy, always posing in a vaguely seductive way, with the crotch of his jeans worn. I wasn't sure he would give in but decided to take the chance. Glad I did.

Have you any interest these days in writing dirty letters to him, seeking to rekindle his pash for you? Or don't you give a shit anymore? No, we kept up for awhile, then stopped writing. No longer have an address for him.

How important was Joe to anyone who gets laid so often as you? He was one of the best lays of my college years. My first steady fuck buddy and a friend, too. Definitely not just another piece of ass. Technique: B. Enthusiasm: A+! (And that's what counts.) While he ate my dick a few times to be nice, he was really just a typical American straight who takes it in the ass. Nice talking to you on the phone — you don't sound like your picture in the *Voice*.

[EDITOR'S NOTE: Superb though this study of a typical American's shit-hole be, it touches upon certain subjects that warrant an additional questionnaire. Had the author not gone abroad on a study grant completing this work, I'd have examined him further on these points: the experiences of Joe's gay roommate in living with three "straights," the details of how Joe "fucked Chip's face," in precisely what way Joe liked "having his asshole played with so much," what Joe said when he "liked to talk about" having the author's cum in his ass, what words the author used to compliment Joe on his body and "rod," and what the author means by "elsewhere" in his comment that they kissed "on the lips and elsewhere." It would be only logical if they kissed each other's assholes, but perhaps they were illogical.]

Young Italian Fireman, Married, Is a Cocksucker, Takes It in the Ass

I will report on the fireman as it is interesting. As follows. I only met him when he was a hot young Italian living in one of the cities nearby. He was 17 and was with a group of youths who would provide sexual favors to the men around. This one was named John and he began to start sucking and would let you come in his mouth from time to time. He had an insatiable sexual appetite and could go forever before shooting a thick load. So he went to college awhile but really didn't like that so he returned to join a semi-pro football team. He grew stronger and bigger and more sexually desirable in all ways. He really began to like to be rimmed. He then announced to me that he was going to get married. I was at this time seeing him about once a week. He had progressed from cocksucking to getting fucked and it was divine. It took me a long time to get him fucked correctly but it happened. His asshole was as delicious as a rose bud and after a lot of foreplay he began to let me in. First it was just the head of the cock and then the shaft slipped in. He would wince and roll about and say how much it hurt him but I persisted. Now married he had a job with the city fire department. Big handsome macho Italian. Lovely ass, nice reasonable cock and an insatiable appetite. Sometimes we don't meet when he is afraid his wife (now pregnant) will find out but he still does it on a regular basis. By the way, lots of firemen are apparently bisexual. I only know one who is totally homosexual and he is an officer in another city fire department.

Youth Lets Priests
Play With His Cock, Shit-hole

WISCONSIN — I was 14 when mother walked in on me and caught me jacking off. Needless to say she wasn't pleased. She called our local Catholic priest and set up a counseling appointment. The time for the appointment was Saturday at 8 A.M. I rang his doorbell and he immediately was there. He showed me into his office and sat at his desk. I sat in a straight chair in front. Along one wall were more chairs and along the other was a couch. He smiled and asked what I needed counseling for. I told him mother gave him all the details over the phone, when she set the appointment. He said he had to hear it from me. I was scared, but was able to tell him I had been jacking off. He asked where and I told him in my bedroom. I had just come from taking a bath. He asked how I was dressed. I told him I was nude. He asked me if I enjoyed being naked and I almost couldn't control my excitement as I said yes. Next he asked how often I jacked off and almost fell off his chair when I said three or four times a day. When the interview was over, he told me to strip. I hesitated, so he repeated his request — strip. He continued that he wanted to examine me. I told him I had a doctor who examines me. We exchanged a few more words and he picked up the phone to call my mother. He said he was sorry he would have to tell her I was uncooperative. I stood up and almost ripped my shirt off — throwing it across the room to a chair. When I unbuckled my belt and lowered my zipper, he smiled and hung up the phone. I sat down to remove my shoes and socks. Then, somewhat embarrassed, I lowered my pants. He told me to take those things across the room to the chair. I returned to the desk only in my white Jockey shorts. He told me to slide them down and step out of them. I bent over to pick them up and threw them to the chair. At his direction I went over and laid on my back on the couch. He brought his desk chair over and sat at my thighs. He had me spread my legs and he rubbed my inner thighs. Next he had me pull my knees up to my chest. He rubbed the backs of my thighs and then bent down to look at my bottom. He made some comments about my body looking good. When he blew on my asshole I immediately got a hard on. Then he put a finger on my asshole and looked at my hard cock. He said, "You sure are hot." I put my legs down when he said to and he masturbated me. I couldn't believe this was happening to me. I was hot and came in a short time. We went upstairs to a bedroom and I got on the bed as he told me — on all fours with my ass high and shoulders down. He used a ping pong paddle on my ass cheeks. He did a good complete job, but wasn't severe. When he had finished we returned to his office downstairs. He again sat at his desk and I sat naked in the straight-backed chair. He noted I had a hard on and told me to masturbate, so he could watch. After coming and cleaning up he told me I could dress. He told me jacking off wasn't so bad and set another appointment for Wednesday evening. He told me not to jack off that day. All mother asked was if I obeyed. I said yes. While it may seem impossible, in a small town of three thousand what else was there for either of us to do. He had the ideal situation, because mother gave him full freedom to take care of (cure) my masturbation. He never gave me a blow job. The most he did was masturbate me.

When I returned to the priest for my second session on Wednesday, he again showed me into his office. He sat behind his desk and told me to strip. Unlike the first time I didn't hesitate this time. I put my clothes on a side chair and stood naked in front of his desk. He had me come around the desk by him and bend over the desk. He played with my ass cheeks and asked me if I had masturbated since I was last in his office on Saturday. I had and told him so. He slapped my ass cheeks a few times. His finger entered my asshole and he finger fucked me. He worked on my hole in silence until he asked if I had a hard on. When I told him I did, he removed his finger and told me to go sit in the chair in front of his desk. As I sat there naked with a hard on, the priest asked me what I thought of when I last masturbated. He cautioned me to be truthful. Since it was true, I told him I thought about the last time I was naked in front of him. He smiled and asked if I had a good time. I nodded. While he sat and watched me, the priest told me to masturbate. When I came, he gave me Kleenex to clean myself up. Then he had me put on a cassock and kneel down. I would put my head on the carpet and he would pull the cassock over my head. In that way my ass was exposed to him and my head was covered up. I assumed he did this so he could see me, but I couldn't see him masturbate. After awhile I was allowed up and would get naked again. We would talk about being naked and masturbating. Sometimes he would masturbate me or have me do myself again while he watched; I had similar sessions with him approximately once a month over the next several years. Then he got transferred. I was lucky to have known him.

Most counseling sessions with the priest were the same, but I'll address several of your questions. Early sessions were marked by — a person shouldn't masturbate, although he masturbated me or had me masturbate during the counseling session. Later it changed to — I should not masturbate without his permission. Once he told me to jack off he wouldn't say anything more until I came. Then, usually — "nice" or "beautiful." Sometimes he would have me shoot more than one load during a session. After the first session, I was hard by the time he would show me into his office — anticipation I would guess. I always wore white Jockey shorts. There was no gossip about the priest, so I never knew how active he was. In contrast boys in phy-ed or out for sports joked about a local barber because he was an alleged cocksucker. Hence, one could have expected to hear gossip about the priest. Once when I was about 16, Father had a priest friend visit and my visit took place at the same time. He took me immediately to his office. I stripped and put on a cassock. Then he took me to the living room and introduced me to the other priest. Father said without explanation that his guest worked with boys and was concerned about their development. While I sat there somewhat uncomfortable, Father explained to his visitor that I was a masturbator and very sexual. The guest had me stand and he came over to me. The cassock pockets were slit, so you could reach into your pants pockets. The guest reached in and since I was nude under it he reached back and felt my ass. Then moving behind me, he again reached in and felt my balls and hard cock. Next Father explained that he had used nudity and masturbation in my visit. Then he said he was going someplace. The guest priest took me to Father's office. Once in the office, he went over and carefully examined my Jockey shorts. He commented how

clean they were. I had to bend over. He raised the cassock and examined by sight and touch. He opened his brief case, got out some lubricant and greased my hole. He stuck his finger up my ass. He felt around then finger fucked me. At the appropriate moment he stuck another finger up my ass. When I had relaxed and was loose, he took me over to the sofa. I lifted the cassock up under my arms, knelt on the arm of the sofa and bent forward. This placed my ass high and exposed. The cassock was over my head so I could not see. The priest moved my legs apart. Then I felt his hard cock against my asshole. He shoved it in slowly. After giving me time to relax, he began fucking me. It seemed to take him a long time to come. After he adjusted his clothing, he helped me out of the cassock and then lay me on my stomach on the couch. The priest massaged my back, bottom and legs while I laid there. After he decided my asshole was closed enough, he had me get up and sit in the straight back chair. He masturbated me. He told me that that should hold me for a day or two. I remained naked and we went back to the living room. We talked until Father returned. Then we went back to his office. I was on my hands and knees again. Father carefully examined my asshole. He massaged the cheeks of my ass and asked if I felt OK. From all that attention, I was hard again, so we went back to the living room. Once there I was instructed to jack off for them again. That wasn't embarrassing, since they both knew what I looked like naked. Father got my clothing from his office and I dressed in front of them. The guest thanked me and told me I had a real hot body. That was all the contact we had; Father said he would keep him informed of my progress.

"A Huge One... I Thought I Would Choke."

NEW YORK — I was thinking back to the good old days at the U. of___. All that tea room action. One afternoon or early evening, horny after class, I went to the basement men's room in the Religion Building. Took a seat in the middle stall of three. One already taken; men coming in and out to use the urinals too regularly for anything to go on. After about 20 minutes of reading the walls, I noticed a tall man standing long at the urinal. Peering through the crack in my stall door, I watched him as he pulled his meat, glancing over his shoulder at the now full stalls. He saw me watching him. He walked over and peered through the crack as I jacked off. Then he pulled back so I could see his long, thick cock. He pulled the foreskin back and forth over the head.

I opened the door. He stepped in and I started sucking; I'd already determined that the other stalls were OK. Someone came in and he clumsily rushed back to the urinals. After that guy left, he motioned me out. We walked out to the parking lot. He asked if I'd like to take a ride. Sure. We drove to the cemetery and parked behind the Egyptian Mausoleum. He pulled out his dick, a really huge one, maybe 11" and very fat. He grabbed my head and pushed it down hard on his dick till I thought I would choke.

"You like these big dicks?" he asked. I couldn't answer. Sucked on that satisfying tool about 10, 15 minutes, then he unloaded in my mouth. Drove me back to school. I ran into him occasionally after that for about a year. When it was established that we would do it in the john, he once took me to his house and fucked hell out of me, which I loved. Turned out he was a professor of English — Sir Walter Scott or some such — and a good friend's advisor. When I saw him in the halls he gave no indication of seeing me. Married. No children.

"There Are the Queers, Grab Them"

CALIFORNIA — I was born into a wealthy Calif. family and am the eldest of four boys I was the only boy in my family left uncircumcised and both my brothers and our Jewish playmates were continually curious about my foreskin (pushing their cocks up my foreskin, etc.). I remember enjoying this special attention and was determined not to be circumcised after my mother's frequent threats, "If you don't wash properly we'll have you cut back like your brothers." Being uncircumcised proved to be my greatest trauma once I entered school — an all-boy boarding school for wealthy brats. A few days after starting school I was in the showers with about a dozen other boys when they spotted my uncut cock and all began to laugh at it. I was embarrassed to death and, realizing that I must be the only boy in school with a foreskin, I went to great extremes during the following few months to hide myself during "naked" situations, in hopes the fellows would forget what they saw and think that I was exactly like them.

Then came the second great trauma (and one which persisted throughout my school years) when the two bullies of my class caught me in the hall and said, "Let's go to the bathroom. We want to show you something." I hesitated but they pulled me in. One twisted my arm behind me while the other yanked open my fly and pulled out my cock. "Look at it," they kept saying. "Look at all that extra skin. Just like the guys were saying. What's it there for?" Then Bill, one of the bullies, pulled out his cock and waved it at me, saying, "This is what they're supposed to look like." Then the other guy said, "We can cut it off for you," and he pulled out a pocket knife. I began to struggle to get away. He put his knife away but began to pull and stretch my foreskin as far as he could, saying to Bill, "Hey, look at this — it stretches way out." They both began to pull on it at once and all I could say was, "Stop. You're hurting me." Then one of them said, "I wonder how he pisses through all that skin?" They led me to a urinal and while one of them pointed my cock, the other said, "OK, piss. We want to see how you do it." Of course I couldn't and got out of it by promising to let them watch me piss someday. But before I escaped they pulled me around the room by my foreskin, saying, "We're going to pull you around by that extra skin until you let us cut it off." Before I got out the door, Bill had dug his fingernails deep into my foreskin, leaving bruises. For all my school years (these two guys stayed in my class all the way through), they tugged at my foreskin every chance they got, even when there were other boys around. I like to think I got the last laugh, though, for as it turned out I eventually developed a bigger cock than either of them and I also became popular because I was a successful competitor for the school's athletic teams and neither of them were athletes. Before puberty, most of the activity was in the dorms (during afternoon naps — many of the boys didn't board) when new boys were pantsed and checked out for size.

I'll never forget the day when little E. came to school, about a year after I started, and my thrill at seeing his cock during his pantsing — the first uncut cock I had ever seen other than my own and my father's. It didn't have a long foreskin (it didn't even cover the top of his glans when soft) but the other kids spotted it and said, "Look, he's got a (author's name) cock." E. became my first real sex partner a few years later just after puberty when we "fell in love." During those prepuberty years pissing contests were the thing. Pissing into

targets and pissing long distance, with awards to the winners, occurred almost nightly. I learned that by pulling back my foreskin I could piss as good as anyone. One afternoon a punk classmate, whom we all hated, was given a chocolate laxative and at night, in the dorm, he suddenly jumped out of bed and ran into the bathroom. We all jumped out of our beds, ran after him, pulled him off the toilet and watched while he did it all over the floor. Then we pissed on him while he sat in it. Poor guy just couldn't stop. I'll never forget how much I enjoyed joining in on the mass pissing.

Then came puberty — jack off time at boarding school. We kept on at each other, "Can you white yet?" We were obsessed at becoming "men," with seeds. One by one we became "men." We had a vacuum cleaner attachment which provided instant hard ons when we wanted to test a fellow student about his "manhood." Some poor guys just couldn't come with seeds for almost two years after I and a few others began demonstrating our "success." While I couldn't win piss contests, I was a whiz at masturbation — same games as with the pissing but the targets were shortened, etc. Monday night was, for those of us with seeds, "who could jack off the most times" contest. Tuesday was "who could jack off the longest without coming" contest, etc. I was still very sensitive about the subject of my foreskin and as we got older most of my fellow students respected me enough not to mention it, except for the two bullies. Masturbation made me one of the boys; I was good at it. New students in our class were soon put to the vacuum cleaner and tested for WHITE. I can remember pumping on more than one frightened, bewildered kid. All those years growing up with those rich, spoiled, sexy little brats in my class, I don't remember one incident of cocksucking. My brother and I sucked each other when we were home on weekends and that seemed to satisfy me. But that summer when E. joined us at my grandmother's summer home on Catalina, my brother and I invited him into one of our cocksucking sessions, and something happened to both E. and me. We couldn't get enough of each other's cocks. My brother soon lost interest and had a puppy love affair with some girl on the beach, but E. and I spent the whole summer sucking, just each other, no one else. We hiked into Catalina's mountains and sucked, we rented boats and went far out to sea and sucked, we found isolated beaches and sucked and in my grandmother's woodshed we sucked. Before the summer was over we realized that we were probably "queer" and that we were in love.

That September I entered military academy. I suddenly found myself getting hard ons in the showers, as did E., who also entered the military school, and we both began to shy away from the other guys, thinking that we alone were "queer." One day after a swim meet in which my class's team competed with the teams of the other classes and we won, I and six other swimmers from my class were showering when the other swimmers (about 20 of them) came in to the shower and started to taunt us, saying, "If you think you're such big men let's see how big you are," "Go on, get your boners on," "Look at J., I'll bet he's never had a boner," etc. Anyway, I got hard quick (despite myself) and gave them a look at my size, which was probably bigger than most of them. But a couple of the others in my class who were small were constantly taunted after the upper classmen knew about the size of our various boners. The upper classmen were constantly asking new students how big their boners were and one afternoon they pantsed about five of my classmates and measured them. One of the teachers had a reputation for his strange forms of punishment, and I happened to be in one of his classes. At first, he would call a student to the

front for talking, etc., grab the kid's belt and pull at it, saying, "Next time I'll strap you with it." As the weeks went by and he got to know us, he began pulling the belts off the kids and giving them a whack across the seat, saying, "Next time we pull down your pants so you can really feel the belt." Sure enough, pants started to drop right in front of the rest of the class and it was always the student's own belt that was used. We all had our turns. Then he surprised us in the middle of such punishment, when our bare asses were turned to the class for the usual strapping, by making us turn and face the class, saying, "I'm going to punish you where it really hurts." And he'd make us pull our cocks outwards while he strapped them (belts were narrow in those days). Talk about this punishment spread through the school and there were mock demonstrations of it in the dorms, but no one dared tell parents or other adults.

My humiliation came when he had me face the class with my pants around my ankles and he ordered, "Scat back." I didn't know what the hell he meant and just stood there. He said, "C'mon, show us your cherry." I died as I "scat back," and he proceeded to belt me across my sensitive, exposed glans. What is worse, I broke down and cried. Talk about E. and me began to get around; the class was at that "anti-queer & make it with the girls" stage. Being a campus athlete shielded me from some of the flak but E. began to get it. The next summer was spent on Catalina and E. joined me for a short time & we resumed our mutual cocksucking. During the following semester, tragedy hit our little relationship. We were in a hidden area of the school grounds sneaking a smoke (big thing in those days) when some upperclassmen came by and shouted, "There are the queers, grab them." They did grab us, pulled off our pants and shouted, "Let's see how you suck each other." They roughed us into a 69 position and tried to push each head into the other one's groin. Suddenly they dispersed as a faculty member was seen walking our way. E. and I decided that we were making each other "queer" and that we shouldn't see each other again. Anyway, E. continued all through school to be labeled as queer, partly because of his involvement with drama & theater, etc., while my athletics continued to excuse me. E. went on to become very square, married with children, joined his father's firm and proved to be anything but queer.

I was sitting in a school bathroom toilet when someone came into the cubicle next to me. He whispered, "Do you like to punch guys in the nuts?" I laughed & said something like, "I don't know, I've never tried it." He slid the bottom half of his body under the partition, lifted his stiff cock and said, "Go ahead, punch my nuts." I made a couple of soft whacks at his balls and he said, "Harder. You can punch harder than that." So I tried. He suddenly jumped up, buckled up and left, whispering, "That wasn't hard enough." I was too embarrassed to stand up and see who he was. For the next few weeks that experience haunted me; I actually enjoyed punching that guy in the balls. I wondered who in hell he was. Then, waiting in the same cubicle one afternoon, in hopes that the guy was making the scene a habit, he came in again and again shoved his body under the partition. This time he had a small rope tied around his balls & he wanted me to pull it & at the same time punch his tied up balls. This time I jumped onto the toilet seat and looked over to see a lower classman who had just enrolled at the school, incredibly handsome, clean-cut West Pointer type, 15 years old (I was 16 by now), dominant personality, very mature for his age, son of a well-known business executive and John Bircher (very active in that society now). He lived with his mother

and younger brother in a Beverly Hills mansion only a few blocks from my grandmother's house.

He invited me over to his house the following weekend to watch him hang his brother by his balls from the chandelier. His bedroom was a nightmare of Nazi Germany mementos. Two boys left alone in a mansion to punch each other in the nuts so often that their sacks were like leather. I spent a weekend trying my best to punch their balls hard enough to satisfy them, finding out that my balls weren't for punching but my cock liked to be roped and pulled, and that I liked torturing the cocks of these two brothers. This relationship went on until I left for college several years later. We often invited certain schoolmates from the military school to Beverly Hills for weekends of ball punching (most of them couldn't take it) but we never did it at school. A few months before I left the military academy a new swim coach joined the staff. He let our water polo teams (of which I was a member) compete in the nude. We had a ball learning how to "drown" a guy on the opposite team who had the ball by grabbing his cock and balls, and to stop a guy from making a good pass by grabbing him just at the right time and at the right place. One day during practice the coach was teaching us a new passing technique when he had to get in the pool with us. We were nude and we jokingly told him that he had to doff his trunks in the pool too. He did and every guy in the pool made a lunge at his genitals, with a wild wrestling match under water resulting. He was good looking, husky blond in his mid-20's and I'll never forget the sight of him scurrying out of the pool with his voluptuous cock and his over-sized balls swinging. I jacked off for weeks remembering that sight. We weren't allowed nude competition after that, but I encountered nude water polo a few years later in college.

Youth Sucks Off His Tennis Coach

SOMEWHERE IN EUROPE — I've been out of touch with the homeland because I've moved into the military investigative services. I'm constantly on temporary assignment from Iceland to Norway to New Zealand. I like to think that I did my small part in selling *Meat* — after my photo appeared in that book I no longer sent pix out with my sex correspondence. Instead, I told ad-responders that they could check out my body in *Meat* to see if they were interested and several wrote back to say that they'd bought copies and enjoyed them very much. I have no patience with guys who say they don't like getting sucked by older men. I'm lucky that my body responses to good mouths don't have any age or racial prejudices, because that leaves a lot of good suckers to me. I've always found older guys better for a lot of reasons: they've had more experience and they suck a hell of a lot better usually; they are more appreciative and never in a hurry for it to end; they have more conversation and can talk about something other than themselves; and in the American sugar-coated society, older men have often lot their natural teeth, and there's nothing better than a toothless suck, not only for expert blow jobs but also for deeper rimming in my asshole. It's amazing how much extra length a rimmer can get out of his tongue if he has no teeth. I like a good mouth working all over my body for as long as my partner can handle it, but I'm above all a face-sitter — lifting my leg for a face to get in there and sitting my bare ass down on a wet

toothless mouth are my favorite activities. I don't suck, fuck or "make love," so many people consider my kind of sex selfish; but those guys who are honest enough to admit that they dig having a muscular, sexy and responsive man available for oral sex have one hell of a good time with me. One of my partners is Ed — mid-60's, intelligent, personable and with the sexual stamina of men half his age. I spend at least a week with him each time I'm back home in the States and his mouth is working somewhere on or in my body 80% of the visit. He's got an incredible mouth — big and wide enough to suck all the toes of one foot at one time and big enough to hold both of my big balls at once, which drives me wild. His long thick tongue is a work of art and when he pushes its full length up my ass it feels as though it will push right out the top of my head. And all this pleasure that he's willing and eager to give goes untapped most of the time because he's "old." Shit, the world's nuts for sure. He licks my body from neck to toes slowly and thoroughly until each muscle is quivering before settling his face deep between my thighs to slurp in my groin for long periods of time. I like draping my legs over his shoulders and scissoring his face between my thighs while that thick tongue goes crazy and his muffled moans of appreciation vibrate through my groin and ass. I've really turned him on to ass-eating and the longer I keep him from it the wilder he goes when he gets it. I usually just let him sniff the crack for awhile and lick the outside until he's at the whimpering begging point, and only then do I lift my leg and shove his face in my ass. He laps and slurps and probes in my asshole and I hold his head firmly in place and buck my ass into his mouth. His tongue makes me wild and my muscle control makes him wild — I massage his face with the muscles of my ass cheeks and squeeze his tongue with my sphincter. I can take or leave shit-eaters — if guys want to eat my shit that's OK with me, but I don't hunt for guys who do it. Sometimes when Ed eats my ass early in the morning he gets shit and he eats it all even though he claims that he doesn't do that with anyone else. He does love piss, though. He's one terrific sucker and one terrific human being; maybe he wouldn't be so hungry for it if he got it more often, so it could be that all these guys who won't get it on with "old men" are doing me a favor.

Officially I'm an Air Force officer (Lt. Colonel); less officially, I'm in military intelligence. I must be in uniform when on military turf and I hate it. Right now I'm spending a beautiful afternoon getting a bare-assed tan on my terrace and it's a good time to answer some of the questions you asked. One of my favorite experiences was one summer when I worked at a raquet club in a suburb of Atlantic City. A thin and homely kid took weekly tennis lessons from me and I felt sorry for him because he was so ugly and was always alone, never with friends. Because I was nice to him, he developed a crush, but I didn't think it was sexual. The last week I was there he didn't show for his lesson, but called the club and said his folks had gone away and he had no transportation, so could I come to his house for his last lesson. I went to his place, an ostentatious house a few miles from the club, and after the lesson he invited me to swim in their pool. It started to hit me then but I said no, that I didn't have any trunks. Right away he said he'd get me a pair of his dad's. I don't know what fuck-shop the kid bought those trunks from but I knew for sure they didn't belong to the little dumpy guy I knew was his father. I also knew from his nervousness that the kid wanted to see me in the skimpy briefs he was offering me and the look on his face stirred the exhibitionist in me. I like having my body admired so I took the briefs and went to change. It wasn't easy squeezing into them and I got turned on by my own reflection when I finally

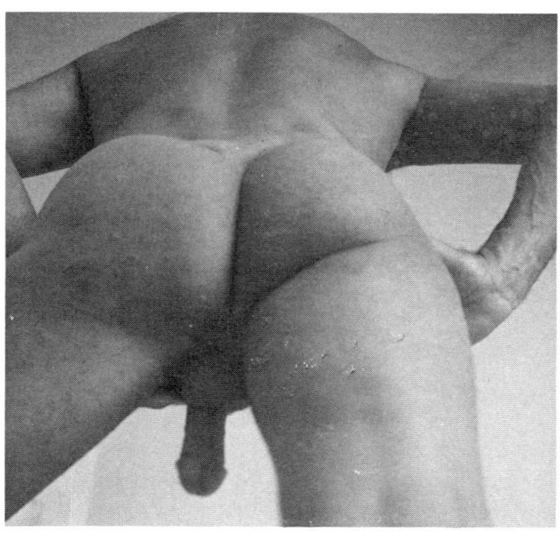

Photo of author of this article

got them on. The material was so thin I could see the outline of my cock and balls clearly and in the back they rode up in the crack of my ass. When I went outside the kid's eyes popped and my whole body lit up like it does when I'm showing it off. I did a couple of laps in the pool and when I came out and stretched on a chaise, the thin material was practically transparent from the water; and my cock thickened from the kid's open staring. I pretended to doze off so he could look his fill and I wasn't surprised when he came and knelt down beside me and bent his head over my groin — no touching, but I could feel his breath going right through the thin material over my big bulge and that was enough to make my cock ooze a thick pearl of heavy top cream right through the briefs. Without opening my eyes, I put my hand gently on the back of his head and eased his face down until his mouth opened. I could feel his tongue lick at the wet spot and he sighed and licked around my cock and balls through the briefs while I stroked his hair and patted him like a puppy. After awhile I asked him quietly if he wanted to take the briefs off me and he nodded his head under my hand. I sensed that he'd never gone this far but when I lifted my ass off the cushions he peeled the briefs off without hesitation. I settled back and closed my eyes again, letting him take his time, and pretty soon he was running his hands all over my groin, rubbing my stomach and thighs until my cock was really swollen. He was fascinated by my big balls; I eased his face down to them and told him to take a taste. It wasn't long before he was wolfing around and licking my balls like crazy. I let him lick for a long time, just stroking his head and telling him he was making me feel good. When my cock started seeping more juice, I lifted his face from my balls and cupped his chin in one hand while I held my cock in the other and gently rubbed the creamy piss-slit all over his lips. He opened his lips when I increased the pressure and the head of my cock went inside his mouth. Normally when my cock finds its way into my mouth my first impulse is to fuck it, but this kid made me feel like some kind of a god. He looked so pitiful and thin, so I just held his chin cupped

in one hand and stroked his hair with the other while he sucked like a baby lamb and looked up into my eyes every now and then. He nipped me a couple of times with his teeth but this clumsy blow job was one of the most exciting I've ever had. I came in his mouth but a lot of it ran out the sides. He liked it, though, and when I pulled out, he licked the cum from my groin and balls. Afterwards he told me that he'd dreamed of sucking my cock all summer and that he'd never done it before. I lay back for awhile and let him kiss my biceps and lick my chest muscles; his favorites were my balls and he moved down to lap at them again for about 15 minutes before I left, but I didn't shoot another wad.

One of my best regulars is a black guy from Ohio. He was an old friend who's a wrestling freak and he comes over once in awhile to watch Josh and me mock wrestle for him. I'm always nude but they both remain fully clothed. I give them the kind of holds they want — plenty of headlocks with Josh's open mouth mashed against my chest while he licks my nipples, plenty of head-scissors with Josh's open mouth mashed into my groin and plenty of pins by sitting on Josh's face. Every time I lock my thighs around Josh's head or smother him with my ass, the old gent cheers. It sounds silly but I get very hot during these "matches" and pretty soon they both get busy with their mouths. The old guy whips out his dentures for some of the best cock gobbling I've ever had and Josh pushes his big tongue up my asshole.

Jim, a psychologist, was an amazing cocksucker, never seeming to have to come up for air when I'd fuck his throat with it all — and I have nearly 9" — so it took some good control to do that. He also liked spit and piss and I've given him plenty. He could swallow piss as fast as I'd let it gush, never spilling any or getting sloppy like some guys. I also pissed all over his face. He also licked my ass clean with his tongue after I took a crap, but that wasn't much — like most athletically active people I tend to "shit clean" as the saying goes and there's never anything really to clean up. He'd get very excited when he did this, though. He was a great ass-sniffer. Christ, I love to have someone sniffing in my ass. Jim sometimes slept with his nose in my ass and I can remember waking many nights and feeling his nose right on my asshole. It was impossible to walk past him in his apartment without feeling his nose push between my ass cheeks for a good sniff. He was a very intelligent and good man, even though he was a jack-ass in many ways. One thing I don't miss is his drug use. I love my own ass but I don't sniff my underpants or stick my finger in my asshole to taste. I *really* dig ass-sniffers and could stay turned on for hours with a nose in my butt. One of my favorite positions is sitting back at my ease in a low comfortable chair with one leg draped over the arm to open my crack wide for a guy to kneel and get his nose in my butt. It's good like this because I like guys on their knees in front of me and I can rub my cock all over their faces while they sniff my asshole and lick it. I also like standing in front of a mirror with a guy kneeling behind me so I can watch him stick his face in my ass. My butt looks great in the mirror. I'm an ass eater's dream man, for sure. First of all I've got the kind of ass that rimmers dream about; second of all I know how to use my ass and how to enjoy it, so guys who eat my ass don't find themselves with a lifeless statue. And finally I can go for it for hours and hours without stopping. One guy told me that my ass was the only one that ever lived up to his fantasies besides those on ballet stages. I'm eagerly awaiting my 12 weeks' leave this summer and I'll be back in the U.S., where the best cocksuckers and ass eaters in the world are still to be found.

Getting A Head

Around midnight entering Cambridge Common, I see a man pissing, but before I can get there, he's gone on; then I notice someone crossing toward the road; he passes three cannons, defending a baby elm tree, where Washington took command of the Revolutionary Army; he reaches the fence among the historical plaques, crosses the street onto Appian Way. I casually cross, enter the way; we meet; I smile and say, "Hi;" he answers under his breath (I almost miss the words), "You give head?"

"Yes," I say and we enter a garden in the corner of Radcliffe College with stone ledges, lots of poppies, various vines, irises — intended to look "sensitive;" a little pond and a stone seat. A man and a woman are sitting there talking about the universe; they keep a careful distance from each other in their philosophy. They don't seem to see us crawl into the bushes and shrubs behind their little enclave.

He's wearing burgundy corduroys with a big brass buckle — about seven or eight inches, shaped like a lion's head. I lick it; the pants come open; no underwear; his hands help; they are giant thorns, rough; I unbutton his eggshell cowboy shirt, button by button; he flops down on the grass and leans against the brick wall, says "eat it." His cock gets very hard, alive; about eight inches, nicely shaped; about as big around as a cucumber; the head circumcized neatly; glistening; I lick it up and down, swallow his balls; I'm going all the way down, up and down; he sits indifferently, almost not noticing; I take his hands and put them on my head; he says, "Oh you like it stuffed to you."

He begins forcing me to take it, as I choke he gets more and more turned on; I roll over so that he's on top of me, fucking me in the mouth. Then I realize how young he is; I'd taken him to be in his 30s; the dusty blond moustache and short cropped hair and his rather bleary eyes had made him somewhat nondescript; now I could feel his every muscle straining; his thigh skin unlike his hands, smooth; he lunged his cock into me; I struggled back holding him with my forearms both pressed against his stomach; he lunged again and again into my mouth; I choked, he said "what's the mater, can't take it;" I go for the balls to get my breath; I whisper, "someone will see us;" he takes my head between his knees and says, "Shut up, and suck."

Suddenly there are blue police lights going back and forth on the other side of the garden wall; the couple are still talking, can they hear us as well as we hear them; I scurry to zip up a little bit; he stands up, looks over the fence and says, "forget it, only Harvard cops;" we go back, me already between his legs, him looking over the fence; more sucking; everything goes into my throat... Then he begins to get softer and lays back and goes to sleep with his cock in my mouth; I lay between his legs and pull both our clothes together a bit for a nap; in all the lunging, we've moved more out from under the shadow of the bushes. I feel very at home resting between his legs, every once in awhile kissing his now detumescent cock...

The male of the couple opposite us now gets up and comes into the bushes to piss. He says, "excuse me fellows;" neither of us look up; the graduate students return to their conversation; my hot rod wakes up and says here suck my ass — a very neat muscular arrangement, I lick it clean, the light brown hairs rubbed down with the spit from my tongue and mouth; saying, "wait a

minute" he goes over to the same tree the graduate student used and pisses; lack of imagination lingers everywhere; he returns and says, "take your clothes off;" maybe I've turned him on to my body; he's been feeling my cock up quite a bit; maybe he likes heavyweight types; I leave my Sears Overall pants on; drop them to my ankles and remove my shirt; he says "bend over" and he begins fucking my ass; he holds my body tight as I move the muscles to enclose his shoves; with the cock nice and shitty, he turns me around and he begins pumping into my mouth.

My mouth is getting tired, but I hold back less and less wanting to give myself totally, to leaving nothing in the space between his cock and my throat — our skins all one piece of thread, spindle, spittle — my fingers go around his ass, adding to the push, moving to his motion, they crawl into the crack and through the hole, go for the prostate gland and rub that little ball-bearing/ silver-dollar shape at the foot of the head in my mouth; he gets hotter and hotter, faster and faster, trying to get all my clothes off; I hold back just that bit, keep my pants.

He comes in a flood, a welling up, a pond released, let go; giant; a full bucket poured, molten milk, wet, mouth, more — in the after flush, I lick the last drops off his cock; he says, "you like that, hugh?" From the taste, I notice he's a little drunker than I'd thought and maybe tripping a bit. He stands up and says, "give me all your money!" Six dollars. Although I didn't want to deny him anything, I had kept my pants on; so he couldn't grab them and go; he searched through the pockets and took the change. "Any drugs?" He'd really worked for his/my six dollars and seventy-five cents. I said, "Don't I give good head?" "OK," he said, "but you take too long." He put everything in his pockets, buttoned up and walked out past the couple. A few minutes later, all zipped up, I followed. The students were still talking in muted tones about the crises of western humanism. Three o'clock in the morning. He went one way. I went the other.

— *Charley Shively*

Interview: Boyd McDonald

[The following interview by Vince Aletti appeared originally in File Magazine, Spring 1980.]

ALETTI: *Aside from the stories, of course, and the headlines, my favorite thing about S.T.H. is the photographs. You seem to favor those rough looking guys from AMG in Los Angeles — any particular reason?*
McDONALD: Because they're so real, especially when they're squinting. Basically, the AMG models are a certain percent of the sailors, Marines and soldiers who were stationed around L.A. from the 1940s on up to today. He's still shooting. I support all kinds of homosexuals, but for sex objects in photographs I prefer vegetables to fruits. The alluring goon type.
All these images of tough, "straight" men and all the accounts of wild sex with seemingly "straight" men — how do you reconcile them with your constant editorial put-downs of heterosexuals? It's a common homosexual ambivalence but it seems very much more evident as a conflict in S.T.H.
It's so difficult that all I usually do is cover it with a slogan, "Love and hate for the American straight." I think it's that, for men like me, men are no good for

anything except sex; they certainly shouldn't be entrusted with governing. Women should do that. But it's hard to get men to have sex because in this culture they are supposed to express their masculinity in sports and war, not sex.

Women are mentioned only in passing in S.T.H. as the absent girlfriends or wives of a lot of your letter-writers or their tricks. When it comes to sex, they seem to not count for very much or they just disappear. What are your feelings about women?

I like them better than "straights" do and I like their children better than their fathers do, but I don't desire women or children. But naturally I don't like women like Nancy Reagan. She had a manicurist flown in from Bev Hills to put five, repeat five, coats of polish on her nails. I can remember when it was shocking to be so greedy as the Reagans. Frank, for instance, one of my classmates, said he'd rather have a small room on the East Side than a big apartment on the West Side, and it was shocking. It's the same with sex. Frank is a homosexual stereotype but he married and has a lot of children. And he went to work at the Opera. It's what he can afford: he can't afford any except official culture, like the Opera; he can't afford to live on the West Side, although it's cheaper; and he can't afford to be homosexual, so he's "straight."

Your sympathies are obvious in the pages of S.T.H., but would you care to define your policies?

It may help a little to say that I use the word "shit-hole" for political reasons. We're not even supposed to use the word "asshole" so I make it "shit-hole" just to be as bratty as possible. I suspect that Victor, who's taking over the magazine, won't use words like "shit-hole," although perhaps I'm too suspicious of him.

Victor's really taking over the magazine?

Absolutely. I told him to put on the masthead "Victor Weaver, Editor." He's been working with me the last few issues so he knows all about it. I chose him because well, it's a snap judgement. I based it on one question he asked. He was doing a questionnaire on a young friend of his who got blown in a car, and Victor's question was, "Who unzipped your fly, you or the driver?" It's a no-lose question. Whatever the answer is, it's interesting. It helps the reader picture the action.

What exactly is Victor's part in S.T.H. right now?

He selects what goes in and pastes it up, from type and photos I give him. From here on he'll decide what's set in type, too, which means...what the magazine will be like.

After all this time — ten years, right? — putting out S.T.H. on your own, isn't it difficult to collaborate with someone, especially if they're in a position to edit you?

Absolutely. Unique work can't be done in collaboration by committee. I'm giving him the magazine utterly, to do it the way he wants. I've always done it the way I want, and lately he killed the two best words I've written in ten years. They are *Embalming Elvis*. I wanted to run his drawing of Elvis Presley on the cover and I had a caption that said it would make an ideal illustration for my book, *Embalming Elvis*. Of course, I don't really plan on doing the book, but I said in the caption that it would be based on hideously embarrassing interviews with the boys in the slab room, and I went to the trouble of mentioning draining the decomposed foods and fluids from Elvis' body. It's the kind of book America would love. But Victor decided not to put his drawing on the cover, and my caption about *Embalming Elvis* was killed with it.

I liked Victor's drawings in Issue 48 — "The Typical American Heterosexual" and his family and that wonderful Halston portrait. Is Victor primarily an artist?
Yes, but as his question shows, about who unzipped the fly, I think he can also do the text very precisely. All you have to be is a real sex hound, like me —I recently jacked off for five days almost constantly, and was in ecstasy, as was Hedy Lamarr; I had a three-day holiday plus I took two sick days from work. Also, you have to be intelligent enough to know that it's all right and that you don't have to do what the church and government says you should. The real sex slaves are the "straights." I think the more intelligent you are the less respect you need, especially from people you don't particularly respect, such as most Americans.
If you're turning the magazine over to Victor, what are you going to do?
I'm going to start a new magazine called *Trans-Lux*. It will have more of my work and less of the readers' letters about their sexual experiences. But *Trans-Lux* will also have my questionnaires about men and their underpants.
Now that you mention underpants — S.T.H., especially in the editorial remarks and the questionnaires, seems particularly obsessed with underpants. Could this be a fetish?
I think "fetish" is too small a word for it. I think if you're crazy about men sexually you're also crazy about their underpants. After all, one of my subtitles is "How Men Look, Act, Walk, Talk, Dress, Undress, Taste, and Smell." I saw a party in FILE — they had a lot of photos of a party, and I wish they'd have a party in jockey shorts, a mock fashion story, "The Return of Underpants" or "The Return to Underpants." The women could wear little panties.
The most erotic photos I've seen were in my brother's college yearbook: a lot of the students sitting around in their jockey shorts. Also my brother-in-law — when he was in the Air Force they took snapshots all squatting down outside the barracks in their jockey shorts. But the best was my cousin, who sent my mother many photos of that Navy equator ceremony — when you cross the equator the first time you take off all your clothes. She had all these photos of hundreds of bareassed sailors which her nephew sent her. I was just a tiny tot but even then I knew a good hard butt when I saw it.
And apparently you've maintained a healthy interest in it ever since — or is sex, especially since you're overexposed to it in your letters from your readers, beginning to bore you?
God, no. I mentioned that I just jacked off for five days. I can't walk a block in Manhattan without seeing someone who makes me wonder what he tastes like, including what his jockey shorts smell like.
Do you think your hard-core gay audience will be equally interested in the Trans-Lux material?
No. Gore Vidal might be — but how many Gore Vidals are there? He wrote that he didn't like the sex parts of *S.T.H.* but that the magazine is one of the best radical political papers in the country. I like it that he didn't say — and, of course, he wouldn't — one of the best homosexual papers. Like, one of the best books written by a Jew, or by a woman. My writing is, as they say in Spanish, "strong," but it's not competitive with the sex material. But neither is Shakespeare or Picasso. Nothing is. The best writing is the writing on the men's room wall, and a lot of my readers write that way. It's gorgeous writing.
Gay Sunshine Press seems like an unlikely publisher for the anthology of your magazine Meat.

It does to me too. Their list is heavy with poetry and serious interviews with famous homosexuals. But Winston Leyland, the publisher of *Gay Sunshine*, is exempt from porn charges, and he's bright enough to realize that the letters my readers write about their sex experiences aren't porn, they're history that no one else is recording, least of all the Gay Liberation movement, which regards sex as unspeakable. Anyway, *Meat* is selling I think at least 20,000 copies and Winston has done a second anthology from my magazine, *Flesh*, which I think is even better. *Flesh* has an intro by my favorite gay writer, John Mitzel of Boston, who has a wonderful hoody style that combines the Mafia with *Variety*. He writes real tough stuff, like Boston is his "turf" and arson is "torching," and so forth. He's just a child compared to me; I suppose he picked up his lingo from 1930's crime pictures on the Late, Late Show.

Have you ever thought about including "straight" heterosexual experiences in S.T.H.?

I'd love to, but "straights" aren't as honest as homosexuals. Homosexual is something you are; heterosexual is something you try to be, or to seem, and part of the attempt is to say only certain things. Homosexuals confess to doing what they shouldn't, what's against the law; "straights" try to claim the rewards you get for being "straight." The only real information I get about heterosexuals I get from connections. Victor, for example, has a friend who tells him about her boyfriends, and one thing she says is that they spend a certain amount of time sticking things in their assholes. I have the impression from Ann Landers that most men wear women's underwear. I think a lot of those fat "straight" businessmen taking a shit in all those booths in the big office buildings are wearing garter belts, and so on.

How do you feel about the all-American macho style — or should I say pose?

I think this *is* their sex life. They act sexier in public than they're able to in the bedroom. If they had much sexual pleasure, they wouldn't have to go around attacking those who do. It's the sex-poor attacking the sex-rich. The people who act above sex are 99.44% of the time not above it, just out of it. It's depressing when you meet someone like Victor or that little guy in New Jersey who's a sort of a patron — he lends me $500 occasionally, which I pay back with interest; he looks like a kid, but he's old enough to have money market funds — and realize all the damage heterosexuals cause, war, boxing, hockey, mugging, rape, theft, crime, divorce, child abuse and think about people like Victor and my little patron, and think that people like Senator Laxalt, Reagan's best buddy in Congress, want to pass laws against them. I turn on the streets to look at a butt I like. I look with admiration; people look at me with contempt — or jealousy. They're more respectable, in quotes. Their hate is more respectable than my love. The two Puerto Ricans who mugged me last summer are more respectable, in quotes, than I. I was minding my own business, wasn't even looking at them, and I have a contribution to make to 45,000 readers, and these two creeps were just out to destroy. They came up behind me and pulled me to the sidewalk. One of them said, "I'm going to kill you." If he had, my dying words to him would have been, "Thank God you're unattractive." They were. It must be painful to die at the hands of someone who's attractive. But I realized while this was happening that I'm better off, that they're deprived and empty. They used the word "man" at least once, sometimes twice, in each sentence to each other, such as "Man, let's go, man." If they felt like men, they wouldn't have had to keep calling each other "man."

"Men Want a Dirty, Low-Down Cocksucker"

GEORGIA — I have a black homosexual friend I've known since high school days. He shocked me recently by saying he hated homosexuals. I know he secretly resents me for I am quite the opposite of him. He's paunchy, prissy, phoney, drowns himself in cologne, deodorant soaps and sprays. He foolishly believes that sex means love. He is baffled that my friends constantly come back for sex and his don't. He has excessive pride. I explained to him that men want a dirty, low-down cocksucker, not someone acting like a woman in the bed. He can't comprehend your magazine. I criticised him for going all the way to Germany and not getting him some German dick while he was in the Army.

When I was about 16 I was well into ass sucking and cocksucking. I started early in life with my country cousins when I was about 11 or 12. The first white guy I ever sucked was about 17 or 18. He was from the working class. This guy and I got together in an old rail Car box not far from the train station. It was one of those hot Southern nights. We both got bare-assed naked. A distant light dimly lighted portions of the rail car. His body was white and succulent in the light and heat. He was sweaty and very musky under the arms and between his legs. His gorgeous dick was thick, about 7 inches. I sucked at most all of his body before busting his full nuts. What a load!

My next experience took place not long after the first. I took a temporary job as a bus boy one night with the idea of getting some white dick. It was a drive-in diner of sorts where the majority of customers were white men, some with their girl friends. I didn't make much money but late that night this goodlooking fellow offered to drive me home. I lived 5 miles from the town and felt sure he wanted sex. About 2 miles out I touched his groin. This didn't alarm him. As a matter of fact he responded with a rigid hard on. I think he was a college fellow because of his manner and dress. I sucked him off on a back road near my home. This man was clean and circumcised. He didn't take off any of his clothes, just took out that beautiful hard cock and let me go down on it. He shot a big healthy load in a few minutes. I was a hot and eager cocksucking teenager. Most of the white dudes didn't object to being sucked off. I love to suck'em because they shoot so quick. There was a young bigfooted white-boy. I fell in love with his large foot print in the field. Working near his home I spotted his dingy jock hanging on the clothes line. I was never so tempted to steal an intimate article of masculine clothing before in my life. I did call his home one weekend, but his "in the know" father was furious. The most tempting white ass I ever saw was actually too big, but its bigness made me hungry to suck it. I would follow him all over town just to watch that ass roll. The seat of his pants always twisted in the damp, humid crack of his ass. I knew it was funky because it looked funky. I wanted that guy's bit shitty ass. He didn't mess around with cocksuckers, although he loved black pussy.

You asked me about my sexual escapades in that industrial city of Akron, Ohio. Well, it was my first trip north from the deep south. I was somewhere in my early 20s. Though the south was not integrated I had had some sexual experiences with white men. It didn't take me long to find out where gays hung out in Akron. There were three main bars: a lesbian bar, a mixed bar

consisting of straights and homosexuals, then a gay bar. They were all on the same street. I scored more on the street than I did in the bar. The best stuff cruised around the block in cars from dusk to dawn. Hustlers also populated the street but most frequented the main street not far away; these were the expensive whores who didn't want to compete with the "free trade" that cruised in cars. I was picked up once by this man who wore a damp jock strap. He smelled clean but the jock strap was somewhat musky. No doubt he had showered yet put back on the jock strap he had worn all day. I suspect that 90% of the guys cruising around were straight. Straight men looking for an eager cocksucker. These men wouldn't be seen in a gay bar. Often they would have me go down on them while they drove around. Most would be already hard but no one had their dicks already out. I have walked past parked cars on occasion and seen young exhibitionists playing with hard dicks.

I had one bad experience which happened in the dead of winter. I had been drinking Wild Irish Rose (wine) in the gay bar (I sneaked it in a paper bag, trying to get a cheap high). I was hot for sex and left the warm bar and went to a book store not far away. Not seeing anything I wanted I lingered out front hoping to be picked up because the street was an extension of the cruising area. It was cold as hell. After a few minutes a car pulled up. In it were three guys — university students. A part of my mind tried to warn me to stay clear. I had never gotten in a car with more than one guy before. Even more suspicious was the Black guy in the car. Two whites and a black. I got into the back seat with the black and we drove off. They seemed to know what everything was about as if they had done this type of thing before. They drove for awhile and finally drove under the viaduct or bridge where they stopped. The Negro suddenly got abusive and started slapping me around. I became frightened. I slipped my wallet out and dropped it on the dark floor of the car near the door on my side. I thought they were going to rob me. As a matter of fact the "coon" did ask if I had any money. I told him no. He then told me to take off my heavy car coat and pull down my pants and shorts. After this he took out a solid hard dick and rammed it dry up my ass. It must have been big for it hurt like hell. He fucked me a few minutes but I don't think the white guys liked what was going on too much. One told the nigger to take it easy. He took his cock out of my ass shitty and made me suck it clean. I was terrified, hurt, humiliated and confused because I hadn't figured a "brother" would do this to me in front of whites. Later, as he pushed me out in the cold, I kicked my wallet out in the snow. I have later found that many niggers put on a show when around whites. It's rather phoney and disgusting.

I have a black dude who comes over from time to time. He is tall and big and always sweaty and rauchy. His beautiful asshole is never clean — very shitty and I love him for being such a careless ass wiper. I love his disregard for regular bathing. He doesn't know that I like bodily filth and I think he would give me more. He is married but it truly a vigorous fucker. I start out by giving him a complete tongue bath, which he really loves. He especially loves for me to eat out his ass — sucking loud and hard. He has a big black dick which brings tears to my eyes because he loves for me to take his big dick deep in my throat. He throws his legs around my head and force fucks my throat but he rarely shoots off this way for he is a natural fucker. There is always cum and a little blood when he finishes fucking me. When he comes to my home it is usually after a hard day's work, wearing soiled cut-offs or tight grungy levis and sweat-stained T shirt. His extremely big cock is rigid and straining at his groin with

lust. He is about 6 feet tall and close to 200 lbs. He is slick black (I am light brown) with short hair. His big sexy feet are naked which adds to his attractiveness; there's that simple countrified air about him which I find so appealing. He is trade but could be more but I don't push the point. I have this illusion about his "straight masculine pride" which I nurse and cater to. He got carried away once and started sucking my big nipples. At that point he could have easily gone down on me. I didn't want this because I felt he wouldn't be able to deal with it.

I met a black male whore in Rochester, New York when I was in my middle 20s. The guy's name was Carl — medium height, fleshy, around 180 pounds, Afro hair style. Nice features, dark honey complexion and clean. I was moving into this apartment house and he was packing to move out. I had no idea the landlady was giving him a room rent free. I later found out that there had been some sort of disagreement. It seemed that Carl was in the habit of bringing very young girls to his room and fucking the hell out of them. The landlady thought she had another stud in me. Which proved a sticky problem later. Anyway, when I first laid eyes on Carl I was immediately turned on. He had a breathtakingly beautiful body. The only thing he had on was a pair of homemade cut-offs. He had a strong fleshy ass which God knows I couldn't resist. He was preparing to go into the basement to wash a few intimate items. We introduced ourselves and he proved very friendly and open. Beautiful smile. From Florida. I'm butch and there is no indication that he knew I was a cocksucker. And at that time I didn't know he was a hustler. Not the established type but a ram-dam predator and opportunist. He was amused because he thought I was going to be his replacement.

A little later in my apartment he was curious and fascinated by my art work. I was more interested in him. I knew I had to act fast because there was a chance I wouldn't see him again. Seeing that he was taken by two ink drawings (18 x 24) of the Sphinx, I propositioned him. Sex for drawings. He was shocked but not turned off or angry. He had thought I was straight. I have always loved men but never allowed them to love me back. During the time I never considered myself attractive to men. Although I was constantly repulsing the attention of women and never could understand what they saw in me. There had been times I have actually had to flee. In the same apartment building I actually got trapped into sex with a woman who simply wouldn't give up. I ended up sucking her pussy because I couldn't get a hard dick to save my life. She was white and I don't understand why she thought I had to be attracted to her because I was black. Because my room was in a mess, Carl took me to his room. He pulled back the spread on his big bed, stripped and got in on his back. His dick was big and circumcised, somewhat dark. It was semi-hard. I was greatly aroused and quickly got naked and into bed. I felt him, rubbed him, caressed him. Kissed, licked and fondled him. He got completely hard. I teased his cockhead and choked on the length of his dick. After hard sucking, I pulled away and lifted his powerful legs. He opened himself completely. And it suddenly dawned on me that he had mistaken my intention. He thought I wanted to fuck him. He surprised me with his giving and passivity. I never cared for fucking a man's ass but I love to suck a man's ass. I greedily ate him out, a thing that tremendously pleased him. As a matter of fact, it was the key that opened up our long relationship. I have no doubt that Carl was straight but he is the type of man who is aggressive, dominating and abusive towards women, yet the very opposite when he's in bed with me.

After I got established Carl would come to see me. Ours was an arrangement involving money. I paid him $10 a load. Despite what I suspected was a very active sexual life, Carl never disappointed me. As a matter of fact if I could afford it I would suck him off twice in one night. He said he was a construction worker but he never seemed to work regularly. One evening he came to visit me with a girl perhaps 16 or 17. At first I thought he just wanted me to see his girl friend but he wanted a place to lay her. I would have done anything to have been in that room to see them. I sat in the kitchen drinking coffee desperately trying to hear him fucking her. I don't think the girl enjoyed it; afterwards she looked as though she had been crying. I'm sure he hurt her for Carl has a dick as big as my wrist. He had taken the sheets off the bed and after they left I examined them and found them quite bloody. After several weeks Carl rented a cheap, small room quite close to my apartment in the same house. Later a young attractive student nurse came to share his room. Some nights I could hear him beating her. This would go on about 15 minutes then quit. Then I could hear the bed springs squeak. He would vigorously fuck her for about an hour. One night all hell broke loose and he raped her. He came into my apartment buck naked, sweaty, smelly and soiled with her juices. His cock was half hard. He wanted me to suck him off. I refused.

Ad Majorem Penis Gloriam

TEXAS — I can assure you that you will find much gay sex going on in a monastery. I remember one day I was in my room shaving & nude when this monk entered my room to let me know that the car was ready (as we were going out). He said nothing but knelt down (a handsome blond man with a big cock & beautiful body) & gave me a blow job, balls and all, that nearly blew my mind. The first time I went to the Baths I was taken by a St. Louis priest. That monastery scene was for real & so is the one that follows: About a five-minute walk from the main monastery we had a summer villa & large pool in a wooded area — very beautiful. In the summer on my day off I would hightail up there fast, strip bareassed & walk about the villa with a hard on. I knew this other monk would follow me up there in about 20 minutes. He was good looking as hell with a fine build & cock. So when he came in I pretended he had "caught" me bareass with a hard on. He just laughed & said would you like to "Indian wrestle," which is wrestling in the nude. So he got bareassed & we began to horse around. When I would brush up to his hard on I would say, "Oh, I'm sorry" & pretend it was an accident. We at last ended up on the floor in a 69 position. The next thing I knew he had my over-heated cock in his mouth & then I started on his and the next thing I knew I had a mouthful of warm cum. It tasted super as I swallowed each squirt. He never liked to fool around in the monastery so we always waited until we went to the villa. This lasted about a month each week until he was sent to another monastery to teach. It was good to know that rabbis, priests & other men of the cloth take heavenly delight in your magazine. Your *M.R.* is the best yet & it keeps me hard all the time.

Young Japanese Fucks "Murderously"

NEW YORK — Let me assure you that the details are factual, my reactions and impressions real. I am pleased that I can write about it because Ron's absence precipitated what was for me a depression that caused me to enter therapy (briefly; it wasn't very helpful). My preference is to fuck a big butch man. At 5'4", 125 lbs., appearing Oriental as I do, I have had some difficulty in securing the right willing partner. Occasionally, however, I am successful and Ron was a particularly hot number. At 6' 1", 190 lbs., a muscular body and a preference for smaller Japanese men, he was ready for action when he showed up in New York unannounced.

Our initial contact occurred some six months earlier when he answered an ad of mine. Handcuffed with his arms behind him, he got me very hot with his tongue licking my cock and balls. He licked slowly, skilfully and with great care until I started fucking his mouth. I withdrew my cock from his mouth and told him to lick my balls again. I put my asshole over his face and had him rim it. With my ass spread, he really got into it and got his tongue up my asshole. It felt good, but I wanted to stick my cock up his asshole, so I turned him over on his stomach and greased his hole and fondled his firm white high round ass cheeks. He was really into the scene and was moaning, appreciatively I think, as I prepared his hole for my hard cock. I moved three fingers easily in and out of his butch asshole, lubricated with Vaseline Intensive Care and baby oil. With his bound arms now in front of him, I gently stuck my cock in his warm, receiving hole, lying over him. I moved my pelvis in short slow motions until he was accustomed to having me in him. He started to move his butt around so I began to thrust in earnest. I pulled his ass up and really went to town with long hard strokes. With every forward movement of my cock, he pushed his ass back. After some time, I turned him over on his back again with his legs up and continued to fuck him eagerly, enthusiastically. His cock was dripping. My own was solid rock from the excitement of his responsiveness.

I fucked his hole murderously, alternating between a frantic pace and a slower pace. Sweat rolled down my face and onto his chest. His moans increased my excitement. My cock and his asshole were all that mattered. After I shot my load, I collapsed over him in exhaustion. My cock began to shrivel and I finally withdrew it. As I lay there on my side, Ron's head moved down to my groin renewing the warmth with his mouth. He wanted, he said, what there was of my cum as it leaked out of my shriveled cock. I realized then that my cock had gotten irritated from all that fucking. He left two days later after more action, several orgasms and some sightseeing.

I began to miss him immediately and in the days that followed I came to realize that I had perhaps fallen for him. I wrote him but never received an answer. I finally reached him on the telephone but our converstion was brief and superficial. It took me several months to get over his effect on me. It's amazing how quickly one is bowled over by the right man and how little details become so endearing; I recall that he had a hole in one pocket of all his trousers so that he could play with himself. I still look for big butch men to fuck and still have the fantasy of fucking a humpy Marine.

Subscriber Refuses to Lick Sailor's Shit-hole

WILMINGTON — Why don't I start with my first attempt at seduction? It was back in the early '50s and there was a big Naval Training Station about 30 miles from where I lived. The guys used to come into town to YMCA dances on Friday and Saturday nights and afterward would be lined up at the edge of town hitchhiking back to the base. After driving past the lineup innumerable times & losing my nerve, I finally decided "What the hell!" and picked up one guy who was standing by himself. He was in blues just molded onto his great body. After some idle chit-chat I said, "Please don't take offense, but would you mind if I just feel your leg?" He did a double take and said I could. After a minute or so I asked him if I could feel his groin and he took my hand and laid it on his hard cock.

I could hardly speak but mumbled that this was the first time I'd ever done anything like that and he said it was OK and did I want to suck him off? We found a truck stop and parked at the end of a line of trucks, where he took off his pants and underwear and I soon had my head between his thighs. He gave me helpful directions on what made him feel good and how to keep my teeth from hurting him and how to use my tongue. He told me to suck his balls, then suck behind the balls, keep going farther, farther. I began smelling some shitty odor so I stopped and he said, "That's OK, don't worry, go back on my cock." After he came, and we continued on to the base, he instructed me in how to talk to pickups to see if they are interested without getting into trouble. I found him another time months later and he complimented me on my progress. I often wonder what became of him and am forever grateful to a very nice, sympathetic guy. He was only 20 and I marvel at his maturity.

* * *

Another time at night I picked up two handsome young sailors and they both got into the front seat with me (Ah, those old wide seats!). I rested my right hand on the knob of the gear shift and let my fingers dangle idly onto the knee of the one next to me. Meeting no resistance, I shifted my hand down the steering wheel, onto my lap & then over to touch his leg. He covered his lap with his pea jacket and I went under it, over his leg to find he had a big hard on. One handedly, without any conversation, I opened his pants, undid his skivvies and took that magnificent cock and balls in hand. At that point he flipped off the pea jacket, exposing us to his friend. The friend gasped, and after a "Jesus Christ!" said, "How about me?" Until we found a place on a back road to stop, there was a confusion of legs and cocks to feel — whose was whose?

Once stopped, I had the time of my life with those two gorgeous gobs. Picking him up shows that I ignored the advice of the 1st one I'd picked up. He said *never* pick up two at once. He also said, "When you pick up a guy, start talking about whether there are lots of girls at the base, wherever he comes from. He will answer either no or yes. Either way, you ask him if he gets his share. If it's 'Yes, I get all I want,' you better change the subject. If it's no, then ask him how long since he had his rocks off, and tell him that if he can't get the real thing he can probably always get a blow job at the base, right? If he says yes, ask him if he'd like a blow job now. If he says no, ask him if he's ever had one

and follow up to see if he'd like to try one. But be casual about it all."

Of course I had some fear when I picked up the two, but both had hard ons and seemed eager for a blow job. The one by the door was a little too far away and he had to help me and I had two cocks and four legs to feel, which got a bit confusing, along with doing the driving. They whispered together & then one of them said he knew a back road near the base & if I took them back to the base, they'd let me blow them on that back road. The first one (next to me) was long in coming. His buddy had got in the back seat, leaned over the front seat to watch & now & then I'd play with him while No. 1 jerked himself. Eventually he came & they changed places. No. 2 came fast as he was pretty worked up by what he'd been watching, and I was disappointed because it was over so fast. No. 1 said he had to shit and did I have any Kleenex. No I didn't, but he said he had to get out & crap. So while he was there No. 2 got hard again and we had a super session.

He was very affectionate (whereas the first one just lay back) and touched me a lot, caressed my head and made happy sounds. No. 1 came back and said, "Are you two doing it *again?*" and climbed in back and lay down on the seat. This time, No. 2 came with 5 times the volume of his first time. When I got home, I found a rock on the floor of the back seat. I guess No. 1 decided he'd better be prepared in case I turned out to be a "crazy." That must have been his outdoor mission instead of taking a shit.

* * *

I lived in the biggest city in Brazil, Sao Paulo, for a few years. Thanks to an early wonderful, romantic affair with a 21-yr.-old advertising model, I learned some of the essential Portuguese expressions that Berlitz doesn't cover. I used these (after my lover moved away) to meet & have sex with guys on the street. The population of Brazil was 50% under 18 years old! The racial mixture of caucasian, latin, black & oriental produces a magnificent people, believe me.

One night I picked up a 17-year-old student & hustler & we went to a little pension where they rent rooms for a night very cheap & don't bother you if you have no luggage. What I love to do is kiss and lick all over the body really getting down to some serious cocksucking. I was able to gauge when to back off to keep Claudio from coming too fast & he went wild. He hadn't very much experience, so he was most enthusiastic over the things I did. I worried that he might be afraid to come in my mouth so I explained carefully in my broken Portuguese that when he came he was to leave his cock inside my mouth. So after he came in multiple spurts and rested a bit he began asking me a question which I didn't understand.

After 3 or 4 attempts, he resorted to sign language, putting his finger to his throat and moving it down to his stomach. At last I understood that he wanted to know if I swallowed his come. I replied "Yes. Now I'm going to have a baby." Claudio went into fits of laughter over this dumb joke, but it ended up with another hard on to produce a brother or sister for his first child.

* * *

I never had but one unpleasant experience with a serviceman — a sailor — and it's still too unhappy for me to relate it — ended up a very enjoyable session in

the car with him calling the police later, tracing my license plate & arresting me at 4 A.M. Here's one, though, with a civilian — a young punk. I picked up this hitchhiker who was 19 or 20, tall & well built, good looking, in tight chinos one night. He had a hard on almost before I asked him if he wanted a blow job and he said he knew a good place where we could park. So he guided me through some back lanes to a field, which seemed very safe — from other cars or cops, at least. So he pushed his pants down & I began sucking this gorgeous cock, when all of a sudden my door opened & someone grabbed me & hauled me out of the car. My "friend" quickly zipped up & got out on his side. Then there were three of them hitting & kicking me. They ran when I began yelling, but they'd taken my wallet & wrist watch & keys to the car.

I was lucky to escape serious injury, but had to get help. The police came, called a friend to come & get me, & they believed my story I made up about the guy wanting me to help him with his car. The cops never caught them, but they did have a fling at a Holiday Inn & bought tires with my credit card.

* * *

I was in Paris once and was, at that time, afraid to go into bars, but was not against trying to pick up somebody on the street. One night I was the object of attention of a cute guy who turned out to be (so he said) a student from Italy. We had a somewhat inconclusive conversation in fractured French, but eventually he & I understood that I wanted to blow him. He said he knew a good safe place near the Eiffel Tower so we took the Metro & ended up in the bushes in sight of the Tower.

It was dark — about 10 or 11 P.M. — and in this clump of bushes was a goddam folding chair! I wanted him to sit down so I could kneel in front of him but he preferred to stand. I knelt, opened his pants, took out his cock which was semihard, opened his mouth — and saw stars! He whacked me on the side of the head, knocking me off my haunches, sending my glasses flying, & pounced on me with his hands on my throat. I kept my wallet & passport in my inside jacket pocket so he had to throttle me first before he could let go to get the wallet & passport. Since he didn't knock me out with that first blow, I did what came naturally, *yelling* "Help! Police!" at the top of my lungs. This was summer, so there were people around & he got scared & took off. Too bad, though, because I was going to enjoy that big Italian cock.

Interview:
Drains Marine, "Hillbillies," Theatre-goers

What kinds of men do you like to suck?
From a teenager, when I was just beginning to jack off, I have always felt my biggest thrill was knowing I had made someone happy. If I sucked a 4" prick and an 8" prick, then had the choice of re-sucking only one of them for a second time, I would pick the prick that showed the most pleasure and emotion. It might sound strange, but my biggest thrill is knowing I have been a good cocksucker and made someone satisfied, or been a good fuckee and

satisfied a good top man fucker. I love to hear a straight telling me what he wants and that I am making him happy. Most of the straights I know are good sexual friends of mine. I know several married straights who claim they are not cheating: "and asshole is not a cunt." I've had spells of Ivy Leaguers, Navy uniforms, truck drivers, in fact every type except queens & faggots.

You have mentioned that you enjoy being called a cocksucker. This requires technique, doesn't it?

I wouldn't take it from a stranger on the streets but I love it from a partner in bed. Years ago I picked up a Marine (straight) in Scollay Square in Boston. He was standing there and I offered him a lift. I said, "Are you hot and bothered?" He said, "Ya. Would you like to suck it?" I blew him twice in the back seat while he moaned. He had a beautiful prick. I suggested that on the weekend we fuck in a bed and get full value. He couldn't do that as he fucked his girl on weekends. So we went to a motel the same night I picked him up. God, he could fuck for an hour. We met the next week at the same motel and while I was sucking him he yelled, "Jesus, you're a real cocksucker. A real good cocksucker." It struck me like a knife, as I had never been called a cocksucker while sucking anyone. The Marine looked at me and smiled and said, "Don't get mad. When you suck me I love it." Then he said, "What are you?" and I gladly looked him in the eyes and said, "I'm your cocksucker." The Marine gave up his girlfriend. For 14 months I saw him twice a week plus every other weekend. Ever since then I've always felt the need to be called a cocksucker when sucking.

In all your travels, where have you made out best?

The Appalachian section of Kentucky, where the "hillbilly" is in full bloom, is a cocksucker's dream come true. I can truthfully state that practically all of the hillbillies I sucked & got fucked by had 7 inches or more plus thickness as well. Many were cut, but a higher percentage were uncut. But seldom did you find an unclean prick. I had many at my apartment, many in cars, especially in drive-in movies. Very few are short winded; they can fuck and get sucked for an hour. The wonderful thing was if the one fucking you thought you were a good fuck he would insist that his pals should fuck you. He would make the date and actually return with 1 or 2 friends who fucked as good as he did. Often I would get fucked while sucking his friend's beautiful prick and when they finished you had it top & bottom and were happy as a lark. I never met any who felt tired or depressed after losing their load. They were all satisfying and if they wanted another round I was always happy to say yes. There was one chap about 25 who had 9" and loved to ease it down my throat. He was married and very gentle; he never tried to gag me. Actually he was an excellent technician. He knew if he wanted pleasure I (his cocksucker) also had to be satisfied. He would play with my nipples and call me his special cocksucker. Then when my throat would tighten he would say, "Boy, your fucking mouth is better than my wife's cunt." This would thrill me so that I would relax and he would slide it in further and would repeat, saying my fucking mouth was better than his wife's cunt. I would shake from joy. The amazing part was all these hillbillies were straight and when sex was over, they treated me as a straight friend.

Where do you go for cock now in New York?

I've sucked many guys who were sitting in theatre balconies with one foot up on the seat in front of them. The positions in my apartment are generally dealer's choice. I prefer sucking them legs spread in bed so I can get to the "hilt" and eventually roll over so he can fuck me in the throat.

Ranch Youth Has "Sweet-Tasting" Asshole, Spinach-Flavored Cum

TEXAS — In the busiest "john" on the state university campus, I picked up an 18-year-old freshman, fresh off the ranch, one Friday afternoon. I was a graduate student. He was flunking out of school already, only two months into the Fall semester. Neither of us had a place to go at two in the afternoon so we took off in my car. He used the term "queer" for other men who had sucked him him off but he was polite to me and used the expression "that way" when referring to me. He wasn't "that way" himself because he had never sucked another guy's dick or had one up his virgin asshole, but he allowed that he was ready for anyone who wanted to suck his dick.

We found a safe place off the road in the hills, parked the car, unzipped his jeans and I soon had his 7" jumping. He was uncut. His hair, both on his head and above his dick, was coal black. His balls smelled strongly of Mennen talc mixed with sweat. His boots were so hard to get off we decided to just pull his pants and Jockey shorts down and leave the boots on. I licked up the fat shaft of his dick to the head. I could taste dried cum and dried piss and dick-cheese underneath his foreskin, but SHIT, that's what I liked about that beautiful hunk of meat. All of this odor and taste made me hotter and hotter and I tried to raise his legs to get his asshole against my lips and my tongue inside, but because he had his boots on and I was laying across his legs, I could not raise his legs enough to get my tongue in his ass. My nose could sense the delights of that sweet asshole.

After 15 or 20 thrusts downward with my hot mouth and my hot tongue swirling around the head as I went down and came back up, he let out a yell and filled my mouth with slick, hot young cum that had a raw spinach flavor mixed with that basic soda flavor, and I gulped down at least three or four good swallows. Being a cum gourmet, I could tell immediately that I had found a good source of the kind of male love juice that I like, and I was ready for seconds, thirds and on and on — so I intended to please this hunk so I could count on re-runs of pure protein, direct from the source. I suppose he was impressed with the way I worshipped his dick and balls, because on the way back to the campus he confided to me that he had had his first blow job in September, right there on campus during "Howdy Week," when he met this "queer" who gave him a quickie at the student union building rest room on the second floor.

Since then he said he just couldn't get enough. Jacking off didn't satisfy him like it used to, and he sometimes got three blow jobs a day when he could find guys willing to do it. He would kneel down and stick his dick under the toilet wall and let the guys suck him off if they didn't have a place to go. He said that he lived in the dorm and couldn't take anyone back there. He had 2 roommates. "Shit, I have to sneak in a hand job when the other guys are asleep — no time by myself almost." He said that of the guys who had sucked him off, none were half as good as I and that he had to get in bed with me for an all night session. He told me he went home every week so he could help his Dad out on the ranch and that he would love for me to go home with him that day if I could. I couldn't make it that week but did the next.

The ranch was 50 miles southwest of the city in the hill country of Central

Texas in scrubby cedar and rock country, very poor land but good enough to raise sheep, goats and some cattle. The house was a big run-down structure and had no indoor plumbing. He told me that his sister and mother used the rear of the west side of the house and him and his Dad used the rear of the east side for toilets. The place was something out of the past; here one just leaned against a tree or rock and shit or whatever. Every week or so, lime was thrown over the remains and turned under by shovel. For bathing, a big metal tub about 2 feet high and 4 feet wide was used, one on each side of the house. A windmill supplied water to the tubs, which were housed in a lean-to about 7 feet long, with a place to hang your clothes.

Before I went out to the ranch, I asked him if his parents might not be leery of me since I was older (I was 26 then), but he said no, they didn't know what "queer" meant so they would not think anything of it. He said they always welcomed strangers whoever they might be; they loved company; it was pretty lonely on the ranch and they didn't get to town often. After Johnny and I rode around the place on horseback awhile, we came back and took a bath before retiring to bed. We got into bed buck naked and played around awhile. I just had to get down under that cover and kiss his ass — that was all I could think of, and the only part of his beautiful body I had not kissed in the car. I slid down under the cover and licked his belly-button, pubic hair and balls and kissed his dick with the foreskin over the head, slowly pulling the skin back to run my tongue around the head and search out the cheese I hoped would be waiting for my hungry mouth. It was there for the taking and I took it slowly.

His dick jumped around in response to my tongue action. As I kissed his balls, he threw back the cover and pulled his legs up in the air and held them with his hands, spreading his ass wide. I could not see his hole in the dark, but the musty odor and pure smell of male ass made my dick swell. My favorite thing, the sex spot that turns me on like nothing else in the world, is a man's asshole. I raised up on all fours and raised his legs back more so I could press my hot wet lips up against his hole. I could feel a slight shudder of his entire body as I kissed his asshole. I darted my wet slick tongue into the puckered hole and he first responded by contraction, but soon opened up to let my thick educated tongue in. I gave him a good tongue fucking for at least 45 minutes or an hour before I finally had to come up for air and wipe the sweat off my body, which was as hot as an August night in Texas by then. I could even feel sweat dripping down the crack of my ass and because the sweat was in my eyes, I had no choice but to stop for awhile and get comfortable again. I played with his nipples, balls and asshole with my fingers.

After about 30 minutes of this, I wanted to go back to my favorite spot. This time I told him to sit over my face and hole his ass cheeks apart, I wanted to eat out his ass like it was going out of style. He did and I did, until my tongue was sore from trying to get it all up his asshole. I had his hole so fucking open I could have driven in a foot-long dildo. His asshole may have been a virgin to a dick but my tongue gave it a good fucking for another hour before I sucked him off. His asshole was a real "sweet" tasting one and when someone refers to a "sweet ass" I know what they mean. Johnny was a sweet ass.

The percentage of my tricks who went "mean ass" is very small. Several years ago I was at one of my favorite rest stops on U.S. 59 (near Lufkin in East Texas). It was around 1 A.M. on Tuesday night and the rest stop is not lighted, nor does it have rest rooms. I usually stopped there to pick up early morning truckers on the way to Houston from Little Rock, Memphis and points northeast. I had had

a big percentage of success with truckers as well as local drivers, but this particular night I met a local Lufkin guy and he was telling me about how mean truckers had been to him. He left finally and by two in the morning I was alone in the place.

I noted that across the highway at the park line I was in, there were some trucks and one pick-up truck, but it was out of reach and one had to come across the four-lane highway to get to our side. This truck came in with a load of chickens for the Houston market and the chickenshit smelled like hell. I was sitting on the picnic tables by the time the driver got through pissing and kicking his tires, and he ambled over to ask me what time it was and to "stretch his legs." (He had only come 30 miles or so, from one of the local chicken farms, but I knew what he wanted.) We got around to talking about sex and he asked me if I had ever fucked a chicken. No, I said, what was it like. He said he would get one and show me if I wanted — whereupon I said no, I had rather you not waste your load in a chicken's ass, how about me sucking it off for you. He said he had rather have a hot mouth around his dick, so out it came and into my waiting mouth with him standing and me sitting down on the table. Even though the odor of chickens was strong, I sucked him off and he pumped me a good load of thick cum. He pulled out, leaving a bunch of chicken sounds, but before I could jack off, the pick up truck across the highway pulled out and came over to my side.

A real farmer-cowboy-redneck type got out and walked to the table and began immediately asking me about the chicken truck driver — what he looked like, if we did anything, and if so, how big his joint was. I said he was about 5' 10", 160 and about early twenties or maybe 19, with a long 8" circumcised. He asked me if it was good or did it feel good up my ass. I said I sucked him and it was good. He had his out by then, jacking it, and told me to get mine out; he wanted to play with it a little. I did and he played with my already hard dick and then I sucked on his dick awhile, and he would suck mine awhile. Then he said let's go down the road, he knew a place under the nearby river bridge that was safe and we could strip off and get in the pick up bed with the quilts in it and have a good 69. I thought about it a minute and said I was going the other way and did not have that much time. He wanted to fuck me, he said, and the truck would be much better, and he could give me a good fuck. He was OK with about 6 ", not too big around but a real clean, nice body. He was about 5' 6", 140 lbs., real nice. He kept trying to get me to go to the river with him. I finally got in my car and he said, wait a minute, so he went back to his car and returned. He stuck his head in the window on the right side of the car and said, "OK, give me all your money, you cocksucker," and he had a gun pointing at me. I said, "fuck you, you asshole," and pushed the window lift up and he pulled his hand out and I sped off leaving him holding the gun.

I stayed away from the place a few months and when I went back I asked the local guy I'd talked to earlier about the guy with the gun and he laughed, saying it was a queen from a nearby town to the south of the park and that one time a guy grabbed his gun away from him and stuck the barrel of it up his asshole and told him if it was loaded he would sure know it soon because he was going to pull the trigger. The guy said relax, it wasn't loaded, and to pull it out and stick his dick in its place — PLEASE! The guy just used his empty gun to frighten guys with so he could have the park all to himself.

"Will You Suck My Ass?"

WEST VIRGINIA — I was glad to see I represented West Virginia in *Meat*. I want the rest of the country to know that Hillbillies are in Man to Man Sex as deeply as the rest of the states and maybe more so with less hang-ups. The first episode I will relate is a recent experience and one I think you will like as you are an ass man. I stopped in at the local roadside park the other night and was sitting on the open door john when in walked a man and as he passed me he looked in and spoke and all at once he grabbed his groin and said "do you want it?" I said I sure did. As he went on around to the urinals he said, "will you suck my ass like you used to?" I said I sure would. At that I recognized he was someone I had had about four years ago for several times. We went out in my car to my favorite parking spot and he pulled down his pants and I went to licking on a nice 7 inch uncut cock which was already semi-hard. I no sooner had it all in my mouth than it was bone hard. I then licked down the hard shaft to the balls and went to licking on them and taking them into my mouth to suck on them. I then started working on down to his ass hole. His pants were hampering my getting to his ass hole good so he slipped off his shoes and pants and presented to me a beautiful ass hole. It was now ready to get to and it was so velvety soft that I could have sucked it all night. I licked it and kissed it and put my tongue up the velvety folds as far as I could. I have had some men lose their hard on while I was doing that but not him. His cock stayed rock hard. I then set back down on the seat and I went back to sucking his cock and licking the head of his meat with my tongue and on down the shaft again to his nuts, which were beginning to tighten up. I took one more lick on his ass hole and then went back up where I swallowed his cock and he started spurting good sweet-tasting cum down my throat. I found out he was as virile as ever after four years and he is now nearing 40 years old. I hope to get him in bed some night where we can have more fun.

One Sunday afternoon I drove over to this college town to see if I could find some fun. I went to the bus station and they had a glory hole and I was seated there waiting for a hard one to show up. Soon a man came in and after he saw me looking through the small hole he went to playing with his cock and he saw I got more interested. He wrote a note and passed it through to me. It said if I wanted to swing on his cock and if I went for rough sex to meet him outside and we would go to his room. I answered back that it sounded good to me. I went outside and met him and it turned out that he was a college professor and was from England. He was returning home the next month. We went to his room and got undressed and he wanted me to use a belt on his ass which I did. His cock started getting hard and when I took it in my mouth that finished the process. I sucked on his cock and then his nuts and licked his ass. He then wanted to fuck me in the ass and I agreed and he used the belt on my ass a few times to get it warm before he put it up my ass. He fucked me hard. He shoved it in all at once and it hurt and he kept it up fast and hard until it was hurting more than it was feeling good. I was a slim 8 incher but my ass wasn't used to taking one. He pulled it out and brought it around for me to suck on again and on the end of his lovely pink-headed cock was a small glob of my shit and as I licked it off his cock jumped and got a half inch longer and I swallowed his

cock all the way down my throat then. I thought it was time to mention something that I liked then so I slipped his pecker out and asked him if he would piss in my mouth and he said he would later, so I put his pecker back in and I think that made him hotter than ever thinking about giving me his piss and he came in spurt after spurt of creamy cum. After he had finished and his cock had softened and he took it out he made himself a cup a tea and about a half hour later he was ready to give me his piss. His cock started to harden up while it was in my mouth and spewing out that good warm golden nectar. By the time he had finished and his cock had soaked in that warm liquid he was hard and ready for another blow job. I gave him a tongue bath over his slim body. I licked down and sucked his toes and I had hold of his cock caressing it with one hand and while I was sucking each of his toes and licking his feet I could feel the throbbing of his cock so I knew he liked it. I sucked out his arm pits and he had the natural smell of a man. I sucked and played with his nipples which I got to harden up. I licked his ass hole and up under his balls and then after taking them in my mouth I went to licking and sucking his cock. It took more work on his cock this time but he soon had a bag full of that good English cum which he unloaded in my mouth.

* * *

I love the smell of a man's groin that hasn't had a bath for at least a day. I love the smell of cock cheese. I love to smell cum whether it's fresh or whether it's dried from the night before. I have this one friend that comes over to the house and I fuck him in the ass and I jack his cock while I am fucking him. He gets so hot that I don't jack much on him. He can almost come with just my fucking him, but when he has had enough I start in and jack him up to a good load and he shoots his load on a towel. I sleep with that towel under my nose all night and I wake up the next morning with a hard on and that good smell is still next to my nose.

NATIONAL DEFENSE:
Sailor Wraps Legs Around Subscriber

FROM A SUBSCRIBER, EAST COAST — You notice I haven't yet got up the strength or courage or whatever to write about the sailor who called the cops. Certain memories are still too painful — like the cop looking at my children's rocking horse when he told me to go with him to the station. The sailor had made a complaint — it wasn't the cop's fault that time. It still is a mystery to me what went through that sailor's head, because he got booked too. I love to remember the experience I'm enclosing here. I've never found anybody since to equal him in total desirability and pleasure. One night I was driving along I-95 and spotted a hitchhiker standing by an exit. It was a young guy about 5'8", slender, wearing jeans, and he had a duffel bag at his side. I stopped and he got in, slinging the bag (a Navy bag) into the back. I drive a stick-shift Honda and the front seats are pretty close together. He settled back in his seat, spreading his legs so that his left thigh touched my hand, which was resting on the gear shift knob. We talked about what he did in the Navy. His breath smelled slightly of alcohol and he admitted that he'd had a couple of slugs of gin in the previous car.

Meanwhile he kept the contact of his leg against my hand. He looked to be no more than 20 (he told me later he was 19) and was very handsome without being beautiful — you know what I mean? Short black hair, good arms, solid muscular legs and no fat anywhere. I asked him about the social life in San Diego — did he have a regular girlfriend? No, he said, he wasn't ready for that and he preferred to get as many different ones that he liked. I asked him if any of them blew him and he said *sure*! He said he loved getting a blow job. One chick worked on him for 2 hours once, he said, before he gave her his load — she was wild! I then asked him if he ever got hard up for chicks out there and he said it happened sometimes. "What do you do then?" I asked. "I have a couple of queers I know," he said, "and one of them is always ready to help me." I asked him if he was horny right now and he said talking about all that sex was making him horny. I said I'd give him a blow job if he'd like and then he said he was pretty short of money and could I give him $20? I thought about it and then suggested that he come home with me so we could have privacy and, instead of giving him $20, I'd take him on to his home, about 25 miles from where I lived. He readily agreed.

So I took him home and he asked for a gin and tonic, which I fixed for him. Then we stood facing each other while I unbuttoned his shirt and drew it off his shoulders, revealing a white T-shirt which I next pulled off over his head. I licked and kissed his chest and nipples and worked my way down to his navel, and was now on my knees. I kissed him all over the fly of his jeans, feeling the hot hard cock inside. I undid his belt buckle, opened the top button of his jeans, and took the zipper in my teeth, pulling it down as I held his thighs and felt his firm round muscular ass. When I opened his pants I pushed them down to his ankles and his beautiful 5" cock stuck out through the opening of his skivvies. I licked the head of it and then gulped it down, swirling my tongue around it. He grabbed my head and pressed into my face, moaning. But I didn't want him to come yet, so I got off his cock and began kissing and licking those muscular thighs and calves. I took his shoes off and slipped his pants off of his feet and went back up, licking all the way. I pulled his shorts down, exposing the most beautiful nest of soft, long black cock hair I had ever seen. He smelled slightly musky, a good clean manly odor, not of old piss or shit. I began devouring his cock hair and then his cock again. This time he removed his cock and lay down on the sofa and I snuggled up along side it with his legs over my shoulders or around my arms, gripping me tight.

He kept telling me how good I was, sucking his cock, licking it up and down, kissing and licking that forest of hair, eating his lovely balls, kissing and licking up toward his asshole. He pushed me further toward his asshole but I stopped and shook my head (my mouth being full of balls I couldn't speak) and he just smiled and said, "What can I say?" That did it. I let go of his balls and headed for his beautifully clean asshole, and relieved to find it so sweet and clean, like all the rest of his beautiful body, I hungrily licked, kissed and sucked his rosebud asshole. He gave little moans. Finally he pulled me back onto his cock and in three full deep strokes delivered his gift in my mouth. His cock never got soft afterward, so I kept up all the activities we'd been doing for another hour till he shot a second time.

His cum tasted sweet and nutty, just like I expected. At times he would apologize because his cock wasn't "very big" but I told him it was perfect and how I adored the sight of it towering over that wonderful nest of cock hair. Once during our second hour he said, "Shit, man, if I had you in San Diego I

wouldn't need any chicks." You can imagine how that spurred me on. He kept drinking gin and tonics and I began watering them down so he wouldn't get sick or lose that erection, but he knew what I was doing and demanded more gin till he'd consumed about half a bottle. Finally I decided I'd better get him to his home. I had thought about putting him to bed and taking him home in the morning but didn't know how he would act in cold daylight. He fumbled around trying to get his skivvies on, gave up and threw them into a corner of the sofa, grumbling that he hated shorts anyhow. (I still have them and enjoy putting them to my face and thinking of his body inside.) He passed out in the car and when we got to his town I couldn't get him to tell me where he lived, so finally he asked me to let him out in the little square in the middle of town. He got his duffel bag out with some difficulty and sat down on it. I asked him if he was all right and he gave me a dazzling smile and said he was OK and thanked me. He didn't know then that I had put $20 in his pocket while he was asleep. I hope he thinks of me kindly, if he thinks of me at all.

"He Always Teased Me By Grabbing His Cock"

By A Prisoner

[EDITOR'S NOTE: The following article is condensed from the Los Angeles publication, Gayboy, which authorizes use of its material when credited to Gayboy.]

You resent always being watched...although sometimes I wasn't watched enough. I was assaulted over 13 times by inmates who tried to force me into sex. They never got any but it was a mental strain having to be on the alert at all times. I had knives pulled on me, rocks thrown at me, verbal abuse. I didn't follow the one rule of the population: Don't be a snitch. I snitched and I'm glad of it. I snitched for my own protection. If someone jumped on me, I wrote the warden. I feel this was the only thing that saved me. I was known for this. So, many inmates who might have jumped on me knew, if I lived through it, I'd tell on them. I used to have sex in my cell with one of the brake-boys. These guys used to throw the brakes so inmates could get out of their cells. They used to break each morning for breakfast and then after breakfast so inmates could get back into their cell, for count. In the morning at breakfast time, the cell blocks were always dark. The lights would go on when it was about time for the doors to break.

This young guy had been in prison for quite a few years. I don't recall what he was there for. I do know he got an additional sentence for setting a black guy on fire with gasoline. The black guy was in terror, so I was told, and threatened to fuck the guy when he got out of his cell. Before he could get out, the guy threw gas on him and set him on fire. He was tall and had a nice build and a large cock. No hair on his chest and a real pleasant personality. Although he had been locked up for years, he claimed he didn't mess around. There was a catwalk behind the cells and he used to walk up to the back of the cell (there were bars in front and back of the cells in Six Block) at night and talk to me.

This was around 5:00 at chow time. I started talking sex to him and he got a hard on. I reached down and grabbed it through his pants. My heart was thumping. I was lining up some trade. So he said he would be up early the next morning. Well, he was. He reached through the bars and shook me, waking me up. I got out of bed — it was still dark in the cell block — and walked to the back of the cell. I reached down and unzipped his pants. He had a raging hard on. Circumcised and smooth. It was also very warm in my hand. Christ he was built. He had a small waist and was over 6′ tall. I just squatted down and he stuck his cock through the bars. He came in seconds.

But within a few days I grew tired of him. I guess it's because I never really liked sex without some kind of feeling of love. The sex need is there, but it's like going to a prostitute for sex. After the sex, there's nothing left. I wanted more. Even in prison, I had to have it my way; I had to choose who I wanted sex with. I couldn't be forced by someone I never liked. I wouldn't have sex with anyone I never wanted to have sex with. And I guess this bugged a few people because they knew I was gay and they felt that because I was gay, I should have sex with anyone who wanted to have sex with me. I was always being abused, either physically or verbally.

There was a real handsome hallboy that helped me take my blankets and personals to my cell. His name was Michael Krowl. Mike wore white clothes since he helped feed the Chronic line. He was just plain sexy. And he had a hard on, which made matters worse. I told him I wanted to suck his cock. He said where? I said right here, the door's open. So he came into the cell and we opened the locker door and got behind it so nobody could watch us. Another quickie. He had a nice fat cock and smooth body. He was blond. He was a gambler and also a pill head. All he thought about was getting high. I used to palm my medication (Equanil) so he could have it. In return, I got his dick. He was nice sex and got off fast. I knew I was being used, but then I was using him too.

Then Tattoo Smitty used to come through the block. He worked in the kitchen. He was a real good-looking guy but he had all those damned tattoos. He was tall with black hair and he had a nice lean body and probably lifted weights. He always teased me by grabbing his cock through his pants. One day my cell door was open and I said, "C'mon in." He did and I took care of him. And would you believe — tattoos on his cock! When I worked at the Quartermaster (where inmate clothes are kept) I had to make a delivery. I stopped in the kitchen to see Smitty and it was just at the right time and we had the chance for sex again. He's another guy whose cock is always real hot. I loved it and him. And he was quite hung, too. There is no way to tell a person just by their looks. I was friendly with a real beauty who was there for murder. You couldn't tell by looking at him that he was a murderer. And he was a quiet, really handsome guy.

This guy, Jim, was working in Civil Defense. I went there, just to get out of my cell. I got more than that, I got his cock too. He was so horny he nearly fell out of his chair when he came. I told him he had a big cock and he said a friend used to blow him and said he had an extra inch he couldn't handle. Jim, at that time, didn't let anyone mess with him either. I guess he just jacked off. But I wanted him and got him. He was later a nurse. I had another opportunity at his cock about a year later. I was going with another nurse, who later turned gay, and had him set up a thing for Jim so we could get together. We ended up in a three-way.

Uncouth Youth,
Has Big, Beautiful Cock

Are you now, or have you been in any other law firm, openly gay? If so, to whom? How was your sexual interest made known? I hate to sound like a lawyer, but your question is objectionable on the ground that it is compound. Just kidding. I've been pretty open in my last three jobs. I let them know I'm gay not by making an announcement but just by dropping a hint here and there, e.g., some fellow says, "Get a load of the neat chick," and I say, "Yeah. Her boyfriend's cute too."
Have you ever been fired for sexual reasons? Yes. I had a boss who thought I was hot stuff for several months. Then, for no known reason, he suddenly didn't like the way I handled cases anymore. I figured the reason for the change was that someone told him he had a queer attorney on his staff.
Have you ever seen any lawyers in your firms into whose pants you'd like to get? I've worked with some pretty foxy attorneys. A co-worker at my last job was 25, blond, blue-eyed and beautiful — enough to make your mouth (or your cock) drool. He knew I was gay and we joked about it. A couple of times we had some drinks and hugged each other, expressing our friendship rather than sex *per se*.
You appear in your photographs to be a valuable representative of homosexuals, in that you're attractive, cool, easy, likeable, loose, open. Do you pass for "straight"? Yes.
I believe you belong to a group of gay lawyers. I belong to a gay lawyers' organization that has 300 members. Most of the members don't know anything about defending sex "crimes" and are far more likely to be arrested themselves than to be defending the accused.
Have you had any bullying from homophobes and fag-baiters? A little, not much. Like most lawyers I'm hyperverbal and can both defend myself and counterattack.
The caption under your photo on your book mentions that you take your son to a park and play softball. Does that mean you would prefer that he grow up "straight?" Life is hard enough without being gay. Consequently I wish my son would grow up straight. I suspect, however, that he's gay.
How often did you jack off as a young boy? Couple times a day.
As a high school boy? Couple of times a day.
In college? Once a day plus whatever other sex I could get.
Now, as a counsellor-at-law? Same as above.
How much sex have you had? Hundreds of men have sucked me off and vice versa. I've fucked a couple of dozen guys. Only 5 or 6 have fucked me.
When you were a kid, did you let dirty old men in their 20s and 30s suck you off? No, but I sure would have enjoyed it. When I was 12 a black dude traveling with a carnival tried to lure me into his trailer. He said he'd give me a dollar if I'd take my pants down. I declined and have regretted it ever since.
In light of your marriage, the question arises, whether you were conscious of interest in men then, and married to resist it, or whether your interest in men didn't surface until later. I've been interested in men for as long as I can remember. I married because my girlfriend was pregnant; because I wanted to lead a normal life; because in the days when I was young there was tremendous social pressure for everyone to get married.

How many men have sucked your ass? How many assholes have you eaten? Not enough to satisfy me.
Please describe your ideal man. For sex, the ideal man is a boy — about 15, blond and blue-eyed, with a perpetual hard on and a tender, pink asshole.
Does it give you a hard on to undress in front of a mirror? No, but it did when I was a horny adolescent.
Do you wear Jockey shorts? Yes.
Do you sniff them when you take them off? I tried sniffing my shorts a few times after reading about it in S.T.H. Could never smell a thing.
Please describe your meat. It's uncut — for which I'm grateful. Average size. I wish it were bigger.
Please list the places where you've had sex. The U.S. Capitol Building; various campers and other vehicles; the Los Angeles National Forest; Union Station in Chicago; churches, tents, libraries, the University of Southern California; the Minnesota State Fair; a bowling alley in Las Vegas; lots of theatres and men's rooms.
Do you during an average day see many boys you want: Now that I'm getting older (40) I am getting more interested in teenage boys. I often see a healthy looking kid in tight jeans and think how nice it would be to eat out his ass. I'd also like to explain a few things about sex for him. Reassure him that it's all right to jack off. Everyone does it. And everyone knows you're doing it anyway.
Did you learn to jack off yourself or did another kid teach you? An older boy with an enormous cock taught me to jack off. The juicy details can be read in the enclosed issue of *GAYBOY*.
[EDITOR'S NOTE: GAYBOY, a Los Angeles publication, writes, "Anything written in GAYBOY may be copied with credit given to GAYBOY." The following article, written by the attorney who is the subject of this questionnaire, is reprinted from GAYBOY.

Dwayne and I had little in common. It was chance and not friendship that led us to sit next to each other in the Junior High School Chorus. After the first practice session, you would have had to pry us apart with a crowbar. At least as far as I was concerned. I was fascinated with Dwayne. More precisely, I was fascinated with the bulge in his blue jeans. We had to share our sheet music, and since Dwayne was big and uncouth, he held the music in *his* lap where he could see it, and not between us like polite seventh graders do . Dwayne was the biggest kid in the class. I was almost the smallest. Dwayne had flunked a grade somewhere along the way so he was older as well as bigger than anyone else. Dwayne and I sat in the back row, at one end, where we were reasonably safe from being noticed. If his cock was not hard at the beginning of practice, a few surreptitious rubs soon had it bulging in his pants. Now and then he'd make it jump. Or press down the cloth around it so it was clearly outlined. I stared — mesmerized — like a rabbit watching a snake.

Things got even more exciting after about a week. Dwayne was evidently feeling extra horny. While new sheet music was being passed out (Brother John's Air, as I recall), he growled at me, "Here, you hold the stupid music for awhile." He grabbed my left hand and placed it on top of his bulge. I looked around. We were unobserved. I cautiously squeezed. Dwayne grinned at me. He didn't look so fierce when he smiled. I squeezed again. It felt terrific. Lying in bed that night, I thought about Dwayne and his enormous cock. *I had to see it.* Very soon after, and very unexpectedly, I did get to see it.

We went out of town on a church outing. Dwayne and I slipped away during

a break and took a walk. In a conspiratorial tone, Dwayne said, "You want some extra chorus practice?" "What do you mean?" I knew what he meant. He looked around. The night was dark. No one in sight. "Come on," he said. We stepped off the sidewalk into a backyard and stood in the shadow of a large bush. "You wanna see it?" I was dying to see it. Dwayne unzipped his fly and wrestled his cock into the open. He put his hands on his hips, displaying it proudly. I was astonished. I didn't know a cock could be so large. I had never seen a hard, full-grown cock before. The size and beauty of it left me stunned. I was in some sort of trance. My blood seemed to burn. Dwayne could tell I admired it. "Go ahead," he said in a generous voice, "touch it." I touched it reverently. Wrapped a fist around it. It was so fat my fingers didn't meet my thumb. "Go ahead," he said. "Jack it." "What?" "Don't you know how to jack off yet?" He grabbed his cock in his large farmboy hand and began to stroke it. He pulled the foreskin back and forth. I had never seen anyone do that. "Hurry up," he said. "Let's see yours before we have to get back." My cock was so hard it felt brittle. I pulled it out of my Jockey shorts. The cool night air felt good on my inflamed cock. "Can you pull the skin back?" I shook my head. "It feels good. Come on, do it to me." I pumped his cock for him. The light from a street light gleamed on the head of his cock. A drop of moisture was caught in the slit at the end. The foreskin slipped back and forth like a well-oiled machine. I was struck by the beauty of it. Dwayne grabbed my dick in his rough hand. "What do you like?" he asked. I was too embarrassed to say anything. And perfectly content to just stand there pumping his cock. He tugged at the foreskin but it was too tight to retract. "Just do this," I said, gently stroking the underside of my stiff prick. "That's all you do when you play with your cock?" I nodded. Dwayne hunched over and began stuffing his monstrous cock into his pants. "Some day when we have more time, I'll show you how to jack off." "Yeh, what is it?" "Tell you later when we've got more time."

After that we talked about sex a lot but didn't do anything for a couple of weeks. At Dwayne's urging, I practiced pulling my foreskin back. Progress was slow. Dwayne kept me enthralled with stories of his sexual adventures. Even playing with other boys, he said, and fucking a girl. I wasn't sure I believed that, but I loved his graphic description and frequently asked him to tell me about it. Our next get together took place at a basketball game. The gym was packed but the rest of the school was deserted. We climbed to the top floor of the school and pulled out our dicks. The place was dark. I could feel Dwayne's cock, huge and warm, just the way I remembered it. He gave me directions. "Grab hold here. Now move it back and forth. Yeah, that's right, only you have to move your hand all the way down to the base of the cock before you start up again. A little faster." I could smell his groin. Not very pleasant but somehow exciting. After a few minutes my eyes adjusted to the dark and I could see his fabulous prick silhouetted against the light from the window. "O.K. Let me try yours. You get the skin back yet?" "A little bit. Not like yours." "Well, keep working on it." His fingers found my cock. He gently pulled the foreskin halfway back. "Ouch!" "Shit," he said. "How are you going to jack off if you can't pull your fuckin' skin back?" "Just do this," I said, stroking the underside of my cock. It gave me a tingly feeling. Dwayne pumped his own cock with one hand and titillated mine with the other. I could feel the excitement building up in me. Dwayne began to move my foreskin back and forth over the head of my prick. "You gotta get this thing loosened up. Shit, you'll never be able to jack off or fuck or anything 'til you do that."

Finds Russians Have Big Fat Cocks

SAN FRANCISCO — RE: your urgent request for information about Russian nookie. Language is no problem. Almost everyone we met spoke English in addition to the international language of the eyes and body english. Many young studs are available. Photos in American newspapers do not do the Russians justice. The average youth on the street is outstanding, very healthy looking. The military stuff is incredible. They are warm and responsive and are just as much into cocksucking as anybody else. Most Russians have big, fat uncut cocks — some with outstanding aroma. Moscow was the dullest place; the toilets near Red Square are smelly and active. Care is advisable; the police disapprove (although we met two cops who were brothers of the flesh). Pickups are in front of the Bolshoi Theater in Moscow. There are no very interesting "bars" in Moscow. The ploy is to "wait" for a bus in front of the Bolshoi. We were also amazed at two flamboyant queens on the Moscow subway who would have been right at home on Polk Street. The other big shocker is the number of beautiful studs who hold hands — quite a bit of this. Saw several sets of soldiers holding hands. The wildest places we experienced were in Southern Russia: Tbilisi and Baku. In Tbilisi, hordes of available teenagers crowd the sidewalks. They are easy to meet and touch. There is park action there. The people in Georgia do not necessarily think of themselves as Russians and are contemptuous of Moscow; they explained that the custom of boys holding hands (which is very common there) is discouraged by "the Russians." They will readily ask you what you like sexually. It's very available. Beautiful people. Mediterranean outlook. Baku, the Tulsa of Russia, has a bar in a hotel where boys dance together and meet. We were shocked when this started happening. Easy to meet boys there also. Men and boys are not just "trade" and no money is expected. They do, however, like souvenirs; they worship all things American and will do anything for Levis. The most common meeting place for Russians and Westerners is the "night bar" as it is called in big tourist hotels that Intourist makes you stay in. There is no nightlife in Russia so everyone just goes to the night bar and gets drunk and sometimes scores. (You can also meet Germans, Finns [delicious], Englishmen and, of course, other Californians in the night bar.) I met a 17-year-old Estonian in Leningrad. He was blond on blond, spoke broken English and explained that he and his two friends (one of whom bedded down with my traveling companion) were in Leningrad from Talin for a "drinking weekend." I let him know right away that I was interested in him physically by touching him (males touch much more and are much more affectionate in Russia than in uptight America) and telling him he was beautiful. We had lots of drinks and I suggested that we go to my room. He was anxious. We did lots of stand-up making out and kissing in the bathroom (he had to use it); I kept stroking his satin chest under his shirt and playing with his nipples. He was "resisting" wonderfully. I got his pants undone and discovered that he, like most Russians and Europeans, was wearing incredibly tacky underwear. It looked like a piece of a curtain in a Baptist parsonage. Anyway, that's not important. He had a fat uncut piece of meat. He was very responsive. I left the Soviet Union with no fear of them whatsoever. They were very friendly and are incredibly curious about Americans. The Russians just want the same things we do: Levis, cars, houses, their cocks and balls sucked. I believe that I relieved international tensions in my own way while I was in Russia through the international network of dick worshipers. It's the politicians and war lovers who fight.

Good and Bad Ass from the U.S. Air Force

TEXAS — When I was a graduate student at the state university, I had my share of hot students, but there was also a meat farm called the United States Air Force Base just outside of town. Early one Saturday morning, about 12:30 A.M., a trick from school called and said he and a friend were hot and he was wondering if I would let them come by for a little action. Of course, my quick reply was HELL YES come on over. I had been with Art many times since I first met him in the basement men's room of the old Geology Building, a popular spot for quickies, when he was a sophomore two years earlier. He had often brought friends by for a blow or a quick piece of ass and this time I assumed he had met another student at his frat house or in one of the many active johns on campus. Art was a muscular guy from Dallas, 6', 165 lbs., brunet, with a long, slim 7", uncut, always hard and ready. He was particularly fond of my long, hot, wet, gifted tongue when it was trying like hell to get up inside his asshole. He claimed I was the first guy he had ever fucked and he loved fucking my ass. His friend turned out to be a fly-boy from the Air Base, who he had met at a downtown bar which catered mostly to fly-boys. The fly-boy was an absolute doll, about 5'9", 160 lbs., with short blond hair, very well built and large muscular arms and, as I would find out later, the most beautiful muscular legs you could ever expect. Between his legs, a good 8" *thick* dick pointed straight out when he dropped his pants and climbed on the bed with Art and I. Art told the guy that my tongue was as well educated as my brain. He told me to "eat out my ass" so I could show what he meant. He layed me back on the bed, on my back, and climbed over my face. Spreading his ass cheeks, he sat down on my face, his asshole squarely over my mouth. I was in my element — FOR DAMN SURE. My nose was right above his asshole and what a lovely musty smell it had. I soon wet each and every one of the dark brown hairs around his hole, savoring the taste of sweet, fresh corn and a hint of the taste of raw potatoes, and perhaps a slight taste of sauerkraut. Ten minutes of my tongue up and around his asshole ended as Art lifted his ass off my face and it was immediately replaced with the beautiful blond ass of the fly-boy. Talk about heaven. A new set of smells and flavors. "Eat out my ass, queer," he said, "lick the shit off of it, you ass licker; get with it, queer ass." It all sounded so nasty and so good. He had more sweat in his ass than Art did, but completely different in taste. Definitely the taste and odor of Lifebuoy soap. After about five minutes he relaxed and I jammed all the tongue I could into his dank, peanut butter tasting asshole, until I had to come up for air as his big balls kept my nose covered. I was certain my tongue had hit his shit and I wiped my tongue against the botton bed sheet as I turned over to get off the bed when the fly-boy lifted his ass off my face. Art wanted to know if I was ready for a dick up my ass and one down my throat at the SAME TIME. I replied, "You got it" and climbed on the bed again on all fours, ass to the end and head to the top where Art had positioned himself, legs spread apart wide. I sniffed, licked and sucked on Art's cock while the fly-boy got his big, thick dick in my ass and pumped like hell. I shot my wad on the bed and then Art unloaded in my mouth. Art pulled out, went to the bathroom and the fly-boy continued to pound my ass for another five minutes, slowing down when he would get close to coming, but finally he shot his load deep inside my ass and gave out a loud holler as he collapsed on top of me, exhausted. I lay in my pool of cum, likewise exhausted. They got

dressed and I served them a cold beer and we talked awhile before they left.

I was awakened later with the fly-boy shaking my bed and then sitting down on it near my head. Another guy was with him, standing up behind him. I could not make out his face in the dimly-lit room, but I assumed it was Art and they must have come back for seconds; I had left my rear door unlocked, so they had simply walked in. But it wasn't Art, it was another fly-boy. The one who'd been here before with Art asked if they could spend the night because they had missed the last bus back to the base. I thought, "Shit, why not," and said (but I didn't mean it) I'm sorry I have only one bed, but they were welcome to share it with me. Soon I had my left and right hands full of hardening fly-boy dick. The new one was an Easterner (New Yorker) — very street-wise and hot. I loved his legs. They were very muscular. His voice was deep, with a Yankee accent I loved. He spoke with authority. Very black hair, dark skin (Italian I am sure), brown eyes and an extra thick 6½" cut dick. His dick was like a fat hunk of baloney and the head of it was large and like a polished glassey silk knob. I couldn't resist sliding down the bed to put my tongue and lips around that beauty. When I worked my way down to his balls I could smell that Lifebuoy soap again. He raised his leg up and with his hand pushed my head into the crack of his butt. Bingo, I was in heaven again, the third time in one night. He kept pushing my head into his ass without resistance from me, for sure. I heard him tell the other guy that he was sure right about the ass eating — this guy knows and enjoys what he is doing. His ass was spotlessly clean by the time he pulled away and he said he wanted it in my ass real bad. I gave him some KY to put on his dick and I put some on my ass and he climbed on top. When he first stuck his dick in my hole I thought I'd die, but that hurt turned to deep warm sensations and I pushed back as he pushed forward. About 25 to 30 strokes later he shot off and left it in until it softened and slipped out. While he was in the bathroom washing up, the other fly-boy moved over and pumped me for 10 more minutes and came inside my ass, pulled out and turned over and went to sleep. The other guy returned after about 15 minutes and wanted a bit to eat. After some ham and eggs, we retired to bed and I sucked him off twice before the sun came up. I finally fell asleep with my nose in his ass. This was the beginning of my Relief Station for the Air Base — most active for the next year and a half until I was forced to move because of just *one* greedy homophobic asshole who tried to shake me down one time too many. He was my favorite and had the sweetest asshole I ever feasted upon, but in the end he was truly a *real ASSHOLE.*

Airman's Ass Sweat Has "Macho" Taste

In my previous letter I wrote about Victor's first visit. He was a real sex machine, about 19 to 20, black hair, dark skinned. He was at his peak of sexuality and could not keep his 6½" prick down. He also enjoyed seeing other guys having sex and I would not exclude the possibility that he was to some degree "gay" himself but just didn't know it yet. I lost my right breast due to a tumor probably because of the abuse Vic made of it with his cigarettes and the biting on it he used to do. I did let him do it so it was my fault for not leaving his company sooner. I was so crazy about him I just couldn't break away until he scared me too much later on and I was forced to get away. Remember this was the early 50s — a real hard time for guys like me. We weren't called gays then, just dirty QUEERS.

I switched to Army tricks after Vic and used to travel to Temple near Fort Hood so that I would not run into Vic in Austin. Had lots of "dog meats" in those days including a German soldier training at Fort Hood one summer — nice fat sausage and its owner could not speak but one word of English — COCKSUCKER. He sure as hell found one. Vic was from Brooklyn, N.Y. Two nights after his visit he came by unannounced at 7 P.M. and wanted a quickie blow job before he was to meet his buddy at the popular downtown bar at 7:30. He was such a doll that I would have sucked his joint anytime he opened his fly. I was so turned on to him. He had such a beautiful deep voice and a teasing manner along with his cock-sure attitude (in command) and his Yankee accent fascinated me also. But he said that my accent turned him on to me also. I gave him a quickie, but before he shot off, he pulled his pants down to his ankles, turned around, bent over and stuck his ass in my face and whispered, "Eat out my asshole — you KNOW you want to. Tell me you do. Go ahead, tell me how much you want to eat out my asshole." I could only say, "I'd rather show you how much I love your asshole than to tell you how much I do." I pulled his cheeks wide apart and within a 15-second search with my tongue, found his pink puckered hole and began to rape it with my stiff long tongue as he moaned and groaned. The sweat was strong, salty, musty and tasted like raw Irish potatoes, so macho I could hardly keep my dick from popping out of my shorts. I stayed in his ass for 5 to 10 minutes while he played with his dick. Then he turned around and put his hands on my shoulders and squeezed with both hands as I put his hard dick into my mouth and sucked out his load in just a few deep thrusts, while he kept squeezing my shoulders harder and harder — so hard it hurt for three or four days afterwards. But at the time I didn't even notice it, I was so hot for him nothing would have gotten my attention from his squirting tool. He patted my ass as he prepared to leave and said he wanted to fuck me the next time. "You got a sweet ass baby and it belongs to me." What a line he had. He strutted out the door so masculine it made me feel like a girl. I was a GIRL alright — he made me one.

I didn't know he meant he wanted my ass just four hours later, but he did, and he wasn't alone. He brought two fly-boy buddies with him about midnight and a couple of six packs as well. His friends were OK in looks and bodies but nothing special but they were MALE and that's all I cared about and Air Force meat was one of my favorites at the time. Vic introduced his buddies to me and said they had to leave the bar because they quit selling drinks and they thought maybe they could finish up their six packs at my place and enjoy a little relaxation to boot. So we sat around the living room drinking beer and shooting the bull, with sex soon getting into the conversation. Vic told me to come into the kitchen with him — he wanted to show me something. He got a glass and pissed in it. He filled it up and got a second glass and almost filled it up also. He left his dick out while he handed me the full glass of piss and asked me if I had ever tasted piss from a real MAN. I said no and asked him why he wanted to know. He said just curious and poured both glasses out into the sink and grabbed ahold of his dick and told me to suck it. I asked him about his two buddies in the other room — they might walk in on us. He only replied, "So what, they know you're a cocksucker because I told them you were. Why do you think they came over with me for? Hell, they want to get sucked off just like I do." So I sucked his dick for about five minutes and he shot off a good load.

He went back into the living room and damned if he didn't tell one of the guys to go in the kitchen if he wanted to get a load off his balls. The guy he told

this to was about 21, 6'2", 180 lbs., and had sandy reddish hair — a few pimples on his light-skinned face but not too bad looking. He didn't say a word but ambled into the kitchen. Vic told me to go take care of him. The guy had his fly open and was playing with his dick by the time I got in the kitchen, so I got on my knees. I felt someone looking at me and turned around and there was Vic about 3 feet away. Vic began calling me a cocksucker, telling me to suck that dick dry, lick those sweaty balls, drink his load, etc. The guy just leaned back and said nothing but he was responding beautifully to my mouth and soon had his hands on my ears pulling my head into his groin, moaning as I sucked all the way down to his pubic hairs. I reached behind him and pulled his pants and underpants all the way down to his ankles and then ran my hand under his balls and into the crack of his ass. He had about 7" of dick and his asshole was surrounded with fine short hair. How I wanted to eat out that blondish-red hair covered asshole, but before I could even think much about it he shot off a good healthy load in my mouth. I almost gagged because I wasn't expecting his wad so quickly. He pulled up his pants and underwear and thanked me and went back into the living room. Vic told me he liked to watch me and that I was doing a good job — that guy loved every second of it. He asked me how the guy's load tasted, was it good, was it as good as his, did he give as much come, and all the time he was asking these questions he was playing with his dick. We went back into the living room and resumed drinking beer.

Eventually the third guy got up and went to the bathroom. He was pretty short, about 5'7", and weighed about 150 lbs., dark hair and cute little ass that filled out his jeans. My tongue really craved for his asshole, because I just knew it was virgin, to a tongue at least, and there is nothing I love better than to get at a cherry asshole with my tongue. After he stayed in the bath for about 5 minutes, Vic told me to go to the bath and "take care of him. He is shy and needs a little coaxing." When I got to the bath the door was partly opened and he was sitting on the stool with his pants down to the floor and his legs spread wide and he was jacking on his 6" dick. He nodded to me to come on in and I did and crawled between his legs and kissed the tip of his dick. I lifted up his balls and ran my tongue across both balls while he ran his fingers through my hair and then inserted his two index fingers into my ears. He pinched my ear lobes and kept running his index fingers into my ears in a fucking motion. Damn that made me hotter and hotter. His smallish dick was not too big around, uncut, and sure was a contrast to the two big fat dicks his buddies had. He had a full foreskin over his dick head. Even with a hard on, only a little of the head showed. I was anxious to search under that skin with my tongue and see if he might have a little cheese for me to taste, but as I ran my tongue under the skin and around the head of his dick, I was disappointed that it was soapy clean. He pulled away from my sucking in a few minutes and got off the seat and closed the bathroom door and leaned over the toilet seat, ass sticking out, and said, "Please lick my asshole — Vic said you did it to him." I said, "Sure I will, and I bet you like it." His asshole was as clean as his dick. He didn't have hardly any hairs around the hole and I got my tongue into him fast. He jumped forward as I stuffed my tongue into his shit-hole and I asked him what was wrong. He said it just tickled, that's all, but to go ahead, it feels great. I got back to it right away and for 5 minutes really licked his asshole good. Then he turned around and stuck his hard dick into my mouth and shot a good load. He patted me on my head and thanked me very much — it was the greatest he had

ever had, girl or man.

It was now past 1 A.M. and after I drove them out to the air base, I returned to my place and had a good jack off thinking of those great fly boys. In the course of a year and a half, Vic and I slept together quite frequently. We had quickies, all night stands, doubles, triples and even had seven of us at a swimming party on Lake Travis one weekend. The last night I spent with Vic was the worst. By now I was afraid of him. He was much too sadistic to have around for long and he was getting worse. One night he made me drink his piss after he had me tied up on the bed. He also would burn my nipples with his cigarette, burn my back as he fucked me, burn my balls and once he even stuck his cigarette to my asshole and fucked it raw. I had to move twice to get rid of him. He would get drunk when he did these things to me but when he was sober he was great. I had to ask some of his friends to leave sometimes because I was afraid they would take part in the sadistic ways he had. I was also afraid I would get kicked out of my apartment if all the noise didn't stop.

I moved in with a gay friend and never saw Vic again. About two years later I was in San Antonio in a bar when I recognized a guy I thought I knew, but I could not remember where. It turned out he was the second airman that Vic had brought over that night, the one I had in the bathroom, and he told me that Vic had been dishonorably discharged for attempted murder of a fellow airman under mysterious circumstances (which I could well imagine). We shacked up that night in the Alamo hotel and we talked about our first meeting back in Austin. This time I must have sucked his ass for three hours. He dearly loved my tongue in his ass. I finally went to sleep with my nose in the crack of his ass and for the time being, I was in heaven.

He Loves to Watch Me Swallow It

TORONTO — Gotta tell you about this thing that happened to me a couple of weeks ago. I was in this can in the basement of a bar. The stalls don't have any doors so when I went in to take a leak I saw this really hunky looking guy sitting on the can. He looked up at me while I took a piss and he seemed fairly interested. I started to play with my cock so he could tell that I was. He leaned back and showed me his dick. It was a real big one so all I could get was the head and a bit more in my mouth. In a couple of minutes he began shooting a heavy load. I swallowed it twice and he was still unloading more. I held his dick in my mouth even after he was through. He said he had something else to give me if I wanted to keep my head there. His cock jerked a bit and he let go a real hot stream of beer piss. He gave me one last squirt and pulled his fat piece of meat back in his pants. He was in his late '20s. He said that watching me drink his piss was a real turn on and if I wanted to follow him back to his place he'd like to drink some more beer and watch me drink his piss again. I liked what he wanted to do so I followed him back. As soon as we got there he grabbed a beer and gulped it down fast. He opened another one and sat down, spreading his legs and opening his fly. He pulled out his meat and told me to suck it. He stood up and told me to follow him to the basement. I got down on my knees and he started to piss all over my face and in my mouth. It was weak piss but nice and hot. He finally ended up fucking me over a trunk in the basement and pissing up my ass.

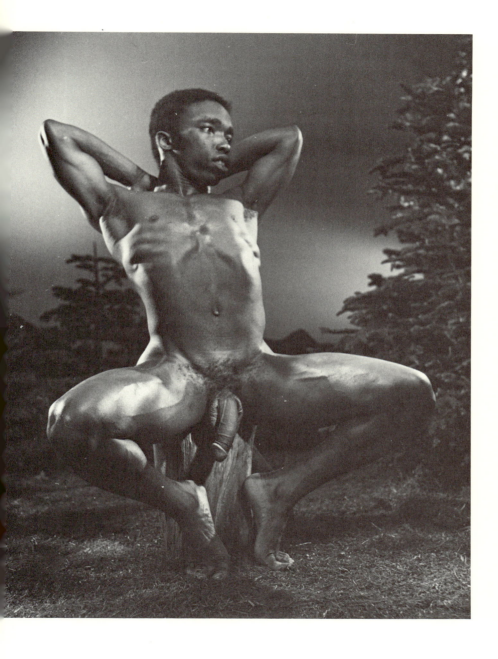

Review: Summers Cox and Some Hasn't

Sir Noel, I see by Cole Lesley's *Remembered Laughter* ($12.95; Alfred A. Knopf), picked his nose habitually, liked snakes, farted so loudly Lynn Fontanne cried "Bravo," and was more candid than most about fondness for watching operations (or as doctors call them, Surgical Procedures). Over cocktails in Bermuda — or was it the Bahamas? — he told "a well-known American actress," to her horror, that her doc had let him watch the excision of her ovaries. There is precious little in this biography of Noel Coward (1899-1973) about another of his interests, homosexuality. One could deduce, from his opinion that anal sex is a pain, that Sir Noel was a Cocksucker, bearing in mind that some homosexuals, but not so many homosexuals as heterosexuals, don't care to go so far as to actually *have* sex. It is at least possible, since he had no money at the time, that he gave something else to the New York cop who caught him bareass at the window — something that pacified the cop to the point where he even insisted that Coward borrow his gun. It is more than possible, given their difference in station, that his "intimate" acquaintance with a Coldstream Guard included acquaintance with the very part the Guardsman used to sire the offspring for whom Coward "stood godfather" — especially when one considers that a classmate of mine had as ushers at his wedding some of the students who had sucked him off. Coward had "a lifelong love-affair with...the Royal Navy," despite the fact that their pants were not as tight as they might be, but there is no evidence in this look that mere love of the sailors progressed to sex with them. Perhpas such things are best left unsaid, but I doubt it very much. "Noel," Lady Castlerosse said as they prepared for a gala aboard Admiral Pound's flagship, "I have a dreadful feeling we've asked too many queer people." COWARD: "If we take care of the pansies the Pounds will take care of themselves." Coward's was a racy, if not necessarily sexy, world. "Who shall I make it payable to?" he once asked. The cashier said, "Summers Cox." "And some hasn't," added Coward's inspired companion, Gladys. At the Palace (theatre), one star said of another's pregnancy, "What a silly girl...In the mouth or up the arse yes, but fancy letting him put it in *there*." Addressing rumors that she was a Lez, Tallulah insisted "she *always* thought about a man when playing with herself." But I thought everyone did, most especially high school boys who murder homosexuals to prove they aren't. Marlene Dietrich was "fairly tiresome...grumbling about some bad press notices and being lonely." Like any ordinary man, Coward complained about the vanity of women, and said to Eva Gabor when she turned up in orange chiffon: "You're not going to wear it you know...If you wear that nobody's going to look at *me*." Backstage, he "slowly poured water from a teapot into a tin can," so that it sounded like "piddling into a chamberpot" to the actresses trying to get through a scene onstage. He asked our greatest playwright, Mae West, what her new show was about. "Wal, y'see, it's about this guy. He's a cocksucker." Coward "had never heard a plot begin with so much promise." Lauren Bacall called Hedda Hopper "a lousy bitch"; worse, Hedda's hat was so big Cole Lesley had to bend its brim so that she could get into the shit-house (or "loo," as Lesley calls it). She emerged more whiteassed than ever; the pot had just been painted. Humphrey Bogart, always the perfect host, told Clifton Webb, "Bring your fucking mother and she can wipe up her own sick." Although his mother was "well over 90 and gaga" when she died, Webb's

prolonged mourning inspired Coward to say, "It must be tough to be orphaned at 71." An inspection of his Paris flat after it was reclaimed from some Nazi roommates in World War II turned up some remarkable stains on the bed, notably on the brown satin headboard which, if my deductions are correct, are a remarkable commentary on the acrobatic agility of the occupants." Efforts to sneak a snapshot of Claudette Colbert's wrong side were unsuccessful and inevitably in a work of this length, there is a clergyman caught "having himself a lovely time" in scanties filched from one of the women houseguests. Coward's own religion was more Christian than the professional Christers, at least as Lesley describes it when he writes of "gentle Jesus, whose teaching Noel admired (and obeyed without consciously doing so) while forever deploring the sins followers had committed for nearly 2,000 years in his name." If the Heaven these people are always talking about exists, we are more likely to run into Sir Noel there than into such hardened old hacks as Billy Graham, Cardinal Cooke and Anita Bryant, who have perverted Christianity into support of "fag"-baiting, football, war and other S/M sports.

— Boyd McDonald

Boys Are Into Jockey Shorts Again

SAN FRANCISCO — It was raining lightly when we left the theatre, so the windows of my Fiesta were fogged. And it was near but not too near a street light. And the seats are upholstered in cloth, not vinyl (cold!), and recline. I thought there and then was as good a place and time as any But J. wanted to drive around for awhile and warm up the interior. We finally parked in another lot of the same mall. His legs are ever so slighly bowed. That has always been a turn on for me. He's beardless and his torso is hairless. His cock is cut, short, very thick. We started out giving each other a hand job from the 69 position, but I very quickly plugged in. He immediately started thrusting his pelvis toward me. One, two, three, and he came, a bland and youthfully abundant wad of cum. He didn't give head but his hand job was pleasurable. A couple passed by arguing about whose purchase was a bigger waste, her boots or his jogging drag (she actually called it that). J. had a cigarette. I thought about how glad I am that I quit, of the subtler range of cock flavors I've discovered since and that smokers aren't even aware of. I wonder if the American Cancer Society would consider that for a theme for their next anti-smoking campaign—"You're Not Getting the Flavor Out of the Cock You Suck!" J. was frisky and deeply interested in being sucked again. Hasn't been sucked since he was a freshman, when he and a friend blew each other. He threw up. His friend threw up. They never tried again. But he did try with several girls. They all refused him but one; she, however, expected head in return. Called him a pig when he said no. He has "always" believed that, with his fat cock, he had something to offer cocksuckers. With complete sincerity, I told him that he had a delicious piece of meat. I could've had him a third time (he was in no hurry to put on his jeans and Jockey shorts), but since we'd arranged to meet again next weekend I decided it would be better not to. That dangle between his legs is hauntingly succulent.

His Underpants Smell Good, Marine Reports

[EDITOR's NOTE: My nose for news sensed a story even before I opened the first letter this Marine sent; under his return address on the envelope he wrote, "Height 6'1". If adorable creatures want their height, or anything else, admired, it is mean not to. I suppose before long they'll be putting their dick size on envelopes, for the benefit of those who can't wait until they open the letter to find it. Here is an excerpt from the youth's first letter, followed by some of the intimate data he divulged in a mail-order interview.]

Are you hard-assed? — that is, do you have a firm butt? Yes.
Are you satisfied with the shape of your butt, as you view it in mirrors? Yes.
Is your butt small, full-sized, or large? Full-sized.
How much hair do you have in the crack of your butt and around your asshole? A small amount.
What colour is it? Black.
Do you like having your asshole licked: Not really.
Have men ever paid you any compliments about your butt? A few at a Gay Bar.
How much hair do you have above your prick? Very little.
What colour is it? Black.
Do you have hairs on you legs, chest and belly? Legs but no hair on chest or belly.
Are your nipples the same shade of pink as your asshole? My Nipples are Pink but I never looked at my asshole to see what color it is.
Do you like to have men suck on your nipples? Sometimes.
Do you like to have men suck on your dick? Definitely. Yes.
Do you like a complete tongue-bath? No. Frenching & my nipples are my extent.
Can you describe a few of the best blow jobs you've had? Too many to sit & write about at this time.
How old were you when you got your first blow job? Fifteen.
Who gave it to you? My Best Buddy.
What colour is your dick? Its white like me.
How big is it? 8 to 8½.
How does it perform? It performs quite well.
Do you like to display your dick at urinals, and so forth? Not really. I am not an exhibitionist.
Do men often make passes at you? Most men are afraid of me being Butch they think I am a cop instead of a Marine. But at Gay Bars they stair & sometimes lick their lips.
Do you get a hard on when a man stares at your dick? It depends on the mood I am in & who he is.
What kind of underpants do you wear: White Boxer Shorts & sometimes Jockey Shorts & jock strap.
Do your underpants smell good? You bet.
Do you like to look at yourself in the mirror? Sometimes.
Bareass? Sometimes.
What position? Standing.

Do you like having your balls licked? Yes.
Do you smell the armpits of your shirt when you take it off: No.
How many times a day did you jack off when you were a teenager? Three times a day.
How often do you jack off now: Once or twice a week. Looking in *Playboy*.
Where do you jack off: Bed.
Do you strip bareass? Yes.
What position do you jack off in? Lying.
Do you like to pose in the mirror? Sometimes in my Jock strap.
Does the Marine Corps issue jock straps? Yes.
When do you wear them in the Marine Corps? All the time, especially working out. P.T.
What kind of underpants do most of the other Marines wear: Jockey Shorts.
Do more men make passes at you when you're wearing civilian clothes: No. There afraid I might jump them.
Did you have any sex in Vietnam? I did it in a fox hole. A little muddy & wet & dirty area but it was well worth it.
Was there any sex or jacking off at Paris Island: No.
Did you enjoy seeing and living with a large collection of handsome young men at Parris Island? I wasn't thinking about it. Just surviving.
Was there much talk about "fags"? No.
Why did you join the Marines: To avoid going to jail.
Were you able to do all of the things required, such as the obstacle course? Yes.
Was it difficult to take the harsh treatment of the DI's? Sure, but I did.
Do most of the Marines exaggerate their masculinity in order to show they're not "gay"? Some do.

Any you wanted but were afraid to seduce? Sure. All of them.
Do the Marines sleep in underpants? Yes.
Is it fun to watch them undress, shower and so forth? Lets say I was aware of it but very careful about checking them out.
Do you have much fear that the Marine Corps will find out about your sex life? Sometimes I think about it, but I really don't have any fears about it.
What would they do if they found out: Throw me out on a U.D.
Do you prefer long hair to the Marine cut? I had long hair but I got used to it being short now.
What kind of work have you done in the Marines? M.P. G-2 Intelligence clerk. Motor T.

Have you met any "gays" in the Marines? I met some bi's.
Have you ever hustled? I've never rented my meat out, but had many opportunities to.
Is there much sex talk in the barracks? Sure — Girls only.
Do you remember any especially handsome or interesting Marines you lived with or saw in the showers? Sure.

How do you look? Good, Fine, Athletic.
Is there any physical quality you wish you could have? Not really.
Do you wish you were a foot taller? No.
Do you wish you were blond? No.
Do you wish your dick was twice as big, or are you satisfied with it? I am satisfied.

What kinds of sex do you like? Bi-Sexual. I dig on doing it with another Bi Couple who are young, or Bi-Male or Bi-Female.
Do you like to fuck men in the ass? Yes.
Do you have a virgin asshole? I'll never tell!
What kind of women do you like? Young tender Blondes with good build & big bust.
What is your weight? 165 solid pounds.
What was your job in Vietnam? Machine Gunner (Grunt).
Did you ever go to a whorehouse with other Marines? Sure did, not in Nam though.
How often do you change your underpants? I change every 2 days.
Have you ever sucked dick? I'll write some separate letters about that.
Was there much horseplay in the barracks and showers, showing their dicks off, kidding each other about being queer, and so forth? Yes.
Are most Marines show-offs? Some are and some aren't.
Do you think the Marine corps, with its reputation for tough guys, attracts a lot of young men who are trying to fight homosexuality, or to conceal it? I'd say yes.
What did most of the Marines among your circle of friends do on leave? Did you do it with them? Or did you leave them to have homosexual sex? Fuck, I'll never tell.
Where have you gone in the past, and where do you go now, for sex? Baths, Parks, Sex, it comes to me now.
What was your high school sex experience? That's a long story. But H.S. Sex was in.
Would you like to get married and have children? At a later time. I'm having too much sex & fun now to get tied down.
Do you respect your superior officers in the Corps? Most of them I give the finger to after they turn around. I do respect all my superior officers even though I don't like all them.
Do you respect your fellow Marines? My fellow Marines yes.
About how many men have you had sex with? I lost track.
What kind of men were they? About 6 different Marines, Navy & Airmen; young men.
What kind of sex? 69 etc.
What is the most exciting sex you've ever had? Having had a Blow Job from my best friend.
What is the ideal sex you would like? A young Bi Sexual Blond Marine — Male or female.

Youth Has "Unbelievable" Underpants, Cop Tells *Times*

A New York City detective, depicted the underpants of a teenage robber named Kenny as "unbelievable," according to an article in *The New York Times*. Police, the paper says, did a strip search of the youth after he was arrested at age "15 or 16." "Kenny stripped to his underpants," the paper quotes the cop as saying, "and they were unbelievable — just black, the color of charcoal. I mean, his mother hadn't washed those pants in months."

Great American Toilets

[A report on a public toilet in a Massachusetts police station. As we left our hero last time, he was talking about a peep hole in one of the shit booths that gave a view of the urinals.]

Sometimes two guys would flash their cocks at each other and then have a jack-off session at adjoining urinals. Other guys, aware of the peephole, liked to stand at a urinal nearby and jerk their cocks into erection purely for exhibitionism.

There was one older fellow with a truly magnificent prick who would give me an eyeful but wouldn't come in my booth: I never got my lips around that beautiful jumbo. Some of the younger guys, too, would do the jack-off bit at the urinal before approaching my booth for sucking.

If my wife wasn't waiting for me, I took time to really enjoy the place. One day I looked in a booth and saw a beautiful blackhaired guy of about 19, sitting there slowly jerking off. When he saw me he dropped his wang and held the door closed. I kept making the rounds, but kept coming back to him. I finally figured that all he wanted to do was watch: he kept turning away all new comers.

There was one husky stud who'd been waving his wang in my direction. Soon I was on my knees tasting his pecker, which was nice, but not nearly as nice as the one in the booth. I took care that the black-haired kid in the booth could see everything as I sucked the stud, who turned out to be a little rough for my tastes. He liked to jam his dick into my mouth and fuck my face like I was a sheep. But I contented myself thinking of the black-haired guy watching through the peephole. A couple of minutes after the guy unloaded in my mouth, the john in the booth flushed and the black-haired guy came out — apparently satisfied. If that was as close as I could come to having sex with him — sucking another cock while he watched and jacked off — well, it was better than nothing.

There was one slightly over-weight but muscular guy in faded jeans and a wedding band who often came in on Saturdays for a quick blow job. He always asked first if I had a place to go (since I'm married too, the answer was always no), then let me suck on his dick. He had a great cock — silky and big — and a particularly big, sweet load of cum.

There was one elderly man who walked with a cane who but who gave a superb blow jobs once he took his teeth out.

There was a rather dissipated looking blond in his early 20s. He exuded a sense of raunchy sex. The first time I sucked on his cock he just walked away from a group of buddies he was with and came over and rubbed his groin in front of my booth. I let him in and went to town on it. His prick was almost too big for comfort but tasted great. He took quite a while before unloading but finally gave me a very nice wad, patted me on the shoulder, smiled, zipped up, and went back to pick up the conversation as though nothing had happened. I saw him many times after that. He needed to show himself off first at the urinals in order to get horny. Once hot he was happy to come in my booth for a repeat performance. He sucked on my dick a couple of times.

Once he stood outside my booth for a long time, waving his dong around. Finally he came and stood right outside my door slowly jerking his prick while I did likewise. Finally he came in and I began sucking on it. He took my hand

and put it on his butt. I worked a finger up his asshole and discovered he had greased it. He obviously enjoyed my finger up his hole and pulled his cock out of my mouth and jerked it as though he wanted to shoot off in my face. But suddenly he turned around and sat down on my prick. It was a wild ride and though I'm not really an asshole man I loved it.

 I went there again today. I went down on a guy with whom I'd had a couple of grope sessions. A tall black guy came and watched. Afterward the black had his hand in his pocket, rubbing his cock, which was large but not unmanageable. We went into a booth and he let me suck on it. He had on jeans with a soft, worn feel. His thighs and butt felt great through them but I didn't get much chance to enjoy them because he shot quickly — right down my throat so I didn't get much of a chance to savor its taste.

"My Wife Thinks It's Cunt I Chase"

ILLINOIS — Last July I took two of my boys fishing and we were on our way home when I decided to stop at a country-side tavern. The only other customer was a middle-age guy dressed just in walking shorts and sneakers. He was on the skinny side, balding, and wore horn rim glasses.

 I ordered a beer and some pop for the boys. The bartender was glued to the TV watching a baseball game, I noticed the guy in shorts looking at me via the mirror. I began to wonder if I could fuck him and with that idea came a hot hard on all trussed up in my shorts.

 I got up off the stool and walked down where he was standing up against the bar. I got behind him and on the pretense of reaching for bags of potato chips rammed my cock up against his ass so he could feel how hard it was. His response was pushing back and working his ass against my fat groin. For a few seconds we stood rubbing against each other. I brought the potato chips to my kids and they saw I had a hard on and a knowing glance passed between them. I discovered when I turned to go back to my hot-assed friend that he had moved to the end of the bar so that all you could see was his torso. The bar blocked the rest of his body from view. When I got down by him I found he had dropped his walking shorts. All he had on was a jock strap. I ran a hand over his smooth ass. As I played with his ass he undid my fly and reached in for some cock. There we stood, me rubbing his butt and he squeezing on my hard cock.

 "Aren't you afraid the bartender will raise hell?" I said in a low voice. "Old Al? It would take an earthquake to jar him away from the boob tube," Hot Ass replied. I worked a finger in the crack of his ass. That hidden notch was greasy, he came prepared. I finger fucked him. He managed to free my cock out of my briefs and hand-stroke it. He bent down and took about six good sucks on my prick and I was about ready to rape the bastard on the spot the way he goaded my dick with suction: But something had to be done to keep my boys occupied so I zipped up my fly and went over to them and gave them quite a bit of silver so they could play the bowling game and order more pop. When I turned to go back to the end of the bar Hot Ass was not there. For a minute I thought he had chickened out after making a fool out of me or that the bigness of my prick scared him off. But I found him in the men's room. He had his walking shorts off but still wore his jock strap. He was greasing his asshole with KY. The door had an old-time eye-and-hook lock so we were safe. I dropped my pants and

briefs and had Hot Ass suck my balls and dick. Then I had him bend over low enough so his hole was at the right angle. He put his hands against the wall to brace himself. The only time he complained was when the head of my prick first penetrated and opened up his asshole. After a few strokes he was with it. He pushed his butt against me, taking all my cock up his hot asshole. As I fucked he put his ass in slow rotating motion. What a sweet motherfucking fuck. His tight asshole was made for overheated pricks like mine. I put my hands on his hips and reamed away with full-length strokes. After 10-15 minutes I popped a load that brought me right up on my toes. The sweat was rolling off both of us. We swapped a few kisses afterward. He gave me a compliment: "Your wife don't know how lucky she is." Hell, if anyone should be complimented it should be his hot asshole, for he put my cock through so many changes I get hard just thinking about it. When I hustled the two boys away from their game and out the door Hot Ass called out, "Hope you'll come back." I answered, "If you'll be here, I will." Outside my youngest said, "Pa, you got a spot on your pants." My cock was still dribbling jass. Just piss, I told him. Will I go back? Your goddam right I will. I will have to take the two boys as my wife thinks it's cunt I chase.

The Beauties of Oregon

OREGON — The Oregon men (and boys) are entirely different breeds from the rest of the States. Most Oregon guys are hiding out in their snow closets, where they are bounded & secured by historical inhibitions left to them by their predecessors years ago. However, under the right (and sometimes not-so-right) circumstances they can be coaxed to do nearly everything you never expected. I've found if you can approach an Oregon male half-way intelligently with conversation about local government, sports and conversation, well then you're practically between their legs (either end — or both ends). Off comes the Pendleton shirt, the muddy Levis, the construction boots, the snow socks, the fur-lined jacket — and the long Johns. Some even *kiss* you a lot. When I have time I'll send you some really trashy stories. However, for now, here's one about our local soccer star (via Great Britain), whom I fucked while both of us were standing up at the rather staid bar of the historic Benson Hotel in Portland. After we'd had a few martinis (I was in the midst of interviewing him) he said suddenly off-handedly — that he'd split the seat of his pants that afternoon & was there anything I could suggest? Naturally, I suggested I locate the slit first off, which I did with my middle finger, finding two of them — one of clothing, one of hot flesh, which had already been greased up with what felt and smelled like Crisco. I lifted his suit coat, and taking out my cock, which was hard as hell by now, pushed it slowly up his hole. This was at the farthest end of the dark bar. There were other customers, but not too many. In only a couple of minutes, I shot my load into the tightest fucking asshole I've ever harpooned. Nobody was the wiser, not even the bartender. Since then I've jacked him off 'til he shoots his cum all over his hard, muscled stomach & the black bush around his thick, uncircumcised joint. Right away I'm down there, licking all that creamy, almond-flavored cum off his body until there's nothing left but the wet, shiny surface of his skin. His fans & I devour his performances — they on the court, me in the sack.

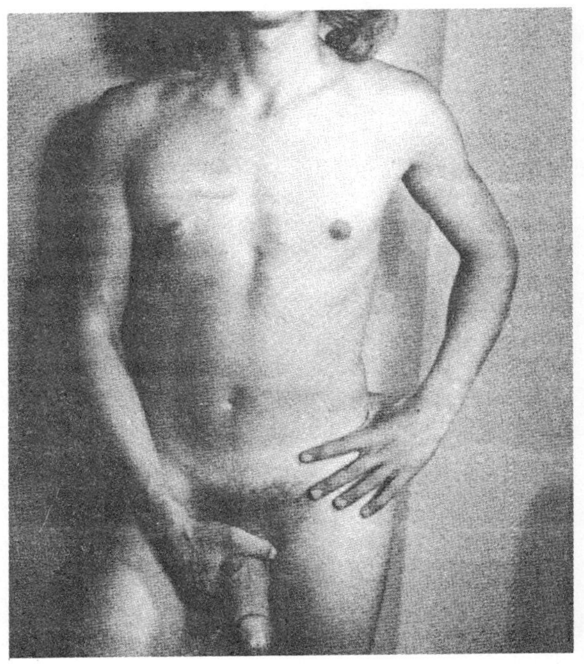

Do You Want This?

LONG ISLAND — I'd estimate that my experiences are about 70% with young men and 30% over the age of 25. I think the age percentages are due more to availability of younger guys than older ones; my preference is for men I know and like, not for age. I am very much out of the closet at home, work and school. I have a son 12½ and a daughter, aged 9. I am 41, 6'2½", a trifle overweight. I was told I looked 23 at work last night. I usually jerk off about once a day, usually just before I go to sleep. I vividly recall the first time I seduced a neighbor boy who was already able to cum and I was 5½ or 6. I am rarely depressed since I came out of my closet and accepted myself as I am, not as others want me to be. (That was at age 33 or so.) I'm occasionally functional with a female but with strictly gay preferences. I have read *Penthouse* and *Forum* for years and initially found them to be the first mention in an open magazine (from the newsstand) of homosexuality in a positive manner. I am married, something I did while still trying to be straight. It took me six years after marriage before I finally (consciously) accepted my gayness. By the time we had two delightful children. I nearly cracked when the initial conscious thought of being gay entered my mind and I realized what I had done and where I was at in life.

I've had sex with four sets of brothers. I'll use fictitious names. The first set

was Mario and his brother Tony. Mario was the first one I had sex with, and is now 28. We are still good friends, but not involved sexually. Tony is now 25 and an acquaintance, who is married with a year-old son. We have drifted apart though he comes by occasionally to chat. Tony was the only one who stuck by me when I was cracking up, and at his young age, I find that nothing short of a miracle. It was one of my best experiences when we fucked for hours on the living room floor.

Another set is Billy and his brother Joey. Billy was my first "lover," though he is now straight. The relationship was mutual in *all* ways, physically and emotionally. He is 26 and engaged to a lovely girl. We rarely see each other but do get together for dinner and a chat now and then. Joey is now 22. He had the biggest cock I've *ever* had. Sexual relationship only. Now married with an infant daughter, I'm told.

Then there is John, now about 30, whom I haven't seen in years, and his brother Sean, now about 24, I see him occasionally. He was a soccer star in H.S. & college before he messed up his knee. His beautiful athletic body is now going to fat.

Finally there are Wayne and his brother David, whom I know now. David is a rather boisterous kid, nice when alone but an obnoxious showoff when around his peers. He is a tough-acting, hard-fighting dude who can be as sweet as an angel when he is in a "non threatening" environment (where he has no pressure to "prove" himself). He comes from a lower class family of five kids. He is good at anything that uses his hands, particularly bike & engine repair. He has little interest in athletics other than pick-up street ball games or an occasional game of catch.

The first time we had sex he was at my house as a "hired hand" helping me clean out my attic. It was a hot July afternoon, hotter in the attic, so we could stand about 20 minutes of work and then adjourned to the living room for sodas & rest. He noted my stack of *Penthouses* and *Forums*, popping a raging erection over the nude females. He already knew of my interest in things "gay" from having seen my gay papers & books and previous visits, though he never looked at them. I noticed his erection through his dungarees, a rather long and very noticeable shape lying upward at an angle across his hip. Having just shared a joint with him, my fences were down and I decided "now or never." So I set his soda down on the table next to the chair he was sitting in and, very gently, grabbed the lump in his pants, saying, "That looks good. Is that for me?" HE was surprised and negative in his *verbal* response BUT slid down in the chair and moved the magazine he was reading to give me a better "shot" at him. His *voice* said "no" but his body language said "YES" very loudly. Since I prefer to let my sex partners make their own decision to participate without too much pressure from me, I went to the other chair to read. After a few moments he moved to the sofa and stretched out still reading *Penthouse*, and with a bigger erection showing. He kept looking at me and rubbing his bulge. I may be slow, but THAT slow I am not. I pulled the drapes, locked the doors, knelt or sat at the edge of the sofa and pressed my "attack." I rubbed the hard-on through his pants for a few strokes and then started opening his belt. He said "don't do that" but helped me get his belt open, pulled his zipper down and lifted his butt so I could slip his dungarees over his ass. His hard on was now really raging and pushing his clean white Jockey shorts *way* out from his hip. He was still saying "don't do that" but helped me pull the elastic down revealing about 7" of beautiful thick cock with a small patch of very light fine hair at its

base. David's body is very slender but also exceptionally well muscled and *very* well defined. His hair is dirty blond. He has nearly bald balls. I started in gently licking his cock-head and he spread his legs, giving me more room to "work." I lost myself in the moment and just enjoyed giving him the best head I knew how. He was so hot he unloaded his sweet cum in a violent, leg-shaking, belly-tightening, loud-mouthed orgasm in less than 10 minutes. Delicious. I enjoyed playing with his balls and rubbing his belly and chest. I complimented him on the beauty of his cock & body and thanked him for sharing them with me. His comment, as he pulled up his pants, was one word, "disgusting." But he sat down and we wrapped about other things awhile, and, as he left, he paused at the door, smiled and said, "Thanks."

Wayne, David's older brother, has been coming over for coffee and conversation for several years. He has a problem with controlling his behavior when he gets a beer in him, or for that matter, anything that alters his mind, and has been in trouble with almost any authority figures around him. He has disappeared, probably to an "upstate" school (we used to call them reform schools). Over the past few years he had several times asked me outright if I were a "homo" and I answered him, "yes." At first he dropped the subject and made much of his sexcapades with almost any girl who came in mind. After a while he started throwing in questions about what gays did in bed, what our life was like, etc. He is an awfully likeable young man. I made no pass at him. One day late in the winter, he was helping me start seeds for my spring planting. We were working in my attic for over an hour setting up the grow-lites and had a running conversation going about my sex life when I was his age. He was comparing his with mine, and as I turned to see a lovely, hard 7" clipped cock, dungarees open and thumbs hooked in the elastic of his Jockey shorts, holding them down under his cock and balls. Being ready for such situations, I opened my mouth and sucked him in to the hilt. He was so hot he came within seconds. Much too quick, but it tasted great. Unlike his brother's, Wayne's cum was rather spicy and thicker; different but also delicious. At first Wayne was very guilty about having been sucked off by another guy, or at least he tried to give me that impression. A few weeks later he was back and ready for more.

Reader, 22, Gets Ass Licked, Sniffed in All Positions

WISCONSIN — When I was 22, I met a man in his thirties in a park near my apartment. After we returned to my apartment and did some cocksucking, he had me lie on my stomach. He began rubbing my lower back and thighs. Gradually his attentions concentrated on my ass. He said he loved asses and continued the massage. He pulled my cheeks apart. Suddenly his tongue was on my asshole. I was surprised, but I loved it. He had me up on all fours, standing bending over, sitting on his face, etc. For five hours he kept me in positions so my asshole was available to him to sniff and lick. I loved the feeling and it sure kept me horny. When I asked him for his name, as he was about to leave, he said he couldn't give it because he was a priest. Unfortunately I never saw him again nor found so dedicated a replacement.

Cocksucking in Contemporary Culture
"Smooth Round & Responsive"

MAINE — I sometimes talk to my sex partners in the rest stops. Usually with the real good ones, a conversation which begins with a compliment and a thanks from me. 95% of the guys are very much still in the closet (& that includes me), so play only at night & in semi-obscurity. But oh, the vigor & intensity! Much more fun than the jaded old pros, I've discovered. I have just 2 *years* now of real action. Played some through adolescence, but limited to co-jerk offs & hugging. No sucking, no fucking. Got married, raised a family, now grown, & finally gave in and did it. Wow — what a joy. Have a lot of catching up to do. Still haven't fucked or been fucked, for example. Tried both under rest-stop conditions, but without success (enjoyment). Am enclosing an essay. It is true. The setting: a partially-wooded section of a Highway Rest Stop in Northern Maine, on a summer night. Several men, including me, were cruising/lurking in the semi-darkness. In one of the more open areas, I could just make out the profile of two men standing close together, front to back; the taller of the two was standing in the rear. Both were fully clothed and the big guy was feeling all over the chest, belly & groin of the shorter guy. Soon both dropped their pants all the way down. The tall guy, who was really a lot taller than his partner, was grinding his hips against the other's butt, and I caught brief glimpses of a big pole poking between the short guy's ass-cheeks & legs. The tall guy was 40-ish, lean, rangy build with short blond hair, tanned face, outdoors look, sort of a deputy sheriff type. The short guy was in his mid-20s, studious type with glasses. He was standing on a mound of earth or a big rock. He was *really* short — almost a midget. He finally acknowledged my watching by gesturing me to come join in. I was very grateful. I stepped up close & could see that he had a dandy full-size cock standing straight out, nice & hard. I took it in hand & worked it gently, then kneeled down (*way* down, that is) and took it in my mouth. It was smooth, round, and responsive — a real good one to suck. My hands ran all over his smooth thighs, belly, and tight balls. As my fingers travelled up under his balls, past his perineum, I felt the slippery underside of the big guy's hard cock moving in and out of the little guy's asshole. I stayed my hand there and enjoyed the feeling, whilst I increased my own sucking efforts. It really was a great situation. Everyone was *enjoying*. Soon I could hear moans coming from the big guy. He clasped his partner real tight and thrust up into guts to unload. I could feel the pumping spasms travel up the big guy's cock. It was great. Then the tall guy bestowed many kisses on the little guy's neck & ears & slowly pulled out and walked away. The short guy still stood there, and I still sucked on his cock. Again I cupped his balls with one hand and with the other explored his asshole. I felt the ooze of semen starting to come out. I stuck my finger in a little way and found that it was warm and nicely yielding in there. I was now eager to move around back and take up where the tall guy had left off, but the short guy had evidently had enough. He gently pushed me away, pulled up his pants, and moved on. Although I was frustrated and super-horny, I was also very grateful for this unexpected three-way enjoyment I had had.

Fraternities:
Life Among The "Straight" Queers

I. "I Had Never Sucked Before"

To be anyone on campus in the late 40's you had to belong to a fraternity. Our Pledge Master had been a DI in the Marines during the last 18 months of World War II. We had to make paddles and they were used often in the house. However, it was always done with the pants on until Hell Week. No one was the house during Hell Week was mandatory. We had to push peanuts across the room with our noses and the brothers were there with their paddles. There were hard ons all over the place during Hell Week. No one was considered "queer" if he got one when he got his ass paddled. Hell Week began on Monday evening and extended thru Sunday afternoon. Monday evening all the pledges were taken to the basement of the house and we were ordered to strip. We were then taken into another room, one at a time, and were ordered to lie across a saw horse. The brothers, who were all dressed, were then lined up and the paddle was applied. I was both embarrassed and excited and as I was taken into the room I got a hard on. I must have laid across the horse 15 minutes before they let me up. I really had a sore ass when they finished with me. Thursday evening was haircutting night. We were allowed to wear jocks that evening. Most of our head hair was cut off. Friday evening was individual night — that is if one of the brothers wanted to pledge a wait on him he could have him. I was picked by one of the brothers who I had not been too friendly with. I was taken to his car and we went for a ride in the country and parked in a lonely spot. He kept the motor running since it was January and Schenectady can get terrible terrible cold in January. He told me to get in the back seat of the car and he followed. He then told me to take off my clothes. He then laid me over his lap and spanked me with his hand. I could feel him getting hard. He stopped spanking me and took down his pants to reveal his big cock. None of us pledges had ever seen any of the brothers naked, unless we happened to walk into one of the bathrooms when one was showering. I had always been interested in men but up until that evening had never had an encounter with a man. Anyway, George played with his cock a few minutes and then he told me that I was going to suck him. I was shocked. I refused. He smiled at me — and said I then had two choices. I could either suck his cock for him and ride back to school with him, or he would put me out on the road naked and I could get back to Schenectady the best way I could. I kept trying to refuse his demand; "queers" sucked cock and I was not "queer." He pulled his pants up and threw my clothes in the trunk of his car. I decided that he meant it so I agreed to his demand. I admit I was hypnotized by the size of his cock.

George was hung, to say the least. I hesitatingly began to suck him — I had never sucked before and as I began to work on him I found it both revolting and fascinating, which I think is pretty much a natural reaction the first time one man takes on another man. As I pressed on in the task it became less revolting I must admit. As I sucked he began to give directions and direct my head with his hands. That was a strange feeling too, because we had had our heads shaved earlier in the week. Here I was in the back seat of a car with a huge cock in my mouth, my shaved head being controlled by a guy I really

didn't know. It was almost too much and when I finally brought him off I began to cry. Most macho types (and he was one) would simply have pulled up their pants, gotten back into the driver's seat and started back to town after getting their rocks off, but George asked me what the trouble was and tried to comfort me. He told me that nothing was going to happen, I wouldn't get syphilis and none of the guys back in the house would know about it.

We had many more "encounters," as he put it, later. He had an absolutely fantastic body on him without an ounce of fat. He quickly broke me in to fucking and he loved to spank. I soon found that I enjoyed taking the belt.

Saturday of Hell Week the drinking began early in the afternoon. About 7 that evening most of the brothers were pretty drunk, and the drunker they got, the more the paddles were used. We pledges had pretty sore asses. One of the brothers who was especially drunk got talking about how exciting it had been to watch the pledges get their heads shaved earlier and he began to suggest more shaving. A table was placed in the middle of the room and a scissors was brought out and a razor. One of the pledges was put on the table on his back and the drunk brother began to cut off his cock hair. One of the more sober brothers decided that if he were allowed to proceed we would probably end up being wounded, so it was decided that the pledges would shave each other of their cock hair. It was pretty horny and every one of us produced a hard on when that razor started working around the family jewels. About 8 that evening George realized that the brothers were pretty drunk and they were falling asleep so he took me out and we slipped away. He had the use of an apartment so we went there and that was the night I got my asshole cherry broken. George and I didn't return to the house until afternoon Sunday, and by then the excitement of the week had worn off. There was some more paddling, but that was about all.

One night, the following year, George asked me if I wouldn't like to go have a sandwich with him. "Sandwich" was a code word we used which meant that we would go to his apartment for sex. George was always the aggressor and when we got to the apartment he told me to strip and get into the bathroom. He pulled out the razor and the shaving brush and lathered my cock hair and took me to bed and used his belt on me as only he could do, and fucked me good. I love being spanked still, and turned 50 last week. I know an absolutely fantastic guy in Baltimore who loves to use a strap — is very discreet and a Southern gentleman in the fullest sense. You would never know to look at him or talk to him that he has a great proclivity to strip a guy down and lay him over his lap and use the strap.

II. Wally Came 7 Times

This is an expecially hot hazing to me. It was told to me by a beautiful guy whom I loved and who killed himself a few years ago. I made him tell and retell me every detail over and over. This took place at the U. of T. in the Fall of 1954. On one day during Hell Week all the pledges had to collect as many signatures as possible from Brothers OUTSIDE the house. This meant that signature-taking was conducted on campus, in restaurants, on the street, wherever. That evening the totals were tallied. The pledge with the most signatures was exempt from further hazing that day. The loser had to sit on the floor with his hands under his ass and head held up while all the other pledges, one at a time,

stripped and, facing him, jerked off on him, being told to aim at his face. He couldn't wash or change out of his cum-soaked clothes all night. Also, for the rest of the night, any pledge having to piss or shit had to ask permission and the loser-pledge had to hold the bucket handle between his teeth for pissers and lie on his back with the bucket on his chest for shitters, then wipe their asses with a wad of toilet paper held between his teeth. Beer was flowing and porno flics were being shown (can you imagine the tacky films of 1954?) on one wall. Periodically a pledge was ordered by a seated brother to come over and jerk him off (the brothers were in shorts or jocks, the pledges naked). This meant that the poor bastard who had gotten the fewest signatures had to crawl over and sit in front of the brother and get a load in the face. Then the pledge who had just masturbated the brother was required to "show respect" by jacking off in the loser's face.

My friend, Wally, said that he came no less than 7 times that night and some of the pledges were forced to come even more often. Toward the end, pledges were begging not to be forced to beat their sore cocks anymore and after as much as a half-hour of pounding away only a pearl of cum oozed out. Wally saw the loser next morning before he had been allowed to shower and said that his face and T-shirt were so stiff from dried cum that his features were distorted. Before he could shower, he was made to strip in front of pledges and brothers, shove the "offending" mechanical pencil up his ass and jack off on his "losing" list of signatures. After he was allowed to shower, all the brothers took a grease pencil and wrote their names on his body. Naturally as many as possible wrote on his ass and around his genitals, and he had to wear their names under his clothes all day.

III, "If I Told on Them I'd Be Sorry"

I'll get into my prep school life in the next letter. But I will tell you something about fraternity life and my initiation. I joined my father's fraternity at UC, Berkeley. My father had been a famous football player. I was determined that no one was going to know that I was interested in other men. It didn't matter in prep school because we didn't consider our little "games" to be queer.

But here I was 17 years old and living with (what seemed to me) real men. All of my fraternity brothers knew of my father and there was a portrait of him hanging in the trophy room. I was at first hesitant to pledge to this fraternity because I couldn't step into my father's shoes as a football player. I was a good athlete, winning my letters in long distance running & swimming and I was on the water polo team. As soon as I realized that not being a football player (I was too slender) didn't seem to matter to the guys in the fraternity I pledged to it.

At first there were about a dozen pledges and we slept in three dormitory rooms in the house (same house my father had lived in); four to a room. One night not long after I moved into the house, I was awakened by what seemed like a wet dream — except that I almost never had had a wet dream in my life; being much too active to let it store up. I shot all over the sheets. The other guys were all asleep and I laid awake the rest of the night wondering how I was going to clean up the mess. But as I lay there I began to realize that just as I was awakening when I shot, I vaguely remember someone running from my bed. I was very confused and bothered by the incident. About a week later I was again

awakened but this time realized that someone was sitting on my bed jacking me off. I pretended to be asleep and I didn't even open my eyes to see who it was because I was so embarrassed. Again I shot all over the bed and he ran away.

One Saturday night when the house was nearly empty, I was alone in my dorm with one other sleeping pledge. Again, in the middle of the night, I felt myself ready to shoot and woke up. This time I was caught opening my eyes and I saw not only the other pledge, who was the younger brother of the fraternity's senior president, but another guy who had his hand on my cock. I was embarrassed and didn't know what to say. Then the pledge, who was very tall & goodlooking, said to the other guy, "Let me blow him," which he did very quickly. I realized that the second guy in the room was the one who had been sneaking in and jacking me off. He was a mid-class fraternity member who had hardly paid any attention to me during social hours. He too was goodlooking although shorter and more slender than me; he was a "personality" boy around the house and was the last person I had suspected. Anyway, the two guys sat on my bed, asked me if I liked getting blowed, etc., whether I was queer, who the other guys in the house were who "played around," and that if I told on them I'd be sorry. There were only about 8 in my pledge class left by the time "Haze Week" came around; there were about 40 in the entire house, some living outside the house. By then I had had sex with two of my fellow pledges and about four of the others. I had been seen nude by all of the pledges, of course, and I had seen them nude, but very few of the others had seen me nude, and I was still very conscious of my family reputation. During the pledge year we had often been paddled but never with our undershorts pulled down.

On the first night of the week when we reported to the initiation committee of about 6 seniors, they made us pull our undershorts down, and as I was being swatted I started to get a hard on, as did a couple of the other guys. The president said, "Look — B. likes getting spanked." They made me go to the front and the paddler was told to give me 50 swats "to see if that'll get his rocks off." I was so embarrassed I almost died and my cock quickly went limp. The next night, again before the committee, we were blindfolded and our shorts again pulled down. Suddenly, they started playing with our cocks and put something on them to make them burn. I quickly got a hard on. They called us up, one by one, and measured our cocks, making derogatory remarks about them ("How in the hell do you expect to make babies with that?" etc.), and the next morning our dimensions were posted on the bulletin board which was always to be read at breakfast.

I was No. 2 in length, No. 5 in circumference, No. 1 (of two) in length of foreskin and at the bottom of the list in size of balls. I had to wear a gold star which said "Skin Champ" the rest of the week to all my classes. The other fraternity guys knew what it meant. Twice again during the week they tried to swat me into an orgasm, as I could never control my erections. Friday night, we pledges ate dinner in our undershorts in the kitchen while the entire membership was present at a special feast in the dining hall. Many of them I had hardly ever seen before, as they didn't live in the house. After dinner they assembled in the huge living room in a semi-circle before the fireplace. We were brought in and taken to the center of the semi-circle. The president then called each one of us forward one at a time, told us to take off our undershorts and he introduced us to the membership. His introduction included our dimensions, to shouts of derision from the audience, especially when I was

introduced as Skin Champ. Then they began having contests with us. One contest was to pour beer down our throats to see which one would piss into ready buckets first. Another was to stuff us with mashed potatoes to see who would crap first. We were made to do push-up contests, etc. All evening my cock went from hard to soft, as did the other pledges, with much discussion about our various conditions. Then we were told to get ourselves hard because they had a live pig in the kitchen which we were going to have to fuck in front of everyone. I couldn't get hard and neither could the others; I guess the idea of the pig was too gruesome. We went through all sorts of embarrassments trying to get hard. They decided to get us hard by using an electric hand massager. One by one we went to one of the upper classmen who pumped us hard with his massager while the whole crowd watched.

They brought out a pig and told us to jack off and the last guy to shoot would be forced to fuck the pig. We all began pumping and after about 5 minutes I won this contest. I got big applause and they smeared my seeds on the poor pig. All the guys came; one took about 20 minutes. He was afraid he would have to fuck the pig, but they didn't make him. Saturday we were taken to the house of our rival fraternity and we went through the same scene again. For some reason it was even more embarrassing, in front of absolute strangers. The pledges from that house were exchanged for us and they spent Saturday at our fraternity house. On Saturday I was hard practically the whole time and got special verbal abuse as a result. Evidently they were told I like to be spanked (which I don't, necessarily) because they paddled the hell out of me, shouting, "Shoot your rocks, B." But I didn't, so I had to jack off while they continued to paddle me.

IV. "We Knelt at the Urinals."

In 1965, I desperately wanted to join a college fraternity just for the opportunity to be disciplined, humiliated and put through "Hell Week." My interest in bondage/discipline as well as my homosexual interests could both be explored without appearing to be gay. I had heard lurid rumors of hazing and degradation during the "7 Days of Hell" and I wanted very much to be dominated. The fraternity was made up of 25 actives and 5 pledges. As a pledge, I was assigned to 5 actives. I was to do their bidding for the whole semester, provided that I passed Hell Week. During Hell Week the house was off-limits for outsiders; the actives had no dates or social outings. Instead, they played out their sexual fantasies on the "slave" pledges. And indeed we were their slaves for the week. Blindfolds were issued and our clothes stripped. We were not allowed to stand and quite often our hands were tied. Only three hours of sleep was permitted each night. We could not use our hands when eating but were issued food in a bowl on the floor.

Breakfast was always the same — we knelt at the urinals which had our breakfast, consisting of a pile of corn flakes liberally soaked with piss. The foul odor of the actives' early morning piss made us almost throw up. Paddling was administered until we finished. It was an unbelievable experience. Today, I still welcome that experience. The actives cut loose with loads of foul piss onto the corn flakes when our blindfolds were in place. We had 30 minutes to clean up every morsel of cereal and *every* drop of piss. Verbal abuse also accompanied breakfast.

Hell Week was long and tiresome. Our asses were red and sore. The final evening, Saturday, each pledge was put over a sawhorse and securely fastened. The blindfolds were put on again. A liberal amount of Vaseline was rubbed in each of the 5 assholes. I felt pressure on my asshole and just as I was ready to yell a cock was stuck down my throat. In an instant, I was being fucked by two of my brothers. As each climaxed and withdrew, another active took his place. After an hour we were released and with a formal ritual we were accepted into the fraternity. I had to do the bidding the remaining part of the semester for my 5 actives. But it was generally light chores, laundry, etc., with paddling once a week. No further sexual abuse was conducted. I never knew whose cocks fucked me during the initiations.

EDITOR'S NOTE: These data on fraternities were supplied by John Barton, who collects them from correspondents, and gives them to various periodicals for anonymous publication.

"2 Hole Pete" Gets Very Good Loads

FLORIDA — I live in a rural area that is growing. Often leave phone # at rest area and have had some unusual calls & several get togethers that proved above average. However do receive mostly JO calls. I left the last message a couple of weeks ago on I-75 about 30 mins. from my house: "Horney — call Pete." Other times, "For best BJ and/or Hot Ass Call Pete" or "Call Two Hole Pete — the Best on I-75." The last one was the best. He called 2 AM. Said he was horney & what did I do. I said what would you like. "I am horney and need a good BJ." I said fine how big. "7." I said fine. An hour went by so I went to bed. 10 min. later the phone rang & he was lost. Took another 10 min. to get here. Was 6'2" or more of real nice goodlooking meat. Come in and said shall we get to it. I said fine. He went in bedroom and started opening his pants and this big 8" cock sprang out. I immediately got down to work. He said it gets big and sure did in short order. It was clean and uncut. I worked my hot tongue and mouth for over 2 hours. He came 3 times with very good loads. He left around 5 AM and was going to Tampa and Miami. Said would be back through. He called the next day & made date for Wed. night. Got here about 6 PM. I worked on it immediately & then we had dinner & again to bed for my ass. I wasn't sure — sat on it at first but finally got on my stomach & he fucked me for over 35 min. It hurt I have never had one that big. He was a talker all through both sex sessions, telling me to suck that big cock, eat those balls and ass, all the time laying back and looking at me at my task. I am this week still recovering from that fucking big cock. I am using Preparation H to ease the soreness. Don't think I will let him fuck me again. I am worried about putting Phone # in rest area but haven't been sorry yet. Had three or four others — will write about them another time. I am married but live by myself during week. Love your rag. Glad to know you get real letters. I go for a couple of weeks & nothing & then a week or two of calls and old reliables every night.

He Said, "Do You Suck Cocks?"

MANHATTAN — Years ago a burly fellow in sweat-stained work clothes followed me out of the subway because I'd been eyeing his ample basket. As he caught up with me on the street he said, "Do you suck cocks?" I replied, "That's no way to approach somebody. Do you think any man would answer 'Yes' to that question? You should be a little more tactful." "Well," he said, "I don't have much time. Do you or don't you?" "As a matter of fact," I said, "I do." And I did.

Conservatives in South Dakota Call Youth "Faggot" Whilst Raping Him

NEW YORK — As to the "Rape in the Badlands," I have been trying to recall the incident over the past week and here is what came to mind: It was a warm summer night — it was just getting dark, so it must have been around 9:00 P.M. I was only about 12 or 13 and was pretty dumb when it came to sex, but I used to jerk off a lot, and thought that I knew a lot about everything, but of course knew very little. Anyway I was walking along a road in this town near the Badlands and this car with 3 young men pulled up. They were probably in their late teens or early 20s. They asked if I would like a ride and I said OK. They were all in the front seat so I got in the back. They were drinking beer. They started telling dirty stories — one I remember was about a guy using a silk handkerchief in lieu of a condom and the punch line was "how would you look if you'd been strained through a silk handkerchief?" They took out their cocks and were playing around with them. They had driven off the highway into the hard packed dirt of the Badlands. My cock had not matured and seemed pretty small compared to theirs so I was sort of embarrassed, and stayed in the back seat after they stopped the car. They got out and told me to get out, too. I thought that they were going to have a circle jerk, but they wanted me to suck them — something which shocked me, as I had never even thought of doing such a thing. One of the guys was so horny he came and then made me lick his cock and stomach. The others were laughing and the second guy made me go down on his prick, He came very quickly and I spit it out. The last guy was the oldest and he had a huge piece of meat and he took a long time coming — forcing me to really suck him and hurting the back of my throat. When he finally came he really thrust my head down hard on his cock and I almost fainted. Then he slapped me around and called me a sissy and a faggot and said that I should go to Hollywood where all the queers lived. The other guys calmed him down and they all got in the car & sped away, leaving me out there in the Badlands. I walked to the highway and then back into town. I remember that I cried and felt terrible. After that I stayed pretty much to myself and never walked out alone. Became a real loner, actually. The next year my family did move to the L.A. area, which seems sort of ironic now. I remember that one of my uncles had been in the Navy and had been in Long Beach. He told stories of going to Persian (Pershing) Square in L.A. to look at the fags. I was a little kid then, but Persian Square sounded really exotic in South Dakota.

The Joy of Gay Shit-eating

TORONTO — I was down in Los Angeles visiting a couple of friends who lived there. I didn't want to stay with them so I was staying at the Tropicana Motel on Santa Monica where a lot of punk bands stay. I had ample opportunity to drive my big renta-car up and down Santa Monica between Vine and Fairfax, the stretch of the city that is lined day and night with whores "hitch-hiking." I'm fussy. No fey or frail thing for me. I like them distinctly blue collar and tough, even rough looking, as mean as I dare, which if I'm drugged up is as mean as they come and normally I want them meaner than I find.

The excitement (no, more of a "charge") of cruising whores, U-turning, slowing to check one out, guessing what he'd be good at, or at least moderately adept at, is a marvelous prelude to the actual picking up, but sadly the whore is often a tame unimaginative waif who doesn't get much into his business. He just wants his bucks and to get the hell out of there and turn the next trick and get his next wad of bucks.

In L. A.., as in many cities, they are cautious about vice cops and I am big and tall and young and don't much look like the sort that "has" to resort to whores (as one punk told me, "Man, why do you pay for it? I would have made it with you for free if I saw you in a bar"). Nice compliment but doesn't the punk realize my scene. I zero-ed in on one stocky youth who looked street-tough. He was dressed in straight boy jock drag of jeans, football shirt in some primary colour with some number on front and back and Adidas and had straight boy long hair and later when I saw him smile saw that one of his front teeth was missing. He initially played hard to get and didn't want to get into my car but did so when he spotted the BLUE JAYS baseball cap of mine on the back seat of my car.

He got in asking me why I support such a bad baseball team as the JAYS. I told him I did so because they, like me, came from Toronto. He came from a small mining town way north of Toronto and was in L. A. after hitch-hiking his way across north North America. He claimed he was hustling cause in Las Vegas he had lost all his money. We talked about unions (I can't remember how we got on to it) and he told me his father was a big union man. He was very slick with his routine and had a droll delivery. He called Hollywood "a bowl of Granola" because you've got your fruit, you've got your nuts and you've got your flakes. We went back to my motel room. I started to undress and he said we best settle the deal. What do you do and how much, I asked. Then, in a smooth faultless delivery he recited the menu:
You jack me off: $25 (no kissing allowed).
I jack you off: $30.
You blow me: $35.
I blow you: $40.
I fuck you: $50.
I fuck and suck you for ¼ hour: $60.
You drink my piss: $75.
You fuck me: $100. Tying up, $25 extra.
You eat my shit: $150.
I fist fuck you: $200.

"What do you want man, hurry up," he said. He seemed anxious and was shifting from foot to foot. "Hurry, man, I need to take a shit urgently if you don't want to buy the stuff." I told him what I wanted — not his shit, so he stepped

into the can, keeping the door open and talking to me while he dumped his load, which he did quickly. He then got up, turned around and looked at it in the bowl. "Damn it," he said, "I held it all day just in case somebody wanted to buy it." He flushed the toilet. "There goes $150," he said with obvious regret in his voice. He had a medium size cock and was a vigorous fuck. He'd lost his front teeth playing hockey. There you go. It's true.

Sucks Youth 1 Hour, Gets 5 Wads

OTTAWA — This little contribution is absolutely true and I thought it worthy of your book. No luck with nasty guys these days; if I don't run into them it is not for want of trying. At the baths, a young blond stud (how else to describe him?) checks in right behind me, looking a bit nervous. I'm slim, bearded, 36. Not too many men about for a Saturday night, but the few guys there give him the cruisy attention he deserves. A young guy, black hair, little brown vial of poppers in hand, stands outside the blond's door but does not go in. I'm pushy. I do go in. He lies sprawled there on his bed, on his back, with a bit of towel over his groin. I stroke the bump under his towel and since he does not pull away, I set to work doing one of the things I was put here to do, because I do it with style and love, superbly and with a touch of the obsessive: sucking cock. The little hairs on his balls and in that delicious little region I love to nuzzle and suck on — just between the balls and where the leg meets the body, on the inside of the thigh — are short and stiff, wiry and black. I licked and nuzzled a bit as a preliminary before losing myself in the pleasure of swallowing the whole shaft of his cock, nose flush to the belly. I barely had time to give his dick a few loving full length sucks before he pushed my head down so that the cock head nestled just at the back of my mouth next door to the tonsils. Cum flowed copiously, more in a steady little stream than in a series of spurts. (Having my head held down while a guy comes turns me on as much as being roughly face fucked. But back to the blond, the star of this tale.) I was surprised and a bit sad that he had shot so fast, but hoped to bring him off again. Little did I know what was in store for me in the next hour. Since he showed no sign of wanting me to leave, I sucked gently and constantly on his beautiful, cut, slightly up-curving dick. Sometimes I rested my head on his stomach, his cock full in my mouth, blissfully happy, as he stroked my hair, which he did throughout. And once I went down and licked and sucked on the soles and toes of his smooth, arched feet (I'm crazy about feet), but I didn't want to leave his cock untended for too long and was soon back up working at it. I hardly took his cock out of my mouth for the better part of an hour. Gentle constant sucking (seemed to fit his mood) and some firm stroking with my right hand, his hands in my hair and now and then pushing me down as he came, and my blond stud on his back came four more times, squirting come down my throat as I felt his spasms rise from the base of his cock, on the underside. (I love to feel a guy come in as many ways as possible — leg muscles tighten, sometimes the toes curl, and I suck away with a hand on each foot.) I wanted to share my five comes in one hour with all devotees of obsessive, tender cocksucking out there. I was really feeling fine when I got up. drenched with sweat. Reality can really put fantasy to shame. Love to all those cocks out there.

Interview:
I've Got a House — a Showplace — Still I Can't Get Noplace

This "straight" man that you kept for three years; when did yoü first lay eyes on him? I first saw him at work, where he had a part-time job.
How did he happen to move in with you? He and his second wife were friendly with some friends of mine. After we'd got together socially a couple of times, I began to like him. He's an immensely intelligent and dazzlingly witty man. I invited him to share my apartment after I'd lost a roommate/lover and his wife had left him. At the time, I wasn't conscious of any sexual interest in him. That developed shortly after he moved in.
You didn't have a sexual "understanding" when he moved in? No. He would pay part of the rent, but less than half. I wasn't interested at first in his putting out.
When you first sucked his ass-hole, was there any feeling that he was surrendering his most forbidden secret to you? I know it seemed strange and forbidden to him. I felt I'd scored a triumph in being able to do what I really wanted to do. I don't deny that his "straightness" enhanced his attractiveness.
Was he ever too dirty? His ass-hole, like the rest of him, was always squeaky clean. He always washed his hole after wiping it (or so he told me). When I told him I'd like to lick his body after he'd jogged, he drew the line at that.
In what sense was he "straight," when his hard cock was in your mouth regularly? He was at pains to let me know that he didn't enjoy "putting out" for me but did it only out of his feeling of obligation; a couple of months after he moved in, he lost his job and he was without money, so I paid for the rent and groceries, and later I started giving him a weekly cash allowance. He screwed women. He said he'd had no previous homosexual experience, and I believe him.
Was it, on your part, mainly a sex affair or a romance? I romanticized it something ferocious.
How old was he? When he moved in he was 35 and I, 38.
Did he have any political compassion? Yes.
Did you ever swallow his piss? I told him I'd like to, but he said he couldn't let me do that.
Why did he live with you for three years? He'd never have denied the convenience, economy, or enjoyment of my company. It wasn't until a couple of years after he'd moved out that he acknowledged he'd enjoyed the sex. He hadn't known that while he was doing it.
How often did you "have" him, in some sense? About 100 times.
Did it ever get tiresome? No. The conflict between us (and there was plenty) was probably a sustaining force.
What positions were you normally in for cocksucking and ass-licking. Almost always he was prone on the floor. Occasionally he stood and I was on my knees. I was *very* ritualized.
Did he seem to enjoy the sex? He couldn't admit - to either of us - that he did, but his cock was always hard. To play his role, he had to be the passive, desired one. Once I had him on the floor, he was a cold fish — but with a hard on. I told him I sometimes felt like a necrophiliac. He couldn't, of course, suppress the spasms which accompanied his ejaculations.

Did he ever feel he'd had so much sex with you he was turning queer? No. I doubt very much that he'll have sex with another man.
Did he have sex with women while living with you? Yes, but he didn't take advantage of all the opportunities (many women were attracted to him) because he feared being impotent. That had been a problem in the past. I've no doubt that his desire for women was genuine, but he had a certain fear which sometimes inhibited him.
Please describe his ass-hole? I found it fascinating but perhaps an impartial observer would deem it only mildly interesting. A rosy-brown rosebud concealed between two solid mounds of flesh. At first he was tense but later was able to relax enough to take my tongue pretty far up. Little flavor or aroma.
How did you seduce him after he'd moved it? Within a couple of months of his moving in and he was interested in learning about homosexuals and what they do. He'd not heard the word "rimming." I said, "Would you like to see what it's like?" With some chagrin, he said he would. So I ate his ass and gave his cock the best sucking it had ever had.
Please describe his cock. Not large — maybe 5½ inches, neither thick nor thin but with a big mushroom head. Cut. I never had to make any special effort to get it hard or keep it hard.
Did his living with you prevent you from jacking off? Certainly not.
How often did you normally jack off while he was living with you? Daily at least. I might have beat off less if he'd not been there.
Why did you only have sex with him once a week? This was the implied "contract"; he'd "submit" once weekly. The day varied from week to week. He knew I wanted it at least twice a day.
How did he hndle his problems? He was usually quite rational (maybe too rational). I think I came to represent all those forces when I hemmed him in, restricted his freedom. He deeply resented his dependence on me.
Was he handsome or were you interested in him because he was "straight"? He attracted me because he was enormously charming and seemed to be in command of himself. He was nice-looking and I think his "straightness" had to do with his allure.
What sort of underpants did he wear? Bikini briefs, usually brighly colored. He changed them daily. Each day he handed me the previous day's pair or left them in my room. There were times when he knew I was in my room sniffing and sucking on them while I jacked off. I'm sure that turned him on, but he expressed amusement at the idea. They smelled and tasted like his sweat with maybe the slightest hint of piss. Occasionally I bought him a G-string or some such. When I was doing the laundry (he did it sometimes), I often sniffed his soiled underpants again — as well as the armpits of his T-shirts.
Would you have liked him as much if he came in and said, "Boy, did I ever suck off some nice dicks in the men's room?" That would have dampened mya rdor considerably. I wanted him to be "straight" except for his relationship with me.
Did he ever, while quarreling, call you sexual names? I can remember a couple of nasty set-tos in which he lashed into me bitterly but he never expressed contempt for my homosexuality.
How did you finally break up? I felt that he handed me a cruel rejection. I still think so but have forgiven him. We remain rather friendly but I'm no longer aware of any sexual interest in him. He married his girlfriend (his third wife). I've spent social evenings with the two of them and he's occasionally come

here for a beer and a chat. We still enjoy each other, but not sexually. I was expecting the impossible, a lasting relationship including sex. He used me, but it was a valuable relationship.
Did he help maintain your Lovely Home? Yes. He did half the work and did any chores I found particularly odious.
When did you put him on an allowance? There was a period of six months when I lost sexual interest in him. I can't remember why. One evening during this hiatus, he hinted that he'd like to be sucked off but I pretended not to get the hint. But eventually sex was reinstated once a week. It was after this 6 month hiatus that I gave him cash each week.
Did you enhance his allure by paying for it? I don't think so but his 'straightness' did.
What do you think of the theory that you were the stronger of the two: you could afford the delights of debasement while he, weaker, had to conform and win the security of numbers, of belonging to the majority? There may be some truth in this.
His "strip teases" are perhaps the most fasacinating thing about his affair. Yes. Encouraged by me, he did blatant strip-teases to excite me (and himself, I think). He found it necessary to smoke dope before putting out. On the appointed evening, he would remove all his clothes but his briefs and sit with me at the dining table. As we smoked, he spread his legs wide apart to afford me the best view of his groin. While I stared at it, his cock hardened and some fluid moistened his briefs. He always asked which regalia I wanted him to favor that evening. That settled, he went to his room to "get dressed." When he passed my chair I grabbed his ass and pressed my face into his groin, sucking the juice from his briefs. He went to his room and returned, typically, wearing a T-shirt and a pair of gym shorts over a couple of other garments (say, a jock strap and a posing strap under the jock strap). I watched from the couch while he strutted round for me and, on cue, rubbed and squeezed his groin. When I asked him to, he stopped before me so that I could feel and kiss his groin and suck his dick through his shorts, etc. He repeated the routine without the shorts, then without the jock strap, then naked. Sometimes (this was his idea) I watch him do calisthenics in his jock strap. The tease done, he lay on the rug (turning over when I asked him to do so) and I had my way with him. I licked his feet, armpits, ass-hole, balls, cock. Usually I sucked him off but sometimes I sucked his balls while he stroked himself to orgasm after I'd sucked his cock a lot (he "held back" a lot). He always pumped his load (usually a big one) into my mouth.
Do you think you put more into this relationship than you got out of it? It was a fair trade off.

EDITOR'S NOTE: I believe this otticle is true but I have difficulty with the authour's characterisation of his lover as "straight." There are a fantastic amount of soft ons or fear of soft ons among "straights" when they are confronted with Pussy or even the thought of it, so that part is O.K. But the house-mate's reliable hard ons when he is with another man suggest that he has a richer sexuality than is covered by the word "straight." I have always thought of myself as the biggest queer in the world, but even I do not wear G-strings, posing straps or other genital regalia, and do burlesque numbers; I do not think "straight" men normally do — not, at least, for other men — and the subject of this article emerges as a virtual male Tempest Storm. But it is my custom to give the contributors their head, as it were.

Youth Seduces Trade With "Dirty Talk"

JAMAICA, NEW YORK — When I was about 12, my mother was always after me to play ball. Unfortunately for me, I lived across from not 2 but 3 parks. I lived on Ocean Parkway between Ave O and Ave P in B'klyn. One particular Friday I was told I had to bring someone home with me as proof of my ball-playing. I of course hated the park and ball. When 6 o'clock came and went, I was desperate so I went up to the first butch guy I saw and asked him if he wanted to make 50 cents as my alibi for the afternoon's supposed ballplaying. He was a doll, black hair, about 14 or so. He came home with me, pacified my mother and we continued our friendship. We ended up in his house and while "fooling around wrestling," he got on top of me and put his cock right in my mouth. We had a 69 of 69's. This went on for nearly 2 years. I can remember him always wanting to kiss me. I would never let him. Then 1 year later when I wanted to kiss him, he was already into cunt, and that was the end of him. When I was 19 I was much more sure of myself. I was on my way home one day when I saw this boy I had known from my public school days named Johnny. He was about 22. I fell in step behind him. He vaguely remembered me. He was a true piece of trade if I ever saw one. Construction boots and all. We had gone up to where he had to turn into his bldg. He was so fucken butch I was frightened to death, but I mustered up enough courage to ask him right out, did he know anyone who gave blow jobs? His answer was an immediate bulge in his pants. I knew I was on the right track so I continued with the dirty talk and cunt etc. He asked me to come up for a beer. We weren't there a minute when he said he had to piss. I said me too. We stood there with 2 raging hard ons. He looked at me and told me to blow him, just like that. It was very exciting. This went on for about 7 years, till I moved away to the island. Every single Thursday, winter or summer, rain or shine, we *never* missed a session. I was more than glad to do him for trade. He would only kiss me occasionally, but I didn't care. He was all *MAN!*

No Such Thing As "Born Straight,"

Pure heterosexuality as a sexual category does not exist, while pure homosexuality does, according to a leading lay analyst.

The analyst — editor of *Straight To Hell* — does not hold a degree in psychology but he holds a jaundiced eye on the hypocrisies, poses, sex substitutes, sex additives, and defenses of the straight and narrow world.

There are such things as 100% heterosexuals, he says, but they are that not instinctively but merely as a conscious choice of a way of life. Most of them do not have what he calls "the balls" to have any except socially acceptable sex. They have sex for the same reason they do everything else — to win society's respect. The Editor does not view society's respect as worth having.

Thus, being a "strict heterosexual" is like living on the East Side, It's not necessarily something you were born to do, merely something you do for status. Heterosexuality is not primarily sexual at all, but mainly social, and therefore unnatural. It is no accident that weddings are reported as "social" news, whereas homosexual couplings are sexual, natural, and forbidden by society.

Youth Sucks Off Brother

VANCOUVER — At 11 I lived in a large house — 7 bedrooms. My brother & I shared a bedroom & our own bath — why we shared I don't know as there were 2 empty bedrooms down the hall. But this day every one was out but the cook and he never came upstairs. I went to take a piss & looked at my growing cock — I turned to the full length mirror on the back of the door for a better exam. I liked what I saw & started to get hard — that took about 5 sec. I began to feel its extreme hardness & found if I put my thumb on top & two forefingers beneath & pumped it produced a great feeling & the more I did it — the greater & greater that feeling. At one point I decided I'd never quit no matter what. I stripped entirely and really got going — I even got the 3 leg stool & sat before the mirror & pumped & played until I "came" (without shooting). It was only a week later that I showed my 4 yr. older brother this trick — and as I played with his cock we both got excited — but he came in a bucketful. Neither of us had seen cum & were a bit scared. Afte that my brother and I did it every night & very often in the afternoon right after school. One day I came home from school & he was in his chem lab (the X-cook's bathroom). He was naked but for a rubber jock he'd made himself. The jock was made from an old inner tube & stapled together. The pouch was filled with hard on & glycerin & he had his hard cock pointing down over his balls & his hand cupped over it working it up & down & it made a beautiful squishy sound. He let me pump him a while — then he let me put my hand inside — as I stood behind & put my right hand around his right hip. Wow — all that skin and hard cock — I had to get as naked as he — what a jack off session this turned out to be. It was only a few nights later I asked him if he had ever had his cock sucked — he said NO — and I showed him & then I couldn't turn him off. Being 4 yrs younger I had to comply.

Farmer, Now Married, Recalls the Jock Straps of High School

Have you always been a farmer? No.
Are you satisfied with farm work? I love the work. Put in long days most of the time.
Your height (6'5") is majestic. Do you attract many admirers because of it? Perhaps my height does draw some. I can't say for sure
What are some of your other stats? I'm 34, married, 190, uncut, 8". I was a high school basketball player and was in the Army. 26 guys have sucked me off and I've fucked 11 girls. I was sucked off by a Baptist preacher once & once had my cock in the high school superintendent's ass.
Is your weight evenly distributed, so that you have a harmonious body, with no parts too fat? Yes.
How does your body look to you in the mirror? Good.
Do you like to admire your body in the mirror? Yes.
Do you ever sit in a chair in front of a mirror and spread your legs and look at your asshole? Yes.

Please describe your body hair. No chest hair. Dick & asshole hair brown.
Do you enjoy stripping? Yes.
What kind of underpants do you wear? Jockeys.
How long do you wear them before putting on a new pair? 2 days.
How do your underpants smell? Like come.
Do you smell the armpits of your shirts? Yes.
What compliments have your cocksuckers given you? I have been told my come tasted good.
How often a day do you jack off? Once.
Where have you jacked off? Everywhere. Indoors, outdoors, forests, fields, barns, bedrooms, toilets.
Ever in public men's rooms? Yes.
What do you think about that makes you jack off? Young men's bodies.
What positions are you in when you jack off? Laying, sitting, standing.
Do you tickle your nuts and asshole while playing with yourself? Yes.
How many squirts do you give when you come? 6 or 7.
Does your foreskin just cover the head of your peter, or is there an overhang? About ¼" overhang.
Please describe your introduction to sex. 2 of my cousins showed me their cocks. We were about 8. They showed me how to jack off.
Please describe your life as a high school basketball player. I was 13 when I first put on a jock strap to play basketball. I folded my dick down but the jock strap gave me such a hard on my cock was so obvious I had to grab it and pull it straight up so the other guys wouldn't notice. After practice we would all go to the locker room and tear off our basketball shorts & shoes & run around in our jock straps. I would have to get into the shower pretty quick and get cold water running on my dick & balls because looking at all those bulges in those other guy's jocks would drive me insane. I was always proud to get in the showers with the other guys because there was a saying in that crowd that I had "the biggest tool in school." All the guys would make fun of anyone who got a real hard on in the showers. We all wore Jockey shorts & I would usually sneak a look at the other guys when we were dressing & undressing. But I also caught them looking at my groin too. My senior year, when I was about 18, we got a new coach, much younger, really hung, and he took showers with us. I'll tell you more about him later but we had several skinny dipping parties at the river at night with 8 of us. This is where I really became a lover of Men, cocks & come. Will write more later. Cock is swelling. Going to jack off right now.

Typical "Straight" Admits Weakness for Friend's Tongue

MONTREAL — I am a 30-year-old so-called "straight," living with a woman, but I have three men friends. One, who is probably the best cocksucker and ass licker in the world, loves for me to sit on his face. He also likes jock straps (of which I have plenty, since I work out a lot). He worships my body for about an hour at a time. I have no guilt, and always feel great afterwards. Another friend, a fashion model, likes to have my prick up his ass. Boy, what an ass and mouth on that guy. And he's so handsome and good looking you would cream your pants just looking at him. Another friend, whom I have known for about four years, likes me to call him "pig," "pig mouth," "fag," or just plain "cocksucker." I have the best of both worlds. I wouldn't trade either, even though my girl cannot possibly do my cock justice like those three guys. They really know their stuff, believe me. My friend whom I've been visiting about twice a month for years is the best sex pig that you ever met in your whole life. I sit in a chair drinking a couple of strong Canadian beers while he's sitting on the floor smelling my sox. He slips off the sox and licks my feet and between each toe, letting me see and hear him. Then he moves up between my legs. I take my Levis off but keep my shorts and T-shirt on. He sniffs around the fly of my shorts, wetting it with his mouth. I keep telling him to show me his tongue and he keeps pulling back and showing me the longest tongue I have ever seen, and he moves it in a circular motion, which, just looking at it, drives me mad, and just writing about it now gives me a hard on. Finally I remove my shorts and call him a dirty cocksucker and tell him I want that tongue in my asshole. He lays on his back and begs me to sit on his face. I refuse for a while, to tease him, and he's never sure if I'm going to let him. That's part of our game. I finally squat on his face and his tongue goes crazy. He puts that long fucking tongue up my hole and I'm all set to cream right away. That is the one weak spot I have, having my asshole eaten, and this guy is the world's best asshole eater. When I can no longer stand it, I jack off all over his face, covering it with cum and calling him any name I can think of. Afterwards, we generally rest on the bed, his head by my cock. We are no longer into the Master/Slave bit, but are quite subdued and relaxed. But when my cock and asshole feel like it we will start the whole scene over again. After coming home, if my girl is asleep in her own room, I go to my bedroom and jack off again, thinking about that fucking tongue. I should be jogging now but I've decided to finish this letter before I get too tied up with my schedule and forget it. Last night after enrolling in my fall evening courses at the university, I strolled up to the mountain around 9 o'clock. There is a place up there that I found only by accident; there must have been 150 guys looking for sex. I stood by a tree for awhile (I'm basically quite shy and am very cautious about making the first move) while drinking one of my two beers. Several guys came over and asked if I wanted any Poppers, and after I said no, they continued on their way. They didn't interest me that much, and I was holding out for something real special. Finally I got up the nerve which only the beer could bring. I saw this stud walk by with about four others following. So I said, "Fuck all this fucking around" and pursued also. The stud I was following took off by himself down a path further into the bushes. I followed him. I finally caught up with him and grabbed him from the back. He turned and smiled, undid my zipper, bent down and took my cock in his mouth — all

this within 30 seconds. Another guy comes up and starts fondling me but my friend told him to fuck off, which he quickly did. We stripped down to our shorts, throwing our pants and shirts on the ground. He was quite a stud, about 6 foot, 175 lbs., about 30, from Pennsylvania. What a mouth he had. He got up from worshipping my prick, removed our shorts and bent over with his hands wrapped around his ankles. I slowly and carefully stuck my dick up his asshole. He went wild and started sucking my fingers, which were wrapped around his waist. His asshole was equal to his mouth. It seemed to have a fucking tongue in there that titillated the head of my prick. It drove me wild. He asked me if I wanted to come in his ass, and I said I would prefer to come all over his face and in his mouth, but if he wanted me to come in his ass, I would most willingly do so. He did. I did. As I was unloading, he sucked my fingers and kissed my hands. While I pulled my cock out, he bent down and took all my cock in his mouth while beating his meat, which was long but thin (mine is long and FAT). He shot his wad with my cock still in his mouth. He got his bicycle from the bushes and we walked back down the mountain to my car. He said he was living with a girl and was out to get a quart of milk. He was the all-American type, just like I'm the all-Canadian type.

Army Recruit in Bad Heat Risks Barracks Fuck

SEATTLE — I was drafted in 1950. In Fort Reilly Kansas I spent a few miserable days. Being an induction center, new men were coming in & out all the time. One night after lights out a new kid from the South who slept on the bunk above me said, "Psst." I said "What do you want?" He softly said, "Put your hand up here." I did and soon felt a nice soft skin and my hand first pulled away because I realized it was his cock. I was curious and so my hand went right back to it. His hand sort of guided my hand all around his cock and what a beautiful feeling it was as it grew in size and stiffened up even more as I fondled the warmth it had. He said he wanted to fuck me and I said, "Someone may be watching." It was in a whole room full of GI's, all recruits. We were very quiet though and they all seemed quiet too so he said, "Let me get down there with you" and he did. He seemed to know what he was doing and I felt him crawl on top of me and he proceeded to find my asshole and since it was virgin it hurt immediately and I quietly said, "No, I can't do it because it hurts." He said, "Don't worry, it's OK" and continued. I just suffered the pain and let him go ahead. I wish I had used a little spit but he went in dry and started working his cock up my asshole until finally the whole cock was in up to the hilt. The pain was excruciating but I wanted his desire to be fulfilled. I wanted to cry out and have him stop but I just suffered and yet enjoyed the excitement of a beautiful cock way up inside me. After he came he lay like a dead weight on me. There was a warm damp sweat between us by now. He withdrew his cock and I was suck a stupid jerk I could have fucked him but I was in such pain and when he offered to let me fuck him I turned him down. Next day even though I tried to be friendly with that good looking boy that fucked me he was wiser and knew we would be parting ways to not bother with cultivating anything. Two days later two hick type boys said that they saw me get fucked and I was embarrassed but I just tried to ignore them because we were all getting transferred to better places for basic training.

Swallows Loaded Trojan

SAN ANTONIO — I like to haunt lovers' lanes in search of used prophylactics. I have quite a collection, mounted in the pages of my private journals, complete with the brand name (Trojans, Sheiks, etc.) and the place where they were found and the date. One night I was in a bath house in L.A. and got into a wild five-way with four other guys, and after sucking the hot cum out of one while being royally fucked up the ass by the other, I retired to the bunks with a big, muscular black who had a prick on him the size of a stuffed tube sock. It was uncut (my favorite) and the foreskin alone would have half-filled a Sheik, the largest rubber made. He wanted to fuck me and although the immense size of his prong scared me a bit, I was eager for more and said yes. Then he did something quite unusual. He took out a package of Trojans and said, "I hope you don't mind, but there's a lot of VD going around, and if I get it my lover would kill me." I got on my knees, as this is the best fucking position if the guy who's giving it to you has a truly enormous ramrod. Very gently, he worked a saliva-coated thumb up my butt, massaging the already spunk-wet muscles until they were relaxed enough for him to put that huge black prick in. He worked it in and out, gripping my haunches with his huge hands, the better to guide his cock, ramming it in up to the hilt. I couldn't believe the difference it made, being fucked up the ass with a rubbered cock — the difference between rubbing your finger over cotton (an unsheathed prick) and over silk. After he'd said thanks and moved on, I found that he'd left the loaded Trojan on the mattress next to me. I tied if off carefully, took it home, and jerked off, slurping his sweet, thick cum and chewing on the rubber as I beat my own 7½ inches. The jet which shot from my cock, and the force of my spasms, were incredible, considering how many times I'd already come at the baths. I swallowed it all just at that sensational moment, not just the thick cum he'd unloaded but the condom as well. For days I worried that the prophylactic might somehow get tangled up in my intestines, as a plumber had once told me that a not-too-uncommon problem with stopped-up sewer lines in houses was condoms. Fortunately, my lines did not get clogged, and I can only suppose that everything came out all right in the end. I also like glory holes. Best of luck. Your publication is the best because it's *true*.

Roman Likes Smelly Underpants

ROME — I find especially useful your articles on raunchy groin-garments — pissy Jockey underpants, stained and smelly bikini briefs, and putrid jock straps I collect underpants, briefs, jocks and prick-panties (new and used). I have a tailor who makes obscene sex-wear for me — like skin-tight jump suits and low-cut bellbottoms in shiny stretch nylon that clings to my groin like a coat of paint and reveals every throb of my nervous cock to the rough and raunchy fuckers who come up for blow jobs. I'd like to hear from perverts with the same depraved obsessions, to exchange experiences, pics and garments or just for obscene correspondence. Your journal is a breath of foetid air in this priest-ridden city. You are to be named among the benefactors of mankind for the wonderful work you do.

Golden Treasury of California Cock

FROM A SMALL CITY — I was in the "Y" and a teenager made it a point to let me see his hard on. He was beautifully hung and uncut. Believe it or not, he let me go down on it almost at once. He took mine also & was a good cocksucker. Said he loved to blow his schoolmates. Had only blown an older man once. It was a friend of his father's. His folks have sent him to a boys' camp in the mountains till school starts. Imagine what goes on in those tents.

* * *

I was about 14 when kids invited me up to the hills. The first time I was reluctant to go. They said we hae fun up there. They all pulled their dicks out. Each one started pulling on his dick. We had a contest to see how far we could shoot our cum. This got to be a regular session, several times a week. We'd go up in the hills after school.

* * *

There's one about 18 I see frequently in the park. Has acted very friendly. He was tossing a frisbee with two friends. He wore a pair of jeans cut off above the knees. Stopped his game to come over. Kept his hand groping himself. He's interested. He said he hoped to see me again. I assume his companions were cramping his style. We shall see. Looks like a football player. He's immense.

* * *

I went to an Italian restaurant near the high school where I learned much about male sex. The restaurant is owned by an Italian I went to high school with. He introduced me to a barful of men. They were plainclothesmen — the vice squad. They ordered several drinks for me. I said, look, you guys will throw me in the drunk tank if I have any more. One big guy said they'd never do that — he could take care of me nicely & put me to bed. I went to the can. He followed. He had 7 or 8 inches of beautiful peter. I got the hell out. I wanted it badly — but not bad enough to take a chance. I wouldn't trust one of those sick bastards. But this guy, who they called Chuck, sent a bottle of red wine to my table later when I was having dinner.

* * *

Our park after 6 P.M. is deserted. It was 101 degrees one day recently and to cool off I was sitting on a bench. Across the grass came what I thought was a Latino or Chicano. On closer inspection found he was an Indian. There are several small tribes in this area. He sat down to talk. He said he ran an Indian shop — jewelry and art objects. His pants revealed a terrific bulge. When he saw me look he groped himself & said his prick had been up all day. He reached in his pants and showed me the head of his dick above his belt line. I rubbed the head with my finger and he groped me at once. My apartment is two blocks away. I had my first Indian. His prick was almost 8". He was practically hairless. He liked blow jobs & also blew me.

* * *

Last summer, before going to a concert at the bowl, I went to the can. There was a young Mexican at the urinals. His dong was hard. I responded at once; mine got semi-hard too. He followed me to my seat in the bowl. He was all

smiles, very handsome. He had a wedding band. His first remark was, "Couldn't we go some place — I'm hotter than hell." He saw me glance at his ring. "Oh," he said, "my wife is pregnant. We've only been married less than a year. I've always made out with men before I got married." I wanted to hear the concert. He agreed to meet me at a certain exit afterwards. I didn't expect to see him again. But there he was. Said he drove around during the concert hoping he'd find someone but drove into a service station & used the men's room & jacked off. But now it was up again. We walked to my apartment, stripped, and I did my good deed for the day. He would only masturbate me but wanted it when I was ready to come. I said "when" & he took it in his mouth. He said he was 23. His uncle had showed him all the tricks. He used to blow his uncle when he was 11. Then as he got older his uncle would return the favor. He came back several times later. Probably the baby has arrived by now and he is getting pussy regularly.

Ecstasy in a Terlet Booth

FROM A PROFESSOR — In the center of Edinburgh is a public men's room, below street level, with perhaps 20 urinals in the shape of crescent, so that when you are standing in a urinal near the far eand you cannot be seen from the entrance at the other end. Also at the far end are 2 stalls. It has become dangerous because of incursions on the part of hustlers, thieves and, periodically, the police. In any event, one Saturday afternoon I was very horny and, since my favorite men's room in the park was closed, I reluctantly ended up in the crescent. Things were *slow*. After about 15 minutes, with just a couple of other men around, an extremely handsome young man, about 18, came in. God was he good looking, and vigorously masculine. He wouldn't come up to the end urinal where I was, but leaned against the wall right near the stall, gazing at me. Gradually he began to fondle himself and, when the stalls emptied out, went into one of them, casting a significant glance at me. I was terrified: having sex with a teenager in this dangerous place? But I followed him into his booth. When I entered he already had his pants down; then he lowered his pure white jockey shorts and oh my God! was he ever beautiful: a gorgeous, full-sized hard on, hard as a rock, sticking straight out. I melted. I was dizzy with desire. I knelt down as if to worship the god Priapus. I grasped his beautiful ass-cheeks and pulled his exquisite cock into my mouth, way down my throat, His body twitched. He groaned in ecstasy. He dissolved against my face, kind of crouching halfway, so that my head was kind of wrapped within his frame. He grasped my head in both hands and rubbed my hair, back and forth, as I sucked hungrily. I couldn't get enough of his cock. Teenagers come quickly (thus probably saving me from arrest); his body begn to have spasms and, when he unloaded, the upper part of his torso simply collapsed on my back. It was thrilling: I was utterly surrounded by him and stuffed with him. I was out of my mind in sexual ecstasy but not so out of my mind that I didn't retreat swiftly to avoid being discovered in his booth with him. I returned to the urinals, where a chap who had been watching enviously when the youth was courting me, greedily sucked me off. I came as fast as the boy had.

Chicago, Chicago!

MASSACHUSETTS — It's two in the morning, but I couldn't wait to share this one with you.

After dinner in Chicago, I headed over to North Wells. Something about the sign in front of a porno shop caught my eye. There was the usual admission ($1, refundable with purchase). Most of the racks visible from the entry were male-female, but I later discovered that the racks you can't see are all male stuff.

I mosied into the peep-show section in the back room. Low lights, sexy guys doors. Oh-ho! says I. I chose a booth and got my quarter into the slot. A picture came on: one guy screwing another. I unzipped and started playing with my cock. Almost immediately I heard a noise to my left. Looking down, I discovered a neat round glory hole. There was a hand beckoning to me through it.

I reached my hand through and beckoned back. The hand was replaced by a nice fat cock, already hard. I crouched down and began sucking on it. It was nice and juicy, and I was really going to town when I heard a voice behind me say, "Suck it, man!" There seemed to be another glory hole to the booth at the right. Then I felt a hand fumbling around for my cock.

The guy on the left had a very muscular forearm. He played with my cock but preferred feeling my asshole. He sucked on my cock (pretty well) but preferred being sucked. He most wanted to fuck my ass — although two attempts weren't very successful.

The guy on the right had a slightly smaller cock — but a very nice one: really hard. His forearm was much thinner than that of the guy on the left. He really liked me to suck him, but got really turned on when — at his whispered request — I rimmed him. He also gave me a real juicy rim job — again, at his request.

Sometimes I alternated between the two guys while the other watched through the hole; sometimes I was in contact with both at once.

I was long since virtually naked. My shirt was lying in a corner of the booth and my pants were down around my boots. The guy on the left had begun the process by undoing my belt; the guy on the right had continued it by unbuttoning my shirt.

After awhile, it became evident that neither guy was going to give me a load. So I decided to cool it for awhile and got dressed.

After leaving the booth, I noticed one particularly hunky guy with a beard standing in a dark corner — I suppose because he is a little over-weight. Why can't guys learn to enjoy what they've got instead of getting uptight about what they don't have? I like chunky guys.

He stepped into a booth and held the door partway open. I stepped in. He already had his cock and balls hanging out of his jeans.

"Suck it," he said in a low voice. I kneeled down.

The door to the next booth opened. A guy entered it, dropped a quarter into the slot, and pulled out his wang. The guy I was sucking on bent over and put his arm through the glory hole, trying to get his hand on the wang. The other guy went right on beating his meat but turned away, trying to elude the hand. He soon left.

By this time my guy was really up, and it was a great piece of meat — the

biggest of the three I had sucked on, with the strongest groin odor. And those great balls banging against my chin. I noticed that there was a face at the glory hole. While I was digging being watched — though not as much as I was digging that great set of equipment sticking in my face — Big Nuts said, "I'm going to give you some piss."

I kept right on sucking to let him know that was okay by me. I could feel him straining to piss — but none came at first.

He took down his pants. Coins jingled on the floor, but he didn't care. He told me to play with his asshole. I got a finger up inside and he really dug it. Then he turned around and told me to stick my tongue up his ass. When he gave me his cock again he managed to squirt some piss into my mouth.

When I had my finger back in his ass he said, "You're going to get a load of shit in your hand." I don't know what I would have done with it if I had — I had nothing to clean up with — but I was so fucking turned on I didn't care.

I jammed my finger up his ass and really gave it a workout, sucking like mad on his cock at the same time. He seemed as excited as I was. When he finally shot his wad we both just about collapsed.

After I'd licked the last drops of cum and piss I got up and we stood side by side, panting.

"You're too fucking much," he said. I gave him a squeeze and said, "Don't forget your change."

He laughed.

It was a little laugh, but its warmth was like a kiss in that dark, impersonal booth.

In Fast and Out Slow

MANHATTAN — I was down at the Christopher St. (7th Ave.) Subway tea room & was looking for a hard fat cock to suck or get fucked by and found a hot TA cop willing to do the job. I was sitting J/O watching one guy blowing this nice looking hard hat, just the type of guys I like, 5'11" or 6 ft., 170 lbs., nice cock & ass & love to mouth fuck a guy. I was still J/O when a guy came in about 26 I would say & took out his cock. I made eye contact & said if you want to piss try my mouth! & he did (I love piss in my mouth or up my ass) & just when his cock was on the way up for a good sucking the TA cop came in. Man did we move fast but I think he knew something was up. The guy that just gave me a load of piss & I got up and started for the door that the cop was holding open. He moved his night stick to come back in to the tea room. He went back outside & got a sign saying closed, then came back & told me to drop my pants. He started to play with his cock. He said OK turn around & bend over. I did. He stuck his finger in first & said it's tight, can you take my cock up there you fag. I said yes. He said first lick the head of my dick and suck it till its hard, then I'll give you a fuck. He got a hard on & told me to wet my asshole & his cock too. When he was ready I bent over & felt that nice hard cop cock at my hole. Man did he know how to fuck & fuck, in fast & out slow, in & out. This went on for a few too short minutes when he let it go. Man did he have a wad. He left & told me to be out of there before too long. I asked him when he got outside if he would call or pass me on to any other cops, TA, city of Nassau or Suffolk. He said no & advised me to keep the story to myself.

Questionnaire

In light of their abuse of wives and daughters, would you entrust your children's education to a male heterosexual teacher? ☐ Yes ☐ No
In light of the Vietnam War, do you think heterosexuals should be permitted to serve in the military? ☐ Yes ☐ No
In light of the high percentage of criminals in Government, do you think heterosexuals should be permitted to hold public office? ☐ Yes ☐ No
In light of their brutality and corruption, do you think heterosexuals should be permitted to serve on the police force? ☐Yes ☐ No
In light of their "make war, not love" mentality, do you think heterosexuals (especially those who suck cock and denounce homosexuals) should be ordained as clergymen? ☐Yes ☐No
In light of the dangers of street crime, do you think heterosexuals should be placed under a sundown curfew? ☐ Yes ☐ No
In light of their abuse of homosexuals in order to make themselves feel big, do you think heterosexuals in the media — TV, movies, books and periodicals — should be arrested for obscenity? ☐ Yes ☐ No
Anita Bryant has red hair on her head. What color hair do you think she has in the crack of her ass? ☐ Black ☐ Red ☐ Brown
In view of the fact that they brought such people as Nixon, Ford, and Reagan into the Presidency, do you think heterosexuals ought to be denied the right to vote? ☐ Yes ☐ No
Do you think heterosexuality should be forbidden by law on the ground that it is socially-induced and unnatural? ☐ Yes ☐ No

Ex-Merchant Marine Forsakes Cunt Juice for Cocks

SEATTLE — Please excuse all of the fucking errors because I've been away from the typewriter since 1974 when I was a merchant marine student. I'm a fucking voyeur, I like to see these guys suck big sonofabitchin cocks at the men's rooms here. Jesus, I'm in love with this blond stud at work, 18 years old. Boy! would I love to suck his fuckin cock and 69 the livin shit out of him and have him come in my motherfuckin mouth until I thirst no more. I use to think that I was straight, but now I know that I cannot get it on with a fuckin floosie. Jesus, how I use to think I loved floosies such as Tracy and Candace (Candy) and Maria but I was kidding my fuckin self. I did not enjoy them. It took a good cocksucker like to set me straight. I don't enjoy fuckin cunt juice anymore. I love cock. Jesus, the men's room scene here is real fuckin good. Lots of suck-in. I have a picture of myself I'm sending you. I'm in my Jockey Shorts fuckin horny as all get out. By the way has a body that just won't quit. Jesus he is near 50 fuckin years old and he has a bod that is better than my mid 20s Bod. His sucky thighs are really outta sight. They are to some cocksucker sweeter than candy. And Maria's pony tail used to give me a rush. I thought I was "QUEER" a long time ago but now I know thanks to some good honest feelings I can express around some truly great human beings like ___ and his friends.

A Multi-faceted Fuck

ILLINOIS — A recent experience in my home town in the Midwest prompts me to write. I'm not sure that I remember everything we said in the right order, but this is pretty much how it happened. Maybe I'll see him when I visit home again at Christmas. I was in the local bar when a good-looking young guy with sandy hair caught my eye, locking it for long enough to show his interest. Unbecomingly shy, I met his gaze as long as I could. After a minute, he looked at me again for perhaps 4 or 5 seconds, and I, feeling very trusting, somehow returned my gaze. He came over and sat by me as if he owned the place. He said his name was Steve. He was 24. He came there often. Yes, I was just visiting from out of town. He guessed me at 23, very flattering as I'm nearly 30. Though our table was in a well-lit part of the bar, he rested his hand on my groin. I was uncomfortable, but his naturalness and ease allowed me to accept it. I had to go to the john. I stood at the lone urinal and was nearly done when the door opened. He grabbed my dick. It got hard. He kissed me but there was a hard edge to it, possessive. Then he walked back to the table. I zipped up, grateful that no one else had walked into the john. He played with my groin again at the table, to my growing embarrassment. Could we go to my house? No, my mother was accepting, but she had her limits. How about his place? No, his "people" might not be too cool. So we drove our two cars into the country. I found a fairly empty road, got out of my car and rode with him, looking for a quiet spot. We found one, out in the moonlight, just beyond some railroad tracks. He unfastened my jeans and pulled out my dick. I started to undo his but he pushed my hand away, saying to leave that up to him. "I want you naked," he said, and started to pull off my T-shirt. I undid my shoes and my pants came off. He told me to put my clothes out on the ground. "You like it when I tell you what to do, don't you?" He had a big smile, which showed him to be handsomer than I'd first realized. I nodded, but I knew he had my number. His hands roamed over my naked body in the car. He stuck his finger up my ass, playing with my dick. I reached for his cock, still inside his jeans, and he smiled and said, "No, not until I say so." He told me to get out of the car. I did, and he came around and leaned me against the hood. He held me and kissed me, again in that possessive way. He undid his pants, taking out his long fat cock. It was incredibly fat at the base, and even though it narrowed, it was still big at the top. "Suck my dick," he told me, and I bent over, taking it in my mouth. He grabbed my head and pushed, and I fought it, not being in the right position. I got down on my knees, and then I could take it. I sucked him for awhile, and then he said, "You like that, don't you? You like sucking my dick," I said "uh-huh;" he had my mouth crammed full with his dick. He pulled my head off his dick and stood up. "I'm going to fuck you," he said. "Get up on the car." I lay down on it, but it was cold. I was on my back. He lifted up my legs and started to put his dick up my ass. My muscles tightened up, so he said, "Put it in there, put my dick up your ass." I got it in a little way but it hurt, so he told me to suck it again. I did, but just for a couple of seconds, and then he pushed me onto the car on my stomach. He tried to stick it in me. It wouldn't go, so I guided it, pushing my ass up as high as I could, and he got it in. He started fucking me and it hurt *real* bad, and I jumped off, my sexual interest suddenly gone. "That really hurt," I said. "I don't think I can do it right now." He scowled, I think, or muttered something, and we got back in the car. He lay down and I lay on top

on him, grateful for his warmth — it was getting cool by then. We lay there awhile, then he asked if I was turned on to him and I said "Yeah." He eased my head down to his cock, playing with my dick at the same time. I really sucked his dick, and then he pulled my head up. "I want to fuck you. Sit on my prick." I sat on top of it and it went in easier this time. I was on it, jacking myself off, and then he pushed me off. I was enjoying it, but he made me get off. "Suck my dick," he said, so I took it again, and he pushed my head down so hard I thought I wouldn't be able to get my breath. I got scared for a second, but it seemed OK, so I kept going until he pulled my head off it and said to get out of the car. I did, and he kissed me and spread my legs and stuck his finger up my ass. "I want to get up in there. Are you going to let me? "Yes, but I've got to go slow." "Do you want it on your stomach or on your back?" "On my stomach." "Good." He pushed me down against the cold metal and slid his prick in. It went in pretty easily by now. "You like to get fucked don't you?" I just said "un-huh." He started to beat me off while he fucked me. A train kept getting closer but Steve just kept fucking me. I got nervous and I lost my attention when the lights of the train hit us, but he just kept it in my ass, slowly sticking his dick in and pulling it out, sometimes almost all the way out, and he'd moan with pleasure every time he stuck it back up my ass. Then he started to jig me faster and I had trouble holding onto the car. "Yeah, yeah," he kept saying, as he really started to buck, and he shot his spunk way up into me. When he pulled out he told me to get my shirt. I started to pick up my clothes and he said, "No, just bring your shirt." He took it and wiped his cock with it. Then he took me and kissed me and made me get back into the car. I wanted to get dressed but he threw my shirt in the back seat and said to leave my pants on the ground. I didn't really like this idea, but I was carried along by my own lust for him. He was nice and tall and goodlooking (I'm short) and I kind of just fell into line with him. He had me sit next to him and he played with my cock as we drove along.

After awhile he said, "I want to fuck you again," which was OK because I was still horny. We parked by the side of the road, maybe a couple of miles from where I'd left my pants, and that thought made me nervous but excited. He had me sit on the hood and looked into my eyes and said, "Sit on it." I lifted up my legs and eased my butt down over his dick again. I couldn't seem to get the angle right so I told him I had to stop. He pulled out and I got down onto the road and started to suck him again. I jacked myself and this felt really good, but when I got going hot again he pulled me up and grabbed me and pushed me against the car. He spread my legs with his own legs and held my arms down and got his dick inside. He moved his dick back and forth slowly in my ass, kind of rocking me slowly. Then he stopped and pulled out. It was kind of cold by now and I went to get my shirt, but he yelled out, "Hey, give me that," and I gave it to him, not wanting to create a hassle because it was too far from where I'd left my pants, and besides, he really turned me on. He was still fully dressed, with just his dick hanging out of his pants, while he kept me naked. "Come here," he said, and we got into the car again. He lay down on the back seat and put his prick back in my mouth.

"I want you to sit on it," he said, and I got on his cock again and slowly pushed it up and down by rocking on it. "That's good, man. Let's see you fuck yourself now." I took his dick up my ass as far as I could and then I'd pull up on it, jacking myself off the whole time. I really got going after awhile, and he said, "After you come I'm going to fuck you again," and I said OK, and started to shoot all over. I wiped it up with my shirt, and with his dick still up my ass, and then he fucked

me until he came again. He didn't want to drive back to where my clothes were, but just to my car. By then I just wanted to get home, so I said OK. When we got to my car, I got out. It had started to rain by now, but he called me back to his car. I went over and he opened the door, shining the car light on me. This road was busier than the one we'd been on, and this made me nervous. He said he'd really enjoyed it. He took my balls in his hand. I got another hard on and he just laughed at me and said Goodnight and drove off. I got my clothes — I was happy to have them again — and when I got home I had to beat off, the whole thing had been so much for me.

"Strangely Delicious"

MANHATTAN — A friend took a West Point cadet to a hotel room. The kid was so hot and pent up that when my friend got him naked and on the bed he shot his load without being touched and it damn near hit the ceiling. It is a pretty picture. Another friend wrote: "Your letter brought back a dozen scenes from Auld Mexico, culminating in a star-studded (forgive me!) night in Acapulco when, finally, Raoul, a bullfighter, offered a pair of firm peach-shaped buns (a great concession, considering the matador/macho tradition). My, God! Wouldn't have missed it for anything. As Oscar once said, 'My only regrets are the sins I never committed.' Would be glad to write it up for *Boyd's*, probably on some rainy evening with a log burning in the fireplace." A masterful type who gave me the works the other night had the most delicious piss. I mean it. He doesn't drink alcohol and here he drank Coke. But what came out of the generous nozzle tasted like sweet slightly salted water. Compared to the other piss of my experience this was not only totally inoffensive but really strangely delicious. I took three loads and to my astonishment liked it better each time. I'm sorry I don't know his name, but maybe it's just as well. Just before he left he told me there was one thing he'd like to do to me he hadn't done during the four or more hours we were together. Would I let him do it? Sure, I said, I'll do anything to please *you*. Then he said, Stand at the foot of the bed and put your hands over your eyes. I'm going to punch you in the gut but I don't want you anticipating the blow. It will knock you out for a half hour or so; you'll just fall back on the bed. Then I'll leave you. I said, Okay, go ahead. He drew back a powerful right — he did have lovely muscles — and I watched him between my fingers. Then he let his fist fall. No, I can't do it, he said, and took me in his arms and kissed the mouth that had just taken his last donation of piss. He lives in a glamorous apt. building with a terrace, etc. He told me he'd like to fuck me on the terrace under the stars. He said he went down to one of those parks at the end of the street one night and there he was approached by a well-dressed dude, not young but not old. Just rather with it, so my informant felt. The gent said to my friend, "Would you like to earn $100?" Playboy asked, naturally. "What do I have to do?" "Well, nothing really," the sophisticate replied; "I'd like you to come to my apartment, take off your clothes and sit naked and let me look at you. And then I'd like to masturbate you with my feet." "So," I said, "did you do it?" "Of course not," he said. "I didn't need $100 right then. Besides, he might have had athlete's foot." I'm sailing for London on the Q.E. II on the 31st, complete with wife. Hot flashes to thee.

Interview:
Rhode Islander Likes Ten Cocks A Day

Have you ever been married? Yes.
Are you a father? Yes.
What is your favorite and most frequent kind of sex? Sucking dick and taking it up the asshole.
What is your sexual self-diagnosis? Homosexual.
How many cocks have you sucked? Many.
How many cocksuckers have blown you? Many.
What is the biggest number of cocks you ever sucked in one day? 10-12.
What is the biggest prick you ever sucked? 9"+.
What is the youngest prick you ever sucked? 16.
What is the biggest number of cocksuckers that ever blew you in one day? About 3, I guess.
How many pricks have you taken up your asshole? Many.
What's the biggest number in one day? 8 or 9.
How many assholes have you fucked? Quite a few.
Do you prefer giving blow jobs or getting them? Give preferably but also take whatever action is preferred by partner at any given time.
Do you like the taste of men's bodies? Yes. Feet, groin, balls, cock, nipples. Clean please.
Do you like the smell of men's bodies? Yes. Clean sweaty smell of any or all parts. Especially when they are sweating.
Please describe yourself. I am white, with a college education. Hair is light brown, eyes hazel. May body is not the most attractive, but not repulsive. I have always been slim and still am. My body has very little hair. I try to keep my stomach flat. Now wear a 31" or 32" pants. I consider myself middle class but prefer not to state my occupation. You may mention my state — Rhode Island. My cock is about 7", balls hang low, ass clean and free of piles or any other growth.
Are you cut or uncut? Uncut.
Do you prefer cut on uncut cock? Don't give a fuck.
Have you ever swallowed piss? Yes, as often as I can get it.
Why do you do what you do in sex? I am only doing what comes naturally — to me.
Do you prefer young guys? Younger men usually have nicer bodies and are more virile.
Do you prefer complete nudity in sex or just a hanging out of the guy's pants? Nudity is far better, but will also take it hanging out.
Do you like the taste of cum? Yes.
What occupational types do you like? Not too fussy if it is an attractive body.
What kind of partners do you like in general? Another homosexual or bisexual. Trade is O.K., but not all the time.
What physical characteristics do you like in another man? Slim, hairless, muscular body. Well-defined pectorals. Long hair. Flat belly.
What personality types do you like? Like someone who knows the story. Cool. Someone young — sweet. I like a partner who likes dancing.
Do you like jock straps? Yes. The odor turns me on.
Have you fulfilled yourself sexually? Sometimes.

Have you fulfilled yourself in your career? Yes.
Where do you meet partners? Toilets, bars, streets, parks.
Do you like love affairs? Yes. Had one which lasted a long time. "Being faithful" is not practical for any length of time.
Who causes more trouble — homosexuals or "straights?" Definitely "straights."
Do you think homosexuals have better morals than "straights" in the sense that they don't bother other people, while "straights" bully others? Yes.
Did you "go" with girls as a boy to conform? Yes, up through college.
When did you first realize you are homosexual? Not until fairly late. I was in my 20s and in the military service.
Have you ever had any sexual trouble? I was once arrested for "unnatural acts" but fortunately it was not while in full action and it was cleared up.
What's your attitude toward hustlers? I have no objection to a male whore. However, two things should be understood. First, he sets his price and sticks with it — does not try to get more during or after the action. Secondly, he should give the person hiring him some quality action.
Who taught you to jerk off when you were a boy? I lived on a farm in Maine. When I was in the 6th or 7th grade, the "hired man" was about 19 or 20. He let me watch the bull fuck a cow and it really turned me on. One day I found him standing on a stool with a big hard on, trying to stick it into a cow. When he first saw me, he seemed a little annoyed, but soon he asked me if I wanted to watch. So he got back on the stool and I sort of leaned on the cow to keep her from moving too much. He jerked his cock a little and then moved the head of it up and down the opening of the cow's cunt. The cow buckled and raised her back slightly. He moved his cock in slowly. He finally got most of it in and then rammed like hell till he shot his load. He asked if I wanted to try it. I did but couldn't seem to get in a good position so I pulled out and got down. He rubbed the juice all over my cock and sort of jerked me a little. It sure felt good. I started to jerk and it felt even better. This was my first real jerk off.
What was your first sexual experience with other boys? I attended a small rural school. I was never athletic and was small and slim — probably kind of cute. There were bullies at school of whom I was afraid but also sort of liked. One day when I was in the 7th grade, someone circulated the information that there would be a "ring dub" in the tool house after school. I was excited that I was asked to come. After school, about 7 or 8 of us went into the tool house. Some were Grade 8 students. When we were all gathered there was much chit chat until it finally appeared the time had come. We sort of didn't look at each other and nothing was happening. Then Bill, who was bigger than most of us, said, "Well, who is man enough to show his cock?" What he meant, of course, maybe without knowing it, was, "Who is homosexual enough to show his cock?" No one opened his fly. Then Bill said, "Carl, why don't you start?" Carl opened his pants and took his cock and then Bill did the same. Slowly, everyone got his cock out and began to fondle it. Then we started to jerk. We all got quite turned on seeing seven others jerking at the same time. The first one to come let it go on the floor. One or two sort of turned around when they shot their load but one turned to another who hadn't come and shot his cream all over the other guy's cock.

Youth Succumbs to Lure of Mechanic's Unbuttoned Coveralls

SAN FRANCISCO — Dear Come-rade, when I was 13 years old, I had a steady relationship with Raymond, the man across the street who ran a garage. He wore coveralls a lot and many times wore nothing underneath. I used to love to watch his body in those loose clothes with the side buttons undone so you could see his hips and *almost* his groin. He must have noticed me staring at him, because he asked if I wanted to go into the men's room with him. I of course said yes. He didn't just take his prick out, he undid his overalls and dropped them to the floor. I just drooled and stared. He pissed and got a hard on, which I reached for without him asking. He wanted to see mine, so I quickly undressed. My cousins and my brothers and I had all been playing with each other for a couple of years, so I was right at home, and with a cock so big as his, with such huge balls and such a nice smelly hairy ass, I was in HEAVEN. Ray played with mine and then asked me to suck him, something I'd never done. I can remember not liking it at first but I learned real fast. After a few weeks, the trip to the men's room became a regular thing. I would lie on the floor and Ray would hover over my face so I could ream his asshole out, take his balls in my mouth one at a time and suck his huge prick. He was always working hard, so he was always sweaty. He wasn't shitty but he smelled strong. One day he brought back some grease and stuck a couple of fingers up my virgin asshole, and I can still remember the feel of his strong tender hands gripping my hips as he first spread my young eager cheeks and pressed his meat against my butt. Slowly, slowly he went in and I took all of it. At first it was uncomfortable, but it didn't hurt. Within a couple of weeks I begged for it. I always jacked myself off after he was done; that was O.K. by me. But I lived for his cock. I had to have it, and he knew it. He never kept it from me if he could help it. First I'd suck him, licking him everywhere. Then I'd lie down and ream him. Then a royal fuck while he played with my cock. This went on three or four times a week for five years until I graduated from high school. I taught my two cousins, my twin brothers, and four other lovers how to suck and fuck and I did it with all of them all through high school also. More on this later. I lived for cock then and I still do. I love hairy assholes, and I could ream for hours. I still jack off a couple of times a day no matter how much sex I'm having.

Cabbies, Cops Have Sex With Boys in Patrol Cars

From An Article By Frank Rose In *The Village Voice* (New York) — Boy towns turn up in strange places: years ago, Tom Reeves stumbled onto one in Baltimore...Subsequent research convinced him that 50 to 70 percentage of men have sex with the boys...One neighborhood boy tells me that cab drivers give kids free rides in exchange for sex. So do cops in their patrol cars. Reeves met one boy, he says, 'who told me I was the first gay person he had met who was not a policeman.'

Dad Takes Two At Once

TEXAS — This is a true story. I cannot sign my name, because I am a businessman, have lived in this city most of my life, am active in Boy Scout work, teach Sunday School, and sing in the church choir.

I have always been fascinated by peters. Even in kindergarten. I liked to look at them all, and if I was encouraged, to play with them, and if they were small enough to fit in my mouth, to suck them.

When I was about 13, my mother began to come down with sick headaches, and my father moved into my room. The bed was not full-sized, but neither of us minded.

The first night we undressed, my father noticed that I was beginning to get hairs around my prick. He gave the hair a playful tug and told me that in a year or so I would be a real stud.

When he came to bed, he was not wearing pajamas. He kissed me on the neck and felt of my peter. I was hard, just from watching. He took my hand and put it on his. It got hard fast.

My father had a rather unusual prick. The shaft was long and skinny but the head was enormous. It looked like a lollipop but tasted better.

He told me that what we were about to do was probably wrong but that as long as we were going to do it anyway we might as well do it right.

He unbuttoned my pajamas, kissed me on my neck and nipples, ran his tongue down my body, and finally put his lips around my dick. I got my nuts off almost immediately.

He told me that I could do the same to him if I wanted to. I never wanted anything more. The head of his peter was so large I had to stretch my mouth to get it in. When he got his nuts off it was not in one spurt, like my fellow teenagers; he came in many short spasms, which were easy to swallow.

Dad asked me about my previous experiences. I told him first about Leroy. Leroy was a senior in high school and worked nights and Saturdays at the local movie house as a projectionist. When I went to the movies I generally spent more time in the restroom than I did watching the film. I met Leroy there. His dick was substantial but not oversized.

He invited me into the projection booth. He changed the reel, locked the door, and asked me how I liked to do it. I told him that I would suck him, fuck him, or jack him off, whatever he wanted; but that he could not fuck me because my asshole was still too small.

I sucked him off, and did the same at every Saturday matinee until he left for college.

Then I told my father about the Jackson boys. Steve was in my grade at school and Mike was about a year older. We had been playing with each other's cocks for a long time. Dad asked what we did and I told him that when we were younger we did everything to each other, but that they had grown up faster than I had and I could no longer take their peters in my ass. Now I usually fucked one or the other and that the brother sucked whoever was being fucked.

Dad was enchanted. He got out of bed, went to the bathroom, and came back with a jar of Vaseline. He lubricated his asshole well, put some on my prick, which was hard again, and told me to stick it in.

I did not like this as much as being sucked off but if he wanted it, I would do anything.

We sucked each other off again in the morning and Dad asked me if Steve and Mike might like to go to the beach that afternoon.

When I asked them at Sunday school they were agreeable. Dad drove us out to a lonely part of the beach and we all went swimming bareass.

Steve and I actually swam but my father and Mike stayed in the shallow water and horsed around. They went ashore. I told Steve to come watch. We found them behind a small sand hill, Dad on his hands and knees and Mike fucking him dog fashion.

Dad had a hard on, but since I couldn't get between his peter and the sand I jacked him off.

He licked his lips and opened his mouth and invited Steve to join.

We repeated this arrangement many times in Dad's office after hours. Leroy joined us when he could.

* * *

Leroy now teaches school and has rented our garage apartment, which is convenient for everybody.

Mike is married and living in Houston, but he comes down every now and then on business. When he does, he stays with me.

Steve is working at a hospital and living with a doctor who has a crooked peter. They are jealous of one another but when one is safely out of the way, I manage to do the other. I am still not much of an asshole man.

Boy Forces Brother To Lick His Asshole

FLORIDA — I've been sucking cock since I was a boy, when my older brother and I used to sleep together. I remember how funky his groin smelled and how big his dick seemed. It took some effort, but I was able to open my mouth wide enough to insert the smooth cut head of his prick and about 2" of his shaft. He never wasted any time with "fag romancing" (as he called it); he just pulled me over to him in the middle of the night, pushed my head under the covers to his already hard cock and used my mouth as a receptacle for his somewhat sweet cum. Since I lived in fear of my big brother (he was the oldest in a family of 5 boys and 3 girls), he was pretty certain that I wouldn't squeal on him and his shocking activities. I really hated him, but he was usually in charge of babysitting me when our parents were out and he would regularly beat the shit out of me so I knew better than to say anything to our parents. He is now a big wheel in law enforcement in Northern Michigan. As time went on he used to order me to suck his balls (the hairs from those balls were forever getting caught in my teeth), lick around his smelly asshole and lick his dick like it was a big hot lollipop. He loved to straddle me while I was laying on my back, stick his prick in my mouth and then pull it out when he was ready to shoot so he could squirt his sticky cum all over my face. Then he told me to wipe it off my face with my hand and eat it. All this (and other refinements) went on *every single night* for two years until we moved into a bigger house and I got my own bedroom. I locked my door. In two whole years of "servicing" my brother, he never once touched *me*. [*EDITOR'S NOTE: This sounds like an ideal relationship; please tell us more — what was said and done, especially the refinements. It's time we got some refinement in this magazine.*]

Successful Cocksucking in Today's Society

NEW YORK — The first time I beat my meat and was successful in cuming was when I just turned 15 years old. I was living with my Aunt and Uncle who had 9 children, 6 boys and 3 girls. The boys' ages were from 9 yrs. to 22 yrs. The oldest was in the service. I did not see him much. All us boys slept in one room, the girls in another. I started playing with my meat when I was about 12 yrs. old. I would do it with some of my classmates who went to Catholic school. They were very strict about little boys masturbating themselves. I would never cum when I jacked off with two or three of my classmates. I don't remember any of them cuming either. I guess we felt guilty about it. They told us it was bad and that it would make us sick and that it was a mortal sin every time you did it, that it would make you crazy. We had to tell the priest every time you did it or tried to, when you went to confession. You also had to tell the number of times.

I was about 14 yrs. old when I started living with my cousins. My mother got sick so I had to stay with them for about 1 ½ yrs. So let me tell you about the first time I cum. There was one double deck bed, 2 of us on top, me & my 9 yr. old cousin & one cousin on bottom. He was about 16 yrs. old. The three others slept on a mattress on the floor. Of all of the cousins I liked this 9 yr. old the best. He asked his mother if he could sleep with me instead of his 16 yr. old brother. He & his brother were sleeping together on the bottom bunk. His brother was big for his age. There wasn't much room for the both of them. His mother said okay but she did not want to hear any talking. So from the first day I moved in I slept with my 9 yr. old cousin. I was still 14 yrs. old and never cum. I would touch my cock once in awhile when my cousin was sleeping but nothing would happen. It was this night that I will never forget that I would like to tell you about. I was just 15 yrs. old then and I had been already sleeping with my cousin a number of months now. Let me give you a description of what he looked like. He was very small for his age. He could pass for an 8 yr. old. But talking to him you could tell he was older. He was almost 10 yrs. old now when for the first time I was playing with my cock that it got very hard. It never got this hard before. This particular night the cousin on the bottom bunk was away. He went Upstate to work for the summer. My 9 yr. old cousin would tell me sometimes that he liked me better than his own brothers & that I was good looking. I did not think anything unusual about this, I would tell him he was cute & kiss him on the forehead. A few times in the park we would play ball together. When we would have to take a piss I noticed he would be looking at my cock. His cock was very tiny next to mine. Well anyway this night I was jacking off, I was in such heat thinking about the way my cousin would look at my cock. My cock was very hard. My breathing was very heavy. The bed beginning to shake a little bit. I did not want to wake my cousins that were sleeping on the floor. My 9 yr. old cousin next to me was sleeping, that is I thought he was. He turned over on his side. I was on my side, our faces were facing each other, I could not see if his eyes were open. It was too dark in the room. I could feel his little body move up against my big hard cock. He only wore a pair of shorts. He had a very skinny body. He did not weigh more than 85 lbs. His body was not very long. I would say it was about 4 ½ ft. I could feel his skinny legs against the head of my huge cock. I stuck it between his knees. I pulled his face next to mine & started kissing him. He put one of his hands

around the back of my head & pulled my mouth next to his. He opened his mouth & I put my tongue inside. He did the same. I came for the first time in my life in between his little skinny legs. The bed was soaked with my cum and it was on his little legs too. He never said a word while all this was going on, neither did I. We never talked about it. I got a clean sheet and put the soiled one in a laundry bag. The Aunt never knew. No one ever knew about this wonderful relationship that began that night & lasted for about a year. It was too dangerous to do anything in bed with him and I wanted him bad. He was still too young to understand.

A week after this wonderful night he asked me why I don't kiss him anymore. I said, "Do you want me to." He said he did and said, "Let's go on the roof." No body goes up there. I said let's go now. I had half a hard on by the time we got to the roof. I started kissing him & took my cock out. It was hard & I started jacking off. I said, lets take our clothes off. He had such a skinny body, a little cock, but a cute face. I liked his tiny mouth. I started thinking what it would feel like if I put my huge cock inside it & jacked off into it. It was such a small mouth that I was not sure if my cock would fit into it. I started kissing him again after we were both naked. I was tongue fucking him in his little mouth and put one of his hands around my cock. He did not know how to do it so I showed him how to jack me off. He didn't know anything. I knew a little about sex from my friends but this cousin of mine knew nothing. He just liked to kiss me. I told him to kneel on his knees & I put my cock against his tight closed lips. He looked scared. I told him it wasn't going to hurt. He said, you have an awful big prick. I said to him, it won't bite you. I told him to pull the foreskin back & forth like I showed him. While he was jacking me off the head of my cock was against his tight mouth. He would not open his mouth. He then began to breathe a little heavy & his mouth began to open a little. With my two hands I pushed the back of his head forward & my cock went into his mouth. He stopped jacking me off so I started jacking myself off into his mouth. With one hand I kept pushing his head forward & my cock was half in his tiny mouth. I was fucking him in the mouth. Tears were coming from his eyes & he was crying. I didn't care. My cock was hard & thick & I was fucking so fast he could hardly breathe, so I pulled my cock out. He said, Please, lets just kiss like we did before. I told him to kiss my cock. He started kissing it while I jacked it off. Just before I cum I told him to open his mouth wide. I shot my cum into his mouth. He spit it out.

He did not talk to me much after this. I asked him if he would like to play ball. He said no. He stopped sleeping with me for about a month, until one night I was half asleep, I felt someone lay next to me. It was my little cousin. He whispered into my ear, I love you & I miss you, lets go on the roof tomorrow. We shared each others bodys until my mother was well again and then I went back home. I was 16 yrs. old now & forgot about my wonderful little cousin. I thought I was strait & liked girls. I didn't want to be a faggot. I started drinking when I was 17 yrs. old & got married when I was 26 yrs. old. I never had a good relationship with a woman. I was never really strait. I thought I was. I was living a strait life. We lived together a year before we got married & had 3 children. It lasted 6 yrs. I never really wanted a woman. I don't drink anymore. I am free. It took me over 30 yrs. to find the truth. I feel like a bird. I am out of the strait prison. I like & respect women but not for sex. I love men. I love to suck cock.

Now I am looking for my lost angel that I met last year. I think of having sex with him all the time. Thats as far as it ever went. I met him last year in the park. He was selling lemonade. I bought a cup from him & we started talking. He said

he was 21 yrs. old but he looks 16. He lived with a 35 yr. old man. He said that there was no sex between them. He had sex a few times & didn't like it. I was afraid to ask him if he had sex with a man or a woman. We went to the beach twice last year. When he goes to take a piss, he tells me to wait outside. He told me he don't like queers. He thinks I'm strait. He never gave me a chance. He always seemed to be depressed when I would talk sex, like I would tell him I never been with a woman since I left my wife. I told him I like to jack off all the time. He said he jacks off by himself. He has sex with no one. He said he doesn't like gay sex. Yet he lived with this 35 yr. old man who supported him, gave him $4.00 a day spending money. He said the man slept in the bed & he slept on the floor. Last time I saw him he said he was working and said he was living alone. This was last year. He knows where I live & has my tel.no. but has never called. I liked him a lot. He's 22 yrs. old now. Hes about 5 ft. 7 inch weighs about 120 lbs. Irish complexion, boys face, brown wavy hair, no hair on face or body, legs, arms. I dont know where hes living any more since he moved. I should have told him about my feelings for him, I should have told him that I would take care of him, that he could have any thing he wanted, that I would be kind & good to him, that I would like to suck his shit hole the dirtyer the better lick his balls & suck his cock. I wouldn't care what size it was, that I would take all he had in my mouth, taste & suck all his cum any time of day he wanted me to, I dont care if he wakes me up in the middle of the night I would suck all the cum he has into my hungry mouth. I'm going to look for this little angel and when I find him take him home with me, where there is no such thing as bad, evil, guilt or hate. But love & love & love & enjoying one another forever & ever. I will find my little angel. I will not lose this one — not like the others.

Youth Has "Perfect" Meat, Seeks "Special" Cocksuckers

LOS ANGELES — I am 22 and have just been introduced to S.T.H. I was introduced to sex 8 years ago in the freezer-room of a store in Houston. I am 5'10½", 140, thin but slightly muscled with good definition. One of the most highly-reported cocksuckers in L.A., a humpy blond middle-aged man named Chuck, and a notorious N.Y. sex maniac named Kerry have each decided I have the perfect cock. It is popular wherever I go. It is only 6-7" but as big around as a silver dollar. It gets real hard and sticks straight up. Since I was 14 I've had about 150-200 guys a year. Until I was about 19 I wasn't into the baths so I got off at the 25¢ arcades in Houston; a truly wonderful couple of years (ages 17 and 18). I met the best Houston studs there as that scene was really hot and still is. When I got back there to visit I see some of the hunks who used to suck and fuck me; they are all older and hotter and still in the bookstores. Living in LA for 2½ years has been a mixed blessing. I have learned the social patterns of the modern urban homosexual and this has stifled some of the Texan lust for prowling and putting in the time it sometimes takes to get something special. Availability here is very high but quality is not as good. I miss Texas meat and I'm homesick for the men who made me what I am. Your magazine takes me back to how I used to be and I am re-orienting myself back to that kind of behavior. If you know of any special hot cocksuckers who want to test my reputation, let me know. They would be a good start on the road back to Texas in my mind. Signed, Almost ruined by the big city.

Cowboy Sucks Off Youth

CALIFORNIA — The summer I was 15 I was working as a cowboy on an uncle's ranch. There was one other hand on the ranch, Joe, 23, blond, *an Adonis*, mustached, tanned, blue-eyed, and great. He became my hero from the first day: he could do no wrong.

We usually worked shirtless. I loved to watch his muscles move beneath his beautiful tanned skin. Every day we went skinny dipping. He was the first adult male I had seen naked. Beautiful! I was fascinated by his cock & huge balls surrounded by blond curls. I loved to wtch his dick and balls swing back and forth as he walked or ran. When he pissed it was like a geyser.

Between dips we horsed around, played grabass, & wrestled. Nearly always, during the fun, he'd make a grab for my dong, which I always managed to evade, and he'd say he'd like to "gobble it" or "eat it." At 15 I was pretty dumb and didn't know exactly what he was talking about. I just took it as a joke.

One day, for no reason, while skinny dipping, I came up with a hard on. I had 7" then: it grew only ¼" more in 25 years. He quickly made his usual grab and this time connected. I wrenched out of his grasp and pushed into the water. Oh, yes, while he did have hold of my bone he made his usual remark about eating me but this time added "now" to it.

As I jacked off in the house that night I resolved that if the chance ever came again I'd just let him do what he wanted.

That chance came a couple of weeks later. My uncle and his family left to spend a day in town. I stayed behind to help Joe do some chores around the barn. We worked for about an hour, then Joe suggested we go up to the hayloft to do something or other — I forget what he gave as an excuse. I followed him up the ladder. We no sooner got up there than he had me down on the hay, had my jeans down around my ankles, & was sucking my cock hard & to the best blast-off I'd ever had.

I loved it. We lay there for awhile afterward — maybe half and hour — talking. Then he went down on me again. Then we returned to our work. I had a half hard on the rest of the day, which many times became a full hard on just remembering the ecstasy he'd given me. That night after hitting the sack I got a real throbber, as usual. I began my usual jack-off, then stopped. Why this shit? I got out of bed and with my boner leading the way made my way out of the house to the bunkhouse where Joe slept. He was real glad to see me & eagerly gobbled my pecker.

This became a nightly routine for about a week. Joe was always so glad to see me, to suck my dick, & swallow my wad. So I asked Joe if I could do it to him. He readily accepted. With his directions I guess I did a fair job. At least he said it was. And I swallowed that first beautiful load of cream. I loved it — the whole bit. After that we exchanged sucks, usually 69. Usually we only did it at night. There were a few times during the day, in the barn or some out-building or isolated place, but only once at the swim hole as we were never sure that someone might not ride up & catch us.

This idyll continued until late that summer. Then Joe was fired for not doing his work. Maybe he wasn't but he sure was doing his work on my cock & thrived on it.

I never saw Joe again. But my heart soon healed when I found there were other cocks around that were available. One was the guy that replaced Joe. He was Joe's opposite — short, stocky, dark, & gloomy, a real sour-assed bastard,

& I did not like him. We were out one day riding or checking cattle when he reined in & stopped to take a piss. He finished first & just stood there holding his cock & watching mine. Then suddenly he got down on his knees, grabbed my cock (which stopped the flow of piss, but I already had pissed all over him), and, telling me to finish pissing, he put my cock in his mouth. I was really surprised. Never had thought of anyone doing that! But what the hell, he wanted it, so I pissed, but only had a little left to give him. I was rewarded with a damn good blow job. Then, thirsty for cum myself, I sucked him off too. His cum wasn't up to Joe's standard but it wasn't too bad and I did need it badly. Shit! I was hooked on cock already.

That was my only time with him since I soon left for home, town, and all that nice stuff in school.

Self Abuse

Agence France-Presse, in a dispatch from Peking under date of July 19, reports that a Chinese sex manual discourages jacking off on the grounds that it results in "overstimulation of the brain, dizziness, insomnia, general weakness, and the erosion of revolutionary will."

Most of these symptoms are causes, rather than results, of jacking off. The only way to get rid of "overstimulation of the brain" is to shoot your wad, and I recommend the same procedure for insomniacs.

The manual offers startling evidence in support of my oft-repeated remark that "straights," by definition, cannot be radical or revolutionary. Only homosexuals — outside the "straight" society and able to see it for what it is — can be.

Sex is the most important thing, more important even than money. Sexual "straightness" is an unnatural restraint. Any social reform must start with sexual reform, which means breaking out of "straightness." The trouble with China's Communists is the same trouble with other socialists, with capitalists, and with other forms of government: they are "straight." Male "straightness" expresses itself in war, violence, and subjection of women and homosexuals. As long as a man is trying to be "straight," he will participate in war or whatever other activities his "straight" society dictates.

All "straights" are Narxists — my word for combining Nazis and Marxists.

Here in dear old America, Jane Alpert recently wrote that her lover, Sam Melville, wrote on their refrigerator, "Wash me." The message was for her. This, and the attitude towards women that it symbolizes, turned her away from the radical group she and Melville belonged to. She says that she does not mourn his death in the Attica prison riot, and she plans to work for improvement in the attitude towards women through women's groups, not "straight" male groups. In these groups, homosexuals are given secondary roles along with mimeographing, coffee-serving women: the "straight" men make the decisions and lead the parades. The radical male, even more than his capitalist brother, needs the social support heterosexuality gives, and his attitude toward women and homosexuals is no better than that of his insurance salesman father.

Only a homosexual knows that the reason society is a shit heap is sexual. Any "straight" radical who is not aware of this is not to be taken seriously.

Boyd McDonald

Interview: Trucker

[EDITOR'S NOTE: This interview was contributed by a STH reader in the South.]
How any other truckers have you had sex with? Easily 700.
You, yourself, were a truck driver? Yes, For almost 15 years. Long distance hauling in Texas and between Texas and Chicago.
What per cent of truckers would you estimate is homosexual — or at least participate? I'd estimate that at least 65% of the office workers in trucking is homosexual or bisexual. Many have been attracted to that industry because of the truckers' reputation. In the early 60s, when I stopped driving, I'd say 40% of the drivers were gay and another 10% got sucked now and then. But the 40% were actively looking for it.
How often did you have homosexual sex when you were on the road? On a bad week, five times; on a good week, every day.
How did drivers cruise each other? A truck would stop at a pulloff — usually a rest area. I'd flash my running lights on and off twice. If the other truck flashed his lights on and off twice, it was an invitation. If there was no response, it could mean he just got sucked off, so there was no need to take it as a personal rejection.
What would you do if he flashed his lights for you? I'd usually start with something chickenshit like "Helluva way to make a living, ain't it?" The other guy would usually rub his crotch in making his reply.
Are there "types" — that is, types of truckers that prefer one kind of sex? Definitely, although in every line of trucking there's always those who will do anything. But bullhaulers, for example, are generally out to fuck you. A bullhauler is a cattle truck driver. They love to fuck a guy's hole raw so if you can't handle it don't try it. Tank drivers generally like to suck or get sucked. Tanks are liquid — gasoline or milk. Milk runners aren't usually too good because they're mostly local runs and the guys don't get hot enough, but I've met some who are good. The long-distance gasoline drivers are good. They're the best cocksuckers and they love having their cocks gobbled. Produce haulers are usually anal, for some reason. They love being packed in the ass.
What did you like best? Mixing it up — all of it. Like a tank hauler in the morning, eating and being eaten; around noon maybe a piece of ass from a produce hauler, and then that night, getting my own hole fucked raw by some bullhauler. I used to love the smell of their sweat as they fucked me. It was really masculine. Really a turn on.
Was there much sex at truck stops where drivers spend the night? Not too much. But we'd exchange truck numbers so that you could get a good cocksucker or a good piece of ass when you recognized his truck.
What kind of guys are long-haul movers — you know, furniture? They're really way out. A lot of chicken hawks among them. I knew one guy who used to take his own teenage son with him on runs during the kid's summer vacation so that the kid could attract other boys at rest areas. His dad would suck the kids off. One truck was pretty notorious — the entire crew was chicken-oriented. They sucked every kid they could get their mouths on along the way. They also liked groups — sucking and fucking with a bunch of young boys.

Would you say most long-distance movers are chicken hawks? No, but a lot of them. But they are way out. The first time a guy ever drank my piss, he was a furniture hauler.
Were you married? Yes. Divorced now. Almost all the drivers were married but they loved to get away from their wives and have it with men on the road. With me the marriage was just a cover. Finally I came out of the closet and got a divorce.
What's your fondest memory? Well, one that first comes to mind was at a rest area in West Texas. I had stopped and had cruised another driver. It was about 3:30 A.M. and we had taken our cocks out and were playing with each other's when another truck pulled in. But I recognized it immediately by the number as a driver I'd fucked once. I told my friend with his cock out not to worry — it was someone I knew. So we just left our cocks out. When the third driver walked over he could see our hard ons and he just licked his lips. He said his asshole had been itching to be fucked all night and he dropped his pants and shorts. So while the other guy fucked his ass he bent over and sucked my cock. He was married and had three kids. After I shot my wad I went down on him. When he began to unload I went all the way down until my lips touched his pubic hair and I moved my throat muscles on the head of his cock. The guy fucking him was really humping hard — slamming it into him. When he shot his load he stuck it all the way up and almost lifted the guy off the ground.
What was the youngest trick you had? Sixteen. He was haunting a truck stop shit house and I could tell he was a trucker groupie — hungry for driver's cock. You can always tell when they look at you, when they know you're a driver; you can tell they've got this thing for truckers. Sometimes it's not so much for you as an individual but for what you stand for, like guys who go for cops, soldiers, sailors, etc. This kid had it. He was scared, even when I got a hard on at the urinal from his looking at it. I sucked him to put him at ease. I undid his belt and pulled his pants down. I'm a good cocksucker. The kid shot rapidly but I kept sucking on it, wanting more, letting him see I enjoyed his cock. I sucked for about 10 more minutes and got his second wad. It was sweet though not as big as his first one.
Did he ever suck you? Yeah — he worshipped it. He did a good job. Later told me he'd had lots of practice on kids his own age. Took my whole load without gagging, although he coughed a bit because it was a big wad. He said it was his first taste of trucker cock.
Are you circumcized? No.
How big is your cock? I have what I call a garden cock — small when soft but it grows to quite a crop in a short time. Soft, it's about 4″ but hard it's 7½″ and it's fat.
How often do you jack off? Usually I cruise to try to find something but if luck is against me I always jack off before going to sleep.
How old are you? Forty-five.
Do you still get a lot of sex? Mostly twice or three times a week. I cruise bookstores now that I'm not trucking anymore. I go around the peepshow booths and sometimes suck cock or get sucked off. Sometimes I bring somebody home with me. Now and then I also pick up a hitchhiker.
Do you miss your trucking days? I miss the sex. I don't miss the driving, though. That gets stale after 15 years.

Royal Navy Unloads in San Diego

SAN DIEGO — Flash! British Balls Bombard San Diego! When it comes to cock, Brittania still rules the waves. A few days ago a Royal Navy vessel steamed into San Diego Port and over a hundred members of Her Majesty's Meat Fleet swarmed into downtown San Diego's gay bars. Eight came into the Press Room Saloon and five were immediately whisked home by patrons eager to sample that superb Anglo-Saxon semen. My friends J. and D., who have been lovers for eight years, took the other three home, stripped the sailors bare, gave them champagne and took turns sucking them. The sailors got sucked all night long and when J. and D. showed up at the Press Room next day their jaws and tongues were so tired they had to sip through straws. My Mexican friend, who runs a travel agency across the border and who keeps in practice sucking off at least three pieces of magnificent young Mexican meat each day, took the other three of the British sailors home from the Press Room. He invited them to take a swim in his pool, but while they were in a bedroom stripping he sucked them all off before the swim. After sucking them all night long, he found the sailors were too tired to be sucked again in the morning, but one of them got out of bed to take a piss and my friend followed him into the bathroom and played with his big uncircumcised British dick while he was pissing. This made the sailor hot again so they went back to the bedroom for one final blow job, to the envy of the other two, who could not get theirs up. Then he took them back to the ship. My friend L., who is a traveling salesman and never fails to find young meat wherever he goes, also took a British sailor home and blew him several times. My Mexican friend married as most Mexicans do to prove his machismo, and divorced after having five children. Now he sucks cock exclusively and there is an endless supply of big, hot, young ones in his town. He looks young for his age and says that it is the frequent cocksucking that keeps him from getting a double chin and those deep lines at the sides of the mouth. One of his daughters married a handsome young American guy a few months ago. Tall, blond, hunky, and my friend showed me a photo of his son-in-law and said he has a gigantic prick. My friend can take only about 7 inches of the thing in his mouth, but he titillates the rest of it with his fingers while sucking as much as he can. The son-in-law visits my friend frequently just to lie back and get a good long blow job.

The Hallowed Holes of Harvard

CAMBRIDGE — There are no homosexuals at Harvard but if you go to the men's rooms at lunchtime you better not need to shit because the booths in the Science Center seven in all will all be filled and there will be men pacing the urinals looking through the cracks in the doors & waiting their turns at the cracks. One day I had a broad-dicked blondie shove it under (all the doors on the inside say KNEEL DOWN FOR ACTION the new motto over *Veritas*) and I was on that dick in a second of course and the black man in the next booth over, on my left, blondie was on my right, starts playing with my asscrack while I'm sucking so I reach in my knapsack & push my vaseline toward him & he greases me up and then the men's room door opens we resume places on our respectable seats then we three are back on the floor and the black man is in my ass and the blondie is in my mouth.

His Balls Slammed Against My Ass

UPSTATE NEW YORK — I can't really explain why I like getting fucked. Just like the feeling of having some guy on top of me and in control. If a guy knows what he's doing and goes slow, plays with my asshole and gets it relaxed, there's not really much pain. If there is it's usually only momentary and doesn't last. It's when a guy slams it in fast and all the way that the pain is sharp but if he just holds it in there a few minutes and doesn't buck around too much that goes away too. Also, my own attitude makes a difference. If I relax my asshole and let him in, the pain is less; if I tighten up and resist, the pain increases.

I met a guy in a "straight" bar near the railroad station. It was late at night and the bar was pretty empty. When he came in he still wore the cap and uniform he wore as a conductor on the train. He was a short, stocky, good looking Italian guy, middle aged, and even with the wedding band on his hand the message in his eyes was clear when he stared back at me across the dimly lit barroom.

I played silent cat-and-mouse with glances just to make sure I was reading the interest in his eyes correctly. When I left the bar he followed a few moments later down the side street to my car. As we sat in the car and got acquainted he let me feel his hard cock and heavy balls beneath the coarse material of his pants. Then he pressed his body over against mine, squeezed my ass tightly and said he wanted to fuck me real bad.

Once in my apartment, he let me strip him down. I got bareass fast and he greased my asshole, greased his cock, put me on my back on the couch, and pinned my ankles by my shoulders.

He plunged his cock right in full force up to the hilt, his balls slamming against my ass. I let out a howl but he held me there. After I got used to his rod in me and relaxed he gave me a fucking that would have turned his wife green.

He moved his cock back and forth in my asshole, nice and easy, slow and rhythmic, stopping whenever he got close to shooting. He'd pull it all the way out, then aim for my hole and plunge the whole length of his cock in me with his full weight. He liked watching that length of his cock slipping in and out of my ass and would throw back his head and moan with pleasure. He kept fucking me like that for about two hours, never coming. When it was time to leave he started a wild, rapid fuck, slamming his cock in and out my ass till I thought I'd be ripped open. With a groan and yell he rammed his cock in so I thought it punctured my stomach and I could feel wave after wave of cum pulsing through his cock and into my body.

That guy gave me the best fuckings my ass ever had. He came by at least twice a week. After he had been visiting me for awhile he wanted me to fuck him so he could see what it was like. We tried it but it didn't work out and he didn't like it. (He had hemorrhoids which made it virtually impossible anyway.) He never wanted to have his balls or cock sucked on. Just liked fucking me.

One time he asked me if he could bring his 18-year-old son along but I refused. He kept coming around alone until I moved out of town.

He never talked about his son except that one time but to this day I wish I'd taken him up on his offer because I still wonder what it would have been like to have that hunky conductor and his son both fucking me.

Every time he fucked me I couldn't help but think about the great time his wife was missing but I was sure glad he was screwing me instead of her.

"I've a Pair of Hot Nuts That Won't Quit"

CONNECTICUT — A large Veterans' organization was holding its state convention in Hartford and I figured there'd be a lot of horny dicks to suck. The guy next to me in the Men's Bar at the Bond Hotel wasn't bad. Late 20s, dark-skinned, coarse but good-looking.

He seemed a little high but not too high to miss me checking him out. He obligingly stepped back from the bar a little and flicked his groin with his hand. All it took was a little chit-chat and he was actually rubbing his groin. By the time he got around to saying he and his buddies were looking for broads he was holding through his pants what looked to be a substantial prick. Looking for broads in a men's bar, they were. Looking to get into my mouth more likely.

He introduced himself as Joe and his buddies as Martin and Floyd. It was several years ago so my memory is hazy but I think Martin was a little younger than Joe, and nice looking, especially in his Air Force uniform. Floyd was older and not very appetizing-looking.

Martin looked right at me and said, "I've got a pair of hot nuts that won't quit. It doesn't even have to be a broad. I'd settle for a blow job from one of the boys."

I blushed and gulped — I'm not sure in what order.

"Me too," said Floyd. "I can't get the old lady to suck on it."

"Shit, Floyd," said Joe, "you ain't got one big enough to suck and besides it's probably too cheesy for her taste." Then he added: "If you had a thick, clean eight inches like me maybe she would suck it for you."

Joe said let's blow this joint (grabbing his khaki-covered prick as he said it) and go up to the room for some beer.

Joe's room joined one shared by Martin and Floyd. Joe's room was completely furnished — even had a drunken Marine, in full uniform, passed out on the bed. A buddy of Joe's and a nice hunk.

"Suck on this," Joe said, handing me a bottle of beer from the frig. "Make yourself at home while I get undressed — no sense going out again and I might as well be comfortable."

Joe did a real strip tease, making a production of it because I was watching him. I bet he never had a more appreciative audience. When he finally pulled off his Jockey shorts I involuntarily gave a slight reaction. I couldn't control it. He was really hung and already half hard. He watched me watching him.

While Joe took a shower — he obviously was hung up about being clean for a blow job — the other two came in. Joe came out of the head drying himself and swinging a beautiful hard on. He loved showing it to us.

Martin asked Joe, "Has he made any — a — suggestions?" I got the picture. Joe had set them all up for me.

"Let's not be coy," Joe said to me. "You swing don't you?"

I guess I showed some of the fear I felt.

"Don't worry," Joe said, "we just want to get out balls drained." Joe gently pushed me down to my knees and put his big prick in my mouth. I sucked like my life depended on it. It really was a beautiful hard on and I wanted to do it justice.

"Jesus," said Martin, watching. "What the fuck you waiting for, Floyd, get those fucking pants off and get in line behind me."

Joe came quickly — a generous load. The bastards had no variety or imagination. Instead of spreading for me on the bed and letting me really give complete service between their legs they just took their turns standing in front of a kneeling cocksucker.

But I'm not complaining. I love cock any way I can get it and all the seduction was done for me by these guys. I didn't have to risk a pass; they were all too eager to get my mouth out of the bar up to their rooms and onto their dicks.

But it was a little mechanical. As soon as Joe pulled his cock out of my mouth Martin came up, held the back of my head in his hands and stuck his long thick cut prick down my throat for draining. I didn't even get a chance to admire what he had. I guess he liked his dick well enough so that he didn't need my admiration. About three minutes of steady sucking and he unloaded, to be replaced by Floyd.

Floyd turned out to be a pleasant surprise. His cock was a work of art. Fat, seven inches, nice loose foreskin. Big cock head and big piss hole. Contrary to Joe's put-down in the bar, his cock was in A-1 condition — no cheese. Tasted fine to me, although those who think cock cheese is the world's most delicious treat would have been disappointed. His wife was crazy not sucking a master prick like Floyd's.

Floyd was beautiful about it — he let me take my time and do all the work. I tickled his balls while I licked around his cock head and into his big piss-hole.

His prick was too fat for me to take all the way. In between vacuum-sucking it and lip-stroking the five inches or so I could take I did a lot of lapping and licking and kissing on his balls and all over his prick, from the base of the shaft to its hot head. He shot a big load after about 10 minutes, registering the longest elapsed time of the three. After he pulled his fat prick out of my mouth he said it was the best — and only — blow job he'd ever had and could use another later. To Joe he said, "How about having him suck Osborne (the Marine)."

Joe unbuckled the Marine's pants and with Martin's help pulled them down.

"Get Jim's shorts down and suck him off," he told me. I did with pleasure. I got his briefs off him and started to suck. His cock was beautiful — uncut and delicious — but it only stirred a little. It didn't get hard.

I sucked him on and off for an hour but never got his juice. He was just too fucking drunk. With a great effort I did get his cock hard once and it was a real beauty. But no juice.

Joe's buddies went to the White Tower for hamburgers. Joe told me to drop my pants and lie on one of the other beds.

"I've got a surprise for you," he said. "I don't want your ass because I've got all the ass I want at home. I want your cock." He leaned down and I could feel his breath on my cock.

"It's cute," he said, "and I want to suck it."

As he sucked on my cock he gave it sensations impossible to describe. I cried out.

"Shut your fucking mouth," he said. He said he'd only sucked one other cock — his buddy in the Navy — and had wanted to have another for a long time and mine was just what he'd been looking for. But he quietly warned me: "If you make any noise or say one fucking work about this to my buddies I'll beat the living hell out of you." To underscore his point he squeezed my nuts and held them tight. "Understand?"

Sex-Crazed in San Francisco

San Francisco — I am a sex-crazed cocksucking pervert. I get off on jockstraps, especially pissy, cum-stained, sweaty ones. There's nothing like drinking a load or two (or seven) of hot piss through a slimy old jock. There isn't anything about piss that I don't like, and I'm turned on by men's natural body odors — sweaty armpits, groins, assholes, cheesy dicks, stinking feet. I'm uncut (8 inches) and when I beat off in a rubber and leave it on after I've cum, the cheese on my dick is fantastic. I really love it when a guy gets turned on to this kind of pig-sex. Far too many queers are caught up in their own middle class prissiness for really trashy escapades. I love jerking off with guys. I especially dig sitting on a guy's face and beating my dick till I shoot a load all over his chest and face. I have a good deal of free time, and much of it is spent sucking cock, eating ass, or beating off with guys in T-rooms downtown. I ran into one guy in a Financial District T-room recently who was wearing traditional young executive drag (pin-stripe suit, tie, wing-tip shoes), but underneath he had one of the dirtiest jocks I've sucked on in a long time. A truly exceptional man. My favorite spot is "Pansy Park" — the section of Golden Gate Park near the Ocean where there's constant sex from dawn to dusk. A fair number of "straight" men (repairmen, truckers, painters) stop off — and I love servicing hot "straights." Usually once they're turned on, anything goes, and I've had more than one "straight" prick piss down my throat. There are also lots of good-looking cocksuckers there at all hours, and the morning joggers there are usually more than happy to have someone lick the sweaty jocks and drink their piss. I have a lover, age 28, who is a sex slave. He keeps my body clean with regular tongue-baths. I have sex at least three or four times a day. If I have the day free, I can easily go to the Park and suck off eight or ten guys, shoot three or four loads, and still come home for a couple of rounds with my lover.

I told him he could do anything he wanted but not to hurt me. I lay back in complete submission.

As he licked my balls, thighs, belly, and nipples, the idea that he had given only one blow before seemed improbable. He was really good at it. He swallowed every drop and refused to stop sucking even after I was completely drained. He got into the "69" position, wrapped his legs around my neck and fucked my mouth, still sucking on my spent cock. Soon he flooded my mouth with spicy-tasting come.

Then he said, "If you know what's good for you you'll get your ass out of here right now." He spat that "now" out at me. He had just blown me but instead of being friendly he now sounded mean.

I looked stunned and he explained, "You don't seem to realize what's in store for you when they get back. And if that Bad Ass Osborne comes out of his drunk you'll really be hurting."

But I suspected that he was more afraid for himself than for me. He wanted me out; he'd sucked my cock. And he was confused. Most masculine, inexperienced stud-types like him, going through the strain of having surrendered to cocksucking, would have taken it out on me afterwards and beaten the shit out of me to regain their lost manhood. Thank God all he did was stand there and look beautiful in his defeat. As I walked past his beautiful bare ass out the door he said only "Thanks."

Lips Around White Meat

CLEVELAND — I got to work an hour early on Monday, March 22 [1982]. I went in a basement men's room and took off all my clothes. That excited me because I wondered if my boss would like to see my roaring hard dick or have it up his white Catholic ass. I jacked off and left my slime dripping on the toilet seat. I went to my favorite porno arcade at lunchtime that day and fed my black dick to a black guy's ass, and then I sucked the hole where my dick had just been. I liked that a lot. I liked seeing my dick in his ass and I liked tasting what I did to him.

Then a few minutes later a black guy had me on my knees and was fucking my shit-hole of a mouth. He asked me if I like to get fucked. I said yes. So he told me to take my clothes off and get on the floor with my legs up. I did as he said and had another nigger dick pounding my nigger ass for about 20 minutes. He didn't say much and finally he shot his scum up his butt. I then sucked my shit off his shit-colored pecker. I had to do that, being the dirty, nasty person that I am. But I still was not satisfied so I stayed awhile more to see if I could find a *white man* to work over both my assholes.

There was a white guy who looked interesting to me. About 45 years old, 6' 2" tall and about 240 pounds. We started at each other for awhile then I walked over to him and asked, "Would you care for having my nigger lips around your white meat?" He looked at me disbelieving so I asked him again. He said yes but that I shouldn't call myself nigger. I told him it's only a word, and we went into another booth. He dropped his pants to reveal blue and white checkered boxer shorts. I knelt down and sniffed them front and back. It tasted of musk and stale piss. I thought it was a very tasty soul food for me. I stopped sucking him and asked if he'd call me nigger asshole or shit skin. He gave me all I wanted. "Suck my cock, nigger boy." "Kiss my white ass, you black bastard." I sucked, kissed, licked and worshipped his white masculinity. I then asked him if he would put his dick in my ass. He had about 8" and it was very thick. I knew I'd feel it going in. That's what I wanted. I took my clothes off and he took his clothes off too. I looked at his naked body and his white skin and I said, "Do it to me, please."

He got me on my knees and jammed his white pole way up my coon ass. It hurt and I loved it. I said, "Fuck me, white man" and he said "you're goddam right nigger boy." In and out, in and out, he knew how to fuck; and my filthy jig ass loved it. I asked him to pull out of my butt and do it between my asshole lips. So he put his meat back in my mouth and gave me what for. "I'm gonna shoot in you nigger mouth, boy," he said. There was a lot of come in his balls. I like sperm from a white man more than anything else I know of. I got to swallow all of his juice. I said, "Please piss in my mouth, I need it." So he did. It was warm and very strong. We put our clothes on and he said "That was good, nigger boy." I think he will be looking for me there again.

That afternoon I just didn't care about anything but dicks so my lunch hour was actually two hours. My supervisor was furious. She said, "Where have you been." I said it couldn't be helped; "I did what I had to do now you do what you think you have to do." She just walked away. A guy I know asked me not to have sex or get off for a week so I would be hot and shoot a lot of slime for him. I told him I never heard of such a thing as not getting one's rocks off for a *week*. That is not natural.

Tim's Steamy Groin

CALIFORNIA — We were in junior high (different schools) when I first noticed him. Bigger than I, with the kind of buns that rumpled firmly back and forth when he walked. Always a winning smile.

I had had a little sex before with another boy — Jimmy. We would go to his clubhouse in the backyard; he'd sit on an old couch with his pants down; I'd kneel in front of his spread legs; he'd slowly flip over the cards in an old "Wolf Pack Deck" of his big brother's (mostly fuzzy shots of fat whores in motel rooms with coke bottles, broom sticks, etc, stuck up their slots, but sometimes a big man's cock), and I would suck on his tiny, short, hard dick.

But Tim was my first real boyfriend. We talked about sex cautiously after we'd known each other a couple of weeks. He told me how guys at his high school goosed each other.

One evening we were walking our bikes over to his house when he goosed me. I didn't like it. A couple of minutes later he made the same playful motion but this time on my balls. This I loved. My cock swelled instantly. That was about all between us that night but when I got home I hit the bathroom fast and jacked off, thinking of Tim's body.

Finally, one Sunday afternoon, we had a full feeling-up session at his house. We ended up rolling on the bed, pressing our bodies tighter and harder against each other, mouths and tongues kissing wildly, hands flying all over inside and outside clothing, shirts, asses, and the hot, firm, wet cocks throbbing inside our Jockey shorts.

We undressed each other slowly piece by piece, our bodies never entirely breaking contact. We lay back side by side and jacked off, cum falling all over our young hairless chests and stomachs.

I remember seeing a pile of his Jockey shorts in a dresser drawer as I left the room. I have been turned on instantly by those classic sexy shorts ever since, whether they're on a shelf, in an ad, or wrapping a package of cock, balls, hair, ass, and heavenly smells. Over the next 5-6 years, Tim and I saw each other at least three times a week. /We played strip poker a lot. We had sex in a tent in his back yard, in his garage, my garage, his bed, my bed, on the floor, on the couch while watching Ed Sullivan (we came during a Julia Meade commercial for Lincolns), in the plum tree at my house, and so on.

After he turned 16 he bought an old Ford. We went to drive-in movies almost every weekend. We'd watch a little of the show, then start inching closer and closer, not saying a word. Then a hand in a lap, then the legs stretched so the lap disappears and the cock has room to grow.

A hand slips into the pants and slowly works down, feeling the Jockey shorts. A finger or two slips into the slot of the shorts. Feels the flesh directly. Maybe a ball, or part of the stiff shaft. If you're lucky the wet cock head would be right there, so sensitive to a slight touch, jerking excitedly and swelling even more when lightly scraped.

Then Undo the belt, buttons, and zipper. On some special nights we would wear button-fly Levis — still the best aphrodisiac ever made by man. Pull the pants down enough so the whole carnival of exciting delights is open to see and touch. Smell the release of the day's odors from a steamy groin. Mingle them with the perspiration of a warm Southern California night.

We'd take turns laying in each other's lap. My head on his well-muscled

thigh. Nose tucked into the folds of his ample balls. Raise my head and close my wet lips around the warm, soft-tasting shaft. Sink it deep into my mouth.

Tim would be quiet at first, but soon the breathing would get heavy and faster. Then gasps and moans. Never commands or words of any kind, but deep animal sensual moans and groans. Then the thrusts of hip-driven cock get stronger. Then the shaft beats and shoots warm, thick, white creamy cum.

Sometimes it would be Tim's head in my lap.

We snatched glimpses of clawing, hugging, humping couples in other cars. I was never much interested in what they were doing. I knew what I had experienced was absolute.

Looks for Girl in Gay Bar

TEXAS — I followed a man into the men's room of a gay bar just in time to see him peel his foreskin down over the head of his cock, slip it back into his pants and zip up. He was wearing a Hawaiian shirt and had a crew cut. I said, "How's it going?" and took out my cock and stood at the urinal as if I had to piss. He said he was looking for a girl and asked if I knew where he could find one. I said I knew where he could get his cock sucked. He said he'd never done anything like that. I told him it felt great and I lived nearby. He said he couldn't do anything for me. I said all he had to do was lie back and enjoy it; I'd take care of myself. He said OK and we went to my place. He seemed a little nervous. Kept talking about girls. He asked to take a shower. I got in with him. He asked if I liked girls. I said yes but not for sex. I soaped him all over, dropped to my haunches and washed his soft cock and long loose foreskin. He never touched me. After we dried off he put on his Jockey shorts and started to put on his pants. I said why not lie down and cool off. He left his briefs on and lay back on the bed with his hands under his head and his eyes closed. He said he wished he could find a girl. I asked him if he screwed lots of girls. He said yes. I asked him if he liked to eat girls. He said yes. I slipped my hand inside his briefs, played with his cock and worked my finger down inside his foreskin. He moaned. His cock got hard. I asked him if a girl had ever sucked him off. He said no. He raised his ass so I could pull his underpants off. I started sucking slow and easy. He moved his hips and kept moaning. I asked him if that wasn't almost as good as screwing a girl. He said yes. I peeled his foreskin back. His cock was about 7 inches long, with a big head; almost too thick to go all the way down on. I asked him if he would ask the next girl he screwed to suck his cock. He said yes. I asked if he'd ever let a man suck on it again. He said yes, but he didn't think he'd let a man screw him. He spread his legs and I started sucking again. I licked my finger and eased it up his very tight asshole. He said "Oh God Oh God Oh God" over and over, then unloaded in several long, strong gushes. I swallowed it all. I looked up. His hands were still under his head but his eyes were wide open now. He said he had to go and started to get up. I asked him to lie back a minute. I held his cock, knelt over him and jerked off, then wiped my come off his stomach. I gave him my number and said to call the next time he was passing through. He said he would. He talked about girls again before he left, but I wonder what he was thinking about while his cock was down my throat and my finger was up his asshole.

Trucker Joins Masturbating Motorist

CALIFORNIA — I was a local freight delivery truck driver in the Los Angeles area and from the high driver's seat of my cab over rig I had a excellent view of drivers in cars. Hell, I've even followed side by side females driving along and finger fucking themselves. Total 3. Nearly every day I had some freight going to a firm in a rural area located about a third of a mile off the main drag down a tree lined narrow road. Almost every time I drove out to this factory there was a guy about 25 in a Datsun pulled off under the trees. He had his seat reclined and was beating his meat. From my vantage point it looked as though his Levis were unzipped and pulled down just slightly and the bottom button or two open on his shirt. One day just as I went by him and looking he was blowing his load with globs of flying cum. It was fucking far out. The next delivery day I got there early, purposely. He was just opening up his pants. I stopped my rig and went over with a huge bulge in my Levis and said, "Let's beat off together." To my surprise and without hesitating he replied, "Okay Pal." I went over the other side and got in & eased my seat back. Then I dropped my Levis and jockey shorts to the floor. That's when I glanced over to see his cock was huge this close up. It was uncut and longer and larger than my 8½". Both of us said nothing. He just looked straight ahead while I was looking at his beautiful tool. Both of us just stroked our cocks. I couldn't stand it any longer and leaned over and impaled my mouth on his cock and sucked it till WHAM! Jeez he nearly blew my head off when he came. He pumped that delicious juice out in both volume and force. It was such a fucking turn on that with just my cock pushing against the seat I came also. But alas all good things must come to a end and after I licked his cock clean he said, "You'll have to leave now man, I gotta go." I have not seen that car again, damn it.

4 Sailors Piss on Chicagoan

CHICAGO — Having lived in Chicago most of my life, I have found several excellent places to suck cock. If you go for truck drivers, I suggest you visit North Water Street, east of lower level Michigan Avenue, behind the *Tribune* docks. The *Tribune* has a paper storage place out there, along with the maintenance garage for their trucks. Around 10 p.m. is the best time, since the truck drivers and their teenage helpers are loitering around waiting for the morning editions to come off the press. You can walk almost a mile east, along the north bank of the river, clear out to the "S" curve on Lake Shore Drive. A small branch of the river crosses under Lake Shore Drive but it hasn't been used in years and the drawbridge machinery has been idle and unattended for some time. A couple of times I have caught boys in there beating off and both times, after I explained that I was OK and that they didn't have to run off or try to get away, they willingly continued. When I slipped down to my knees, my own stiff cock in my hand, and began sucking the cocks, I never encountered any resistance. Most of the newspaper pressmen, truck drivers, etc. who are old enough to drink hang out at one of the several bars within a block of the paper, at Rush and Grand Avenues. One place there, supposedly "straight," is always filled with horny men looking for relief around 2 a.m. I have never yet

failed to take someone home from there, with the understanding that they were going to be strictly trade, which is the way I like it best. About two weeks ago I blew one of the teenage helpers in the back of the truck while we were going down Grand Avenue.

Another excellent pick up spot is the Northwestern Railroad station at Canal and Madison Streets every weekend night about 12:30 a.m. The last train for Great Lakes Naval Base leaves about 12:25 and invariably a few sailors will show up too late, or too drunk, to catch the train. Any cocksucker with a car will find a sailor or two willing to put out in exchange for a ride back to the base by morning check-in time, to avoid being AWOL. When they find that all I want is a load of sailor sperm shot like a gusher down my parched throat, they readily agree to a short stopover at my place on the way back to the base.

On Labor Day weekend I went to the terminal about midnight Monday and had four young guys in desperate need of a ride back to the base. I make my terms plain from the very beginning, so that nobody is offended later on or can claim they didn't understand. I told them I wanted the four of them to strip me while they were in uniform, fondle my cock and balls and ass, then with me on my knees they were to form a circle around me with their pants lowered and shove cock into my mouth one at a time and come. Afterwards a shower of hot piss from all four in unison, using me as a common trough-type urinal, would refresh me for the 40-mile drive to the base. All were happy to oblige, and I urge other Chicago readers to visit the depot for good, wholesome cocksucking. An experienced cocksucker can score every time at the Museum of Science and Industry. When I lived south, not a weekend passed that I did not score with one or more tourists coming through town. But that's a complete story in itself, which I will save for another time.

Human Urinal

PHILADELPHIA — I never seem to get enough piss. There is a glory hole toilet on the Atlantic City boardwalk which has a hole on each side. One is on a paid side, the other on a free side. These mean you are able to get cocks stuck in from two directions. I try to get in the middle toilet because the other free one is very busy so I'm sure of getting plenty of cocks through it. The last time I was there I stayed about 2 hours and swallowed a lot of cum and drank a lot of piss. When I drank the piss from one guy he said he had a friend outside so he asked him to piss but his friend just wanted to piss all over me instead of in my mouth. I just had my shirt and swim trunks on. My trunks were down to the floor so I just took off my shirt and let him do it. I thought he would never stop. There was so much of that delicious rich golden piss. Two other guys watched and got so excited that they started to do it after he finished. These two both came in the booth together and at the same time let go with what seemed like gallons of piss. One aimed it at my head and face while the other one pissed all over my stomach, chest, cock and balls. After they finished I got both their loads of cum to swallow. I was very pleased and satisfied while drying myself with toilet paper. I forgot to mention that while these two were pissing I aimed my own piss up over my chest and stomach along with their piss. You can see how much I love piss. In fact just writing this has made me horny enough to fill a glass of my piss to drink now.

Youths Wave Pricks to Taunt "Fag" Pitcher, But He Wins, 8-1

FROM A LAW STUDENT — Between cruising everybody at the Law School dance and sitting in the lobby getting signatures for a gay rights petition, I managed to get a number of people uptight about being seen even talking with me. So not everybody was sure what to do when I showed up for a touch football game Sunday at noon. I was great. I made a pair of interceptions, caught everything thrown my way, made lots of good plays on defense, punted the ball far and high my only kick, and guided my team up the field for a touchdown on my only series at quarterback. I had a great day on offense and defense, no more than 12 hours after the Law School dance, where I tried to make most every one of the other 13 men on the field. Many of the men at the dance wore three-piece suits, which bother me politically, but a handsome man looks about five times better in one of those things. Most of the men were trying to impress the other men with their clothes and dates. So-called "straight" men are always dressing to impress the other so-called "straight' men. I was into a lewd and lascivious trip that ought to have gotten me kicked out of school. I cruised my civil procedure professor (his wife wasn't there and I asked if that meant he was free after the party). I patted the asses of a number of guys I have been admiring. One of my classmates told me I had a pensive look and asked what was on my mind. I told him I was thinking about how good it would be to suck on his cock. He said that was interesting. I asked about 25 men to dance and not one of them would. As far as I know, I am the only full-time faggot on any of the teams I play on. But the other teams in the softball league make jokes and teased that we were a team of fags, just because of me; I wore the words "gay power" on my sleeve. Of the other men on my team, Richard is one of the best kissers I have every known, is married, and he asked me specifically not to kiss him the day we played a game (1) which was attended by some of his students and (2) which was attended by his mother-in-law. That was my team in the city league. As for the team I play on in the University intramurals, I am the only faggot, and again, we get a lot of shit about being the faggot team since I play with my "faggot" shirt on, which I do in order to make the other players realize that this is a faggot with whom they are dealing and who is *beating* them. When we win the university intramural summer championship (which my team has done the last three years in a row), they have to suck on the fact that the shortstop is gay or the pitcher is gay or the left fielder is gay (I have played these three positions). They also have to deal with the fact that they are therefore not even as good as faggots in those activities by which they have traditionally been able to convince themselves that they are "men." The guys on my team can't patronize me either because I am always one of the top two or three batters. Last summer I batted .591, tops on the team; this summer I batted .523, again tops on the team. I say that to brag, goddamnit, just like them. There is a team in the city league that really hated us. They were a team of high school boys. The one who was the piggiest was the one who was the cutest. I think he was piggiest because he knew how cute he was and he had to put on a performance for his teammates, since he was in the most precarious position. We always had hot games, full of nasty razzing and acrimony. They would especially concentrate their verbal abuse on me. They would pull their softball pants down to their knees and wave their

cocks at me and tell me to suck it. I offered to and then they pulled their pants back up and wouldn't let me. One guy I hated on that team was the right fielder. I would laugh at him and say, "Come on over to my house, hon, and I'll teach you how to use a stick properly." We had to play them in the last game of the season. I pitched the best game of my life and nothing they could do worked for them. After each of their batters failed to get on base, I yelled out "Next," and laughed at them. They were boiling. We beat them, 8-1. They wouldn't even shake hands with us after the game. Their cute right fielder threatened to attack me if I tried to shake hands with him. We used to go to a local quarry after the game and have a nude swim. I couldn't possibly describe all of the fine cocks and balls I was drooling at (which they all knew I was drooling at, too).

Urban Affairs:
"20, All Waiting For Me"

DETROIT — Although I come from a middle class, pretty well to do family, I was always attracted to a rough, lower class bunch of guys who used to hang around the park not far from where I lived. I wanted to be a buddy of theirs but I never had quite enough guts to approach them. I remember being about 14-15 when I went to the park, hoping against hope that I would be noticed and maybe get to know these guys. I remember five or six kids, 15-16 years old, standing in a bunch behind an old tool shed, and one of them noticing me.

He turned to his buddies and pointed at me. They all started to move toward me. I wasn't able to move. They were like a circle around me. None said a word.

The biggest of them, a husky blond about 6'1", stepped directly in front of me and grabbed my dick, which by now was hard. He kept holding it and turned to his friends and said, "Hey, look, I found it and it's stiff. I think this guy needs action. Shall we jack him off?"

His buddies said yeah, let's. My heart pounded. I didn't know how to react.

One of them grabbed my shirt and stripped it off while the other five held me down solid. Then he unbuttoned my pants and took them off and they all saw me in my jock shorts hiding my stiff dick.

"Let's take that off too," another dark haired, strong looking dude said. He grabbed the waist band and pulled my jockeys off and my dick popped up.

One of them said, "Hey, he has his foreskin — this is going to be fun."

The youngest, about 13, came over and played with my balls. One 15-year-old grabbed my hard on and said, "Let's see how fast we can make him come."

The other guys held me down while he pulled the foreskin back and forth. I couldn't hold back, even if I'd wanted to. My cock itched to beat hell and I popped a load so fast and far it was all over a couple of guys' hands and faces.

They told me as punishment I was to report to them every Monday, Wednesday, and Friday, and if I didn't they would find me and really take care of me.

I did, out of fear, go back, and there were about 20, all waiting for me. The story of what happened is something else and almost impossible to repeat.

Try! — *EDITOR.*

S/M at B. U.

NEW JERSEY — I am glad there is a publication which gives me the chance to tell of an experience I had as a pledge to a fraternity at Brown University. Before initiation we all had to spend some free hours each week working at the frat house — serving meals, cleaning and generally catering to the whims of Brothers. For any mistake we would "assume the position" — bent over to get our asses whacked with the paddle.

None of the members but one would paddle us on the bare ass so we wore heavy pants and several pairs of undershorts and the beatings were not so bad. But the one guy, Randy, was a mean bastard and would make us drop our pants and shorts and beat our naked tails till we yelled. He seemed to pick on me especially because I was taller than the others and than him.

One night I was supposed to clean up supper dishes while everybody went out to some bash. When I thought they were all gone I grabbed a beer, which was forbidden, and sat down to watch television. Suddenly Randy came back. He caught me red-handed, called me a "fucking sneak," and told me to fetch the paddle. As I walked from the room he almost lifted me off the floor with the hardest kick in the ass I ever got.

When I came back with the paddle I was scared shit. He told me to bare my ass and bend over. Then, did he ever blister my hind end with that paddle, I screamed and cried, begging for mercy. But he wouldn't stop. My ass went from pain to numbness, till I couldn't stand it and jumped away. We argued and he told me If I was chickenshit I could get the hell out and forget about the fraternity.

I didn't want that or for him to get the best of me so I apologized and decided to take anything he dished out. He made me strip altogether and then marched me bareass upstairs, smacking my already sore behind all the way up. He tied me hand and foot on a bed and lit a candle. First he teased the soles of my feet with the flame, threatening to really burn them. They did burn once or twice and I let out a howl.

He ran the lighted candle up my legs to my groin and set my cock hair on fire. He would put it out when the flames grew big but by the time he finished practically all my manly hair was singed to stubble.

He turned me over and I thought he was going to tan my ass some more but instead he spread my hind cheeks and started dropping hot wax from the candle on my asshole. Many didn't hurt but a couple of real hot drops hit my sensitive tail pipe right on target and made me jump.

At last he asked if I was ready to obey and I said yes so he untied me and made me get on my knees and take his cock in my mouth and suck on it. I was never so humiliated in my life. There were tears running down my face as he ground his hips and dug his prick deep into my throat. All the time he was calling me "Cocksucker" and "Fag" and saying "Suck it, Mary." The only thing I was spared was his coming in my mouth because I choked and gagged and turned red so he slapped my face and told me to get downstairs, put on my clothes and get back to work. On the way downstairs he booted my ass again and almost sent me sprawling.

The initiation that came some weeks later was also a pretty bad time.

Toilet Star Wears (A) Levis, (B) Jock Strap, (C) Scumbag

CALIFORNIA — I had a most delightful experience Christmas day. Driving from El Lay to San Diego to visit family, I had a flat tire in the middle of Oceanside. I managed to get the car to a service station and as the attendant was repairing the tire I had about half an hour to kill. I decided a good jack off would help to pass the time. I headed for the men's john, went into the toilet cubicle and although the door had a latch on it I failed to lock it and the door was ajar about an inch. So there I sat working on my hard seven incher when in walks a young blond kid wearing a lite blue pullover, tight Levis and tennis shoes. I'm sure, since the door was ajar, he could see I was working on my rod, so he just stood there with his legs spread, massaging the bulge of his groin. This was too good to pass up so I opened the door a bit more and motioned for him to step in and told him to close and latch the door, which he did. He stood there in front of me with a slight smile and said nothing. I reached up and rubbed his bulge and said, "I'd like some of that." He just said, "Be my guest." I unzipped his Levis and as I was sliding them down, I was delighted to see he was wearing an exceptionally white swimmer-style jock strap (I later learned it was called Pro-Duke). It was the most appealing jock strap I've ever seen. When I lowered it, lo and behold, up pops about a 6½ incher encased in a very tight-fittin transparent rubber. I couldn't believe my eyes. Beautiful sight that it was, though, I started to remove it and he said, "No, leave it on! I prefer to be sucked with one on." When I asked him why, he explained that there was a guy he met here every Thursday and the guy likes to suck the kid off with a rubber on. He then went on to say that his friend was to have met him here today too, even though it was Christmas Day, but he (the kid) had been delayed and was late, so his friend must have already been there and left. Well, this young cock was too gorgeous to pass up, rubber or no, so I went ahead and dined on rubber-covered tube steak. He really did need it I guess because he moaned, his whole body shuddered when he came and his knees started to buckle out from under him, so I had to hold him by his hips. As soon as it was over, he was in a hurry to get out of there and he adjusted his jock strap and Levis. I said, "What about the rubber?" As he started to remove it I said, "Let me have it. I'll get rid of it for you." He left but I kept his loaded rubber. Later that nite I licked his juice out of it, then rolled it onto my cock and had my second blast off of the day. I would gladly service him again, so long as he lets me keep his scumbags.

Scat

I sucked assholes for years. One day I got my tongue inside a guy's ass, and when I pulled my tongue out a little piece of shit came with it. I didn't want to spit it out so I swallowed it. I liked the taste so I said, "Do you want to give me the rest of it?" He didn't even know he'd let some shit slide out. I love to have a guy sitting in a chair with his asshole exposed and see the hole open up and a turd slide out slowly and eat it that way.

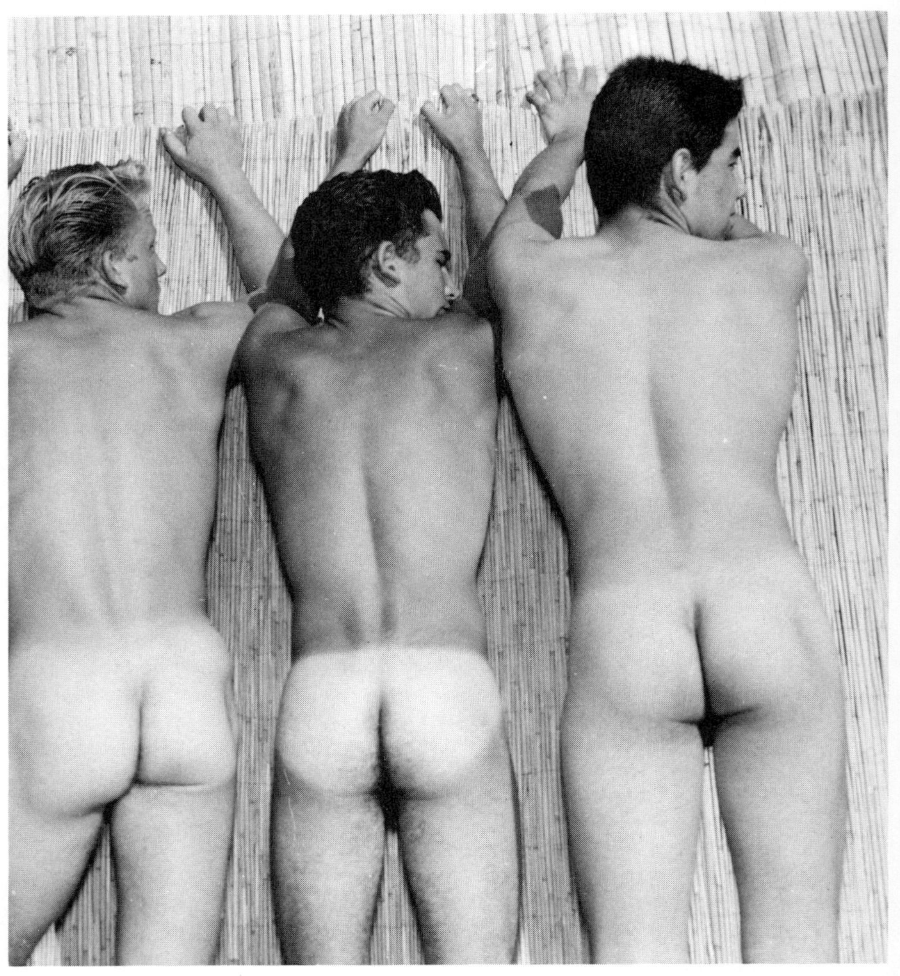

Interview: Sucks 15 Youths in Woods

No bars, baths anymore but not dead: now at 43 I got a built in supply on my job at a boys' school. They're really hot and I've been able to enjoy sucking some nice dicks with loads of cum. I also have a place in the forest with a college nearby, and term offers up some lovely college men. On weekends I hit tea rooms & book stores, so who is old at 43 and I don't expect to be old at 65 or what have you. I've been sucking since 15 and figured I've serviced thousands and still at it. I don't buy the men who at 45-55-65 say they can't get anybody to have sex with them. One has to get out and look and bars, baths are not for you, but there is a big world out there and a lot of Dicks need service.

You mentioned that you've sucked off thousands of cocks. What's the biggest number you ever sucked in one day? 15 in their late teens or early 20s. Had to stop after rain started in the wood of a country club.
Have most of your partners been clean? Most were. A very few were dirty or had a strong smell.
Have you often tasted cum you didn't like: Very few had cum I didn't like.
Have you tasted any cock cheese you didn't like? Yes, I only found very few with cock cheese that I could enjoy.
Have you had much trouble? Had a few rejections and insults, hit once, bitten once. Apt. robbed once and caught by vice cop I put the touch on, but I went to court and won.
Where have most of these blow jobs taken place? Rest rooms of mews, theatres, parks, rest areas, shopping malls. The rest at my apt. and a good many in the car.
What degree of nudity is there? Usually all drop their pants, and I can feel their lovely ass.
Do you like to get sucked off yourself? I used to always want to be sucked off, but now not so much because of the high rate of VD.
How often do you jack off? At one time three times a week, but now usually only once or twice a week.
How were you introduced to sex as a boy? I was staying overnight with my cousin and he said, look over here. He was jacking off, so I did it. I was 12 then. Me, a cousin & a stepbrother were just playing around and got into sucking each other, and then I told a friend and we did it; then there was this 13-year-old boy on my paper route who I talked into it, and I was well on my way, but really came out in the Air Force. I went in at 16 for 6 mos. At first I spit it out but then tried it one time and liked it.
What's your technique for seduction? I mainly sit down over a cup of coffee and talk them out with hinting to see how they respond, then I'll invite them to my apt. —that is, if they are not negative to the hints.
Isn't there danger that some of the boys at school will rat on you just to show they're "straight"? This school is more a youth jail, so they have as much to lose as I do. Also, when the boys get mad they call just about everybody fag, so no one pays attention to it. They don't want the mess any more than I do. One has to know how to cover his ass.
What percent of the students you've had sex with do you think will lead the "straight" life? I'd say 90 percent and 5 percent will go bisex. The other 4 will be gay.

Have you had sex with a lot of men who are leading the "straight" life—married men, fathers, and so forth? Yes.
What kind of underpants do your students wear? Jockey shorts.
Are they clean? Yes.
Do you lick anything besides dick? Always suck balls and nipples. Rarely ass; I use the finger.
How do you seduce men in toilets and book stores? In rest rooms they show it. In the book stores you ask if it's OK to watch the movie with them. Most are straight and drop their pants to the floor. Most are from the working class.
Please describe yourself. I'm in good health, 5'7", 140 lbs. Light brown hair. Usually friendly.
What is your blow job technique? I always tell them they got a nice Dick. As for sucking, I go all down, off and on, also run the tongue around the head and push it in the hole.
Do you care about dick size, or is it the whole man you're interested in? I go for build and personality mostly.
How long does the average blow job last? 3 to 5 minutes and longer.
Do you prefer cut or uncut cock? I prefer cut cocks, but they will not turn me off if they are uncut.
What are your other forms of recreation? Reading magazines, TV, music, camping, walks.
After sucking so many cocks, do you think you will begin to get tired of it? It is still thrilling. The cocks are just as good as ever.
Have you ever had any cocks too big to handle? About twice.
Do you consider it an advantage to be a homosexual? I would not say it is an advantage, but just as good as any other life there is to be had and I've really enjoyed life and will to the end. I'm not lonely, very seldom get bored and I don't buy the sin bit. I'm just as good as anyone, maybe better than a hell of a lot of them.
Have you ever had more than one piece of meat in your apartment at the same time? Yes, off and on and once a group of 10.
You mentioned that you sucked off 15 youth in the wood of a country club. Were they strangers? Yes. I met them in a bus station rest room and took them to the wood.
How did you pick them up? They just show their Dicks and I ask, you want a BJ, and let's go to a safe place.
What position were you in? Most stood and a couple laid down. I was on my knees.
Were all 15 there at once? No.
What degree of nudity was there? Most just took their pants down. Two took all their clothes off.
Were they all good conquests? All worth blowing. Glad I didn't tire out too fast.
How long did these 15 blow jobs take? It took me about 8 hours for all 15, to have the sex and go back to the rest room and get another.
When did they have a hard on—as soon as they pulled their dicks out or did it have to be worked up by sucking? Both.
Were you tired of sucking at the end of your 8-hour session? My neck and jaw only.
Did they try to act "straight" and superior? Just friendly teenagers. Some said thanks, some said they enjoyed it, some said I could suck it all day.

What did you do when the rain started? The rain started on the last one, but I kept sucking till he shot and we were both drenched, but he didn't seem to mind and said it was great.

You mentioned that you've had a few men who were smelly. How did you handle it? Most I went through with it, as the meat was too nice to let go. Some bothered me and some I told I had a sore tooth so I just jerked them off. Once I ended up with four Army men when my buddy left as he was afraid. Once a guy left me miles from the city to walk and it was cold, 15°, but I got a ride. Once two young moving van drivers took me in the van on the mats for sex. While I sucked one I played with the other, and then sucked both dicks at one time.

How were you caught by a vice cop? I was in a park. It was entrapment. He was a college kid. He asked me for a light, I gave him one, but he came extra close to me. I walked away and he came up again. I felt his meat. It was hard. He then pulled out his badge and said I was under arrest. All he said after that was, don't you read the papers, 14 were trapped that week. I said I was out of town. I figured I was ruined so I said to myself I'll fight it all the way, as the other 14 got 6 months and/or $200 fine and their names in the paper. I got out on bail after 3 hrs. and had an Atty. in another city, who knows I'm gay. In court I told the judge it was an accident; I stated my back was to him and he came up so close it startled me and when I turned around my hand brushed him. The vice cop was not at court. I pleaded to suspicious person and was fined $20. The Atty. was $200. It didn't hurt me otherwise.

Professor Sold as Slave

Two rough-looking H/D riders saw me standing in the station and offered me a ride. I was roared down the highway to a garage-like stable, stripped, blindfolded with a rubber section over which a gas mask was placed with a tube going into my mouth. My hands were chained to beams overhead, and I was whipped with belts on my back and butt and felt liquid pouring down the nozzle into my mouth. I realized it was piss and voices told me many more bikers were now present. Leather and chains with weights were attached to my sex parts, and I felt hands pulling the hair under my arms, around my cock and rectum. Then an intense tingling heat made me realize my hair was being burned off.

Several times my legs were raised, and I was fucked. I must have had several quarts of beer piss forced into my mouth. A sharp pain shot through my ears as they were pierced and rings inserted. My tits were pierced and rings put in and thumb tacks studded my ass prior to intense beating with studded belts.

I awakened next morning to find a fine looking boy ready to take me to L.A. on his H/D. Only later did I see the words "MALE" and "WHORE" on each side of my butt. When he dropped me off, he said, "We know your name, address and employer, and we have pictures of last night, so don't try anything ever against us."

The brand gradually wore away and my tits healed. From time to time I am sold for sex by one or the other of the several who send someone through town. An odd experience for a Phi Beta Kappa who had planned to be a priest and is a sedate college professor! But I am advertised by these guys as a supreme piece of ass. At least six have sold me at times. One has made over $1,000 on me. For a full professor to be sold to anyone at any time is degrading, yet exciting.

The Rogerian Method

Sniff my asshole, fag. You read my interview now smell of the *real* thing. My asshole is available for sniffing, $20.00 for 20 minutes. You can smell my asshole (1) clean (2) smelly (3) shitty. I also make hot cassettes and have some nice used shorts, jock straps, etc. For a list of what I've got send $2.00 to: Roger

* * *

[EDITOR's NOTE: Rotten Roger is blatantly a mail-order hustler, but a gifted and ethical one; in sending me some of the replies to his notices in S.T.H., he discreetly removed the names and addresses of his admirers.]

Roger Sir,
Seen your great story in the Manhattan Review. I am a groveling type faggot. Wish I were there to tongue shine your Boots! Please send me your list of used gear etc.
On my knees.

Hi Roger. Rec. your wonderful shorts and loved them. I sucked kissed and licked them for an hour or more, then raped them around my hard prick and jerked myself off. I have them on right now. I only wish I could suck and lick the ass and cock that was in them before me. I would like to have some of your pictures. Please try to make them all with a hard on and one of your hairy asshole. Which I would love to get my tongue into. Call me all the dirty names you can think of. I love to be called cocksucker and all things like that. I have sucked a lot of cocks and suck a lot of assholes and love it. I have had a lot of guys give me a good hot golden shower. They piss all over me and some times right in my mouth. I love that too. I am now going to jerk off in your shorts again. Wish you were here. I would get my tongue away up your hairy asshole. I would love to get your load of hot creamy love juice in my mouth. Keep all the faggots happy.

Roger — I'm into the jock scene, in that I love to worship, lick & sniff and service horny jocks. I'm 5'3", small build, 120 lbs., red hair, blue eyes, 6". At 29, I look much younger, maybe 23. I have a few tapes that I have made of a jock scene with a buddy of mine from Notre Dame U. We have a scene where he stands in his sneakers & sweat socks, muscular legs spread apart, jock strap pulled to one side, while I get to sniff and lick his big balls while he beats his meat. Eventually I get fed his big hot meat, down my throat and on my face. I worship with words as well as lips & tongue. Basically I play the "worshipping punk" or the "adoring sports fan" who would do anything to please. My partners in this scene have usually been verbally aggressive, getting off on showing their masculine attributes, talking dirty in a show-off way, teasing and provoking with flexing & exhibiting. Let me know about the possibility of getting together at the end of April.

Hi Roger. I have an absolute fetish for rubbers. You said one guy liked for you to answer the door wearing just a Rubber. Since you say you make hot cassettes, you can make me one (if your asking price isn't too damned high) telling how you like to use Rubbers for your sex life. No, I'm not a fag. I enjoy women as much maybe more as men. I just happen to dig Rubbers. P.S. If you decide to make me a cassette *I only want to hear how you like to use Rubbers! Nothing Else!!!*

It Swayed As He Walked

SAN DIEGO — At 12, the love of my life, or one of them, came wheeling in. We were just moving in when I first saw him climb out of his old klunker in the backyard next door. The best looking hairy tanned guy I'd ever seen running around in raggedy-assed cutoffs and sneakers. I was going bananas trying to figure out just how I could see *all* of Happy (although he didn't leave much to the imagination in his cutoffs). Our folks solved the problem. They began going out together and Hap was to be my "baby sitter." I was to spend nights when they were out in Hap's quarters over their garage. The coy one, I went into the bath to get into my P.Js. "Jeez, isn't it about time you grew up?" he said. "Wearing those damn things to bed is kid stuff." I promptly peeled and climbed between the sheets to play possum. He watched the 10 o'clock news and got up to go to bed. I just barely cracked my eyes to watch him strip. Nude, he was even more beautiful than I'd been able to imagine. So nice and long and big. He had that kind too where all that extra skin came down over the end. It even swayed back and forth as he walked to the bed. I'm sure half the night went by before I was sure he was asleep. Ever so easily I worked my way over next to him and ever so lightly rested my hot clammy hand on his cock. Boy, just barely kneading it got it bigger and harder. I was scared I'd woke him up when he rolled in my direction. I froze. But he said, "Don't quit. That feels good. Go on." He started feeling of my bare butt. He slipped a finger in my crack and wiggled it around my hole. I sort of rolled around. He was beginning to move back and forth and his dick was getting sticky. He went to the bathroom, shook hair oil all over his dick, brought the bottle back to bed and told me to roll over on my stomach. I wasn't surprised when he got on top of me but surprised is an understatement to describe how I felt when I discovered that it hurt *so* bad. I tried hard to squirm loose. But he held me tight. "Lay still, It'll feel real good in a little bit." He was right. Pretty soon it did feel good. Ever so slowly, he shoved more and more in until he was pushing real hard on my butt. I never felt so good, just laying there with him deep up inside me. The harder and faster he began to pound the better I liked it. I began helping him, humping my tight, hot, virgin asshole up and down to meet his thrust. First thing next morning we had a conference: our "fun" was just between the two of us; no one was to know about it. We fucked every damn chance we got, sometimes even jumping in his klunker and hiding out somewhere, or going over to one of his buddies. At first this really upset me. I loved to have Hap fuck my ass but I didn't think I wanted anyone else to. It hurt my feelings too that he'd told anyone else about our secret. But it turned out that it felt just so good whether it was his cock or another in my asshole. His buddies liked it as much as he did. The best times were when 3 or 4 of us would go out somewhere and they'd take turns. Some of them would do it more than once. They never did anything with each other, though; just stood there and watched and played with themselves.

His Gym Pants Fell To His Ankles

LOS ANGELES — I am enclosing an item I wrote in the laundromat. We had for a brief time here a male massage parlor. It was called Selma's after Selma Avenue, which runs through Hollywood and is a street popular with male hustlers. The massage parlor was located on Melrose Avenue in a mixed residential-business area. The building was an inconspicuous single-story. The sign in the window said: Massage Parlor — Male Masseurs. I pulled the door open and stood in a small lobby. The light was dim; the furnishings cheap and worn. The place was deserted. I waited half a minute. Nothing happened. Should I leave? The desire for sex was pushing me forward, but on the other hand I am easily intimidated. Was it safe? Could I afford it? What if I got mugged? I turned to go, just as a friendly but rather weasely fellow appeared in a curtained doorway. "Hello, Hello. What can we do for you?" "Well, I thought..." "Best massage in town. Good looking male masseurs. Twenty dollars for half an hour; $35 for a full hour. They'll give you the full treatment. Really take a load off... your shoulders." I reached into my pocket. "Your ad says..." "Oh, you saw our ad. Terrific. Terrific. Entitles you to a $5 discount." In spite of the sleaze of this fellow who talked like a used car salesman, I liked the place. Usually I was different about sex, but this place was different. There was no pretense. The proprietor took my $15 and steered me through the curtains into a cubicle. There was a rubbing table, a smaller table with bottles and towels, and a single chair, tilted back, on which sat a bored looking young man chewing gum. "This is Jerry. He'll make you feel real good." Jerry stood up and took charge. "Hang your clothes there (pointing to a hook) and climb up on the table." Jerry was about 25 or so, a decade younger than I. He was of average height, stocky but not fat. He wore a black T-shirt and baggy grey gym pants. He was good looking without being handsome, had a relaxed and friendly manner. "You been here before?" I shook my head. "Didn't think I'd seen you before." I lay face down on the table. He began rubbing my back. A quick once over from shoulders to heels. He then spread warm oil over my back and began a very sensuous massage. His hands were sure and knowing. After working on my shoulders and back for about five minutes he began to play with my ass and upper thighs. Occasionally his finger tips would dart into the crack of my ass or touch the area just above my balls. I wiggled my pelvis and spread my legs to give him complete access. I couldn't wait for him to start doing things to my throbbing cock. I reached under my body and staightened out my hard cock. He continued to play with my ass, running his hands up and down the crack of my ass, playing with my balls and running fingers around between my legs in general. Probably seeing that I was about ready to explode, he slapped my ass in a friendly way and said, "Turn over." I did. My dick was rock-hard and pointed toward my chin. He ignored my hard on and began rubbing oil over my chest, belly and legs. From time to time his hands brushed against my balls and cock. He took my hands and positioned them over my head so they rested on the edge of the table. Then he stood at my head and leaned forward so he could rub my belly and thighs. As he rocked forward his bulging groin touched my hands. I waited about ten cautious seconds, then began to play with his hard prick. Immediately he walked to the edge of the table so his groin was only inches from my face. He jerked the string and his gym pants fell to his

ankles. He was wearing a black bikini which covered only part of his fat, red prick. He tucked the bikini under his balls. This caused his cock to point straight out, like a cannon. It was my favorite kind of cock. Long, fat and torpedo shaped with the head the same diameter as the shaft. It was not cut, and I pulled the foreskin back and began to suck the head. He reached down and took hold of my cock. "If you want me to take care of this, there's a tip involved." It turned out there was a fee schedule. For another $5 you got jacked off. For more money you got more exotic tricks. I willingly gave him the $5 and continued to suck his fat piece of meat. I wished my own cock were exactly like his. While I sucked he jacked me off. He put more warm oil on my cock. It was a juicy and noisy jack off and I wanted it to go on and on. I held back as long as I could. Then shot what felt like a gallon. He was very considerate, held on to my cock even after I was through coming, then fetched a warm towel and cleaned me up. He did not come himself. He handed me my clothes, gave me a friendly pat on the back when I was dressed and urged me to come back soon. I planned to go back when I had more money, but within a few months Selma's closed its doors. That was five years ago.

Gang-Sucked

One day when I was 11 I sneaked over to the bare-ass area of our local swimming hole used by the boys 14-17. Thee were three boys in the water horsing around. I dove in and headed underwater for Jim. When I swam up behind him he was standing bare-ass, his legs spread. I started through and he closed his legs on me, locking me in a vise. The next thing I knew he had me in a scissors lock but instead of a mouthful of feet, I had a mouthful of cok and balls — in our struggling I had twisted myself around. Jim kept his legs tight around my neck but floated on his back so I could come up for air. Jim's big cock and balls flopped in and around my mouth as I gulped for air.

The other two guys laughed and Jim said, "The kid must like it the way he went after it." Jim's cock got iron hard. Every time I opened my mouth for breath he would poke the tip into my mouth. I'd gag and he and the boys would laugh like hell. The three of them pushed me up on shore and into a clump of leafy sumac trees. They argued about who would be first. Jim said he discovered me so he got first shot.

He spread a towel out and forced me down on my knees. Bill asked, "Has your brother let you see the white stuff he can milk out of his cock?" "No. He doesn't even let me see him naked any more." Jim said that if a young boy drank the white stuff, it would go down to his balls and help the cock and balls grow faster. While he was explaining, he kept rubbing the head of his cock across my lips. "Just suck it nice," he said. "Don't use your teeth." It was hot and hard and delicious. "Stop fucking around," he said. His voice was hoarse. "Suck it!"

All of a sudden he started moaning and groaning. He pulled my head against his crotch while ramming his prick as far into my throat as possible. I felt it explode and choked on the jism he was shooting into me. I took the other two and went back for seconds. From that day on I followed those three around like a faithful puppy. I'd get on my knees and beg them to let me suck their cocks. By the time school began I was sucking eight or nine guys, some as often as four or five times a week. Jim once pumped three loads a day, five days in a row down my throat.

Connoisseur Sniffs, Kisses Whore's Ass-hole

MANHATTAN — I have always been into paying for sex even as a young man (I am now over 50). I felt more in control that way. Four years ago I was sent a young street hustler by a bartender friend who worked at a seamy Ninth Avenue bar. The kid was on probation and on pot. He was constantly being thrown out by his mother, who often called the police to assist her, and many's the time he appeared here with bruises, cuts and once a missing front tooth due to a gang fight. He looks terrific, very butch; has a muscular body that is not overdone. Before he quit school he was on the wrestling team. His strong Germanic face is surrounded by a lion's mane that is held back by a kerchief headband *a la* American Indian. His clothes are a hodge-podge of wornout military and patched Western, always having a faint masculine odor. Our routine was that after he came by bus from New Jersey, an hour's ride, he would always just glance at me, grunt some sort of salutation and head straight for the bathroom to take a shit. That done with, on comes the TV, usually Popeye or the like. He then plops on the bed, resting his head in the cup of his hands, indicating that the show is about to begin. He says nothing. We never did really talk or exchange views except when he was heavily stoned or when, after our numerous breakups, he would call and condescend to use his beguiling boyish charm to con his way back into my affections. It always worked. In the beginning he liked to jerk off while I was on my back underneath him sniffing and licking his soft pink ass-slit. He would then come all over my face. I forgot to mention that before we got to this position, while he was lying on the bed, I would with great pleasure undress him. First off were his dusty work boots, then his usually non-matching athletic socks. I would kiss his feet and lick in between his toes. Next, the unbuttoning of his washed-out plaid shirt with its musky fragrance. He would sit up with outstretched arms obediently (the only time, I might add, he was obedient), letting me pull off his mildly sweat-stained T-shirt. As he lay back I would nestle my nose in his intoxicating hairy armpits. While rubbing his stomach and chest, I would slowly tongue-bathe him, not forgetting his nipples. He lifted his rump so that I could pull off his pants. I would then softly chew his cock through his piss-marked Jockey shorts, all the time being treated with a pungent whiff from his manly groin. Through the years I would kneel in front of his spread-eagle position at the foot of the bed as if at an altar, and after his prick got hard with the help of my salivary glands, I would prop up his bare ass on a pillow for me to worship by licking and kissing his ass-hole, fresh from just having taken a crap. The stench is heaven. While he held his legs up in the air, I would sometimes jerk him off, fingering his ass-hole. His hot creamy juice would shoot all over his hard teenage stomach. I would promptly lap it up like a hungry calf. Then there were times when I would lick his thighs, cup his large sack of balls in one hand and start nibbling at the base of his seven-inch prick. I'd lick slowly up his cock shaft, making sure to tongue all around and under its hot-pink mushroom head, as per his instructions; then go down completely on his shaft with much compulsive slurping, my mouth and head going as if turned on by a generator that's out of control. He always gives a healthy load but sometimes likes to pretend disinterest by having a smoke and looking at girlie magazines. But more often than not, he is a wide-eyed, interested sergeant gruffly giving

orders as to the proper way for me to suck or to take it easy with the balls, no fingers up the ass, etc., etc. Usually, after being separated for some weeks, he would return to do the thing I like best: to be fucked in the mouth. I would lie on the bed naked. He would squat over me fully clothed with his aromatic groin pushed in my face until his tool hardened, at which time he'd pull it out and stick it into my waiting warm mouth. I particularly like this position, for I could then see his entire body suddenly jerk and watch that strong, handsome face grimace as he shoots his wad. In his arrogant way, he can't help but ask in a husky tone if I enjoyed it. I, of course, politely reply that it was delicious, which, to me, it was, tasting like tapioca pudding with just a pinch too much salt. His reaction to this is a self-satisfied, shy smile. Unhappily, at this writing, I have not seen him for some time. I lost my patience along with some money. So I think this time our parting is for good. It certainly was great fun and I wish him all the luck.

The Case for Big Cocks

SAN FRANCISCO — I'm a sucker for a big cock. I don't hide that, either. I know a guy who says, "There are two types of men: size freaks and liars." I don't mind being called a size freak. What else would you call it? My other craving is foreskin. Sorry to say I am cut. I love foreskin. I crave foreskin. I use the strong word "crave" because my feelings are strong on the issue. Fortunately, I guess, many men don't care and it is easy for me to find men to suck me. But my preference is to do the sucking. Get a big uncut dick in my mouth and I could go for hours. There is one quality about my dick that most men like: it gets *very* hard. I had never thought it was that unusual until I started to notice others. All hard ons, it turns out, are not equally hard. I've had good reports about the smell and taste of my meat, ass-hole, cream, piss and briefs. I always smell my underwear when I take them off. And sometimes I bend over when I'm sitting on the toilet to get a good whiff of my briefs. I always wear them a few days so I can build up a good perfume for myself and the men who like to bury their noses in my briefs. My brand is Munsingwear. There are lots of gay-owned and - run places here where you can go to get plenty of sex. But I eschew them for a different type of experience. I like to find my men in the 25¢ peep show houses and mixed straight/gay porn stores. They are different here than they are in New York. In New York there is too much surveillance; the staff is making sure nothing happens and they are too intent on making sure the tokens are always dropping. It's a little more lax here. These places are usually frequented by a wide variety of men: some gays, but lots of heterosexuals, some married, who don't get blown very often and really appreciate good head. I am also a very Equal Opportunity cocksucker when it comes to age and some of the other features than turn off lots of fussy gays who will only go to bed with a *Blueboy* or *GQ* model. My type of men is not rigid (only their dicks are); I can't confine myself to only one hair type or color of eyes or height, weight, etc. The appeal has more to do with something that tells me this is a hot man. I'm not sure what to call it, but I know it when I see it. There are three main areas where there are good peep shows: Mission Street, the Tenderloin and Broadway. The one near Broadway is within walking distance from the Financial District, where lots of business types work. I suck 'em pretty well and they appreciate it.

Youth Reaches Into Reader's Jockey Shorts

LOS ANGELES — One night when I was feeling restless and couldn't sleep, I decided to go to a sex shop in my neighborhood. As soon as I walked in, I noticed what I first took to be a child, a young Chicano, in the homosexual book section. I was pretending to look at the glossies a few feet away from him when he came up to me with a magazine he had opened to a picture of one guy fucking another in the ass. He said, "That's nice, isn't it?" I nodded assent. His hair was very short and I figured he must either be in the service or just out of jail. He said, "Do you want to do this?" I said sure. He had such baggy clothing I couldn't tell what his body would be like. I took him to my apartment, sat next to him on the couch and asked him how tall he was. He was so tiny. He said 5'3". I asked if he'd made it with any guys before and he said he had when he was 12. He said he was now 18. He was a little drunk and nervous so I reached over and stroked his chest and started pulling off his baggy shirt and pants. I discovered a beautiful, muscular, hairless little body, with a tattoo on each arm, "Connie" on one and "Mary" on the other. I asked him about them and he said they were old girlfriends. I asked him about his short hair and he told me he had just gotten out of prison on a charge of armed robbery. He said he'd had plenty of opportunities for sex in prison but had avoided it. He had a respectable cock on his little body, with a nice full bush of cock hair. He had the beginnings of a moustache and the most heavy-lidded bedroom eyes I'd seen in a long time. His boxer shorts were so big they came down to his knees like culottes. I took him to the bedroom and got under the covers with him. He was affectionate as a little kid and at times as I cuddled and held him it felt as if I had a prepubescent child with me. I asked him if he had ever sucked a cock. He said no. I told him he ought to try it, that it tasted just like putting a finger into your mouth. He tried for awhile and seemed to get into it. When he started pushing his little ass against my dick I got some KY jelly and started to loosen his hole with my finger. As I inched my cock into it he asked me not to hurt him. I had to get him on his back, since his small size made most other positions impractical. When I started to move my dick in and out he pulled my mouth down onto his and got me to go faster and deeper by clutching my thighs on the downstroke. He let loose of my lips and started shouting "Fuck me." I was so excited by then that I couldn't keep from unloading. He asked me to leave my dick inside him and try to keep it hard for a little longer. At the same time he stuck his finger in his hole and started to jerk off. He shot a healthy load into his belly button. I licked it up and tried to kiss him but he moved his lips away. As soon as he shot his wad he was anxious to leave. Four days later at two in the morning I heard a knocking on my door. It was Jorge again. Even though I had jacked off twice before going to bed, I couldn't resist him, so I sat him on the couch and figured I would just talk to him a bit. He put his arms around me and while he had me against the couch reached into my Jockey shorts and started playing with my dick. It got hard and strained against the cotton. He asked, "Can I sleep with you?" After I screwed him for awhile he told me to wash off my cock and jerk off in his mouth because he'd always wanted to taste another guy's sperm. I kneeled with my legs on both sides of his neck and shot my wad into his mouth while he jacked off. After shooting off he suddenly wanted to leave.

Jacking Off in Vietnam

SAN FRANCISCO — In Vietnam on guard duty in the foxholes we'd strip down to just our jocks and boots because of the heat at night. Some of the guys would be bareass, with their uniforms handy, but most were in combat boots and jocks. The moon would be full and guys would stand up and start jacking off and you could see the sweat dripping off them. They would shoot and the cum would be milk-white in the moonlight. You'd hear a low groan as the guy came and the others would laugh softly. Most of the guys were straight, but they had no aversion to jacking off in front of each other. It was considered manly and not the least embarrassing ("What's a guy to do with no girls around?"). Two or three guys, bareass but for their shoes, would get in a foxhole and have a JO session and shoot over the rim of the hole. Guys would crawl naked out of the foxholes in the middle of the night with big piss hard ons and sneak in the bushes and piss. You could watch the yellow streams sparkling in the moonlight. In camp during the hot summer one guy used to sleep bareass in a hammock with his cock sticking down through the mesh. Most of the others wore just T-shirts. It was too hot and humid to wear any clothes at all. They'd walk to the latrine with their cocks swinging and their big piss hard ons sticking out. In the barracks you'd see them with big piss hard ons sticking up as they lay on their backs with their legs spread and their assholes showing. Sometimes they'd jack off and just let their sweaty T-shirts soak up their cum and stay in bed and go to sleep.

He Whispered, "Kiss My Ass"

FROM A PRIEST — I was 11 years old, living in Chicago. We had been given free tickets to a concert for young people. Neither of my parents could go — so I was allowed to go alone. After the concert I took the "L" train home. Several stops later a man in his 30s sat down beside me. I ignored him and looked out at the lights in the houses as the train sped along. I became aware of his hand, on the seat, pressing against my rump. He was obviously drunk. I pretended to read a pamphlet, and was scared as hell. His hand kept pressing until it was partially under my rump. I was happy when the stop at long last arrived. I left the train and started down the stairs. Fear — and — interest — swept over me. I deliberately slowed down, allowing all the other people to move ahead. About halfway down the stairs the man from the train paused by me. He wanted to know if I had a light. At age 11! I said no, so he produced his own. He offered me a cigarette. At my age, in those days, it was sinfully wicked. I accepted it and we loitered, talking. He asked if he could come home with me. I told him my father would be angry. Another train arrived and the people passed us. We slowly made our way down the steps and I followed him under the "L" tracks, which was also an alley for neighboring houses. For awhile we just stood there in the semi-darkness just touching our bodies lightly together. I began to tremble. His hand touched my pants, opened my fly and pulled out my cock. He fondled it. I looked up at him. He was strange and handsome. I said, "What's that for?" He said, "Don't you know?" He gently grabbed my hand and put it on his cock. It was just there when he pressed my hand to it. It was the first time I felt a warm cock in my hand. I enjoyed it. I played with it. I was still frightened, but I enjoyed being with the man. He put his hand on the back of my neck and gently pushed me down. I opened my mouth and sucked in his cock. Each time an "L" train roared above us the lights from the train would light us up. Anyone could have watched us. But I was oblivious to where we were. There was a nice warm smell coming out of his pants and his full-blown cock was a wonderful thing to go down on. I slipped my hands around his thighs and felt up his ass. I liked the way it felt. Soon he indicated I should rise and we walked down the "alley" to a more secluded place. Both of us had our cocks sticking out of our pants. It was a turn on for me, though at time I did not know or understand exactly why. We stopped by a group of garbage cans in the darkest part of this "alley" and I fondled his cock and balls again. I remember the soft warm feeling and the nice smell. He pulled down his pants and I sucked on his cock again, totally unaware of anything else. He pulled away, turned around and whispered, "Kiss my ass." I was embarrassed, but I could not resist. I leaned forward and buried my face in his crack of his ass. It was not what I expected. His buns were nice and warm, and the smell was strangely exciting. I kissed his ass and began to lick it, instinctively and without being told to do so. Again, it was not all as I had imagined. It was beautiful. He took my pants down and told me to bend over. He slowly started to shove his cock up my asshole. It sure hurt, but I did nothing about it except endure. It was still a strange mixture of fright and an erotic turn on I couldn't resist. My face was pressed against a garbage can and he was ramming my bottom. Soon he blew his load (or I believe he did). He pulled his cock out and had me suck it clean. He asked what I thought of it and I said I didn't like it. He laughed quietly and hugged me to his stomach. No one had ever hugged me before. It was nice to be

hugged. He wiped his cock with his handkerchief and gave it to me and said, "Keep that for a remembrance." Then he reached into my pants and played with my cock and asshole again. He put his hand to my nose and said, "Smell." I breathed in the sweet smell. "Now go home and be back in a week." He walked away and I felt a great loss. I wanted him to love me. No one had ever hugged me or been nice to me. As I walked home, occasionally smelling his handkerchief, I was horny as hell. At home, I went to the bathroom and cleaned out my mouth, then went to bed and played with myself, smelling his handkerchief. Later I was embarrassed, I put the handkerchief into our "garbage burner" and watched it burn. I went to bed frightened, vowing never, never to return to the "L" stop. But four days later the urge returned. I couldn't wait until Saturday. When Saturday came I waited and waited in our "alley," until disappointment made me return home. I never saw the nice man again. But since that night, I've had a fondness for assholes, coarse language and smoking. I have nothing against cocksucking, but it runs second or third to my interest in assholes. I enjoy rimming a kid and listening to him swear and talk dirty, but a man's ass is even more exciting. This is a true story — nothing changed or added.

"He Made My Legs Shake"

MANHATTAN — What I still consider to be the single most exciting sexual experience of my life took place late one moonlit night in the meat rack on Fire Island. I had been in the erotic labyrinth for two or three hours sucking cock like crazy but hadn't gotten my own rocks off yet. I was still horny, but I was also tired, so I headed back to the house in Cherry Grove to go to sleep. I entered a fairly large clearing on my way out and saw coming towards me a body like the Michelangelo David. I won't ever be able to have this man, I thought, but I was stoned and stuck my arm out to let my hand graze his hard stomach as we met. The next thing I knew I had been engulfed in his muscular arms, locked in a passionate kiss, his tongue probing deep into my surprised but willing mouth. Suddenly the guy was on his knees in front of me. He undid my belt, pulled down my zipper and yanked my jeans and jock down below my knees. Oh God, I thought, I'm going to get the shit shaken out of me. I thought he was going to throw me to the ground and fuck me, but instead he started to suck me, at first caressing the head of my rock hard dick with his tongue and then taking the whole 7½ inches. He gave me the best blow job I've ever had, making every bit of my cock tingle with pleasure. As he licked and sucked on my cock, he tickled my balls, making me moan and my legs shake. My eyes were closed. An inhaler was thrust into my nose. I took a hit of popper and really began to fly. I opened my eyes and saw my benefactor give a snort to the hunk who was blowing me. I looked around and saw that about 50 guys had gathered around to watch me get sucked off. This turned me, and I think the guy who was sucking, on. Every now and again one of the spectators would give us each a good hit of amyl, but none of them tried to get into the act. Some were jerking off; some were sucking; some were just watching. After I came he continued to suck and lick me until my cock became so sensitive that I reluctantly pushed him off me. He stood up, kissed me, and slipped from my grasp before I could find out who he was. I pulled up my jock and jeans and walked away. A guy said, "Was that you who was in trouble?"

Interview:
Hotelman "Had" Bus Boys, Watched Cops Coupling

MANHATTAN — I used to work at Hotel. Used to suck some of the bus boys. Also used to have peepholes, and once saw two 17th Pct. make it together. We gave them free rooms when they chased whores from hotel. I scraped mirrors between conn. doors, and also used to watch couples fuck.

I was asst. mgr. at this hotel and one of the boys (from Colombia), married, about 21, used to check out my meat at work. I invited him out one night, he came to my pad, I wound up fucking him; but it was through him that I used to suck off 2 or 3 of the other bus boys regularly. Usually in a room at the hotel.

Bus boys sound like high quality pieces of trade; did you find them to be? Definitely.
What ethnic group were they? Puerto Rican, Colombian, Cuban.
Please describe them. Typical young Latinos, dark, short (except for Cuban, who was big, stocky), early 20s.
Did they disrobe completely? Always undressed completely. Colombian was mutual sex — others trade only. The Cuban (biggest prick of all) used to fuck me occasionally.
Did they have hard ons before you began sex with them or did you work them up? Usually hard to begin with.
What positions? Usually lying in hotel rm. bed.
What kind of underpants did the youths wear? Jockey shorts.
Were the youths clean? Usually clean — sometimes a little funky.
What did they say and do whilst being blown? Just usual horny moans.
How big were their dicks? Averaged about 6-7 inches, except Cuban, who was about 9 inches and it was fat. He could come 2-3 times. Said my mouth was like his wife's cunt.
Were they nice boys or rotten? Couple were married. Often used to see them with their girls. Puerto Rican boy was fired for stealing.
Were they on the make for anybody, or just someone they knew and trusted like you? A couple of them would go with anybody I think. Cuban was more selective. I still see him occasionally, though we're both married.
Did they ever try to recover their lost heterosexuality after having homosexual sex with you? Never any trouble after sex. Latins are much more liberal, I've found, in this respect.
How did you know the two men you saw having sex were cops — specifically, from the 17th Precinct? Working as manager, I used to give them Rooms. Knew them quite well.
How did you observe them — peep hole or two-way mirror? Both.
Please describe them. One Aldo Ray type (maybe Irish, Italian or Polish), one Ty Hardin type, stocky, blond.
What kind of underpants did they have — Fruit of the Loom boxer shorts? Jockey shorts again. By the time I saw them they were in Bed. It was afternoon, light from window shone in room. No lights; beer bottles on dresser. TV on.
Did they kiss or just mechanically get down to sex? No kissing, Just 69. One rimmed the other for a long time. Beautiful Polish ass.

What were your feelings when you saw this? Surprised, excited & incredulous.
Was it an attractive scene or repulsive? 99% attractive. Used to give the same Polish cop a room for him and his girlfriend. He would eat her for hours. Then she would let him fuck her with his fat cock, and he'd come 1-2-3.
What vibrations did they give off as to being "gay," "straight," or both? Non gay. One was particularly anti-gay in comments.
Were they "dirt" (vice) cops? No, not vice, just patrol cops, who would come to hotel when we had a robbery or something. One used to work for hotel on his night off as hotel security.
What kind of sex did they have with each other? Just suck, suck, rim & suck. Speaking of peep holes, it was much groovier for me personally to just watch a cop by himself in a room, sometimes jacking off, or just lying nude watching TV.
You mentioned that through peep holes and two-way mirrors you watched cops in rooms which your hotel gave them, and that you saw one cop rimming another for "a long time." How long? Sporadically — off and on — about 20 min.
Your mentioned that the cop being rimmed had "a beautiful ass." What was beautiful about it? Chunky, solid. A little hair. Beautiful shape. Average crack. Hair visible in crack.
What position were they in for rimming? Both on bed, one lying with legs up while his buddy does it. Also later on the one cop sitting on bed, legs on floor, the other on hands and knees on rug lapping it up.
What position were they in for cocksucking? 69 Position. Also one on the rug sucked the cop sitting on the bed between rimming sessions.
Did the cop being rimmed cooperate by making his asshole easily available? Opened his crack with his hands. Could see him pushing hole in his partner's face.
Did the rimmer seem passionate or just mechanical? Did he caress any of the cop's other parts while rimming his asshole? How did he rim? Like he would never rim again. Not a lot of head movement, but savoured every taste. He was jerking his own tool at the same time and caressed the other guy's belly and legs.
How did they such each other's cock? When they finally got in 69 position, they started out gradually. The rimmer took the other guy's large cock to the base. His partner pulled back several times — didn't wish to rush. Rimmee only took half the other guy's cock. Alternated with hand-mouth.
Please describe their bodies. Both reasonably chunky (not fat) with semi-muscular natural bodies. One had quite a lot of dark body hair. The other average hair.
How did it all end? The rimmee shot his load. The other guy jerked himself off while he licked his partner's balls and groin.
How do you know the two wore Jockey Shorts, if they were bareass when you first espied them? Because their shorts were on the floor. One of them wore heavy utility socks during the action, which also turned me on.
How long did you observe this pair? One time I watched about 25 min. Another time I just got glimpses.
You mentioned that you saw one of these cops laying a woman. Which one? The one who got rimmed.
How did his butt look as it moved up and down in fucking? Unbelievably

attractive. It turned me on really more than when the two guys had sex. In fact I jerked off twice while watching him eat and fuck her cunt. He ate for about half an hour, then shot fast.
You mentioned that the two cops didn't seem homosexual. In what way can two male cocksuckers, one of whom also gives the other a rim job, not seem homosexual? Just attitudes. Both could be athletes. Didn't have the hungry, desperate look that guys in baths or piss houses have. But it's hard for me to be objective, since I had seen them as cops around the hotel for so long.
You mentioned that one of them was a "fag"-baiter. Which one? The one who got rimmed.
What did he say? One night I was wearing fag perfume. The rimmee said, "That's the same shit the fags wear on Third Avenue." Sometimes when I would walk out for coffee and they would be driving around, the rimmee would say, "Be careful of the queers." Sometimes he would say, "Hi, Mary" to the Third Avenue gays.
What do you think of a man who sucks cock and gets his ass rimmed by another man making cracks about homosexuals? He never really offended me, because I never took the cracks seriously. Plus he always was joking about everything, not just gays.
Would you have liked to get in bed with either or both of them? Would have loved to rim and suck the rimmee, and especially would love to have fucked him, which I'm sure was what he wanted. Would have like to 69 with the other, as he was a wild cocksucker.
Why didn't you make a pass at them? If I had, any future voyeuring on my part would be finished.
Can you describe their pricks? The rimmee had fat pinkish cock about 8 inches. Beautiful shape. Brown pubic hair. Other guy had about 6½, not so fat. Black pubic hair.
Were there any signs of love or affection, or was it just sex? Just sex.
Did they talk much? Smile? Laugh? They laughed afterward. Giggled like kids. Couldn't hear dialogue. They watched TV and drank beer.

Finds Mr. Right In Peep Show

SAN FRANCISCO — Where in the fuck is the next issue of *S.T.H.* They have the hottest shows in town. Every night at nine there is a live show. When I say live I mean live. Everyone has their pants down jacking off and the man on the stage comes out in the audience and lets us all suck on his dick and sometimes takes some hunk on the stage with him and they have sex and come all over each other. By that time all of us are so hot that we are coming all over ourselves or the man next to us. It is really fun because no one is inhibited and all either suck or jack off. Last night I went to one of those quarter movie places that San Francisco has so many of. There was a man that was about 40 and in a business suit. He was on his way home to his wife and stopped by. Well I motioned him into my booth and when I unzipped his pants and tood out his meat I was amazed. It was about 9 inches. His balls were fat and his foreskin and dick were perfect. I asked him if he could meet me sometime and go to a hotel room and he agreed. I also asked him if he ever let it get cheesey and he said no one ever wanted it that way. I do!!! I also asked him to piss on me but I will have to train him to do that too. God, he was the best I have had in ages.

Cock-crazed Boy Prodigy

I'm amused when I hear of men seducing helpless boys. I went looking for men. They were frequently hesitant because of my youth; I pressed the point. I may have been 12 and they 25, 30, 35, but it was I who seduced them. I told myself it was a phase, a substitute for girls, but all along I knew what I wanted and was determined to get it. Lately I heard of a 12-year-old picked up on Christopher Street who had been giving head under the boardwalk in Asbury Park or some such milieu since the age of nine. I have always gone for older men and I can well remember what it's like to be a teen on the make. I began furtively reading my father's medical texts about the age of ten. The book that touched me off was a thousand-page tome entitled *Prostitution and Morality*, a Sexology book of the month which arrived when I was 11. The chapter on male hustlers, complete with case studies and interviews, was a revelation. It talked about movie house balconies, public men's rooms, parks; and I suddenly realized what all those men were doing hanging around the men's room in Sears and what that big hole in the stall was; the motives of those guys in the balcony of the Paramount, where I was frequently to be found at Saturday matinees, suddenly became clear.

So at the age of about 11 or 12, I went over to Sears and took a seat in the last stall. A guy in his early 20s came in and ran his finger along the bottom of the hole in the wall between my stall and the next, but I didn't know what to do. Eventually he got on his knees and slid his cock under the partition. I looked at it for a minute, and then reached down to touch it. I was enthralled but had no idea how to proceed. He muttered that I should suck it. I hesitated a minute, then got down on my knees and put his cock in my mouth. My career was launched. By the time I was 14, I was regularly cruising men's rooms in department stores, movie houses, the public library (which had the highest quality meat). That was also the year I began hanging around the pavillion in the park, and started going home with men. I refused to admit to myself that I was crazed for cock, though that never stopped me looking for it most nights of the week and frequently all day on the weekends. I blew soldiers on leave at theatre tearooms. Occasionally one would blow me, though usually they stood soundless and as near motionless as possible, wanting only to be serviced. They seemed so old to me then, though I'm sure none of them was over 20. I loved to suck their cocks, fondle their balls, caress their thighs.

Canadian Re-discovers Vidal

TORONTO — Congratulations on the latest issues; it just keeps getting better and better. I have a few experiences I must send, but I don't have the time at the moment. Are things getting more and more hectic, or is it just a case of discovering more and more things that need to be done? I can't understand people who say "I'm bored." "I'm boring" would be more appropriate. I must thank you for re-turning me on to Gore Vidal's writing. My first exposure to him was the essay "The State of the Union" in *Esquire* in 1976. I still have the issue. Then in one of your issues you quoted some stuff from his *Matters of Fact and Fiction*, which I bought. I've bought two more copies as gifts for friends. I can't think of any writer I admire more, and with whom I agree so much. What a mind the man has. Thank God he's the way he is.

I Gagged But I Loved It

JAMAICA, LONG ISLAND — Here is a true experience I had when I was 15. Up to this time, I had only experienced sex with kids my own age. I lived in the Flatbush section of Brooklyn. There was a bar on McDonald Ave. that had the roughest guys imaginable. I used to go there at odd times of the day and nite just to drool at the windows. One day right after school around 3:30 I saw this garage mechanic come out. He was about 30, Italian, black hair. Not handsome in the "pretty" sense, but so damn masculine, I was frantic. I was completely mesmerized by him. I hadn't the vaguest idea how to cruise or what to say so I just followed him down the street. He walked a few blocks to an auto repair shop, and much to my amazement, jerked his head and groped himself as if to say follow me. He took me in this little wooden shack and without a word, locked the door and took off his pants and underpants. He had a beautiful fat uncut cock, about 7 inches, and the biggest pair of fat balls I'd ever seen. He pulled me down and gagged me with that fat gorgeous meat. I gagged but I loved it. I ws then *told* to eat his balls and ass. I had never done this but I took to it like a duck to water. When he had come, he told me to come back in a couple of days. I sure did. I loved it. I learned to eat his ass like an expert. He loved it. But not more than me. This went on at least twice a week for 4 years. He also introduced me to 3 or 4 friends, who also loved getting blown. However he was the very best. I went back there years later but the place was torn down and Frank was gone. What a man. I can still remember the smell of oil and car grease like it was yesterday. I tried to duplicate this scene with other gas station types but nothing came close to that filthy dirty gorgeous hot Italian.

Diplomat in Drag Seduces Queer

I am completely and delightedly queer. A few weeks ago I boarded a train in Penn Station, bound for a disarmament conference in Princeton. A man who looked the very definition of Mr. Straight Bureaucrat took the place next to me. He was in consummate corporate drag: grey pinstripe suit, briefcase, short hair and pallid, pinched expression. A wide wedding band as well. He opened his brief-case and pulled out a sheaf of State Department documents on the Iran-Iraq Crisis. He propped his forearm next to mine on the arm-rest. Slight-but-distinct pressure, which I noted but ignored. Later he let his head fall back against the seat, closed his eyes and "napped." His hand was draped over the edge of his brief-case, which still rested on his lap. His fingers hung suspended just above my left thigh. Centimeter by centimeter, these fingers lowered until they grazed the creases of my pant-leg. By now, I realized what my straight neighbor was up to. I was ENTHRALLED. Thrilled at this private seduction taking place in public train, I lowered my *New Yorker* to provide cover and raised my left leg to meet the pressure of this gentleman's fingers. As soon as he knew I was cooperating with him he carried on his advances with steady determination, still feigning sleep. I watched my fellow passengers and the archetypically frumpy conductor pass in the aisle as my neighbor squeezed my leg, ran his fingers up the inside of my thigh, pressed my balls and, finally caught my cock, pressing and stroking its turgid length through the cotton of summer weight pants. His face was a mask of icy composure; my groin was on fire. His caress was unspeakably pleasant. He worked his hand between my

pants and shorts. He was able to wrap his fingers around my wet cock, with only the camouflage offered by my *New Yorker*, without provoking the attention of any passersby. Using the lubricant I had by now secreted in abundance, his fingers began stroking my cock. In less than a minute a stream of cum, ineluctable, dizzying erupted and spilled over his fingers and my Brooks Brothers underwear. I saw not a trace of this exquisite event betrayed in his sleeping expression. I withdrew his hand and pulled my blazer over the conspicuous blotch, the damp stigma of my delight. When I got off at Princeton I turned to my deceptively-costumed comrade and repeated a line from the pre-recorded message broadcast throughout the train at each station stop: "Thank you for riding Amtrak." He smiled shyly and I was gone.

Submarine Officer Sniffs Sailors' Black Socks

As you recall your Navy submarine service, what images of flesh come to mind? Sailors in their underpants. Underpants were normally called "skivvies." As there were no showers on board, we didn't see much bareass. You waited until you got topside and usded Mother Nature's seas all around you or took a quick sponge bath. Water is always a crucial item on board a sub and everyone conserved it.

What kinds of underpants did sailors wear in thos days — World War II and the Korean War? Three-snap boxer shorts —white.

Did the sailors sleep in their underpants? We had double-tiered bunks against the hull of the boat. Someone was always sacking out and the closeness of a sub's interior makes for removing all but shorts and lying on top of blankets and sheets. Lots of nice legs, some in their black socks. Big feet encased in stinking and sweaty socks — Jesus, but I would linger as long as I could talking with a buddy off duty just so I could inhale that sexy man stink of socks worn several days in clammy shoes or boots. Whew! I still can smell them — were they ever sexy. And I'd get an instant hard on rubbing up against their bunks.

In such close quarters, was there a heavy smell of men? The stink on board was composed of diesel fuel fumes, oil from lubrication of machinery, foul air as recirculated in the boat, burning electrical apparatus, bodies and unwashed armpits, groins and feet. Jesus but it was a sexy smell.

Were you able to beat your meat when you wanted to? Yes, whenever I felt the urge. As an officer, I had my own quarters — a green draw-curtain covered the entrance to it, but pretty damn small.

Did you hear of the others beating their meat? The men were always beating their goddam meat, some quite unashamedly, and the new recruits quickly caught on. It was not unmanly to jack off. On the contrary. Some were a bit bashful, but when nothing was ever said, it was done, mostly when lying in their bunks, sacking out. You could hear the tell-tale slap of an eager hand beating the hell out of a cock.

How long did the sailors wear their underpants before changing? Lots of us wore our skivvies a fucking week or more. No laundry aboard. Each did his own in a bucket and dried it near the engine room, where heat from the batteries would dry them quicker.

Were any sailors ever caught jacking off and derided or reprimanded? Not really. It was a widely accepted practice.

Sucks Workers' Cocks, Shit-holes

MANHATTAN — I have always enjoyed sex with "straight" guys who enjoy having their pricks sucked. I'm also constantly amazed how easy it is to get these guys to unzip their flys and take out their meat. Some of my success must be attributed to the way in which I approach them. With repairmen working in the building where I live, the approach is to prop open my front door so anyone passing by in the hall can look in and see me sitting on the sofa in the living room reading fuck books. I also get off more on "straight" fuck books than "gay," so if the guy does stop to watch I just get up and walk to the open door with one of the books in my hand and ask the guy if he likes looking at fuck books while I shove the book in his face. If, after looking at the book, he seems like he might be interested, I invite him in to look at more books, which then usually leads to a blow job from me while he looks at the books.

Several years ago I was sitting on the sofa nude jacking off when I heard footsteps on the roof above my apt. I decided to check it out so I put on some cut-offs and with one of the "straight" fuck books in my hand I went up to the roof. What I discovered was a very interesting Italian cable TV repairman checking out the cables. He noticed the book I had in my hand so I showed it to him. I told him I was downstairs looking at fuck books and if he wanted he could stop down when he finished and look at them too. He said he would so I went back down and dropped my cut-offs and sat bare-ass on the sofa with the front door propped open. I heard the roof door slam and footsteps coming back down the stairs. I looked up and here was this sexy Italian again with moustache and tight jeans standing in the door and asking if he could come in. I got up and brought him into the living room where he sat on the sofa and began looking at the fuck books. Since I was naked and playing with my meat, he eventually stood up and dropped his jeans and said, "I'm getting horny, too." He pulled out his prick from his white Jockey shorts, sat back down and started playing with it. I asked him if he wanted to get off. At first he acted surprised, as if to say, "What do you mean?" I told him I would give him head if he wished. I bent over and started sucking him. I looked up to him and asked if he had ever had his ass eaten out. He said no and I said, "Want to give it a try?" He stood up, turned around and pulled down his Jockey shorts, revealing beautiful, firm, round hams. I took my hands and spread his ass, putting my tongue in his shit hole. He was very clean except for a slight, exciting, musty smell of shit. As I ate his "virgin" ass he became more excited and now he was bending over even more, allowing me to really get my tongue deep into his shit hole. During all this he was jacking off and looking at the fuck books laid out in front of him and I was beating my meat, too. As he left, I assumed I would never see him again, but much to my surprise and delight he suddenly appeared last February when I needed my cable box fixed. We repeated the scene.

One morning I looked out my window and saw this sexy Puerto Rican Con Ed worker at the house across the street. I wanted to make it with him but realized it probably wouldn't happen. Later, not thinking about him anymore, I went downstairs to run an errand. Returning home, I saw him coming up the street towards me. In my very straight-forward manner I asked him if he wanted his cock sucked. At first he didn't realize what I had said or maybe he couldn't believe his ears. When I repeated my offer he smiled and asked if there was any money involved and I said no, but that I could show him some

175

"straight" fuck films and give him some beer and a joint to smoke. With this offer he agreed and came upstairs with me. While I put on the film he looked at some of my fuck books. Without much trouble I got his pants down and started sucking on his big, brown, uncut prick. He shot almost immediately. However, the second time I saw him on the street it didn't work out quite as well. I did get him up to my apt, but while I was sucking him I asked him if he liked having his ass-hole eaten, at which point he got upset and left without even letting me finish him off. If only he knew the pleasures of a hot tongue in his shit hole.

Not all of the workmen I try for accept but still the number of them that do makes the tries worthwhile. I have sucked off several of the supers who clean the hallway outside my door. There have been some painters and plumbers who have seen me through my open door and have stopped to look at my "straight" fuck books. When I ask them to join me in beating their meat they decline but still many of them watch me until I shoot my load all over the floor.

My hottest ongoing scene has been with the "straight" exterminator who comes once a month. I know this one is "straight" because I've seen him on the street with his wife and kids. When he first started coming to our building I would have my fuck books out and would be sitting bare-assed on the sofa when he rang my buzzer. Several times I tried but could never get him to join me in jacking off. One Saturday I decided I would get him no matter what. Maybe the time was right for him too because he seemed to linger longer in my apt. I asked him to take out his meat. He refused but I kept on insisting. Finally, as he was leaving, he said, "Make me an offer." Now I realized what had been his hangup all along; many Latins feel if they get money it doesn't make them "queer." So I offered him $10 to let me suck him and for him to fuck me. As if he couldn't get to it soon enough, he rushed back into my apt, and dropped his pants. There before me was what I had been waiting months to see — a big, stiff, uncut piece of meat. Right away I was down on my knees and sucking it. He told me to grease up my ass so he could fuck me. I quickly did this and he shoved his big dick up my eagerly awaiting hot ass-hole. Man, did he know how to throw a hard fuck into a guy's ass. I bent over and pushed my ass up against his groin as much as I could so I could get every inch of that hard prick up my shit hole. As he left I handed him the ten-dollar bill but it seemed like he had almost forgotten about it. For the next several months each time he would come to exterminate he would have me suck his prick and there was never any mention of money. Once I had another trick in bed with me when he arrived and the two of us went down on him at the same time. What a turn-on it was for him — two "queers" sucking his prick and balls at the same time and even putting their tongues up his shit hole.

Wedding Vows

MISSOURI — I am sucking a 19-year-old that will be married next May. The engagement has been announced. I asked if I could still suck his ass & cock after he was married and he said, "It is yours forever." His bride-to-be won't suck him. So if nothing happens, I'll still get it at least twice a week. She is working and that makes it handy for him. He works too but not on bad days (construction work). She works wet or dry days. He has a beautiful body. And the nice thing about him, he wants a blow job again within an hour after the first one.

"I'll Do Anything You Want"

HOUSTON — This encounter got me off, partly because I knew I was taking advantage of this slightly drunken young man. Last night I was out carousing. Stopped by a book store. Not much action at first but I noticed a black guy leaning against the painted black plywood walls. I went into a booth next to where he was standing, inserted a quarter but left the door open so that he could get in. He came in and felt me up while I watched the movie. He mumbled something unintelligible. After he repeated it several times, I finally understood that he wanted me to go somewhere else with him so that he could watch me fuck some unknown third party. I said I wasn't interested. I cruised the hallways some more and found a young thing standing in the corner. Without any provocation or invitation, he reached out and felt my hard dick through my pants. I let him feel me up for awhile. Then he suggested we go into a booth. Once inside I sat down and he fell to his knees and instantly began slurping and sucking on my cock. It seemed he would choke, but this was obviously an experienced cocksucker. After a few moments I stood up and jerked him by the hair into a corner. Then while he was pinned in the corner I rammed my dick in his mouth as hard as I could. He moaned and said "Fuck my mouth. I'll do anything you want. You can fuck my mouth, my ass, beat it on my face." I said, "O.K. Let's get out of here and go home so I can beat the shit out of you. Are you sure I can do anything I want?" "Oh, yes, anything. That huge dick of yours." We left and he followed me home. He was a wild driver. As soon as we got home I pulled his pants down to his ankles and threw him down on the bed. He moaned and told me to tell him what to do. I pulled him by the hair up to my dick and said, "Suck it you little shithead." He slurped and gulped it down. His drool ran down my cock. I sat on his face and told him to lick my ass. After he did this a long time I got my black belt and whipped his ass. With each whop he moaned and writhed on the bed. Red slashes appeared on his ass, a young ass with little hair. He begged me to fuck him but I never got around to it. While he stuck one finger up my ass I jerked off and came before I really wanted to. He sucked the cream off my dick and chest. I got his 'phone number; I wanted sometime to fuck his ass brutally. I told him he ought to see how real men fuck and he agreed. He went off into the night and said he would call soon. He never did, but he had given me his number and I called him a few times but never could get him over. I decided he had been wild that night only because he was drunk. Too bad so many men (both straight and gay) have to get drunk before they can have the degrading sex they want.

Sailor Makes Pass at Step-son

My step-father, who was a Chief in the Navy, and I were not friends during the first year of my mom's marriage to him. He was 29, ten years younger than my mother, and only 14 years older than I. And a hell of a nice guy, easy going and affable. The reason I didn't like him was that he seemed physically coarse to me and offended me. He was a type that I adore now. Robust and well fed, but never fat or even plump, he ate and drank and farted with great gusto and his face was always rosy. He liked me and wanted to be my friend. He knew from the beginning that I was gay, while my mother knew only when I told her a few

years later. But I loathed him like the perfect ass that I was in those days. The first physical overture came before he had married my mom. They'd been living together for a few months, so when mom went off to Las Vegas to divorce her previous husband, he continued to spend his nights at our house to look after me. The very first night that we were alone together he asked if I would like to sleep with him. I was aware that it was, without doubt, a sexual invitation, and oddly enough, I was neither shocked nor suprised. Damn it! I also knew that his offer was an attempt to win my affection, and I still turned him down. What a fool I was. Even though I came to love him, and to let him know it, he never again repeated his offer, nor was there ever any indication that an overture on my part would be welcome. Not, at least, until the very end of his marriage to my mom. That was some 10 years later. One night when mom had already gone to bed, my step-father and I were shooting the breeze over beer. He was one of those black Irish types. For the life of me I can't remember how we got onto the subject, but he was suddenly telling me that during virtually the whole of his marriage to my mother he had had a male friend who gave him regular blow jobs. That really did surprise me, for he was a real ladies' man and cheated on my mother right and left. Well, we talked about gay sex (we never had before) and I learned that he also liked to have his ass sucked. I was ready to do it on the spot and my hand was soon nestled on his groin, atop a hard-on of some good size. But alas, it came to nothing. I was uncertain as to how far he should go. There was never another opportunity. Not many months later he left for good. I do, however, have a treasured sexual memento. Some six years after our "near miss" in the kitchen, I was browsing through the porn collection of a guy I'd met in a Hollywood bar. All of a sudden, there was my step-father, posing nude for the camera, smiling and flourishing a hard on. My friend gave me the photo, and I've shed both tears and sperm many times while looking at it. What a beautiful picture. He was a fine, healthy man, with a big, beautifully-shaped prick and something in his face, his eyes that made you know he'd be a good juicy piece of trade.

Hawaiian Seeks Counsel on How to Abuse Himself

HONOLULU — I play with my peter a lot. I have been practicing at it for years, starting with the help of the boys' and mens' illustrated articles in the Sears and Monty Ward catalogs, especially handsome cusses. I am not aware of having achieved any special expertise in the art. Do you offer any advanced courses to help me? The only specific advantage that I may have is that I am ambidextrous, which reduces the wear and tear on my right hand. I impatiently await any help which your readers can provide.

[EDITOR'S NOTE: I envy this man his ambidexterity, as I indulge in self-abuse relentlessly, sometimes even finding it necessary to relieve myself at the office; and as a result, while my right arm is that of an Arnold Schwarzenegger, my left is that of Phyllis Diller. There's everything to be said for self-abuse, but nothing that can be said about it; I suspect we all know exactly how to do it extremely well.]

Boy Sucks Married Soldier in Out-House

SAN FRANCISCO — The first time I came off was when I was fucking my Cousin in the ass. We had been playing around with each other for some time, jacking each other off and sticking our cocks up each other's ass just a little way. I think I was 13 and he was 12. Anyway we lived in Columbus, Georgia. The houses there have no cellars; they sit high up on brick columns. We crawled under the house my Grandmother lived in and were playing around and he asked me to fuck him up the ass as he liked to have cock up his ass most of the time. I gladly obliged for I liked to do it to someone but not have it done to me. We fucked for awhile and I noticed it felt better to me than it ever had before. When I pulled my cock out it was still oozing from my first cum.

The first time I sucked off a man was when I was living with my Aunt in Columbus. I was 12 at the time. We had no inside plumbing. Just an old out-house that sat over a gully about a block from the house. My Aunt started renting out rooms to Soldiers and their wives after the Army started to send them South just before World War II. She rented out two rooms to this Soldier and his wife. One night my Brother and I were in their Apartment when the electricity went out. The soldier asked me to come with him into their kitchen to see about the coffee he was making. After the door was closed he grabbed me in a Bear Hug and felt me up all over. He felt my ass, my groin, rubbed my nipples nd asked me if he could have a kiss. I didn't answer, just reached up and kissed him on the mouth. He had a moustache. He stuck his tongue in my mouth and pulled my tongue into his. He put my hand in his fly and asked me if I wanted to see his Cock. I said I sure did want to see it as it felt enormous. He turned on the flashlight and took it out. It was huge and smooth and circumcised. (At that time I didn't know what circumcised meant.) He asked if I would like to kiss it. I said I did. He said for me to meet him at the out-house later. Later I told my Brother I had to go and take a shit and left for the out-house. The soldier was there waiting for me. He had his pants down around his ankles. He told me to sit on the hole while he stood in front of me. I slurped and licked his cock. I really liked the taste. I have always been able to swallow any cock after I got it slippery with my licking and sucking. Never had any trouble breathing. I suppose I am just a natural born cocksucker. After a short while he asked if I wanted to swallow the cream. I said no. So he took his cock and moved over the second hole and let it fly. His wife was pregnant at the time. I found out later that she had twins. Do you suppose I missed a double load that night.

Today's Recipe

Ingredients: 20 cans, B & M beans
20 cans, Spam Serves One

Remove the cubes of fat from the cans of beans and the jelly from the cans of Spam. Discard the Spam itself and the beans, or give them to heterosexual neighbors. Heat the cubes of fat; eat the jelly cold, like jellied consomme. Both the fat and the jelly are exquisitely seasoned gourmet items concealed in the coarsest possible canned food, in the same way that the coarsest peasant may have concealed in his pants exquisitely flavoured meat, both front and rear. To compensate for the fat, serve with a salad composed of ultra-lean lettuce.

Sports:
Coach Plays With Player's Pecker

TEXAS — I used to play football in high school. My football coach would always contrive to share a hotel room with me when we traveled to another team. In the room when we went to bed he would play with my dick, which was bigger than his. Mine was 8 inches even then and has grown since.

It used to shock me that he played with my dick because he was a "married man" and had just had a fourth kid. Little did I know about "married men." His dick has only about 5½ inches. He tried to get me to play with it but I wouldn't.

About 15 years after I left high school I ran into him in a "straight" bar in another city. He kept talking about sex and saying I must be much more sophisticated by now. Although he was about 45 he was in perfect physical shape, 200 pounds of solid lean muscle. By then I was bigger in every way and much more muscular and I had plenty of sex.

He tried to play with my dick again and was surprised to learn that it had grown almost two inches since I was in high school. I wouldn't play with him so he suggested that we two good buddies go out on the town and get sucked off. I was curious. He found a too-eager guy who wanted to blow us both. It was no challenge. You did not wonder if he would do the job and you did not know with anyone that eager whether you were really wanted for yourself. No possibility of a lasting relationship. I saw my ex-coach come in two minutes. He thinks he's butch.

New Hope for the Older Queer

NEW YORK — At the advanced age of 54, I've just had one of the three best cocksuckers I've ever had in my life. Or maybe the ones I had when I was young were as good, but I didn't take full advantage of them. Once when I was young, wearing just a jock strap at the baths, I walked past the locker of a handsome young guy with tan skin and green eyes who was dressed, ready to leave. He looked up. I walked by again. He said, "Tell me what you want and I'll do it." If I'd had any balls then I'd have told him to kiss my ass, and he undoubtedly would have. Instead, I just sat down and he knelt and blew me. An ordinary blow job. It was less than I wanted and probably less than he wanted. Also when I was young, before piss-drinking became so popular, a nice young guy blew me at the baths and sat on the floor afterward while I sat on my bunk and talked awhile. He said he was a real slave and drank piss and everything, but I didn't take him up on it. It was rare then. But about 10 years ago a guy was blowing me at the baths — a tough guy with a crew cut — and told me to call him a cocksucker. I did, and it was fun, and since then, if they seem to want that, that's what I give them. They're usually the ones who invite it. This new man I just had liked to use language like "cocksucker" and be called names and so when he was blowing me I'd say sweet nothings like "I'm such a dirty son of a bitch I need a cocksucker as dirty as I am," and he'd say, "Let me be your dirty cocksucker. Make me your dirty cocksucker." I asked him if he was going to kiss my ass whenever I wanted it, and he said yes. I asked if he thought I could make a real ass-kisser out of him, and he said all right. And so on.

Rude Italian Sits Bareass on Reader's Face

MANHATTAN — I'm especially interested in straight assholes since the first asshole I ever kissed — out of a total of maybe three — belonged to a straight. One night in Everard Baths, I opened the door on a couple of men rooming together, second floor. I'd seen them come in and watched them go to and from the showers. Probably truck drivers, I figured. Their first visitor left, and that was when I opened the door and went in. Both men were in bed, on separate cots; the shorter, younger man, probably Mexican, had been taken care of by the first visitor and was on his way out. The other man, obviously Italian and a real hunk of macho, in his early 30s, had been watching. The light was on and his legs were spread; his hand gently played with his dick. When the Mexican left I shut the door behind him and sat down on the bed next to the Italian and lowered my head to go down on his cock. I was very hot because straights of his calibre weren't all that common even in the Everard. But after a minute he pushed my head off and said, "No, that ain't gonna work." I was disappointed, thinking he might be through with me. The Italian got up and told me to lay down on my back, so I knew he had other plans for me. I did what he asked. He climbed back in bed and squatted down over my face. He positioned his crack directly over my mouth and lowered his ashole to my mouth. Without even thinking I began to kiss it, over and over. Soon I began to lick it and suck on it, because the texture of his hole was like nothing I had ever felt with my lips and tongue before. Satin. The taste was slightly bitter. Musky. Unforgettable. Soon he began to rotate his ass. After awhile he lifted his ass and looked down at me. 'I like the way you're doing that," he said. "Now go crazy!" I could see his big uncut cock swaying above me in an upright position as he lowered his ass onto my face again. When we made contact my tongue went wild. I wanted to shove my tongue all the way up his asshole, following with my nose. When I felt and heard the rhythm of his hand on his dick, I put my own left hand on his massive right arm (which was doing the work) and held on. Soon he came and I could feel the muscles of his asshole contract and expand as he unloaded. I won't ever forget him. You sound like you know what you're doing every step of the way and I get turned on just imagining the way you smell.

Extraordinary Sailors Hook Up in Charleston

CALIFORNIA — When I was in the Navy about 12 years ago, I was stationed on an aircraft carrier in Portsmouth, Virginia, and wangled myself two weeks at a training school in Charleston. I lost no time in taking advantage of the sexual delights of Charleston. After several nights of carousing, I met a sailor named Max who was stationed in Charleston and who lived off base in a trailer. One night Max and I were driving around when we spotted a very drunk sailor hitch-hiking back to the base from town. We stopped, I got out, he got in the front seat and I got back in beside him, so that he was between Max and me. He was a great beauty: 18 or 19, blond, small but muscular, with a peach-fuzz mustache and a skin-tight white uniform. He didn't raise any objections when Max and I each put a hand on his legs, and so I suggested that since he was

drunk, perhaps he'd rather be in the back seat, where he could lie down. He agreed. Max pulled over, the sailor got in back — and I got in back with him. He stretched out as we started up again, so that his thighs lay on my lap, his groin bulging in those sailor whites just inches from my hand. As he mumbled about the places he's been and the drinks he'd had, I slipped my hand from his knee to his groin. I soon had his cock rock-hard. He pretended not to notice. "Hey Max," I said, "let's go to your place for awhile." Max, who had been watching in the rear view mirror with such intense interest that we nearly ran off the road, was only too glad to oblige. "Where're you takin' me?" the sailor asked, boozily. "I'm suppose t' be back at the base." But he wasn't exactly struggling to get away, and still had a hard on. Clearly, bodily pleasure was winning out over fear and scruples. He came into Max's trailer and as we were stripping him on the bed he said only, "Listen — you guys can do what you like. Just don't hurt me and make sure I get back to the base by morning, okay?" For the next hour Max and I took turns: one of us would fuck the sailor while the other blew him. His prick was just average-size but stayed super-hard throughout: that kind of young-hard dick that pointed up, towards his chin. He loved getting screwed. The harder we fucked the more he moaned. When, at the end of an hour, he finally shot his load, with me fucking him and Max blowing, it was all we could do to stay connected because he was thrashing about so violently on the bed. Max was afraid the neighbors would be wondering what was going on, so we dressed him and hurried him back out to the car as soon as we caught our breath. As we drove him to the base, he admitted he'd had a good time, though he'd never have thought to do "those things" on his own. He even asked Max for his phone number, but Max was beginning to be freaked by what we'd done and fear of the Navy finding out, so he gave him a wrong number. At the gates of the base, the sailor waved goodbye as we drove off in a hurry.

Baptist Boys Do It, As It Were, in Church

SAN FRANCISCO — I grew up in a small — very small — Mississippi town. I can remember sucking dick as early as age six, but didn't really get into it until I was 11. My cousin, who was 13, told me he was going to show me something that felt good so he pulled down my pajamas and blew me. I had my first wet dream when I was 14. I was sleeping with my father at the time and I didn't know what had happened. I just tried to gingerly slip out of bed to wipe off my soggy pajamas. I had absolutely no sex education, but fortunately, did have a strict conservative Baptist upbringing, which means I got lots of practical sexual experience via the church. I had to go to church every fucking Sunday for years. All the boys did. So we could sit way in the back while the preacher droned on and play with each other and jack off. Once while we were standing for a hymn, I was trying to unzip one of my friends' pants and I was shocked to look up and see his older brother staring at us. It was okay, though, because I had done it with him too. This was all when I was about 14. The church provided lots of queer activity since it was constantly organizing events for all the teen boys to be thrown together. These "religious activities" usually consisted of opportunities to spend the night camping out or something with your buddies. We had one game called "Squirrel." What does a squirrel do? He grabs nuts. I got into my first three-way when I was 13. My cousin and I and a

friend used to play in the hay. Hay was stored in a barnloft and we would go up there and make out. You itched a lot after, though. We were once attacked by red wasps while doing it. I have been sucking my own dick for years; I started as a teenager. It requires a long dick and flexibility. Not only is it great when you're lonesome, it can be a turn-on for others. Every time I've ever revealed my ability to do this, my sex partners always want to see me do it. Eating your own wad of come is a really exciting experience plus you are in total control and can make the blow job last a long time. Also just shooting off in the face is really gratifying. I have had many other experiences which I will write about later — getting my cock measured by the roadside in Arkansas; having a 14-year-old pull off my swimming trunks at a public beach; blowing the three sons of the Baptist preacher, etc., etc. Perhaps you should send me a questionaire.

[EDITOR'S NOTE: Absolutely. Practically all of the scenes listed briefly here warrants thorough examination. I know from my own boyhood in a Lutheran church, and from sleeping with the minister's son, that church activities can be as exciting as St. Mark's Baths.]

Visiting Airman Removes Pants to Avoid Wrinkling

VENICE, CALIFORNIA — What I'm looking for is some great ass shots. The asshole shots that I'm looking for are of models bent over, showing their luscious holes. Now, I'll tell you of a real experience that happened a couple of years ago in L.A. It was a hot August day. I was in one of the parks. All of a sudden, the most beautiful gorgeous young male walked by, reading a newspaper. He was in the uniform of the Air Force Academy, which fit like a glove. As he walked by, I decided to follow him. He sat on a bench quite a ways from where I had been. I said, "Boy, it's sure hot. Do you mind if I sit down?" After a little chat, I suggested we go to my hotel room as it was air conditioned. Had a bottle of bourbon, asked if he'd like a drink, he said, "OK." He must have had 2 or 3. He said he was going to be sick. He went into the bathroom. I followed & did what my mother used to do when I got sick. One arm around the waist, the other hand on his forehead. That way, when he threw up, there wouldn't be so much retching. We were both fully dressed. I positioned myself so that while he was getting sick, I kept pressing my cock against his ass. Finally, he stopped. I left him alone & went back into the room. He came out of the john stripped to the waist. He asked if he could lay down on the bed. To keep his pants from wrinkling, he took them off, leaving him in a pair of briefs. Put cool compresses on his forehead. After the 3rd or 4th compress he pulled me down on the bed and thanked me for taking care of him. He slept awhile. When he awoke, at my request, he spent the night. I stripped off his briefs. He was built. We had a great night, fucking and sucking. He was fantastic. Just 19.

"Straight" Discovers His Dick Leaks for Man at Airport

SAN FRANCISCO — Am 34, 5'9", 174#, light brown hair & eyes, 8¼" cock, muscular build, and very good looking. Nationality is Italian/Dutch and originally from Chicago, but moved to San Francisco 11 years ago. I love ASS! Am a very aggressive lover, but much into love & affection for my partners. Clean sex and cleaned assholes are a must. Christ, there's nothing so beautiful as a man's hole, smelling so beautifully, fresh from a shower. No aftershave necessary — just the clean smell of soap and the chemical reaction of a man's body. Kissing and tonguing armpits, nipples, navel, cock (smaller the better), balls (more important than cock), inner thighs, hard ridge underneath ball sack, and the best — sweet & fresh asshole. Another erotic area of men, at least for me, is the back of the knee. Consider myself supremely fortunate that nature gave me thick saliva (sounds goofy) that makes it *unnecessary* to have to use lubricant to fuck my men. Also fortunate to be double jointed and able to fuck & suck at the same time. The combination of my spit and profuse leaking (pre-come fluid) causes no problems for my men when I enter their bodies. When I first switched to men (age 22) my excessive leaking caused much embarrassment as my partners thought I'd already come and the peak was deflated. Also embarrassing that the piss slit of my cock is wide enough to put the tip of an index finger into. Have learned over the years to not be so sensitive when comments about my excessive leaking and cock opening are made. Smaller cocks are preferable to me because while buried inside my man I like to suck the whole package, cock and balls, and smaller-cocked men seem to have a more intense and profuse climax than guys my size and larger. I am not a cocksucker. Odd statement, but I consider it valid in that it's a means to an end and a catalyst so that I can fuck them. Most important that we both come, although over having to suck cock, the ideal situation is the action of my cock rubbing their prostate gland to produe a naturally timed climax while kissing.

Prefer 2 main positions: (A) partner on his back with me between his legs and his thighs on my shoulders so that we can kiss throughout our love making, and (B) me kneeling with my partner sitting on my cock and having his legs wrapped around my waist and our torsos embracing tightly so that I may kiss his lips, ears, eyes, chin, nose and eyebrows. When I said I was not a cocksucker I don't mean to put down anyone or to indicate I think it demeaning, it's just that I would never go to one of our numerous sex clubs or baths to suck cock only. Just doesn't interest me to only suck cock and not be able to fuck the man. Further, also do not enjoy having my cock sucked. The feeling is just not exciting enough for me and it's very hard to keep a hard on due to my lack of interest. The feel of a man's asshole and internal muscles grasping, clutching, and allowing me (my cock and tongue) inside his most personal body features produces waves in me of tenderness and caring that are incredible. ___ has been after me for the last 5 years to do a J.O. film for him but my Midwestern roots still make me too shy to even have a nude picture taken. Just can't seem to get the nerve.

I was married at 15 yrs. old and finally got smart at 22 and got divorced. Had 2 children, both boys, and both dead at 6 yrs. old & 18 mos. respectively. My wife was 6 yrs. older than me and taught me my preference for assholes. My

ability to fuck and suck at the same time was developed through my ex-wife. Used to sink my cock into her asshole and still be able to lick and suck her pussy lips without pulling out. All very exciting but somehow never fully satisfying. Something left me wanting emotionally and physically after climaxing.

About our 5th year of marriage (I was 20) I developed an understanding that the female form lacked the firmness & texture my inner self fantasized would be preferable. At this time I was playing (singing) a small Las Vegas cocktail lounge called the Black Magic on weekends. Part of my deal with the club included round trip plane fare from my home in Chicago each week. The influx of beautiful women and men in Las Vegas is abundant and more & more my appraisals of beauty strayed to men over women. Smoothly rounded firm asses encased in sharkskin slacks together with form-fitting polo shirts set off by dark hair slightly greying at the temples became a constant image for me while fucking my wife.

The Las Vegas airport provided the opportunities to see these pretty men and fuel my desires. Finally, upon arriving one weekend for my gig, I saw a beautiful & exotic man at the airport of Caucasian/Eurasian parentage and about 15 years older than me. Our eyes met, held and sent sparks. More than anything, I wanted this man. Thank the fates he struck up a conversation with me 'cause I was so scared I could never have started things. I could feel the pre-cum juice sliding out of my cock and into my Jockey shorts as we stood there talking. I must have had a hungry look as he smiled sweetly, offered me a ride and took me to his house. Christ, I'll never forget the terror in my guts, confusion and crazy excitement upon first getting to his apartment. This man relaxed me with his eyes alone; subtle changes in eyelashes, lids, eyebrows and expressive emotions paraded in this man's eyes and made his intentions clear. Once at ease, I leaned close to him and kissed him and warmed to the task of parting and exploring his tongue, teeth and gums. A new expressn from his eyes — shock! He knew I was straight and yet I kissed him. Never once with him nor with the thousands (not exaggerating) since him have I ever felt revulsion at kissing a man. From the first kiss I knew what he wanted ...ASS. Incredible hairless skin satiny smooth on the surface but rippling with muscles just underneath. Ass globes of perfect design with a narrowness filling me with wonder and desire. My cock was leaking so badly he softly said, "I wish you could have waited." I assured him it was only my natural lubrication and entered him slowly and tenderly. Intense pleasure — more than I'd ever felt. So many different emotions, lust, tenderness, safety, oneness and the luxury of this man desiring me as much as I wanted him. On 2 successive trips I spent the weekends with him and had him to the club when I was singing. All my taboos of old & my dread at the double life started taking their toll. I ended the relationship, stupidly, and continued my "ideal family man" ruse for the next 2 years and through the devastation of both my children dying. After dealing with my loss I was finally able to tell my wife of my affair in Las Vegas and the direction I needed to follow. After reaching 24 my true sexuality developed fully. I love being gay and yet seeming straight.

Cop Arrests Man After Having Sex with Him

This is an excerpt from the journal of a New Yorker, who has opened his diary for STH just as he has opened his thighs for other men who want to put something between them, such as their tongues, dicks and those sorts of things.

SEPTEMBER 9, 1963. — I had gone to the Soldiers and Sailors Monument on Riverside Drive to be serviced. As it happened, I was not serviced, for, shortly after midnight, when things would have begun to pick up a little, a plainclothes cop snuck into our midst. He arrested a drunk who had been on his knees doing him. The cop pulled his prick out of the guy's mouth, pulled a pair of handcuffs out of his back pocket and put them on the guy's wrists while he was still on his knees in front of him. "All right don't move," the cop said, but naturally we all scattered like cockroaches. Later I was picked up on Riverside Drive by a Cuban and taken to his room on 74th Street and serviced there.

JULY 29, 1963. — R. and I went up to the shrubbery behind the Soldiers and Sailor Monument. One boy got blown by another but the cops came and scared everybody away. At one point I was groped by a big bruiser of a man, all in blue denim, but I moved off instead of standing still to be blown because R. was with me. If I'm to be unfaithful to D. I don't want anybody that he knows to know about it. If I had been in the bushes alone, I would have allowed the man to blow me, and later, alone, I actually picked up a trick in the neighborhood. (I later found out, from friends who had picked him up in Kelley's Bar on West 45th Street, that he sometimes hustled.)

JULY 30, 1963. — At midnight I returned to the shrubbery behind the Soldiers and Sailors Monument. As I entered the Sacred Grove I saw nobody but in the darkest recess I found an orgy — perhaps eight boys — and I joined it, allowing myself to be blown while I felt and kissed a tough Puerto Rican who was standing next to me. More and more boys and men arrived and the sex got wilder and wilder. Several times, boys got fucked bent over and leaning against trees and there was a black boy, not more than 16 or 17, who never stopped blowing guys. He blew about a dozen while I was there. They would be standing around playing with their dicks and when he finished one he would turn to the next. The bushes are sexier than the baths; everyone is young. Lots of teenagers, probably students and neighborhood kids, some of them tough, who just go in long enough to get their rocks off.

AUGUST 23, 1963. — Last night R. and I saw a gang, a real gang, in Central Park looking for someone to victimize. They were very fierce little boys in their early teens armed with sticks. This evening the same gang was roaming Riverside Park, shouting "Let's get the faggots." If the cops cared to distinguish between people who are actually dangerous and people who are perfectly harmless, their presence in the parks might not be so useless and infuriating. The municipality provides salaries, patrol cars, searchlights and even police dogs so that some perverted cops can spend their evenings lurking in the bushes in order to nab harmless homosexuals.

WEDNESDAY, 6 NOVEMBER 1963, 9:16 A.M. — I am up so early because I went to bed after dinner last night; and I went to bed so early

because I didn't get any sleep the night before. The reason for my not sleeping the night before is that I spent it in jail. Frustrated and wanton, I had set out after dinner to find some sort of trick. Two or three men on Central Park West tried to pick me up but they were unattractive. At 72nd Street I went over to Riverside Park — it was now about 11:30 — and inside the park I walked up the Sacred Grove. It was a cold and windy night. Along came an ultra-butch leather-jacketed type, a little advanced in years; he bent down to blow me. Suddenly he ran away. A butch black man, rather good looking, dressed in an overcoat and looking a little too much like a plainclothes cop, approached and began to wave his cock at me. We had begun a little hanky-panky when two suspicious-looking men in raincoats appeared over the crest of the hill. The black man and I supposed they were cops and we crossed the meadow and continued where we had left off. The two suspicious-looking men eventually followed along. This time they came right up to where we were and I got a good look at them: they did indeed look suspicious and I was scared enough to say to my black friend, "Let's get out of here." On our way out we passed a couple of boys on their way in, one of whom seemed breathtakingly beautiful in the dark. I stopped to stare at him. The black waited for me. The beautiful one leaned against a tree. I stood right in front on him, staring. The two cops were still in sight too. I looked from them to him, trying to make it clear with my eyes (impossible in the dark) that I liked him but was too scared to stay there. I rejoined my black friend. He asked me to go home with him. I refused. Then the beautiful boy came up on the terrace too — as I later found out, because he was following me. He took a position, where I stared at him doggedly. After ten minutes my black friend realized I had dropped him and had the kindness to go away. I called to the boy to come and sit down beside me. We chatted for awhile, me making periodic excursions to the balustrade to look down to where the shadowy figures of the cops still lingered alone in the darkness under the trees. My new friend turned out to be Cuban and his name was Ernesto. I decided that while he was cute enough to play with in the park, he wasn't worth taking home, so we went toward the bushes again. Suddenly I saw the two cops emerge from the bushes, walking faster than normal. I said to Ernesto, "I'm sure they're cops — we've got to leave the park quickly." We arrived safe and sound on Riverside Drive. I paused to catch my breath and at that moment I heard a voice behind me say, "Hey, you." I turned around. They had already grabbed Ernesto and were putting handcuffs on him; one of them took my right hand and handcuffed me to Ernesto.

Police Station Nookie

I was feeling horny today because it had been over a week since I'd had any sex. I went to my favorite john — the one in the police station I've written you about before.

My favorite stall was empty — the one with the peephole on each side, the left one giving a view of the row of urinals and the right one looking into the booth next door. The stall has no door (the only one in the place that doesn't).

The guy in the stall next to me motioned me to stick my business end under the partition. We had been eyeing each other through the peephole and his

cock was beginning to ooze. When my knees and cock were under the partition, he gave me a few jerks on my cock and then tapped my thigh as though somebody was coming. When I got back on the throne and looked through the hole, I saw him wiping up. Apparently just the touch of my prick had been enough to make him come.

After he left, a guy with a muscular build, a tank top, tight, white bell-bottom dungarees, and sandals came into the empty stall next door and stood there, peering through the hole. He was carrying a parcel, so he didn't look like plainclothes fuzz, and though he was handsome in a toothpaste-ad kind of way, he made me nervous.

I gave him a show, but people kept coming in to piss, and instead of sitting down he would retreat each time a guy came in. Finally, in a moment of calm, he got up enough nerve to come around in front of my booth and take out his pecker. By this time I was really hungry, and I got my mouth around it as fast as I could. But the urinal traffic was pretty heavy and he kept retreating.

On the third attempt we really got into it. He was all tensed up — his thigh muscles were like stone through his jeans, and he kept fucking my face in spasmodic jerks.

I was trying to make up my mind whether to come when he did — I was just about ready — but he decided for me by shooting a huge load down my throat very quickly. That was O.K. by me, because I was hoping to make it with Bulgy Groin, a guy who hangs around there a good deal, and who was there again now. He has a good-sized cock, and today he was wearing the kind of jeans with exposed buttons down the fly that really emphasize the groin — and he'd apparently done a subtle bleach job on them so that he looked like a basket with a man attached. He wears sneakers and moves silently, so he's hard to keep track of, but I know from experience that he likes to get it out and get it hard at the urinals when he knows somebody's watching.

After Tank Top left (in a big hurry — a guilt-ridden would-be "straight," I guess), Bulgy Groin made a number of passes past my stall, without indicating that he was interested. He finally moved in on one of the urinals and I could see he was whacking on it to give me a show.

It's a beauty, curving upward somewhat and with a real juicy quality. Cut, but you can't have everything. His slightly loose jeans would flop around his groin as he massaged his cock (I like that) and at one point his hips started to buck like he was ready to come.

A couple of times new arrivals interrupted him. Then when they left he'd appear silently at the urinal, press up into it until he got hard, then slowly move back and give me a show.

I couldn't take it any longer. I pulled my pants up, but didn't do up the fly or the belt, or my shirt, which I had opened in the hope that my bare chest and belly would catch his eye as he came past my stall at some point. Without making a sound (I wear construction boots that are as quiet as his sneakers) I moved to the urinal next to him.

He was startled when he realized that I was there, but kept on whacking and looked down at me while I did the same.

Finally he reached over and took hold of my cock and I took hold of his. By this point I was boiling, a week's accumulation of cum was screaming to get

out, and the feel of his beautiful prick in my hand was just too much. Even as I kneeled down in front of it I could feel myself beginning to come.

I knew I was going to shoot all over my pants. I also knew how dangerous it was to go down on him there. But I didn't care. I *had* to get my mouth around that fucking cock and I *had* to come. It didn't take him long to shoot in my mouth. By that time my own load was all over my hand and my pants.

I retreated to one of the booths and mopped up as well as I could.

There was a sort of street fair going on outside. At one booth what appeared to be a father and son were selling paintings. As I passed by, the kid looked at my groin. My cum stain was pretty well dry by now, but he smiled to himself. He looked away quickly. He knew, damn him. But I was glad he knew.

Sucking Cock at Danang

Editor's Note: The only glory in Vietnam was the glory holes. The mere fact that we print these pieces does not mean that we supported this shameful war.

Although I had plenty of opportunity to suck cock at Chu Lai, I seldom took advantage of it. The famous Americal Division Headquarters Compound was a close knit unit and I was scared to death word would get out about me. I sucked my hooch-mates' cocks and assholes (we slept six officers to a shack) but I actually turned down their offers to supply me with some of their buddies. I took frequent chopper trips to DaNang and flew in and out of Saigon so I did most of my cocksucking with men off the base. The airfield john at DaNang was so busy there were guys waiting around to be serviced. At the barracks head one night I got brave enough to stare openly at a good looking young stud. He looked right back, scratched at the bulge in his shorts and headed for the shower. When I stepped into the shower he was alone soaping a very long hard cock. He looked at me, left the shower running and moved over near the door so he could see anyone approaching. He just stood there, legs apart, smiling, his beautiful hard prick bobbing slightly up and down, beckoning to me. I pointed to his cock and put my finger into my mouth. He nodded yes. Immediately I was on my knees. His cock was incredibly fat; I had to really open my jaws to accommodate it. I took it all the way in and when I pulled back to where I just had the head covered I'd swish my tongue into the rather large piss hole. I really tried to swallow the whole prick but it was so fucking thick I think the most I ever managed was five inches. I got so damn hot I turned him around and ate the shit out of his asshole. I'd been at it only a short time when he said, "I'm coming." I turned him around quickly. Just in time. He came in quarts. Quite a bit of it spurted down my throat but I was determined to taste the stud's stuff so I withdrew a little so the next jet hit the back of my mouth. He didn't buy that. He slammed it to me two or three more times, then stopped. He had very sweet cum. He abruptly pulled his glorious cock, still hard, out of my mouth, wrapped a towel around himself and took off like a shot out of a 105. I made several more trips to DaNang and scored every time.

AIDS RISK REDUCTION GUIDELINES FOR HEALTHIER SEX

As given by Bay Area Physicians for Human Rights

NO RISK: *Most of these activities involve only skin-to-skin contact, thereby avoiding exposure to blood, semen, and vaginal secretions. This assumes there are no breaks in the skin.* **1) Social kissing** (dry). **2) Body massage, hugging. 3) Body to body rubbing** (frottage). **4) Light S&M** (without bruising or bleeding). **5) Using one's own sex toys. 6) Mutual masturbation** (male or external female). Care should be taken to avoid exposing the partners to ejaculate or vaginal secretions. Seminal, vaginal and salivary fluids should not be used as lubricants.

LOW RISK: *In these activities small amounts of certain body fluids might be exchanged, or the protective barrier might break causing some risk.* **1) Anal or vaginal intercourse with condom.** Studies have shown that HIV does not penetrate the condom in simulated intercourse. Risk is incurred if the condom breaks or if semen spills into the rectum or vagina. The risk is further reduced if one withdraws before climax. **2) Fellatio interruptus** (sucking, stopping before climax). Pre-ejaculate fluid may contain HIV. Saliva or other natural protective barriers in the mouth may inactivate virus in pre-ejaculate fluid. Saliva may contain HIV in low concentration. The insertive partner should warn the receptive partner before climax to prevent exposure to a large volume of semen. If mouth or genital sores are present, risk is increased. Likewise, action which causes mouth or genital injury will increase risk. **3) Fellatio with condom** (sucking with condom) Since HIV cannot penetrate an intact condom, risk in this practice is very low unless breakage occurs. **4) Mouth-to-mouth kissing** (French kissing, wet kissing) Studies have shown that HIV is present in saliva in such low concentration that salivary exchange is unlikely to transmit the virus. Risk is increased if sores in the mouth or bleeding gums are present. **5) Oral-vaginal or oral-anal contact with protective barrier.** e.g. a latex dam, obtainable through a local dental supply house, may be used. Do not reuse latex barrier, because sides of the barrier may be reversed inadvertently. **6) Manual anal contact with glove** (manual anal (fisting) or manual vaginal (internal) contact with glove). If the glove does not break, virus transmission should not occur. However, significant trauma can still be inflicted on the rectal tissues leading to other medical problems, such as hemorrhage or bowel perforation. **7) Manual vaginal contact with glove** (internal). See above.

MODERATE RISK: *These activities involve tissue trauma and/or exchange of body fluids which may transmit HIV or other sexually transmitted disease.* **1) Fellatio** (sucking to climax). Semen may contain high concentrations of HIV and if absorbed through open sores in the mouth or digestive tract could pose risk. **2) Oral-anal contact** (rimming). HIV may be contained in blood-contaminated feces or in the anal rectal lining. This practice also poses high risk of transmission of parasites and other gastrointestinal infections. **3) Cunnilingus** (oral-vaginal contact). Vaginal secretions and menstrual blood have been shown to harbor HIV, thereby causing risk to the oral partner if open lesions are present in the mouth or digestive tract. **4) Manual rectal contact** (fisting). Studies have indicated a direct association between fisting and HIV infection for both partners. This association may be due to concurrent use of recreational drugs, bleeding, pre-fisting semen exposure, or anal intercourse with ejaculation. **5) Sharing sex toys. 6) Ingestion of urine.** HIV has not been shown to be transmitted via urine; however, other immunosuppressive agents or infections may be transmitted in this manner.

HIGH RISK: *These activities have been shown to transmit HIV.* **1) Receptive anal intercourse without condom.** All studies imply that this activity carries the highest risk of transmitting HIV. The rectal lining is thinner than that of the vagina or the mouth thereby permitting ready absorption of the virus from semen or pre-ejaculate fluid to the blood stream. One laboratory study suggests that the virus may enter by direct contact with rectal lining cells without any bleeding. **2) Insertive anal intercourse without condom.** Studies suggest that men who participate only in this activity are at less risk of being infected than their partners who are rectally receptive; however the risk is still significant. It carries high risk of infection by other sexually transmitted diseases. **3) Vaginal intercourse without condom.**

BOOKS FROM LEYLAND PUBLICATIONS / G.S PRESS

☐ **PARTINGS AT DAWN: Anthology of Japanese Gay Literature.** Brilliant collection covering 800 years of Japanese culture. Illus. $21.95.
☐ **OUT OF THE BLUE: Russia's Hidden Gay Literature.** 400 page anthology of stories, articles, photos—New Russia & earlier. $21.95.
☐ **THE LEGIONNAIRE.** Erotic novel by Tom Kvaale. $16.95.
☐ **THE MILK FARM.** Erotic novel by Luc Milne. $16.95.
☐ **MUSCLESEX A collection of erotic stories** by Greg Nero. $16.95.
☐ **CRYSTAL BOYS** The first modern Asian gay novel by Pai Hsien-yung $16.95.
☐ **MEN LOVING MEN: A Gay Sex Guide & Consciousness Book** by Mitch Walker. New revised edition. 40+ photos. $16.95.
☐ **MEATMEN Anthology of Gay Male Comics.** Tom of Finland, Donelan, etc. Large sized books. Circle books wanted. Volumes 1, 2, 3, 4, 5, 6, 7, 8, 9, 10, 11, 12, 13, 14, 15, 16—$17.95 ea. Vols. 17, 18, 19—$18.95 ea.
☐ **OH BOY! Sex Comics** by Brad Parker. $12.95.
☐ **ENLISTED MEAT / WARRIORS & LOVERS / MILITARY SEX / MARINE BIOLOGY / BASIC TRAINING: True Homosexual Military Stories.** $16.95 each. Circle books wanted. Soldiers / sailors / marines tell all about their sex lives.
☐ **SEX BEHIND BARS / BOYS BEHIND BARS / THE BOYS OF VASELINE ALLEY** (3 Vols.) by Robert N. Boyd. $16.95 each. Circle books wanted.
☐ **MANPLAY / YOUNG NUMBERS / BOYS BOYS BOYS! / STUDFLESH / BOYS WILL BE BOYS / EIGHTEEN & OVER:** True Gay Encounters. Circle books wanted. Hot male-male sex stories. $12.95 each.
☐ **LUST** and **HUMONGOUS** True Gay Encounters. Vols. 1 & 5 $16.95 ea.
☐ **LEATHERMEN SPEAK OUT** Vols. 1 & 2. Ed. Jack Ricardo. 50 leather dads & sons, slaves & masters reveal their S&M sex encounters. $16.95 ea.
☐ **SIR! MORE SIR! The Joy of S&M** by Master Jackson. $16.95.
☐ **THE KISS OF THE WHIP: Explorations in SM** by Jim Prezwalski $17.95.
☐ **KISS FOOT, LICK BOOT.** Foot, Sox, Sneaker & Boot Worship/Domination Stories. Edited by Doug Gaines/The Foot Fraternity. $16.95.
☐ **TRUCKER / SEXSTOP / HOT TRICKS / MEAT RACK:** True sex stories. Circle books wanted. $12.95 each.
☐ **ROUGH TRADE: True Revelations** Vol. 7. Hot sex stories. $16.95
☐ **ROCK ON THE WILD SIDE: Gay Male Images in Popular Music of the Rock Era** by Wayne Studer. Illustrated. $17.95.
☐ **GAY ROOTS: Anthology of Gay History, Sex, Politics & Culture.** 100+ writers. Illustrated. 1000+ pages total. Vol. 1: $25.95; Vol. 2 $22.95.
☐ **HIGH CAMP: A Guide to Gay Cult & Camp Films** by Paul Roen. $17.95.
☐ **AUSSIE BOYS / AUSSIE HOT** by Rusty Winter. $16.95 each.
☐ **MEAT / SEX / CUM / JUICE / CREAM True Homosexual Experiences from S.T.H.** Boyd McDonald $16.95 each (5 vols.). Circle books wanted.
☐ **MILKIN' THE BULLS and other Hot Hazing Stories** by John Barton. Stories of military school, sexual hazing, etc. $16.95.
☐ **ORGASMS / HOT STUDS / SINGLEHANDED:** Homosexual Encounters from *First Hand*. $12.95 each (3 vols.). Circle books wanted.
☐ **GHOST KISSES Gothic Gay Romance Stories** by Gregory Norris $14.95.

TO ORDER: Check book(s) wanted (or list them on a separate sheet) and send check / money order to Leyland Publications, PO Box 410690, San Francisco, CA 94141. **Postage included in prices quoted**. Calif. residents add 8½% sales tax. Mailed in unmarked book envelopes. Add $1 for complete catalogue.